Bo...
ac...

they met.

✛✛✛✛✛✛

The Forest Lord rode at the head of his army, a borrowed bow taut and ready in his skillful hand. Calmly he dismounted, and took his place in the ranks of the archers.

"Stand fast. Do not release until red armor passes between you and that stand of poplars in the midst of the field. Remember to aim high, to reckon the distance."

Calmly he watched the stand of poplars. His troops began to rock and breathe deeply and draw their bows, all eyes straining for a flutter of red.

Then a column of red-armored troops broke from the ranks and rushed toward the archers, roaring and shrieking, their weapons raised.

"Now!" spoke the Forest Lord, and three hundred arrows launched in unison . . .

✛✛✛✛✛✛

THE
BALANCE
OF POWER

Also by Michael Williams

A FOREST LORD
A SORCERER'S APPRENTICE

Published by
WARNER BOOKS

FROM THIEF TO KING
THE BALANCE OF POWER

MICHAEL WILLIAMS

WARNER BOOKS

A Time Warner Company

WARNER BOOKS EDITION

Questar® is a registered trademark of Warner Books, Inc.

Cover design by Don Puckey
Cover illustration by Edwin Herder
Map by Teri Williams

Warner Books, Inc.
1271 Avenue of the Americas
New York, NY 10020

 A Time Warner Company

Printed in the United States of America

First printing: December, 1992

10 9 8 7 6 5 4 3 2 1

For Gali R. Sanchez,
the original Ricardo

Acknowledgments

The third volume of a trilogy is both the most challenging and rewarding, as I certainly found in the last breathless weeks of completing this manuscript. As always, the words do not become a story, and the story does not become a book, solely through the power of one person.

I have my agent Scott Siegel to thank, profusely and deeply, for his resourcefulness and his moral support. There's also Brian Thomsen at Warner Books, who liked the project from the start and whose help has been invaluable.

Thanks to John Hale, who clued us in to St. Anthony of Portugal, and to Professor Joseph Summers, whose brilliant introductions to seventeenth-century English poetry have found their way into this book. I hope this story is worthy of him, and especially of the poetry he taught me to love.

Speaking of the poets, there are quite a few of them whose time-honored words have formed the spells, songs, and incantations of the Thief to King trilogy. I thank them all: William Shakespeare, Ben Jonson, Christopher Marlowe, Sir Thomas Wyatt, Sir Walter Raleigh, John Donne, Edmund Spenser, Geoffrey Chaucer, Robert Herrick, Edgar Allan Poe, John Skelton, Henry Vaughan, Thomas Lodge, Andrew Marvell, Charles Baudelaire, the Countess of Dia, and of course, Anonymous. Several of the poems are my own: I hope they gain luster from their shimmering company.

Finally, my wife Teri has helped guide these books from their inception with essential work in all stages of the process. The Prologue and Epilogue of this book are her words and hers alone, and it's fitting that she begin and end this book, since so much of who I am begins and ends in her.

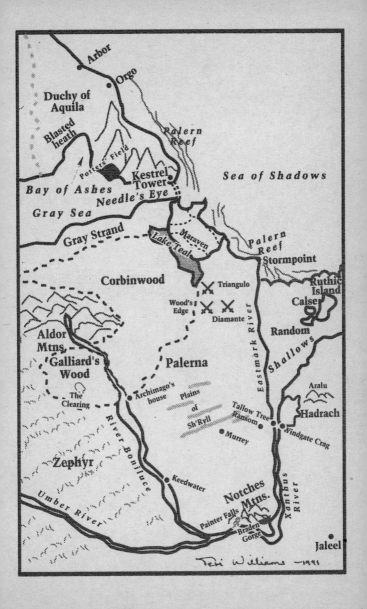

≺≺≺ **Prologue** ≻≻≻

Anthony the Shepherd whistled merrily to himself down the rutted path to his cottage and thought of the hot meal his wife would have waiting for him. He had been a fortnight in the uplands, gathering in the lambs and strays of his small flock to bring down to warmer pastures. Though it was still summer in the valley, and the corn and pumpkins had not yet ripened, in the higher parts of Palerna, heavy frost already appeared with each dawn. Anthony lifted up a sickly late-born lamb and nuzzled its cottony neck. "Mistress'll likely keep you as a pet. Yer not fit fer nothin' else." He laughed at the prospect of yet another tiny thing underfoot in the cottage. Three small children and now twice that many animals.

Only a mile away from home, Anthony stopped suddenly and searched the sky. There was no smoke. Merlys never let the fire go out. Never. He softly put down the lamb and ran for all he was worth.

The door stood wide and there was no answer when he called her name as he reached the threshold. He stepped inside warily. Merlys was sitting in her usual place by the hearth, staring into the cold fragments of the burnt-out fire. He moved toward her and called her name again. She could have answered him yesterday, but not now. The buboes covered her hands in her lap and her eyes were frozen open in surprise.

He stifled a wail and turned to the children's pallets. On each one lay a small covered form. The Death had been thorough.

Anthony buried them together behind the cottage by himself. He dug another grave beside the first and went into the hut to clean the hearth and sweep the floor; the next family to use his home would at least know he had some pride in it.

When he had burned the sweetgrass and spread a new rush floor, he thought he felt the first symptoms of the plague—the blurred vision and the fever, and a faraway rhythmic drumming in his ears. Anthony sat down and waited, numbly thinking about what would become of his sheep, of the tiny new lamb that Merlys would have loved into health and sheltered over the winter. He walked outside to look for the little creature and found it nursing at the permission of his best ewe, alongside her own lamb. There was a stream nearby that hardly ever froze over, and maybe enough for such a few sheep to eat if the winter was a mild one. They would survive.

Anthony waited five days for the moment he would wrap himself in the blanket and go out to lie down in his grave. Then it became clear to him that he would live, that the Death had passed by him or through him and not taken him. He wept for an entire night, finally falling to sleep in exhaustion.

He awoke to that same rhythmic drumming he had believed to be in his head days ago. This time it was very loud, and clearly outside of thought or hallucination; indeed, it was outside his door.

Anthony rose and peered down the footpath in front of the cottage. To his profound amazement, more people than he had ever seen stepped to the military beat and followed a young man on horseback. The tramp and shuffle of hundreds of roughshod feet was hypnotic, and Anthony found himself wandering closer to the passing army with each thump of the hide drum. When perhaps two hundred had passed by him, a man from down the path, Anthony's closest neighbor, pulled him into the parade with a shout and a smile. "We'll storm Kestrel Tower and rout the Witch! Are ye with us, Anthony?"

Anthony stared vacantly at his friend and then looked back at the diminishing cottage. He had closed the door. The fire was out. The sheep would survive. He picked up his feet and put them down again to the drumbeat and never looked back.

When Gabriel of Murrey got up from meat, he whined about his indigestion. His father Albert had no patience with his only son's plight because he himself *always* had indigestion. It was a family tradition, just like his trade. Every male in their line produced heartburn and candles, and Gabriel had no right to air his complaints on either time-honored family duty.

Albert scowled and burped and returned to the shop in front of their living quarters. Three hundred candles to make by the week's end for the village. Because of Dragmond's trade bans, he would be paid in pigs and other indigestible things. If Gabriel didn't stop moaning over his stomach and mooning over the latest news of Brennart the Pretender's approaching army, they would never get the work done. And Albert's six daughters had to be fed. Why, he peeved, did he have only the one son to help in the shop? What little help he was.

"I'm going now, Father." Gabriel's voice was tinged with a certainty Albert had never noticed before.

"Nah, nah. You're goin' nowhere but to the butcher's for rendering fat. We're far behind today," said Albert, dismissing the boy's remark.

"No. You don't understand. I'm going to join Brenn's army. I'll be a hero and make something of my life. I'm truly going, Father. I'm sorry. Maybe you can get an apprentice." Gabriel turned and moved out into the street.

Albert did not look up to see him go. The boy was making that talk every other day. Gabriel was only eighteen, and Albert knew what kind of romance other things and other lives held for young men. He had himself wanted to join Aurum's service years ago. But the men in his line were always chandlers. It was the way of it.

Albert waited on Gabriel for the rest of the afternoon and when he rose from the dinner table, the boy was still not back. Albert's stomach promptly soured and he walked into the vacant shop, grimacing at his discomfort and his growing surety that Gabriel wasn't coming home. "I hope they feed you good, boy," he muttered, as he locked the door. Then he thought again, and left the latch up.

The wet clay slumped and shredded in Unferth's distracted grasp. It was the twelfth jar he'd ruined that morning.

"Gar, Unferth! Hold your eyes to your work! I ain't peddlin' no more for you 'til you get your mind on it!" came the voice under the potter's wheel. A short barrel-chested man emerged, his face splattered with bits of earthenware and his tunic wet and filthy.

Unferth laughed at the dwarfish apprentice and let the wheel spin to its own stopping. He got off the bench and threw the collapsed jar into the scrap heap, rinsed his hands in the trough, and relaxed against the wall of the pottery. The other six apprentices glared at him over their own work, and he smiled cheerily back at them.

"Nice jobbing, boys. You'll make up for me easy," Unferth teased. No one laughed.

From the direction of the Master's wheel a low and boding voice said, "I'll make up for you, Unferth. I'll hire somebody else!"

Unferth chuckled again, this time a little more privately.

"Yeah. Sure you will. Nobody left in this burgh to hire. All gone to the wars. You're stuck with me, old man."

The old man hoisted a six-pound biscuited pitcher and hurled it straight for Unferth's head. It crashed within an inch of its target, but Unferth was already at the door to the street, and he didn't stop there. The last thing he heard was the beginning of the Master's favorite speech. The one about how Unferth's five other Masters—the tanner, the wheelwright, the baker, the fisherman, and the gravedigger—had all said not to take Unferth on. How he would never amount to anything and how he could never stick to a job long enough to learn it.

Unferth threw back his head and crowed, but the sound was lost in the commotion of the town square. An army was marching through. Someone handed him a makeshift pike. He raised it high and crowed again.

The Master could stick his speech.

* * *

When Brenn saw Corbinwood, he stopped and dismounted. Only when Galliard made it plain that it was safe to enter the deep forest could his thousand dusty, footsore, and determined troops fall out and rest. All along the march, their ranks had swelled as if by magic. Indeed, that was the rumor, that the Pretender could make twenty men out of one, but it was not so. Brenn knew that each of his soldiers was first something else in life. Each of these people had personal reasons to fight, and a common one to fight against. Ravenna and Dragmond had taxed and starved and whipped them into desperation. They were united behind Brenn because he offered them hope.

Galliard's whistle put Brenn back in his saddle, and he turned the black stallion to address the long line of his ragtag army. The days of rough travel had made companions out of strangers, and a leader out of Brenn, though he did not know at what point he had become more king than thief.

"We will defeat Dragmond and the Witch by speed, cunning, and desire," he began, intending to explain to them his vision of victory.

"What about takin' the Tower tonight?" a raw voice shouted. "We've come this far and we want to finish it now!"

Brenn drew on patience he had not realized he possessed, and smiled only a little. "Who speaks?" he asked.

"Gabriel of Murrey, sir!", was the instant reply.

Brenn found the face and saw that Gabriel of Murrey was very nearly his own age. And he looked exceedingly young for what lay ahead of them all.

"Gabriel. You shall have your fight after you've had your rest. I need you to be fit and hearty, and the Tower is another day's hard stepping from here. Will you wait with us, Gabriel?" Brenn broke into a huge grin.

Heartily embarrassed, Gabriel nonetheless grinned back and nodded as the two young men beside him poked him in the ribs and cuffed his neck.

"We will enter the forest," said Brenn, thinking better of his long speech. "Go gently, for it is a living thing. Divide into tens and pitch camp. Keep the fires small and cut no tree unto its death. You are the best fighting force in Palerna!'' he shouted down the line.

A mighty cheer rose from the ranks and the Palernan army, under Brenn the Pretender, moved into the forest's fastness.

≺≺≺ I ≻≻≻

Ravenna shivered and looked out over the battlements of Kestrel Tower. A sharp wind from the Sea of Shadows unsettled the winter morning, diving across the ashen waters.

She turned and faced the wind, listening to the voices it carried from Cordoba and Leon, from Provence and the Sicilies, soft voices brimming with Latin and knives. Above her, huddled on the spires and crenels of the ancient tower, a dozen black birds rumbled and coughed.

Over the city of Maraven the Great Witch gazed, her black eyes scanning over Grospoint and Wall Town and Teal Front, past the walls and south to the shadowy distances of the Gray Strand, where the rising sun glinted faintly on the red armor of General Helmar's Second Legion.

Good, Ravenna thought. *The old bastard has them out early.* She smiled grimly, squinting in the unfamiliar daylight.

Below her, at the very edge of sight, the legion wheeled in the dark, volcanic sand.

Ravenna leaned forward, clutching the stone crenels for support. It was maneuvers only, those men on the beach: an announcement of their presence to the expectant eyes that no doubt watched their movement from nearby Corbinwood. For by night, the Strand was dotted with watchfires and campgrounds as the Pretender's rebel army narrowed its stranglehold on Ravenna's city.

Ravenna sneered. It was a snot-nosed boy at the head of a ragged legion of cousins and alchemists and thieves, these rebels—more a traveling circus than a redoubtable army. The peasants who swarmed to the boy's banner would crowd the ranks, would rob him of speed and efficiency.

And he was young and green, and heir to a thousand mistakes.

The Great Witch shook her head distractedly, dismissing the voices on the wind, the sullen choir of ravens. The Watch dared not attack by night, and by day the enemy removed themselves, retiring into the fastness of the woods, the sheltering and deceptive darkness where they drifted like wraiths.

Each day, the Gray Strand changed hands, as the armies locked in a strategy of watch and wait.

The Watch lieutenant, on horseback, raised his arm menacingly, and the columns branched and dispersed amid the innumerable smoldering campsites. Dodging in and out of sight through the rising smoke, the soldiers spread out to comb and cover the dark, sandy terrain.

All of this took place in quiet, or so it seemed to the Witch. A mile from their menacing rehearsals, she was far from earshot, and it was strange to watch the drills and exercises, the obvious shouts and orders and calls that tumbled into silence before they could reach her across the distance and the black span of water.

It was like a scene enclosed in a dome of glass, or rising from the heart of her candles: a scene that she watched through fire and chanting, enacted at the great remove of magic.

But the sounds encircling her nearby were unsettling, anxious. The wind and the rumors of the Mare Nostrum, the ravens above her murmuring and boding . . .

. . . and below her, the whine and gibber of a dead king locked in his bedchamber.

I shall think of that later, Ravenna told herself. *Later, when my thoughts have gathered and Captain Lightborn is at hand to . . . advise and . . . instruct.*

She shook her head. It was as though the glass dome had descended to smother her, or the candle fires had moved suddenly, uncomfortably closer. She reached for the green vial of acumen dangling from the chain at her neck, for something had shifted inexplicably in the distant blending of sunlight and sand and shadow.

Something was happening on the Gray Strand.

Out on the dark sands, the Viscount Halcyon coughed into a silk handkerchief and ordered his troops to pass even nearer the wood's edge.

Appointed commander of the Second Legion over the objections of the General himself, the young aristocrat had distinguished himself in drill and maneuver, though he had yet to face an enemy soldier. Helmar had maintained he was too green, too inexperienced to command a legion, but the viscount's family riches and the Great Witch's delight in discomfiting her thorny old general had secured Halcyon's appointment.

He had spent a week patrolling this country, on horseback in the midst of his trudging infantry. He had heard the grumblings of the troops, seen their uneasiness in the long inaction of the autumn, and this morning he had decided to hunt down the rebels, to give swift and daring pursuit.

Halcyon loosened his sword in its sheath. After all, he thought the green-clad rebel troops of Brennart and the traitorous cousins had to go somewhere at sunrise. Surely, if the Watch looked closely and shrewdly enough, they would find innumerable passages into Corbinwood—entries into the honeycomb of pathways and trails that some said had marked the great forest for centuries.

Whatever the path or entry or trail, Halcyon had no intention of following it himself. He would stay here, at the water's edge, out of the range of bowshot, of javelin.

The rebels were few, were undisciplined, were woefully equipped. And still the viscount lost three, four men a day to the deadly bowmen who roamed the edge of the woods, as invisible and elusive as wraiths. You would see them for a moment—a flash of green upon green in the recesses of branch and needle—and it was like a bird had alighted only to spring suddenly into the air and vanish in the heart of the forest.

No, let the Watchmen flush out the quarry.

Halcyon leaned back in the saddle. His handkerchief smelled

of cinnamon and cloves, and for a minute, closing his eyes, he was reminded of a bakery on Teal Front—a safe and expensive and exclusive shop that catered to . . . expensive and exclusive tastes.

He opened his eyes as the wood's edge bristled and opened, and the rebels moved slowly out of the forest.

Halcyon sighed in delight and disbelief. It was all too easy. He guided his horse into the covering smoke of the campfires and shouted to his lieutenants.

There were no more than fifty of the rebels. Ragged and green-clad, they observed the Watch from a distance, taunting the city boys with their wild silence. Most of them carried shortbows and light sabers and makeshift spears—Zephyrian cavalry issue at best, but more likely unreliable weapons hastily crafted in country shops and smithies. Next to the Spanish swords of the Watch, the blades looked like toys.

Silently and quickly, as though some enormous tactical error had uncovered them, the rebels slipped back into the foliage. One of the cousins was among them: Halcyon was not sure of names, but it was the short, soiled one—the digger.

He had tunneled into trouble this time, the viscount decided gleefully. Quickly Halcyon shouted to his captains, and a hundred men rushed toward the spot into which the enemy had vanished. If they were quick enough . . . bold and resolute enough . . .

For a moment the edge of the woods was a chaos of leaf and red leather, as the first ranks of the Watch plunged into the thick undergrowth, the ferns and junipers around them unnaturally loud with birdsong.

Something is wrong here, Halcyon thought, *dreadfully wrong but I cannot figure what it is* . . . He searched his memory of strategy and tactics urgently, almost frantically—the dusty accounts of *coup de main* and *guerre a outrance* from the French military texts in his father's library. . . .

Something is wrong here and it is not those words and it is simple, but I cannot . . .

Then the forest exploded with cries and shouts, with the deadly music of bowstrings. One of his lieutenants fell in a whistling rain of arrows, and after him a Watchman, and another, and another.

Guet-apens. Enfilade, the viscount remembered in horror.

Swiftly, shrieking and dropping their expensive weapons, his troops turned from the lip of the woods and raced onto the black beach. A barrage of arrows followed them, and six, maybe seven tumbled into the sand and the ashen campsites. Halcyon edged his horse into the water, drew his sword, and shouted to his other lieutenant, motioning his archers into range.

In a daze, as though he were drugged or enchanted, the lieutenant complied with the hasty orders. The first line of archers knelt, bent their bows; the men behind them stood at attention in the military stiffness instilled by the viscount's maneuvers. But it was no maneuver on the sands before them: It was war this time, their first sight of the enemy, and their knees churned the sand as they fumbled at the bowstrings, as they whimpered and cursed. His gloved hand trembling, their lieutenant reined his horse through their ranks, murmuring encouragement and appraisal.

With a shrill outcry the rebels burst from the woods, pursuing the scattering Watch. They were young, these pursuers—young or surprisingly old, and at closer view they were even more ragged. Flushed skin showed through the green patchwork of their tunics and leggings, and their feet were bound in rags instead of comfortably shod.

In alarm, Halcyon realized they were far too close. Hastily, he coaxed his horse farther up the beach, away from the rebels and the clash of armies. There, safely situated by the ruined foundations of the ancient lighthouse, he paused, shifted in the saddle, and squinted back through the smoke at the developing skirmish.

Then the smoldering campsites that littered the beach in the hundreds burst suddenly, unexpectedly into new flame.

It caught the Watch off guard. A dozen men, perhaps a score, were burned by the flaring, and the archers startled, their arrows launched uselessly into the sand, the air, the rising flames. Moving swiftly, as though they had expected this all along, the rebels weaved through the fires and crashed into the midst of the archers, their light swords flashing and plunging home.

The smoke rose around them, and Halcyon turned from the

dark sounds of metal on metal, of metal on bone. He spurred his horse east on the beach, squinting uneasily through the smoke for the dark looming walls of Maraven and the tower beyond them.

She is watching, I know it I know it . . . but perhaps the smoke . . . the distance . . .

He heard a horse whicker out of the haze. For a moment he thought of Lightborn, of reinforcement . . .

But then he saw the green armor, the dark flashing flanks of the horses.

Flanc. Pince. The deadly maneuvers of mounted troops.

The Black Horse Cavalry.

The enemy surrounded him in a second, cutting off all escape. Desperately Halcyon raised his sword, but the commander, a dark Alanyan, his long hair knotted in a single braid, leaned gracefully in the saddle and sent the weapon flying with a casual flick of his saber.

Halcyon watched the sword fly into the smoke and darkness, then turned in horror as a gauntleted fist crashed into the bridge of his nose. He toppled from the saddle, breath and light leaving him as he struck the sand. Dimly, hazily, he saw the cavalry move by him, rushing in a gallop toward the sound of battle.

Then the Viscount Halcyon of Teal Front, of Orgo, whose holdings at Ransom and Painter Falls he neither heeded nor recalled, recalled nothing else as the darkness passed over him, black as smoke and volcanic sand.

She saw the burst of flame from her perch in the tower.

Ravenna shielded her eyes as it exploded over the Gray Strand, silver and swirling and fierce. Blinded by the sudden torrent of light, she whirled from the balcony and stalked into her chambers, toppling the nearest of the encircling candelabra. With a curse she righted the bronze stand and staggered to the center of the room.

Lightborn. She would call Captain Lightborn, who would . . .

The witch knelt on the marble map of the subcontinent. She breathed deeply, collected herself, then slowly traced the outline of the slate Gray Strand with her pale, sinuous fingers. The morning sun was framed now by the east window of her cham-

bers, its light glistening red upon the black parapets of the enormous East Balcony. Ravenna stroked the map slowly, coldly,
and thought about the Pale Man . . . about the limits of her trust.

Not yet. Despite his name, Lightborn was dark and shadowy
and undefined. He had risen rapidly through the ranks of her
nephew King Dragmond's guard, and now, after Dragmond's
death in a grisly magical accident, seemed to be at her side when
she least expected it, looking into her business with that pale and
canceling stare that seemed to mock all of her best efforts.

His was the voice in the back of her thoughts who ridiculed
her best plans, made light of her strategies.

And yet she could not rid herself of him.

No. Not Lightborn. She had to know more before she trusted
the infamous captain.

But trust was a low commodity in Kestrel Tower, as the
War of Succession—what all of Maraven had come to call this
struggle with the renegade wizard Terrance and his brat the
Pretender Brennart—moved tentatively into its sixth month.

Ravenna shook her head angrily. There was a time, when
Dragmond sat the throne, that she could trust in his stupidity,
his gullibility, and use his bloodline and his gender to establish
a claim to dominion. But now he was dead, and the landscape
before her was murky, peopled by mysteries:

The seasoned General Helmar, too shrewd and independent
to bend to her authority, too steeped in his antique notions of
honor and truth . . .

The weak aristocrat she had set in command of the legion on
the Gray Strand, simply to gall that seasoned general . . .

The girl Faye, whose friendship with the Pretender was the
boy's first memory and bond, whom Ravenna had kept silent
and compliant by the terrible strands of enchantment . . .

And then the Pale Man himself, the presence in the shadow
of the castle.

Below her again the king cried out.

What was passing through the dead country of his thoughts?

Did the dead dream? And if so, of what?

Ravenna shuddered. Quietly, she pulled back the gray sleeve
of her robe and extended her bare hand. Suddenly, blue fire
sprang to life in her palm—a wispy flame no taller than her

fingers. She rose and glided toward the nearest candle, chanting a Provençal curse designed to vex and discomfort the lot of them.

> Qu'ist son d'altrestal semblan
> com la niuols que s'espan
> qell solels en pert sa raia
> per qu'eu non am gent savaia.

Satisfied, Ravenna imagined them all as clouds: Helmar, Halcyon, Faye, and Lightborn obscuring the depth of the glorious sunlight. Smiling, she held the wick to the flame in her hand and muttered yet another incantation—the one that would guide her, as it had always guided her, through the flame to the heart of their dreams and thoughts.

There she would find out what had befallen the viscount, what lay dangerous in the thoughts and ambitions of Helmar and Lightborn and the charmed girl.

What, if anything, coiled in the mind of Dragmond.

"By each spot the most unholy . . ." she began, the words so familiar as to be effortless.

> By each spot the most unholy,
> In each nook most melancholy
> There the traveler meets, aghast,
> Sheeted Memories of the Past:
> Shrouded forms that start and sigh
> As they pass the wanderer by . . .

The wick caught fire, and the Great Witch smiled bleakly, fumbling at the glass vials that hung from the chain around her neck. Instantly, uncannily, Ravenna's gray eyes deepened and glittered and turned a fathomless black, as she opened her mind and imaginings to the hearts of those she would watch . . .

and suddenly, the candle sputtered and went out.

Desperately, the witch lifted the wick to the flame once again. The chamber filled with a blue smoke that smelled of violets, and Ravenna shook her hand angrily, painfully, as the flame in the center of her palm singed her skin.

What is it? she asked herself. *This has never . . .*

She turned to another candle, and yet another, as the room filled with smoke and the smell of burning tallow. Over the map of the continent Ravenna staggered, wrestling with the pain in her hand, vainly trying to light the taper that rested in a silver candlestick above the lapis outline of Alanya.

It, too, sputtered and died in a rank column of blue smoke.

The witch howled in dismay, and turned next to the Umbrian candle, dark above the southernmost reaches of the map. In turn, it refused the flame she offered.

Ravenna fell to her knees in the center of the map. Her gray robes billowed about her, as her black hair cascaded over the marble floor.

Outside the wind stirred uneasily, the voices rising out of it thin and parched like the scorched thickets of the dragonridden Aralu, thin and parched and drear and mocking . . .

Luogo e in inferno detto Malebolge . . .

. . . Je meurs de soif aupres de la fontaine . . .

. . . los muertos . . .

"Lightborn!" she screamed, her voice shrill and breathless in the smoky air of the chamber. "Lightborn!"

Three floors below her, the Pale Man raised his cold eyes to the ceiling and smiled. He stretched and leaned lazily against the mantel of the fireplace, warming himself by the banked flames. The girl he was watching stopped at her tasks, propped the broom against an oaken bench, and brushed the brown hair from her eyes.

"M'lady calls you, Captain," urged the girl. "I reckon she expects you quick, on account of her shouting and all."

"She'll call again," Captain Lightborn said huskily, and stretched again. His eyes played lazily over the girl's taut body, as he imagined the firm dark legs beneath the folds of her skirt, the sweetness of her, the soft electric sweetness of her skin. "Ravenna has . . . an expanded sense of the dramatic."

Slowly he fingered the hilt of his dagger, his thoughts involved and heated, as again and yet again the Great Witch called his name, her voice rising in pitch and in volume until the ravens, startled by the shrieks from the chamber, rose ponderously into the brightening Maravenian sky.

<<< **II** >>>

Brenn had declared the war from Galliard's old clearing in Corbinwood. Gathered around him were upward of a hundredscore men, chiefly farmers and woodsmen from the Palernan outregions, and though Ravenna would call them *rebels* and *insurrectionists*, they were the Palernan army in their own minds, gathered to defend the nation against the terrible encroachments of its own capital city.

For twenty years Maraven had drained the Palernan countryside of grain, livestock, of lumber and of manpower. King Dragmond had oppressed the country people with high taxes, had seized their most promising lads from the farms and made them soldiers in the Maravenian Watch, and for years the Palernans had endured these oppressions, chiefly because the taxes and impressments were gradual, growing slowly through the decades, and because the money was reasonably good in return.

Then Maraven sent them the plague as well.

The Death passed through Palerna in the summer of Brenn's apprenticeship with Terrance. It roared over towns like Diamante and Irret, Abertaw and Durain, and it struck the caravans that skirted the Plains of Sh'Ryll. All in all, it killed over half the Palernans, and suddenly Maraven, with its towers and flint walls, became a black and glittering symbol of death, returning plague for bounty.

Maravenians were treated coldly in the little villages now. All city folk were quarantined at the edges of the village, guarded in smoky, remote campsites, and there were accounts of tax collectors tied to a rail and tipped into bogs. But though the wayfarers decreased, the taxes continued to rise, and with them the hostilities.

Finally, the Maravenians collected money, grain, and livestock as they had collected the village lads: the King or the Great Witch closed out commerce with the countryside, instead preferring the trade of the harbors, of incoming ships and more exotic goods. Villages such as Keedwater and Bara were all but abandoned, and instead of the plague, Maraven now dispensed starvation.

When Brenn crossed over the Eastmark River on his way back to Corbinwood and inevitable battle, the Palernans flocked to him. Some said it was because of something kingly in the young man's stature, but most marked it down to simple vengeance: they had scores to settle with Maraven.

And so the War of the Throne had its beginnings.

For the six months that followed Brenn's arrival in Corbinwood, as July passed into September and October, and the trees of the great woods turned yellow and red, then suddenly, dismally bare, the rebels warred with the Watch by challenge alone, and by distant, menacing maneuver.

At the head of the cavalry borrowed from the Zephyrian athelings, Ricardo became the stuff of legends by the campfires of the Watch. His Black Horse Cavalry, claimed the Maravenian troops, were wraiths or mirages or perhaps even eidolons like those that haunted the Plains of Sh'Ryll. Whatever the truth, the western horse soldiers and their Alanyan commander rode out of nowhere and glided back to nowhere, leaving in their wake a litter of casualties and looted supply caravans.

The cavalry made war most swift and elusive, bold and in broad daylight, thwarting General Helmar's plans for a sustained assault and causing shortages of food and commodities inside the city. The citizens of Maraven grumbled for lack of spices and salt and finally grain. The general's temper grew hotter and shorter, and in the disheveled city, rumors arose that King Dragmond had gone into seclusion and that the Great Witch Ravenna stewed in the topmost rooms of Kestrel Tower, caught without augury or plan.

Through the autumn and winter, though no major battle had yet been joined, the tide of the war was clearly with the Palernans. They patrolled the Gray Strand with little or no opposition, and at night, a thousand watchfires dotted the black sands, men-

acing points of light that glared at the Maravenian walls like a
legion of angry eyes. They patrolled the beaches in lackadaisical
dozens, sometimes even helping the fishermen draw in their nets
or pointing out strange tidal arrangements to Ravenna's hired
retemancers. Often the Maravenian guards, gazing over the
southern battlements of the city wall, would see their green-clad
adversaries strolling the black sands or the brown plains. From
a distance they looked lean and elusive, like forest animals or
the sun-hardened Parthian warriors of the far west. Sometimes
they encircled a fire, sometimes they patrolled and sometimes
merely wandered, often tantalizingly just beyond range of the
Watch's best bowmen.

By January, the ancient General Helmar had left his Teal Front
villa entirely and virtually established headquarters on the city
walls. Sullenly, he followed the uneasy Strandward stares of
his own shivering officers, ice forming on his white, drooping
moustache as the troops on the battlements saluted him and
then marveled and worried. Through a shimmering, newfangled
spyglass from the Netherlands, Helmar watched the movements
of Brenn's army in the boy Pretender's first and tentative maneuvers.

He itched for warm weather and decisive campaigns.

"I'll have him on the Plains or on the Strand," Helmar muttered, handing the spyglass to the lieutenant at his side, who
fumbled the instrument in his mittened hand. "Steady with that
thing, Danjel. Yes, I'll have him then, for I'm three times his
age and three times more used to the waiting."

He nodded sagely at the bundled, shivering officer beside him.
Danjel wrapped the blanket more tightly about his shoulders,
inwardly cursing the old man's vigor and doggedness.

"I can draw him from the woods come spring," Helmar said.
"Drew out Namid and Macaire before him, and they were both
seasoned partisans."

Lieutenant Danjel rolled his eyes.

"And it doesn't matter what advice the Duke or the wizard or
Baron Namid give him. He's eighteen, and eighteen makes for
fire and error."

He clutched the battlements and looked long into the sky.

"When the spring comes, he's mine," the general muttered

absently, his words half lost in a cold, rising wind off the Sea of Shadows. "He's mine."

Danjel began to stamp his feet to find some feeling in them. This business was troubling, interesting. There was no hint of battle-lust in Helmar's voice. And he seemed *resigned* rather than resolved. Why, one would almost think that the redoubtable General Helmar had lost his edges.

It was something the Captain should know.

In March, when the sun had moved firmly into the Sign of the Lamb, heralding the beginning of Dragmond's eighteenth year on the throne of Maraven, the Pretender's army moved onto the plains south of the city, shifting and forming ranks at the farthest margins of Helmar's sight. With his Dutch spyglass he could see them, and Ravenna, drugged and kindled with acumen, counted their numbers from her chambers in the Tower.

Four thousand. Two hundred score. Numbers matching too well against the vaunted Maravenian Watch.

Who would have thought it possible? they asked themselves, general and witch, as the King's army gathered at the South Gate, assembled on Hadrach Road by the southern shores of the sea. Who would have thought it possible, those numbers and banners, the allied legions from Zephyr and Alanya, and the strange, nodding lights over the camp before daybreak?

Helmar shuddered, though spring had come sudden and un-timely warm to the shore. Out across the fathomless darkness he looked, to the campfires and the cascading lights in the southern sky.

He clutched his sword and gathered himself, awaiting the movement of armies. The Battle of Diamante, the histories would call it. The first amd bloodiest battle in the War of the Throne.

Diamante, for the little village six miles south of Maraven, a cluster of a dozen houses that figured so prominently in the first hours of the conflict, around which the infantry milled and clashed and locked in the deadly morning hours. Diamante, named by the Portuguese trader who founded the town in a place where the morning sun glittered on the dew . . . like diamonds.

Diamante was a hard stone, indeed, testing the mettle of both armies in blind Fortune and a shifting seaside fog.

All sight was clouded and angled and dim on the day of Diamante. When survivors gathered to tell stories of the war years later, they learned how different was each view of the fiery and faceted battle.

From the walls, the Maravenians saw the Palernan army march from the woods, traveling east onto the plains in numbers heretofore unimagined. The Great Witch, perched at her balcony as the evening descended, bright-eyed and jubilant from a fierce dose of the green *acumen*, saw them five miles away, the Pretender in the midst of a forest of motley banners.

She thought reconnaissance would be easy, that she would not lose sight of Brenn and his legions, but as she leaned on the south balcony, her dark hair lifted by a warm and directionless wind, suddenly they vanished into the mist and night and distance, and no drug could recover the sight of them. Though Ravenna chanted and concocted and peered into crystal and claridad and candle, all she could see to the south was a blazing amber light.

Below her, in the cluttered and dusky streets of Grospoint, Captain Lightborn mounted his white horse quietly and unceremoniously.

Aides and lieutenants flurried about him, handing him documents, briefing him on logistics, troop positions—on the ghostly, elusive presence of his rival to the south.

Lightborn's troops were afield already. Nine hundred infantry camped just east of Lake Teal, and another six hundred lined the old Hadrach Road south of Stormpoint. They had grown easy and soft with winter waiting, but messengers raced from Kestrel Tower with orders to mobilize, to arm, to prepare for skirmish if not for battle outright.

Calmly the Pale Man took the reins in his teeth and slipped on his white gloves. Around him, like an insistent high wind, the words of his advisers cautioned and lectured and buzzed. Cavalry had been sighted just north of Tallow Tree, Lieutenant Meresin reported, but whether they were Helmar's reconnaissance or a genuine threat from Umbria or Alanya he did not know.

Lightborn shook his head in disgust, waved the tall blond man away. Lieutenant Agares, full of misgiving and trouble, tugged at his stirrup, reporting that a squadron of Watch had verified the sight of a hundred traitors, no farther than a mile east of Corbinwood—the vanguard, no doubt, of a monstrous and formidable army.

"Traveling west?" the Captain asked calmly.

"I . . . I did not think to ask, sir."

The white-gloved fist crashed into the lieutenant's face. Agares pivoted, rocked on his heels, then fell to his knees.

"I suspect you will think to ask in the future," the Pale Man murmured.

Lightborn leaned back, righting himself in the saddle. Two of the Captain's aides stepped toward the fallen lieutenant, extended their hands . . .

then stepped back, thinking better of kindness.

Lightborn nodded to his mounted escort of two dozen men, then galloped through the city and Grospoint, down the rows of abandoned, reeking slaughterhouses where the night and the wild dogs and the thieves and things darker still haunted and stalked. Along Hardwater Cove, he rode, the smell of blood and metal and death receding, his gaze on the misty road ahead.

Back in Ships, the great bell atop the bronze-domed Burghers' Hall tolled midnight.

Glancing over his shoulder, the Captain thought he glimpsed a light on high, faint but steady against the rocks of the Aquilan coast.

That would be Kestrel Tower. Her chamber. Her balcony. The corpselight rising.

Captain Lightborn smiled grimly and sang to himself, a tune faintly recollected from his childhood, borne to his remembering ear by his mother's vanished voice.

> Dans quel philtre, dans quel vin, dans quelle tisane,
> Noierons-nous ce vieil ennemi,
> Destructeur et gourmand comme la courtisane
> Patient comme la fourmi?

He laughed softly, fingering the dagger at his belt. The young men riding behind him shuddered.

Lightborn stood up in the stirrups and shielded his eyes. Ahead, somewhere in the rising fog, lay the wizard's abandoned tower, searched from roof to cellars by his own most capable bodyguard. And just beyond the tower lay the East Gate, and beyond that, the dusty, unkempt road toward Hadrach and his assembled roadside army, who awaited his guidance and presence, he knew, with a strange mixture of eagerness and dread.

The Pale Man sat back in the saddle and rode on, his speed redoubled. Meresin spurred his horse to keep pace with the commander, and the others followed suit. Above them, lost in the clamor of hoofbeat on the hard dirt of Cove Road, the call of rider to rider, the faint sound of wingbeats wheeled overhead, and the dry cough of a dark bird guided unnaturally through the black depths of a seaside night.

Out on the plains the Palernan army settled for the night, its fires banked and its movements cautious and quiet.

Brenn crouched by a central fire, his cousins Galliard and Sendow standing over him. Around the three of them the soldiers moved and mingled, as though it was not unusual to keep close company to the rightful king and his family.

A young girl emerged from the guarded tent closest to the center of the camp. Modestly dressed in a plain green robe, she was nonetheless resplendent, gliding across the shadowy campground like a leaf sailing over a meadow. Quietly she knelt beside Brenn and drew four glittering stones from a little blue velvet bag at her waist.

"Cousin Lapis," the Pretender exclaimed quietly, with a merry half-smile. "What brings the fairest of my family hence?"

Lapis frowned. She brooked no talk of her beauty when she was about serious matters. She set the four stones in front of her regal cousin, explaining swiftly as she placed them on the campground.

"The blue one to the north, sire. The red one to the south. White to the east and black to the west. On cleared ground like the points of a compass. That is what the Umbrians tell you. Now for the light."

"This collection expands daily, coz," Galliard teased. "Where do you . . ."

"Hush!" Lapis ordered, pointing to a spot of light that sparkled and swelled in the center of her makeshift compass. "The crystals draw light from the points of the compass and . . . you can tell by the shadow when there's something . . . out there. Can even get the shape and size of it, when the moon is right and the skies are clear. Good for tactics, to watch the movement of our troops—and theirs—by day and night."

Slowly the light spread to the edge of the crystals, which now marked off a glowing green square, no larger than a book, in the center of the campsite. Brenn stared into it. There were the walls of Maraven, the rocks of Stormpoint at the easternmost edge of light, the smaller circular shadows that no doubt were the villages of Diamante and Irret.

"There!" Galliard exclaimed. "That broken line north of the circles!"

He and Brenn exchanged solemn glances.

"Helmar," Brenn whispered. "The old bear is out of hiding."

It was not the best of news, and yet it was the news they had expected and prepared for in the season of training deep in Corbinwood. If Dragmond's great general was aware of rebel movements on the plains of Palerna, he could not stay holed up in Maraven for long.

"Ricardo said the Maravenians are five thousand strong north of the villages," Sendow insisted.

"And I believed Ricardo when he told me," Brenn replied.

"Would that we had a clearer sight of it," Galliard complained, squinting at the wavering map. "Were it not for this fog—"

"The fog is nothing but our friend," Brenn said confidently, stirring the glowing wood with the blade of his sword. "Though by all signs Dragmond *must* know that we have left the forest, and now I expect he's eyeing to locate and number us."

"One can hope he blinks, sire," Sendow remarked impassively. "And that the fog holds."

Galliard nodded and turned from his cousins. Bracing himself against the night air, he stepped away from the fire, and for a moment he blended into mist and the dark of earliest morning.

Brenn looked up in concern. "I don't believe it will return."

Galliard stepped back toward the fire.

"The curse," Brenn explained. "The Lifting is over for you, Galliard. That's what the business in the East was all about . . . the dragon, the Aralu . . ."

"And the Bag of Ladra you . . . carry with you," the Forest Lord replied. "I know. I know you have lifted the curse. It's just that . . ."

Sendow and Lapis nodded briskly. They turned to Brenn, their pale eyes glittering.

"When you live with a curse for as long as we have," Sendow said, his northern accent crisp and clipped, "you . . . live about its edges, and you shape your life in its presence."

"Until it is lifted," Brenn replied. "And after that . . . I suppose you fill its absence the best you know how. But you don't abide by it anymore." He returned with a shrug to stirring the fire. "But it's only the Greeks that insist their kings be philosophers," he added with a smile. Galliard and Sendow looked uncomfortably at each other, wondering if the former thief had stolen a history book in his travels eastward. "Whatever you do about the curse, I expect you to be at other things come sunrise. Helmar's already afield, my scouts say, and Captain Lightborn will not be far behind him."

The rightful King of Palerna met the troubled gaze of his cousins, then turned serenely back to the glowing arrangement of crystals at his feet.

"At sunrise we shall send two hundred troops toward the villages."

Galliard nodded. It was a good beginning—cautious, yet not idle.

Brenn peered into the map of crystals and light, and nodded slowly. "We shall see how the general receives us. If Helmar meets us with a greater force, our troops will fall back, draw his attack. Then we'll flank him on the open plains."

" 'Tis an old ploy, sire," cautioned Sendow.

"Oh, it is," Brenn declared calmly, his gaze still at rest on the green glowing map. "And yet it works in every alley, Sendow. In every cul-de-sac and box canyon, from the days of the Philokalians all the way to last spring in Wall Town. The Goniph once told me there's a trap both ways in newfangledness, that ever looking for the new makes you quarry to the old."

Sendow shrugged. "The morning will tell us whether your Goniph is right this time."

"So it will," Brenn agreed, and was silent as his cousins drifted away to their beds. It was a feeling of surpassing calm that rushed over him there at the campsite as the sentries changed for the last watch of the night—a feeling like the Whelming at the hands of Glory, but deeper, milder, and more confident, and he spoke softly to the deepening darkness. "So it will, and I shall answer for it."

Miles east of Brenn and the glowing maps, four hundred Black Horse Cavalry stalked through rekindled light, the eastern horizon ahead of them purpling with first sunrise.

At the head of the second column, his tall horse overshadowing the squat Zephyrian ponies, Ricardo glanced to his left and counted the watchfires. By a traveler's swift arithmetic he guessed that the forces on the Hadrach Road were at least five hundred, perhaps six or seven.

Enough to give Brenn trouble by noon.

Gently the Alanyan lifted the reciting owl from his shoulder and whispered something to the bird—words lost in the soft rustle of hoofbeats over the plains. Immediately the owl took wing, soaring west and south toward Brenn's encampments. Smiling, Ricardo watched the bird flash out of the moonlight into the dwindling mist, an odd stream of chatter and poetry trailing it into the darkness.

"May the wind speed you well, my friend," he murmured after the owl. "And may your new song gladden the ears of the King."

The Zephyrians riding with him frowned. It had been like this since they mustered at Aldor in the early fall: the Alanyan had seemed a tangle of riddles and contradictions, far more like a traveling player or a vendor of miracles than a commander of cavalry.

They had watched him since, had followed and watched through the lightning raids on supply caravans, where Ricardo would lead two dozen cavalry against fourscore guards and emerge unscathed, delicately stealing the horses from the very traces of their wagons.

They watched through the ambush and shock attack that had defended the Gray Strand from the Maravenian Watch, where Ricardo had led them across erupting sands, guided at night by the odd little owl now sent back to the Pretender, and in the day by a strange, high-flying eagle he called Bertilak.

And by now, through raid and skirmish and downright battle, the Zephyrians had come to recognize that this juggler was a warrior of considerable invention, his strategies so wild, so harebrained that an officer such as Helmar could neither predict nor fathom them, so that when the dust had cleared and the black horses had passed once again from containment and view, what had seemed foolish not an hour before seemed either remarkably lucky or brilliant. The Alanyan did what he intended.

They watched the bird vanish, wondered what mystery it carried, then followed their commander as he turned northward toward the encamped Maravenians, the rising sun a red blade's edge on the horizon.

Lieutenant Danjel was jostled awake by the rough prod of the general's boot in his ribs.

"Wake up, son. Sunrise, and they're mustering south of us," Helmar rumbled. "The other side is moving, and I need you to carry orders to Lightborn."

Danjel scrambled drowsily to his feet, stumbling dangerously near the campfire. The general's strong hand restrained him, steadied him, and as he stood blearily at ease, rubbing his eyes and shifting his feet, Helmar scrawled a hasty list of commands on the back of a supply order.

For the Palernans were moving at sunrise, a wide green column snaking north to Irret, where it was rumored the villagers supplied them with water and milk and eggs. They marched on to the more perilous ground of Diamante, where the ramshackle circle of a dozen huts had been suddenly abandoned when their owners had discovered that the paths of battling armies joined on the village green.

"It looks simple from here," Helmar muttered. "Like a textbook on tactics—simple but formidable. The lad's designs are old and sound, not like those of the lunatic horseman he employs . . ."

The muttering trailed off, and Danjel broke the silence as a flushed sergeant brought forth a white stallion, saddled and ready for errands.

"Simple, you say, sir? How do you mean?"

The lieutenant was all ears. He would carry more than the general's scrawling to the pale Captain in the north.

"Sortie and retreat. An old alley dodge, worthy of a good thief. Which I understand the Pretender was in his recent boyhood."

Danjel suppressed a frown. Surely the note of admiration he heard in the general's voice was . . . something he had imagined.

"What we do is simple, Lieutenant," Helmar continued, laboring over the letters, the crumpled parchment. "Strike'im with twice the numbers, then dig in at Diamante. Above all, follow the other side nowhere."

With a flourish, the general finished his letter, quill poised in the air. He handed the soiled document to Danjel, whose face was a mask of trustworthiness as he folded the document neatly and placed it in the pouch at his belt.

He would open it on horse, when the sun was higher.

"Wait in the village," Helmar repeated. "Let the Pretender come to us, and break himself on our resolve.

"For now, he must think his ploy is working."

Garmund's Spear was a peasant squadron from Murrey, and like most villagers, sworn to the Pretender early. Their commander, a tanner named Garmund, had first heard of Brennart when the lad marched through Murrey on the first morning of July. By nightfall, the tanner had pledged his right arm, his money, and two years of service to the cause of the rebellion.

Garmund was also an active recruiter: young Gabriel the Chandler threw in his stout bow with the tanner, and a half-dozen villagers also offered allegiance. The rest of the company, thirty strong, was filled by farmers and villeins from the outlying regions. Hope of a better life was all the coaxing they needed to leave the old one.

They had chosen the company name for its drama and martial ring, had drilled with bravado and noise at the edge of Corbinwood. By now these peasants, though they would never be soldiers, handled their spears with some familiarity, and Garmund and Gabriel had passing acquaintance with the language of strategy and tactics.

They were the first troop into the hushed and menacing world of Diamante. Its thatched roofs rose out of the mist like a dozen dark cairns. Diamante was unholy ground: vacant and shadowed, smokeless, soundless, awaiting some sudden and dire change.

Softly, Gabriel began to sing, as he slipped his bow from his shoulder.

> The forward Youth that would appear
> Must now forsake his Muses dear,
> Nor in the Shadows sing . . .

"Hush, now, Gabriel!" Garmund hissed, waving fervently at the lad. "Leave the song, and search them huts."

Gabriel nodded, suddenly possessed with the seriousness of the morning, the quiet approaches, the possible presence of the enemy. He strung his bow soundlessly, his eye on the nearest of the thatched roofs . . .

then beyond it, to the northernmost edge of town, where the mist was rapidly shifting, reddening, taking form. . . .

"Garmund!" the young man exclaimed, and the north of the town erupted in purple flame and war cries. The peasants fumbled with their pikes, stumbled into each other, gaped at their commander, and through the black billowing smoke surged a hundred armed swordsmen, buoyed by the heat and the flickering blades and the bone-shivering roar of their voices, bearing before them the crimson standards of His Imperial Majesty, Dragmond of Palerna.

* * *

The first reports reached Brenn shortly after sunrise.

By then his commanding officers were dispersed. Thomas and Sendow had returned to their legions on the western and eastern flanks of the army, and the Forest Lord Galliard, whose troops bore the brunt of the evolving battle, stood bravely in the center of a three-mile line extending from the margins of Corbinwood across the plains to Irret. The Pretender sat with his staff of cousins—Lapis and the large, philosophical Ponder—in a stand of poplars three miles south of Diamante. The three of them shared a frugal breakfast of brown bread and water, awaiting the scattering of mist and the first news of the battle.

Soon Brenn saw the smoke rising from the north, and despite his gathered family, he felt terribly alone. He had never thought of war as a commotion of messengers.

By midmorning, as the smoke billowed and the plains to the north rang with outcry and metal on metal, the first rider approached, and the cousins rose to greet him, setting aside the maps of light and the speculation.

"I have sobering news, Your Majesty," the messenger proclaimed. "Your cousin Galliard, Lord of the Forest and Duke of Aquila, regrets to inform you that the village of Diamante is occupied by the enemy. Shortly after sunrise, two Maravenian legions—the Twelfth and the Seventh, our intelligence has it . . ."

"Alas!" Ponder interrupted. "Two hours into it and the Watch has us on the run. We'll be guests in the Tower by noontide!"

Lapis fastened her towering brother with a fierce scowl, and he fell silent. Brenn said nothing, but nodded for the messenger to continue.

The courier, a sandy-haired man of law from Keedwater, dismounted uncomfortably. His knack with a horse had put him in awkward surroundings, he feared, for he had heard tales of how monarchs killed the bearers of bad tidings. The Persians had done it, and the Pharaohs of Aegyptus. Azriel of Partha was the worst, having seized the captain who brought him news of his defeat at Ansari and poured molten silver down the poor wretch's throat. Wiping the dust from his doublet, the messenger swallowed and pressed ahead with the news.

"The Twelfth and the Seventh, as I was saying, sire. Helmar's best, and they drove your volunteers from Diamante with scarcely a scuffle."

"Shameful!" Ponder leaned forward, pushing his spectacles to the front of his nose. They were a gift from his younger sister, who had invented them and given them name. They were designed for the big man's most precious pursuits: the left lens was thick, through which he could read the finest inscriptions in scrolls and books and manuscripts, while the lens over the right eye was thin and clear for distant visions. Crouching before the glowing map, his eyes distorted by the variegations in the glass, the blond giant closed his right eye and traced the path of the armies with a long, meaty finger.

"Lapis's map shows them south of Diamante, sire. Headed this way."

It was Brenn's turn to swallow, to press ahead. Taking a deep breath, he stood to his full and most commanding height.

"It goes . . . as planned, cousins," he announced. Lapis nodded, and Ponder, his eyes still on the map, broke into a wide and delighted grin.

"Whatever Helmar told them, sire," the big man proclaimed, looking up at Brenn with triumph and amusement, "they've cast aside in their hunger for Palernans. I suppose that Sendow and Thomas . . ."

Brenn nodded. Sendow and Thomas would advance their archers and darken the sky with arrows. Straight into the jaws of Galliard's thousand the Watch would stumble . . .

And the trap would close behind them.

Gabriel rested amid the hayricks and fumbled for an arrow.

He had fired once, twice, a third time into the tumbling smoke of the huts, but nobody had returned the fire, so at Garmund's orders he had backed out of the village with the rest of them, to a spot in a southern pasture where the tanner had stopped, bound his own wounded leg with a torn scrap of tunic, and called for Garmund's Spear to assemble about him.

There were fifteen of them now, their number halved from what it was at sunrise.

Kneeling, squinting into the smoke, Gabriel kept watch while his comrades rested. The heat of the day had transformed the field around them. It was not just the fires in the villages and pastures, for it was more than seasonably hot that April morning, with the air shimmering like the edge of a flame.

Gabriel exhaled slowly, nervously, trying not to blink lest he miss a movement in the smoke, a flitting form in the shrouded ricks. He wondered inanely if an arrow could find its target through that watery shimmering air, or was it a cover of sorts, like the fog this morning or the smoke in the village, where the air itself conspired to hide target from target, to stir the confusion of armies until Watchman and Palernan were indistinguishable and therefore more deadly, stumbling across each other at close quarters, where dagger and fist would settle the business.

He coughed as another swell of smoke passed over. Behind and at some distance, Garmund paced in the midst of the shaken company, waving his spear dramatically, trying desperately to rally them. By then even the stoutest of them, the tanner's own apprentice Harald, realized they had been overrun.

Outside Diamante, where the cottages gave way into open fields and pasture, they passed the first of their comrades, wounded by a sudden, knifing movement of Captain Lightborn's Second Cavalry. The trained Aquilan horsemen had rushed over them like a storm on the open plains, their long knives bared and their horses swift and fearless as the fabled steeds of the Huns.

The cavalry had descended, struck, and raced on, leaving behind some thirty wounded Palernans. A few were dead, Gabriel saw at once, but others clung to life, groaning and sometimes swearing, and some were quieter, calling for friends or wives or mothers or just for water. He stopped, there in the open field, the red-armored Watch in full sight through the smoke behind, and had started to hand his waterskin to one lad, but Garmund stopped him, saying *Gabriel, look, the shaft's passed through the boy's gut, the water will only make him suffer more*.

Appalled, the chandler looked at the arrow buried in the boy's stomach. He would learn later, from a kindly barber surgeon who served as a pikeman with the Spear, that when you took a wound like that, the water poured through you like through a sieve.

He wondered what it was in dying that would make even water turn against you.

Shaking his head, dismissing the ghastly image, he peered steadily into the surrounding smoke. The old pikeman, Josce, quietly joined him.

"All caution, Gabriel, m'lad," the old man urged. "All caution and a tight grip on the nock' ere you see red armor out there in that smudge of a hayfield."

"They're all about us, Josce," Gabriel replied, a dry urgency in his whisper. He raised his bow then lowered it, as a rooster, terrified by the battle and smoke and commotion, rushed panic-stricken between the haystacks. "By the Four Winds they're here and over there, and I'll . . ."

"You'll do no such thing," the old man soothed, his deft hand on the lad's shoulder. "No such thing, that is, lest ye see that armor. . . ."

Gabriel nodded and relaxed, and Josce turned away, back to the clustered company and the makeshift treatment of Garmund's wounds. Left alone in his dangerous vigil, the young man tried to remember the martial songs he had learned with such relish back in Murrey. The one about the forward youth, there was, and the one about Agincourt, all blustery and rhymed and colored with banners and blood.

"Tell me not . . ." he began, and cleared his throat.

> Tell me not, Sweet, I am unkinde,
> That from the Nunnerie
> Of thy chaste breast, and quiet minde,
> To Warre and Armes I flie . . .

The song dwindled into silence, drowned out by the nearby crackling of flames, the shouting and scuffling in the shifting smoke. Gabriel listened bleakly. After a single morning the war had lost its tune.

Unferth the Apprentice crouched in the smoky cornfield. Red armor and green robes danced lethally at the edge of the churning fog, and out of the gloom came the cries of the wounded.

His plan for desertion had not worked all that well.

He stepped from the line and slowed to a walk, an amble, as his fellows passed by. There was Walter the farmer and Dexter the clerk, Alan the confectioner and the two lads from the outlying village whose names he could not remember.

They were a brave lot, and he was sorry he could not go with them.

Unferth laughed and sprinted off in the other direction, back toward Irret where the fighting was distant, the houses were abandoned, and food was plenty.

But Irret seemed to shift in the haze ahead. Soon Unferth was lost. The smoke had tricked his senses, and he circled the same wheatfield for a long, confusing hour, driven slowly toward its center by the advancing Maravenian army.

Now the battle surrounded him, clamor and commotion on all sides. A Maravenian swordsman burst from the smoke and charged, his weapon raised menacingly . . .

only to fall as a Palernan arrow lodged squarely in his neck.

Frantically, Unferth looked around for cover, for a passage to freedom. When neither availed and the Maravenians drew closer still—so close he could make out their words, their names—in sheer desperation he drove the head of his pike into the ground and climbed up the shaft, entangling it awkwardly in his cloak. As the Watch burst into the clearing, Unferth posed grotesquely, hoping they would mistake him for a scarecrow, would pass him by.

He could not believe his good fortune when they did.

As the battle wound away from him, the failed apprentice twisted on the pikeshaft and laughed softly, reveling in his first success.

The sun burst through the cover of cloud and smoke as the videttes of the Black Horse Cavalry reached the top of the hill.

Ricardo leaned over the rippling neck of his horse and gauged the animal's fitness. Churros was scarcely winded, though he had traveled the morning at a brisk canter.

'Tis good, Ricardo thought contentedly. *Good riding and good comradeship. 'Tis all that cavalry promised.*

He lifted the spyglass and peered into the gray swirl of smoke to the south. There, half obscured by the settled fumes, by the dust they raised and by their own rapid movement, Dragmond's army hovered at the edge of sight.

Lightborn's Sixth and Eighth Legions, Bertilak had told him. Led by the Pale Man himself. They had embarked at sunrise from their position on the Hadrach Road, and goaded by their sinister commander, had erased the miles like a moving hand, their forced march swift and merciless and awe-inspiring.

Ricardo winced and turned in the saddle. His cavalry would be hard put to overtake Lightborn.

From the northern hills, it appeared that if the Black Horse Cavalry did not attack the Maravenians, Lightborn's legions would crash into the middle of the Palernan lines, supporting Helmar's Twelfth as wave after wave descended on the village, broke through into the hayfields south of Diamante. . . .

"Captain? Captain?"

The company adjutant, Mashoba, held out his hand for the spyglass. Behind him, the ten remaining squadrons—sixscore men armed with shortbows and long knives—sat poised and expectant on the backs of their black horses.

Ricardo coughed, handed Mashoba the glass. Now was the time for the mask of serenity.

"Lieutenant Mashoba," he said quietly, his voice scarcely betraying his own rising excitement. "The time has come to see the elephant, as they say in my home country. Give the order to advance. We'll do this boldly, like they do in the Zephyrian saber charge."

A charge that would take them straight up the back of the vaunted Maravenian Sixth, he thought, against troops seasoned in the border wars with Zephyr, their new commander an officer famed for brilliance and cruelty and a strange, almost supernatural sense of survival.

Hastily he called for Lesharo and Angeda, the Zephyrian officers. The two men approached, the squat legs of their ponies churning soundlessly up the rise. Ricardo gasped at the speed and the silence, taking note as always.

One of them—he believed it was Angeda, though for the life of him he could not affix name to commander—had but one eye. It was said that when Namid lost his eye on the Gray Strand twenty years back, this one had blinded himself out of loyalty.

Churros pricked his ears as his rider gave a low whistle.

If they were ever to become our enemies . . .

Briskly, jovially, Ricardo explained the unfolding assault: The Maravenian legions were on a double march, but according to the birds that were Ricardo's reconnaissance, Lightborn had made the tactical error of marching the men too long too quickly. Four hours at a trot in heavy armor was enough to wind all but the most athletic of soldiers and horses, and these were aristocrats—exceptional fighters but used to a softer life and longer leave. They were straggling, the sharp-eyed Bertilak maintained. Spread over two miles of flat and hazy grassland. No doubt Lightborn planned to regroup within sight of Diamante, but for now his forces were scattered and vulnerable.

Lesharo and Angeda would each take four squadrons, sixty men apiece, and riding swiftly in a wide circuit, intercept the Eighth Legion, encircling it before it could join with Helmar's troops in the village.

"Thereby taking the Eighth . . . out of the conflict at hand," the Alanyan concluded, "and leaving Lightborn and the Maravenian Sixth . . . to my attentions." He sat back in the saddle confidently.

The Zephyrians nodded, and with no word, no praise for the commander's tactics, no assessment of terrain or numbers, wheeled away to their respective squadrons.

Ricardo shook his head. They were weapons themselves, sharp-honed and unquestioning, taught from infancy to be *the Atheling's talons*, the *long claw of Zephyr*. Thought was a hurdle to them, a barrier like rough terrain or a wide river.

As was compassion. He would not want to be a straggler in Lightborn's legions.

Ricardo watched the columns snake into the rising dust, then, with a gesture he knew was overdone, too dramatic, drew sword and flourished the long blade before his cheering cavalrymen.

Libra, the ancestral sword of Aquila, glittered there in his hand. The sword that legend said would *single out the crown of the line.* Following the directions of a curious dream, Ricardo had snatched the ancient weapon from the throne room of Kestrel Tower, that night in June when he and Galliard had carried off their foolhardy raid on the strongholds of Maraven.

They had ridden away singing, Galliard and he, singing the old *idle fyno* song the reciting owl had taught him in his alchemical days with Delia, and yet when they reached the edge of the woods, Galliard placed the sword in his keeping, soberly telling him that it was his "by right of dreaming."

Now, almost a year later, Ricardo stood in the stirrups on a grassy, treeless knoll, and as though charmed or enchanted or otherwise bedazzled, raised the sword to the recovering sunlight. The weapon's inscription, *Libra potestatis sum,* blazed into his eyes as a beam of light cut through the morning clouds. He had enough chemist's Latin to know that it read "I am the balance of power," but beyond that, the sword was a mystery.

For the life of him, he did not know why it had fallen to his keeping. Nor, for the life of him, was he certain that what he would do next was not the depths of folly.

From the moment he raised his cavalry, Brenn had decided to pattern it along new lines: the troops were lightly armed and armored, used mainly for reconnaissance and protection, for little raids and for great disruption.

Ricardo knew all of this. He also knew that, no matter your courage or skill, a charge such as this was reckless and rash if you rode unarmored into the jaws of a well-equipped Maravenian legion.

The Palernans were outnumbered, perhaps overmatched. Surprise and speed might be their deliverance, as the Pretender had said on that momentous day in Corbinwood.

"Charge!" Ricardo thundered, and kicked Churros into a headlong run down the hill.

Mashoba nodded dispassionately and charged, and if the Zephyrians found the orders foolish, even suicidal, not even Bertilak the sharp-eyed eagle could have known it from a look at their faces, where the flat, impassive grasslands reflected in their dark and shallow eyes.

Ricardo knew these men would never be his friends: stony and single-purposed, they did not distinguish between the thoughts of the heart and the deeds of the hand. Swords were their only poetry, their only subtlety and accord.

Impossible to live with, Ricardo decided, they nonetheless were men with whom you might be proud to die.

Not that he intended to do so.

Descending from the hills, as the horses gathered speed and the red line of the Maravenian troops loomed closer and closer over the acrid plains, Ricardo felt the same exultation, the same sense of adventure and simple joy he had felt on that June night by the Gray Strand, as he and Galliard rode home from their raid on Kestrel Tower. The foolish song sprang to his throat, and he sang it at the head of his galloping army.

> Ha ha! Ha ha! This world doth pass
> > Most merrily I'll be sworn,
> For many an honest Indian ass
> > Goes for a unicorn.
> > > Fara diddle dyno,
> > > This is idle fyno.

> Tie hie! tie hie! O sweet delight!
> > He tickles this age that can
> Call Tullia's ape a marmasyte
> > And Leda's goose a swan.
> > > Fara diddle dyno,
> > > This is idle fyno.

The Alanyans and even some of the Palernans took up the song, but soon it was drowned in the clamor of hooves, and a bloodcurdling Zephyrian war cry rose from the midst of the company.

Soon the Maravenians ahead of them began to turn, as their ranks collapsed on each other and slowed. Finally a handful stopped, then more, and an order rose up from somewhere in the red-armored lines. From their midst a score of archers stepped forth and leveled their bows.

* * *

He scarcely knew how to hold a sword.

Anthony the Shepherd stood in the midst of a desolate field, torn between following his comrades and running away forever. The war whirled like a hot wind around him, buffeting him from skirmish to skirmish. Boys, Palernan and Maravenian alike, looked up at him with frail, terrified eyes, and as he reached to console them, to protect them, they were sheared away from him by the surge and eddy of the battle.

He had thought of dying in a good cause, to lift the thrall of Dragmond and Ravenna from his precious land, how it would be sweet to fall in the vanguard, delivering wronged Palerna . . .

But that was all words now, all the vain imaginings of a man in love with departures.

At Diamante it was different, and the new images confused him: he could smell something turned in the air, the smell of death that should not have come so soon, even in the torrid heat of the burning hayricks. It was as if these boys had died before they crossed into Corbinwood or left the walls of Maraven, died back when he was waiting for them at his plaguestruck cottage, not knowing he was waiting for them yet, and the sheep were sleeping and scattered like rocks around the meadows and the banks. It was as if they had died back then and did not know it, and now that the dying was over they wanted to hasten through the first of the death, to be free of the whole terrible business.

When Lieutenant Mashoba recalled it that afternoon, his stomach turned and his hands grew unsteady.

The first volley of arrows had fallen short, and the captain kept singing, his sword raised and the big Umbrian stallion never breaking stride as he galloped into the downpour of arrows. Mashoba was the youngest of the officers, so he was sure that inexperience made him long for cover, for a stand of trees or brigantine armor or a kite shield as long as his body.

And the arrows tumbled about him, tunneling through the air like they were tearing it open. *We are someplace under the water*, Mashoba thought to himself, *we are not moving fast enough*, and he gave his pony a kick in the sides, propelling the stout little creature to the middle of the charge.

Then the boy in front of him called out—a brief, quiet exclamation, so softly Mashoba was surprised he had heard it over the hoofbeats and the Zephyrian war cry. The boy toppled back into the path of the pony, who hurdled his lifeless body effortlessly. And then the village ahead of Mashoba grew bigger and bigger through a haze rising out of the ground, until the huts were afloat on a river of fog and fire. In the midst of it wandered the Maravenians, a grim, bloodred array of shapes, dim as eidolons and turning, turning and kneeling, their bows raised obscurely in the smoke . . .

And another whoop arose in the Zephyrian ranks as, out of the banked fog beside them, a wave of green washed over the Maravenian Watch.

They emerged from the fog like wraiths, the long pikes readied, the red armor weaving through the gray tendrils like blood in cloudy water.

It was an omen Gabriel could read.

Calmly he let the first arrow fly, then a second and a third. A man fell over at the edge of his sight, and for a moment the fog seemed to swallow the red shadows once more.

The lad leaned against the hayrick. Perhaps the battle was circling around him. Perhaps the rumored reinforcements from the north had come.

"Too much supposing," he told himself grimly, and nocked another arrow.

And again they came, no doubt, to emerge from the thickly clouded plains into a hayfield, where a lone chandler from Murrey raised his bow and fired with mortal accuracy. A second man, then a third dropped before the young man, and he steadied himself, kneeling and raising his green hood against the smoke that rose again from all sides of the hayfield, replacing the soft fog with a choking, acrid murk.

Somewhere behind Gabriel a voice cried out, metal struck upon metal, and a long scream lanced out of the twisting darkness. He was tempted to turn but held his post.

"I must not. Garmund gave me orders," he proclaimed aloud, then startled at the sound of his own voice, at the tumult and noise that followed.

For in front of him the smoke blackened and billowed, and faintly the wicked light of a dozen fires began to illumine the burning landscape. Somebody shouted from the midst of the flames—a triumphant cry that spoke of *the Black Horse*, of *victory*.

And from the heart of the fire came a rider.

Gabriel lowered the bow and sighed. The man approaching was not in red, but a dust-covered, soot-covered white. He weaved in the saddle and shielded his eyes against the smoke, then, looking down at the young archer from Murrey, flashed him a winning smile.

Gabriel smiled in return, though he felt a strange tremor at the roots of his hair that spread down his neck and spine.

"We have them on the run, lad," the rider said, his voice cool and unruffled. "Dragmond'll lick his wounds in the tower before the day is out."

Gabriel wanted to toss his weapon into the gritty air, to whoop triumphantly and joyously. But the man before him was an officer . . .

and needed aid. The dusty man slumped in the saddle, reeling dangerously above the hard ground.

Gabriel dropped his bow.

"Looks like you'll be needin' a lift down, sir," he said quietly, reaching up for the man in the saddle.

A white-gloved hand and a dagger whipped out from the dusty folds of the rider's cloak. Off guard and weaponless, the young chandler felt the sharp, piercing blade against his neck, felt a strange, vicious tugging . . .

and then felt nothing. Saw and heard nothing.

Gently, as though he lowered a sleeping child into a bed, the white rider lay Gabriel on the ashen ground. Then, glancing about cautiously, shielded by the roiling smoke, he sheathed the long knife and dragged the body unceremoniously into a nearby cluster of hayricks.

Faintly audible over the crackle of flame, a laugh rose from the shadowy mounds, and the burning hay swirled upward in a hot wind.

Then a man emerged, wearing a green cloak. Effortlessly, he mounted the white horse and reined the beast north, into the circle of flames. From the saddle another laugh rose, cold and insinuating, a memory of winter. As horse and rider were lost in the black billows of smoke, a strange song trailed them, as haunting and opaque as the surrounding clouds.

Dans quel philtre, dans quel vin, dans quelle tisane,
Noierons-nous ce vieil ennemi,
Destructeur et gourmand comme la courtisane
Patient comme la fourmi?

All the afternoon, as the battle reeled southward, the general paced along the shores of the Sea of Shadows. His aides labored to keep up with Helmar's pivoting stride, a hitch earned dearly on the black sand of Gray Strand a generation ago, in Macaire's Invasion.

Back then, he had laughed at the circling fires, at the waves of Zephyrian cavalry. He had held a thin line along the beach from the old lighthouse to Barco's ferry. At the helm of a half-beaten army he had held it bravely, doggedly, for a fortnight at the cost of a thousand men. But Macaire was defeated, returned west, and for years the city had been safe.

That had been a summer of clear nights, when you could watch the enemy feint and turn at a distance of miles. That had been another beach entirely.

Now, in a maddening blindness, Helmar heard out the couriers, shaking his head.

This will not do at all. No, no, this will not do at all.

Out in the depths of the battle, the smoke was no longer moving but settled into a monstrous, lonesome mist and crying, inside of which he could begin to distinguish the fallen trees, the dark things moving . . .

"Danjel!" the general bellowed, extending a gloved hand. The lieutenant produced the spyglass crisply, and wordlessly Helmar peered through it, guessing vainly at the arrangement of the Pretender's army.

He dropped the instrument to the sand in disgust, in resignation.

"Blind! I have *no idea* where they are," he said, his voice as flat and bare as the beach around him.

Fully aware he was the last line between Brenn's army and the Maravenian walls, Helmar had set up a makeshift defense, just west of Stormpoint at the margins of Hardwater Cove. He gathered his cavalry into a single division. They stood at the shoreline, dismounted, some of the men ankle-deep in high tidal waters.

They were prepared to mount at a moment's notice, to move rapidly over the black sand to any point along the general's position, where their presence might prevent Helmar's worst nightmare—encirclement by Brenn's quickly moving forces.

There were not enough of them to defend the city. Most were scattered far afield.

To the landward side of the cavalry, the general stationed the regular infantry, the Third, Fourth, and Fifth Palernan Legions. These were stout men from the north of the country, bolstered by Aquilan officers and mercenaries, screened to the front and flanks by veteran crossbowmen. Flanking the crossbowmen in turn, established at the most vulnerable tactical positions, were the crack Twelfth and Seventh, already blooded that morning among the houses and hayfields of Diamante.

Where the Sixth and the Eighth were, he could not guess.

Helmar looked over his disheveled legions, and his warrior's spirits sank like a schooner run onto the Palern Reef.

Less of them. Grievously less. And disorganized, almost routed at Diamante. This will not do at all.

The Pretender's cavalry was unnaturally swift and unpredictable. Though the smoke was clearing now, it was still sufficient cover for a band of Zephyrian horsemen and their dauntless Alanyan leader. They could sweep out of nowhere, as far west as the Tower of Varthing or even Atheling's Pier, and it would be impossible to mobilize, to counter their slashing assault.

Galliard and Sendow especially would be shrewd commanders. Aquilan aristocrats spent half their days at tactics, and the young men would wait, just long enough, until the cavalry had crashed like a meteor into his westernmost legion . . .

then strike. But where? If they struck now, followed up their victory, the Maravenian cause was utterly lost.

For the first time in thirty years of soldiering, the general was lost and scattered, awaiting the cavalry, the fierce Alanyan in the vanguard.

That same Alanyan paced in Brennart's encampment, his dark face purpling with an anger scarcely contained.

"Regroup?" he asked, incredulous. "But . . . but, sire! We have scattered the Sixth and the Eighth, and if Helmar's officers had not been tough old veterans, we'd have even routed the glorified Twelfth in the town this morning! They're whipped! Demoralized!"

He groped for more words, but could not find them. He leaned sullenly against the sweaty flank of his horse.

Before him, Galliard bent over the glowing map, trying to make sense of its mysterious swirl of lights.

"Had we the magic to know his number *here* . . ." Galliard offered, pointing a slim finger toward a purple spot at the edge of the map.

"But we don't, cousin," Sendow interrupted, never the one for conjecture. "The magic we have is what lies before us. We have no Terrance, no Archimago. Nor do we have Cousin Brennart's . . . celebrated Faerie Queen."

He glared at Brenn, who would not return the gaze. None of his cousins, it seemed, shared his belief in the faeries, nor had the lifting of the Curse lifted their doubt. It was curious, as though something within each of them warred at the mention of Glory and the old Folk.

Would that Delia were here! Brenn thought wistfully. Delia, who alone of his friends had seen the Faerie Queen in full majesty, commanding a magical barge in the midst of the Eastmark.

But then, where were the faeries? It was all well to descend in a translucent globe of gold, a transforming light that covered a boy king and his reluctant subjects, bringing them into unexpected alliance. But where was that light, now that the news of battle was urgent?

"No," Brenn said finally. His three commanders stared at him, with expectation and not a little doubt.

"No. Our soldiers are exhausted. The battle has taken a terrible toll—four hundred, perhaps five hundred good men, who this morning sang of victory and war's glory." He seated himself on the ground. "To press farther would be . . . cruelty. It would be to do . . . as they do in the North."

He waved his arm vaguely in the direction of Maraven.

"A wise and compassionate choice, Majesty," Galliard said, staring coolly at Ricardo as he spoke. Sendow nodded and motioned to Jimset, whom he would send by horse to Thomas' company of archers, ordering them to pitch camp for the night.

In silence, Ricardo vaulted into the saddle. He nodded, regained composure, and rode off to join his company as Galliard and Brenn watched him ride away.

"You know full well that he may be right, Brennart," Galliard whispered, setting his hand lightly on his cousin's shoulder.

"We haven't the magic to know, Galliard," Brennart answered, unaware that he had lost his one great chance for a swift and total victory. Shielding his eyes against the westering sun, for the first time fully visible in a clear summer sky, he murmured softly to himself. "I wish I knew where they were . . . Glory. The faeries. Terrance.

"Especially Terrance."

Brenn walked through the camp in the aftermath of the battle, hearing scattered conversation, boasts, and insults rising from the tents of the men.

Their spirits were still unshaken, buoyant, and their distant joking reassured him. He stopped at the edge of one campsite and craned into the smell of food, the warmth, the noise . . .

and suddenly, he thought heard his own voice rise from the midst of rising laughter.

"Go gently, for it is a living thing. Divide into tens and pitch camp. Keep the fires small and cut no tree unto its death. You are the best fighting force in Palerna!"

The laughter dissolved as he stepped into the firelight. It was a company from Bara who scattered at his approach, leaving one man, his back to the Pretender, who continued to mimic and rail, his right hand cleaving the air comically in a parody of Brenn's unpracticed speaking style.

"We will defeat Dragmond and the Witch by speed, cunning, and desire . . ."

"The rest of it is even more eloquent," Brenn interrupted, and laughed to see the man blush, stammer, and stumble to his feet.

"Oh, a *thousand* pardons, Your Majesty, if ever you were to think that I was imitatin' you it was not that it was me imitatin' a man I heard imitatin' you and the joke of it was that he didn't sound like you at all he sounded . . ."

"Enough," Brenn said with a smile. "Your name, soldier?"

"Araven, Your Grace."

"But it's actually Unferth, is it not?"

The man bowed his head. " 'Deed it is, sir. Didn't want it published abroad so's the news'd reach my family when you behead me for mockery."

"Behead you? A talented chap such as you? There's always a use for these guises and voices, Master Unferth. In the coming days, I shall expect you at my immediate call."

Unferth's look of relief was no guile, his breathed *thank you* no voice but his own, deep-felt.

Far to the south of the fighting, the wizard rested in the blackened branches of a claridad tree. A battered straw hat pulled down over his eyes, Terrance slept lightly, the half-emptied flask of Zephyrian gin rocking precariously on the blasted branch, tilting back and forth with the wizard's snores.

It was the perfect time for experiment, Dirk supposed. He crouched at the foot of the tree, and nimbly withdrew the book from its supposedly secret pouch in the wizard's sack.

The months at old Archimago's had been less than interesting, especially given the company. Dirk missed Brenn, and Ricardo, and Faye up in Maraven, though the rumors had it that she had gone over to the Great Witch. He missed Glory and Lapis and the friends he had made in the depths of Corbinwood.

The glamor of being chosen for Terrance's new apprentice had sustained the lad through autumn and even into the winter. Some of the more simple spells had to do with noise and lights and fire, and that kind of magic Dirk took to readily, seizing every chance to startle the horses or dazzle Old Man Archimago and his scholarly apprentices Glendower and Vergil. At first it had seemed a romp—a holiday at the edge of Corbinwood filled with tomfoolery and practical jokes, with the wizards removed in abstruse conversation for hours, during which time he could do very well as he pleased.

And there was a roof, and food aplenty, and good stories of an evening. It was a settled life, but steady, and after the nights in Maraven when the dead walked and the Great Witch ruled, and after his near-deadly wyvern's sting of last winter, being settled and steady seemed greatly to his liking.

That is, until Terrance stepped up his training. It had started when the eagle passed over and dropped the green, glowing fruit on the wizard's head. When he regained consciousness, Terrance had pocketed the strange, bright apple, breathed a thank-you to Galliard into the foggy river air, and instantly redoubled Dirk's studies and tasks.

Dirk grumbled that the blow had damaged the wizard's faculties. Now the fireworks and incandescence were set aside, replaced by long and subtle spells that took weeks to learn and sometimes an hour to recite, where every word had to be precise in pronunciation, in tone, in inflection, until they sounded like no words Dirk had ever pronounced before.

Then, after all that sweating and memory and blabber, the spell went off and nothing happened.

Oh, something happened, all right. At least, Terrance claimed it did. Said that *the fabric of history was woven anew or unraveled,* whatever that meant. Said that Dirk had a gift for this very kind of spellcraft—a gift that, in years of training, would bring him great delight and bring great good to the world.

Dirk wasn't sure, however, that all that greatness was worth the years of training.

So, assured that the wizard was sleeping, the lad tiptoed from beneath the shadow of the claridad onto the sunstruck bank of the Boniluce. He scrambled down the riverside, still muddy with the water's recent swell, took off his shoes and dangled his feet in the river, leaned back, and began to read.

He was looking for something about explosions . . . but it was all poetry in front of him, abstract stuff about astrolabes and compasses and *the seed growing secretly*—heady stuff, Master Terrance maintained, the likes of which Brenn could not have mastered in a ten-year apprenticeship.

He sat the book on his lap and sighed.

It was his great good fortune, however, to have attached himself to that fellow in the tree. Archimago made his prentices *step lively,* and even though the old man was slothful himself, his stilted, rickety house was spotless, and whatever he decreed came to pass within the hour.

Like the damned machinery in the shed.

Dirk closed the book, leaving it unread for yet another balmy summer afternoon. He closed his eyes and thought about the contraption—a German bed of cranks and wheels and a strange rotating belt—and how Glendower and Vergil had struggled in setting it up. They were so pitiful, so at sea amid the cogs and sprockets that he'd half a mind to offer his own help, seeing as there had been a time when he'd been handy with a latch.

But Terrance said no, ordered him away. He had grown used to following the wizard's orders and expecting no explanation, but later Terrance had told him the thing was for *making* books, for *printing* so that you wouldn't have to copy your words by hand and you could have a dozen, two dozen, perhaps even a hundred of the same book that varied not a jot from page to page.

It was a thing that made Master Terrance shudder.

"Just imagine, Dirk!" he exclaimed, teetering on the black branch of the old rotting claridad, lifting the flask until the refracted sunlight shone through it and spangled the surface of the Boniluce with bright blues and violets and deep reds. "Imagine the . . . the *lockstep* of letters!"

Dirk had let the wizard brood and bode, had come to the bank to read and ponder and watch the Boniluce switch and tumble southward on its way to join the Umber. The two rivers flowed farther south and westward until they joined the Eastmark in that shadowy high country they called the Notches, the home of oracles.

Dirk sighed. A year in the open, away from the confining walls of the city, and he found himself thinking in expanses—in large geography that sorted ill with the tight places he had inhabited as a Maravenian thief. He looked up into the heavens, where the afternoon sun had passed through a cloudless sky to settle on the dark treetops of lower Corbinwood, and he wondered what the sky looked like where Brenn was, far to the north.

He had heard of Diamante. Archimago's guests, the three gentlemen from Europa, had brought the news when they arrived yesterday morning. *A momentous standoff to the north,* the Spaniard Saavedra had called it with a frown, leaning his gaunt frame over the neck of his horse as Glendower stumbled forward, helping him dismount. The other travelers, the Englishman and the Irishman, stood back silently; men of peace and more sparing of words, they let the Spaniard tell of the battle.

Brenn, it seemed, had brought four thousand troops to the field and, facing an army of nearly twice that number, had defeated it soundly with a daring, almost reckless cavalry attack to the rear guard of the Maravenian Sixth and Eighth Legions. His one mistake, according to Saavedra, had been not pressing his advantage: Helmar had regrouped on the seacoast, it seemed, and with the monumental defenses for which he was fabled in every tactical book of the age, had secured the beaches for Dragmond and Ravenna.

"The Eighth?" Terrance asked, eyebrows raised in delight. "Then our boy hit . . . *Master Lightborn* with the whipping end of the cavalry!"

"But we heard that Lightborn escaped," Edmund the Irishman said, dismounting nimbly from the horse and brushing the dust from his cloak. "Heard he vultured the clothes from an archer and made his way home to Helmar, decked in green and silence."

All of them—travelers and wizards and apprentices alike—mused over missed opportunities, and the night and morning had passed in the telling of stories, when the Irish bureaucrat took Dirk's wondering thoughts from the wizards at hand with tales of a knight's adventures through a transparent, sunlit landscape, where all the people and creatures he encountered were the eidolons of a god's imagining.

It was like traveling in a diamond, Dirk marveled, or over the crystalline Plains of Sh'Ryll. He listened rapt and fell asleep curled on Archimago's high bookshelf, awakening in the early hours to the bickering of wizards.

Terrance and Archimago stood below, glaring at one another over the German machine.

"You were always wary of new things, Terrance of Keed-water," Archimago scolded. "Ravenna was always the more inventive."

Dirk craned forward to view the dueling enchanters. He had seen the Great Witch once, dark and beautiful in a gondola on moonlit Lake Teal. Since that time, her name had always taken his notice.

"She was the smarter, too!" Archimago grumbled. "Would've seen the virtues of movable type while you were still muddling with runes or glyphs or . . . or . . . *cuneiform*!"

Terrance was silent, his long fingers ranging across the surface of the contraption.

" 'Tis neither Ravenna nor this . . . *machinery* that concerns me now, Master Archimago," he replied quietly.

"The *ortografye*, then," Archimago muttered. "In the spells."

Terrance nodded. "Do what you will with the *vocali*, the *consonanti*, the *unciales* you taught me half a century ago," he said coldly. "I assumed then that they had something to do with the magicking of things."

"Overrated," Archimago replied tersely. "Inaccurate, most of 'em. And unpronounceable for the young ones. Glendower and Vergil liked to *never* learn 'em."

"And yet you taught them ortografye," Terrance urged. "Thought it was important *then*. How long ago was that? Six years? Five?"

Archimago nodded bleakly.

Dirk rolled over on his back. A green parrot, who had perched beside him on the shelf to gather the sun from the high window of the cottage, startled and fluttered out into the morning sunlight.

The lad stared at the raftered ceiling, his thoughts racing.

So *that* was why Terrance was such an overlord when it came to the pronouncing of spells. Why you could not say "thow" when the spell read "throw," why "roote" was two syllables instead of simply "root." Why you had to make your voice rise on a word in some spells, keeping it down when the same word appeared in another incantation.

It was all so serious and powerful—hardly the course of study he had imagined when he signed that damned devious writ of Terrance's, the scroll where the letters changed with each reading, sometimes right before his eyes.

No, he was in for a long tour of duty. Longer every time he looked at that blasted document.

"Think how lucky you were, Terrance of Keedwater," Archimago protested, his white summer robes rustling against the side of the machine. "Think how many lads live so far from a wizard that their hopes for apprenticeship fade in those distances. Magic will never be their way of life, nor will they brighten the world with the gifts of their enchantments."

"And *this* is supposed to remedy that?" Terrance asked dramatically, waving his arms over the contraption.

"Printing will spread the magic far and wide," Archimago pronounced. "It says so in the plans and diagrams the merchant brought with this . . . this *press* from Europa."

Terrance reached for the documents in question, and the old mage handed them to him reluctantly. Even from his perch some ten feet above them, Dirk could smell the bright odor of trickery.

But still, he had no idea who the trickster was.

Terrance seated himself atop the press and unfolded the documents. He puzzled and muttered, and held them up to the light.

"My German is none too good," he admitted, and looked again.

Dirk leaned precariously over the shelf, clutching desperately with knees and toes as he stretched over Terrance to sneak a read of the plans in question. He sighed: he had no German letters— his Palernan was not all that good when it came to reading—and the diagrams on the pages were swirling, incomprehensible.

"But," Terrance concluded, folding the document triumphantly, "I recognize the mark in any language."

"What mark?" Archimago asked uneasily, his eyes turning toward the parrot, who had settled amiably in a flower box upon the windowsill.

"The *silver* mark, you old fox!" Terrance replied with a bitter laugh. "The coinage of Anglia, of Germania and Gallia, the little coin with the tyrant's voice! You have no more concern for the future of magic than you do for . . . for that *chamber pot*! And yet you piously plan to sell book after book to gaping rustic boys with a yearning for magic, when the only magic will be how you feed your pockets with their foolishness!"

Dirk smiled mischievously. Suddenly he had great respect for the old weasel.

"Now, Terrance . . ." Archimago began, clearing his throat and pushing feebly against his former apprentice, trying to move the younger wizard off the precious machine. "Surely you can see that two goods can be turned in this . . . this arrangement. That what fills my pockets fills their rustic hearts with magic and their rustic heads with knowledge."

Dirk could hardly keep from laughing. The old man was thoroughly corrupt.

"What is this?" Terrance asked coldly, like a stern schoolmaster reproving a wayward student. The document still lay upon the press, its ink newly dried. The younger wizard reached around the stubborn Archimago, picked up the vellum in question, and, holding the printed page at arm's length, read it aloud.

> Then doth the daedal earth throw forth to thee
> Out of her fruitful lap abundant flowers,
> And then all living wights, soon as they see
> The spring break forth out of his lusty bowers,
> They all do learn to play the paramours;
> First do the merry birds, thy pretty pages
> Privily pricked with thy lustful powers,
> Chirp loud to thee out of their leavy cages,
> And thee, their mother, call to cool their kindly rages.

Terrance smiled. "I remember this one. Always liked the first two lines of it, the beauty of the spellcraft. It worked on flora and fauna, and as I recollect, served *you* well in other matters."

Archimago blushed.

"Where did you get this version?" Terrance asked quietly.

"The Irishman," the old enchanter muttered. "Brought it with him in a commonplace book he's keeping."

Terrance sniffed. "And in Europa they think the *Irish* are the mages. I recall it otherwise."

He rose from his seat on the press and raised his hands. Dirk felt the chill rise at the base of his neck as Terrance spoke, spread through his body until his very knuckles hummed with surprise and rapture.

"The first line was the same, more or less," Terrance said, clearing his throat. "A vocale's difference is all. But the less is certainly more for the magic's sake."

> Then doth the daedale earth throw forth to thee
> Out of her fruitful lap aboundant flowres,
> And then all liuing wights, soon as they see
> The spring breake forth out of his lusty bowres,
> They all do learne to play the Paramours;
> First doe the merry birds, the prety pages
> Priuily pricked with thy lustfull powres,
> Chirpe loud to thee out of their leauy cages,
> And thee, their mother, call to coole their kindly rages.

The words settled lovingly into the room, and it was all the magic's difference. Startled again, the parrot leapt from the flower box as the plants bloomed with a new and sudden profusion, blossom cascading over blossom until the walls of the cottage were covered in violets. Airborne and jubilant, the parrot burst into song, its harsh voice magically sweetened, repeating the first two lines of the incantation,

> Then doth the daedale earth throw forth to thee
> Out of her fruitfull lap aboundant flowres,

and more abundant still, the flowers burgeoned and blossomed until the room was blue and fragrant and Archimago, brushing the leaves and petals from his precious German contraption, cried out in frustration and woe. Terrance laughed and began the incantation again. Dirk laughed as well, laughing until his shoulders shook, shaking the unsteady bookshelf so that the both of them, shelves and mirthful prentice, toppled into the center of the room.

Still laughing, and schooled as a thief in a dozen falls, Dirk rolled harmlessly out of the way, as the unstable shelving crashed into and splintered the celebrated press of Archimago. The old wizard sputtered and fell silent, gaping forlornly at the wreckage.

"The magic of this world, I suppose," Terrance announced, leaning against the flowery windowsill and gathering his breath, "is safe for another generation at least."

It was the Englishman's night at Archimago's cottage. The chairs had been drawn into a circle by the prentices, and the violets cleared and the bookshelf righted.

Nowhere was there a sign of the notorious press.

"I see what you were after, Master Terrance," Dirk whispered companionably, as he seated himself beside the wizard.

"You do?" Terrance asked, arching his brow ironically. "And what might that be?"

"Well, sir, it's your defense of the old ways, as I see it. Of the old ways being proof against newfangledness, and good in their own right, else they wouldn't ha' lasted to the new times. Least that's the way I see it."

Dirk sat back, smiling contentedly.

"Oh, that wasn't what I meant at all," Terrance whispered mysteriously, his eyes alight. "It's something else altogether, and you of all folks should know that a word must bend its way through a keyhole." He turned from his apprentice, masking a mischievous grin, and watched the Englishman sit and draw forth a copy book, poring over notes and loose pages, setting pen to lines and stanzas.

"Just like a forest warden," Saavedra quipped. "Pruning the property's edge."

The travelers and the wizards laughed, but Geoffrey remained silent, poring over the pages as if he had heard nothing. Then he began to read, slowly at first, then more vigorously, in a jaunty and cadenced English that Dirk had trouble following at first. But quickly and completely, the little Maravenian found himself drawn into the story.

"Arcturus," he whispered reverently. "Arcturus and Anglia . . ."

Geoffrey's story was a tale of changes and transformation, set in an Anglia when faeries still roamed the land, holding their circular dances in the depths of the forest and conducting the *specula*, the magic schools, in Devon and Cornwall and Wales and Iona.

Arcturus, the legendary king, had a knight in his service, who, unlike most of the others at the Tabula Rotunda, was a servant less to his king than to his own desires. The young man, it seemed, discovered a young woman beside a forest pool, and, taking advantage of the solitude and her vulnerability, raped the poor creature.

It was as simple and as brutal as that. But the girl, distraught and disheveled and murdered in that deep way beyond words that falls to survivors of violence, went to the court of Arcturus and accused the knight in question.

Now, the king was furious, all ready to slay the youth on the spot, had not Queen Gwenhyfar intervened. The lady, it seemed, willed that the young knight be handed into her custody, to do with *as she pleased*.

"Wonder if she'll *torture* him?" Dirk whispered bloodily to his master. "Or d'you reckon she'll . . . *poulardize* the wretch?"

Terrance winced and silenced his apprentice with a firm push, as Geoffrey continued, quoting his story from memory now, eyes lifted to the ceiling.

The queen in the tale set a task before the young man: within a year, he was to return to her and tell her what women desired the most.

"As simple as that?" young Vergil asked incredulously.

The older men glared at him, and Dirk stifled a giggle.

"Well, now, if the young Maravenian finds my prentice so . . . *amusing*," Archimago observed dryly, "then perhaps he can give *us* the answer before Master Geoffrey finishes the tale."

"Get on with it, Master Geoffrey," Terrance snapped, his stare grown suddenly intent. But Archimago would have none of it, goading the little thief, fixing him with a steady gaze until Dirk, nettled beyond endurance, offered a guess.

"Money."

"Hardly!" Archimago sniffed.

"And what would *you* say, Master Archimago?" Terrance asked wryly, his gaze still on the Englishman.

"Wantonness," the old wizard offered, then blushed as all of his apprentices, former and current, snickered.

Honor, the Irishman offered, and Saavedra maintained it was freedom. Terrance said nothing, but continued to stare sharply at the Englishman. Glendower, glancing soberly at his master, declared that what women no doubt wanted was *not to be contradicted*.

Vergil, baffled by the whirling answers, declared that he had no idea.

Which, Geoffrey maintained, was precisely the dilemma of the young knight as his year's search came to a close. All of these answers the knight had heard, and a good deal more besides, but the more he heard the more confused he became.

It so happened that, as the lecher returned to Arcturus' court, he came upon a group of maidens dancing in a circle, deep in the fastness of a wood.

"Faeries!" Dirk breathed, and Archimago wheeled about to scold him.

Geoffrey, on the other hand, looked directly at the boy and winked.

Faeries it was, evidently, for the Englishman told how the young knight waded into the midst of them, then stood back in dismay as the lot of them vanished, leaving in their stead a hideous old hag, who croaked and rattled as she asked him his business.

The young knight told her of his year-long quest, and how that quest had come to naught, and that he returned to Arcturus' court, to face whatever sentence the queen might imagine or devise. The old woman offered to help him, to give him the answer that would save his miserable and confused skin . . .

on one condition.

All of the men groaned.

"Best accept a woman's decision than suffer a woman's condition!" Saavedra declared, and the Irishman and Archimago laughed, while the prentices looked on stupidly.

"Go on, Geoffrey," Terrance urged. "Come to the point."

The Englishman puzzled at the wizard's intensity. He cleared his throat and continued, telling the company about the knight's arrival in Arcturus' court, how the lad stood boldly before Gwenhyfar and her assembled ladies and declared, as the hag had told him, that the one thing women desired the most was . . .

"They want the balance of power," Terrance proclaimed with a triumphant laugh.

"You guess well, wizard," the Englishman said. " 'Tis sovereignty."

"I do not guess at all, Geoffrey," Terrance replied quietly.

"What?" Dirk asked a little too loudly, rocking back in his chair.

Above him on the buttressed bookshelf, the parrot squawked amiably and hopped from volume to volume.

"Sovereignty," Terrance repeated. "Power. Rule." A slow smile spread across his face.

Geoffrey returned the smile, and continued. It seems that the young knight's answer was the right one—at least according to Gwenhyfar and her ladies-in-waiting. The knight was acquitted of his crime and turned to leave the court in triumph . . .

. . . only to be stopped by the hag, who stood before him and demanded her *condition*: that the young man take her as his loving bride.

The three apprentices cried out in dismay and covered their faces. Then, surprisingly, Dirk peered through his fingers to see Terrance rising, throwing belongings into an old leather rucksack.

"Well?" the wizard asked pointedly, staring at his apprentice.

"S-sir?" Dirk stammered.

"We're off to Maraven, then," Terrance declared. "Get your things together, boy!"

The two of them rustled about the common room, gathering clothing, food, parchment, and vellum, while with a strange half-smile, Geoffrey finished the story.

He told how the hag offered the young knight a hopeless choice on their wedding night: to have her young and lovely and unfaithful or old and ugly and true.

"Old and ugly," the Irishman said. "For with those flaws comes the greatest virtue, which is a holy and a loyal heart."

All the rest disagreed.

"He should answer neither way," Terrance decreed bitterly, folding a robe first one way then another, then giving up entirely and cramming it into the bulging rucksack. "He should say, 'Whatever you please, my dear'!"

Geoffrey laughed delightedly. "And so he does!"

"Please, Master Terrance!" Dirk urged. "Let us stay for the end of the story."

"Yes, stay, Master Terrance!" Geoffrey echoed. "For you've yet to hear of the great transforming."

"Transforming?" Terrance asked, pivoting about and sitting on the rucksack, shifting his weight as he tried to buckle the thing shut. "Well . . . prithee, speak, then!"

And Geoffrey brought the tale to a conclusion. Before the startled and delighted young knight, the woman transformed into a bride both fair *and* true, for her choice, her sovereignty, had been granted by her husband in full. The listeners applauded, and only then did Archimago rise and urge Terrance politely, halfheartedly to stay.

But the wizard would have none of his old master's blandishments. Together he and Dirk saddled their mounts—the same rugged horses they had brought with them from Corbinwood a year ago—and they left Archimago's house as abruptly as they arrived, impelled by some curious crisis that Dirk had yet to fathom.

Sitting uncomfortably in a saddle too hastily arranged, the lad goaded his horse to match strides with Terrance's long-legged stallion.

"Where are we off to now, sir?" Dirk asked, as the stars in the northern sky spread before them.

"To Maraven, as I told you," Terrance replied impatiently. "We'll be there by this time of night tomorrow, and it's good that we'll arrive in the darkness."

He turned and regarded Dirk openly, flashing a brief, ironic smile.

"We're going home, lad. Home so we can welcome the lot of them if they come. *When* they come."

His big steed raced away from the shorter horse, and the little thief coaxed his mount to follow. Catching up to Terrance at a hilltop overlooking Archimago's grounds, Dirk looked back over his shoulder to the stilted cottage that hovered over the glittering current of the Boniluce.

He would miss the slow peace of the southern woods, the sense of a time freed from time.

Below, in the shadow of the lofty cabin, Glendower and Vergil were at work repairing the press.

<<< **VI** >>>

Terrance and Dirk rode north, skirting the edge of Corbinwood, and to their east they saw the fires of the rebel encampments. The wizard was always ahead of his apprentice, awkward in the saddle, trailing cups and scrolls and vials so that Dirk was hard-pressed to keep up, stopping as he did every league or so to retrieve yet another dropped item. Once the claridad fruit dropped from the wizard's robes, but it was easily found and recovered, glowing by the trailside in the dim evening shadows.

The once-fertile plains of Palerna had been razed by the movement of armies. Miles of trodden fields and gameless forests bore witness to their haste and hunger. Despite Brenn's professed care for the farmers and farmlands, his troops were like all others in their need to eat, their bent to forage.

"But it won't always look like this, will it, Master Terrance?" Dirk asked. "After all, don't grasslands grow back? Don't farmlands . . . recover?"

Terrance smiled sadly.

"Of course they do, city boy. But they're years in the growing, and in the meanwhile, what do the farmers do with an empty and trampled land?"

* * *

They reached the first encampment by midnight—a bivouac of the Black Horse Cavalry set far behind Brenn's lines, where the wounded were quartered until they gathered the strength to rejoin the army or return to their homes.

It was like a dream of fever—fragmentary and shadowy and crimson with blood and flame. On the level plains, with neither wall nor tree nor rocks to stop them, the shadows cast by the soldiers standing in the firelight seemed unnaturally long and large—the shadows of ogres or monsters.

Terrance and Dirk weaved through the clustered wounded, through the stern Zephyrian guards. All around, on cots and pallets or lying on bare ground, were the heroes of Diamante. Boys Dirk's age and men far older than Terrance were gathered by the firesides. Some were blinded, some were nursing the stumps of severed hands or arms or legs. Some had suffered no visible wound—not even a scar or a bruise—and yet these were often the most pitiful of all, staring vacantly at the flames, at the sky, at nothing at all.

A smell rose from the midst of the encampment—the rusty broken smell of spilt blood.

Dirk winced as he saw girls among the wounded. Girls, and lads no older than eleven or twelve.

"Brenn has much to answer for this," the little thief muttered.

"Pardon?" Terrance asked distractedly, leaning in the saddle to catch the words of his new apprentice.

But Dirk fell silent, nor did he speak until Terrance roused him awake at dawn, handed him a cup of lukewarm tea, and goaded him again into the saddle.

" 'Tis Maraven by nightfall, lad," the wizard urged. "As we planned when we set out. But first I must have a word with you."

Dirk looked up at Terrance, who seemed inexpressibly older.

"There is something you need to do," the wizard ordered. "In which you need to join me before we leave this forsaken place."

Slowly, Dirk shook his head.

No.

"That is not the answer," Terrance declared, and there was

no urging in his voice—only the sharp, steely edge of command. "Do as I say. Hold your hands thus . . ."

And the wizard taught the apprentice the art of soothing the wounded. It was all they could do in the encampments, for the King's Touch of healing was beyond the power of even Terrance, and even so, they could ease the pain for only a dozen or so— only a dozen until the strength of the healers gave way and they wounded themselves in the effort.

Dirk crouched above a delirious young girl, placing his hand over her fluttering heart. She had taken a spear wound in a skirmish just north of Irret, where Lightborn's Eighth Legion broke momentarily through Sendow's lines. Stalwart in the ranks then, she was gasping now, gasping and gibbering and shrieking to the world that she was sorry, so sorry, and that she would do nothing wrong again if the pain would just stop stop stop. Dirk placed his hand above her heart, and he thought of green, of the leaves in Corbinwood and of grasslands in the spring, no doubt like those near the little hamlet from where, judging by her accents, the poor creature had come.

"She's from Garmund's Spear," a Palernan youth offered, standing over Dirk and the girl, casting a purple shadow over the red and fitful light.

"Move back!" Dirk muttered angrily. Surely there was something in what Terrance had taught him that would heal her . . . would bring her . . .

"Last of Garmund's Spear, she was," the boy continued. "The rest of 'em is dead up at Irret."

The heartbeat began to fade. Dirk rifled his thoughts desperately for a spell, a chant, but the tremor beneath his hand grew fainter and fainter until . . .

"Gone," he breathed desolately.

"Last of Garmund's Spear," the boy repeated. " 'Twas like the plains up and swallowed the lot of 'em."

Terrance approached the standing boy, his weeping apprentice who still knelt over the body of the girl.

"Grief is a luxury that healers can't purchase," he declared coldly. "There's a lad at the next fire with a stomach wound. Go to him: think of grasslands and leaves."

He clutched Dirk's shoulders firmly and locked eyes with him.

"This . . . misery of yours will have to end shortly, for by midmorning I intend to leave here, to pass through Diamante and the Maravenian lines. I will need your voice and your Wall Town accent to guide us through."

Thunderstruck, Dirk stared at the wizard.

" 'Tis no time for morals and blaming, Dirk," Terrance explained. " 'Tis a time, instead, when the best good can be done by passing through."

And pass through they did, the smoke encircling them until it seemed to the young men of the Watch that the two riders emerged from a hellish dream with healing and mercy in their hands.

Dirk did as Terrance instructed, announcing to the men who stopped them that he was the apprentice of one Valerius, a Parthian healer sent personally by the King of Partha to his Esteemed Brother in Royalty, Dragmond of Maraven, in order that said Valerius might attend to the illness of *some in Kestrel Tower*. Grumbling over the privilege of royals, the red-armored Maravenians stepped aside to let them pass, and Dirk and Terrance would have been safely to Maraven by nightfall had it not been for the Aquilan sergeant, a sly mercenary who asked for the papers that authorized Master Valerius.

"Summons?" Terrance asked, shifting uncomfortably in the saddle. "Y-you ask to see the papers of a man on an urgent mission?"

"Because these are urgent times," the sergeant insisted politely, "and because these are the front lines of an army, through which spies often attempt to travel. We have to examine your authorization, sir. It's common procedure." The mercenary's eyes raced probingly over the two riders.

Dirk gave Terrance a quick and secretive glance. The wizard coughed, fidgeted, and fumbled in his robes for a document that never existed. He drew forth an inkhorn, handing it to the sergeant, then two books and a compass.

"How long will this . . ." the sergeant began impatiently.

"Perhaps *this* is what you're looking for, sir," Dirk interrupted, reaching into his own saddlebags. With another glance at Terrance—this one more direct, more desperate—the lad produced the writ of apprenticeship and flourished it before the sergeant. " 'Course, you'd have to break the king's own seal. Sealed document, you know, from the Parthian king himself. So's someone can't tamper with it."

The words tumbled into a great silence. Suddenly it was the sergeant who coughed and fidgeted.

"Perhaps . . . my seeing the seal would be . . . sufficient, gentlemen," he replied uncertainly.

Dirk fingered the wax, broken long ago in Maraven by another apprentice, and breathed a quick prayer. He slipped his thumb over the fragments that still lay clinging to the parchment, and as he handed the scroll to the sergeant, whispered a brief incantation.

> This ae night
> This ae night
> Fire and sleet and candlelight

He felt the wax melt beneath his thumb, sealing the document again.

The sergeant took the scroll, frowned, and examined it.

"Of course, it's the Traveler's Seal," Terrance added quickly, and Dirk, who had scrambled beyond his wits too long, sat back in the saddle and breathed a long and thankful sigh.

"Traveler's Seal?" the sergeant asked, turning the scroll one way, then another.

"Of course, sir. If the traitors found a document sealed with the Parthian Eagle, how long do you think 'twould be before they opened it—not to mention opening me and my prentice?"

The sergeant nodded, but Terrance was not through.

"What cares the Pretender for the penalty that falls upon those who open the king's correspondence?" the wizard asked with a hearty laugh. "If he doesn't stop at treason, why should he balk at a *slightly* less capital crime?"

The sergeant looked back at his men, then brusquely handed the scroll to Terrance.

"Pass through," he said, and stepped aside, his rough face unreadable. "Arnaud, escort these gentlemen to the other side of our lines. May your journey be swift and safe."

On past the ranks of the Watch the wizard and his apprentice rode, a skeptical young soldier walking beside their mounts, guiding them through the watchfires and the tents and the stacked spears of the vaunted Eighth Legion. Twice Terrance stopped to tend to the wounds of the dying, and on a third occasion, too wearied to soothe yet another, he ordered Dirk from the saddle to kneel by the side of a young trooper from Wall Town. Solemnly, Dirk set his hands to the brow of the lad, who looked up at him once and, smiling as though he recognized the boy attending him, passed into the next world clutching a sheaf of letters.

"Yes," Dirk muttered over the dead boy. "Ye may be a soldier and I . . . well, I may be what *I* am, but we're Wall Town boys at the end of it—the kind the rich folks throw on the burning."

Then Terrance was at his side, a firm hand on his shoulder, and they rode from the camp, leaving the fires behind them, their only light a small white lantern dangling curiously from the brim of the wizard's hat.

For a mile or so, Dirk said nothing, lost in dark meditations. The war, he decided, was large and purposefully beyond him, for it was the duty of country boys and lads from the slums of the city to fight for a change of kings that would change the lot of those boys very little. . . .

Again, Terrance's hand was on his shoulder. While Dirk had brooded, the wizard had reined in his horse and waited. Their horses walking abreast now, the two travelers continued toward Maraven in silence.

"That writ," the wizard said hesitantly.

Dirk nodded. "An old Tarrochio trick. Costs the player to see the cards." And he started to explain the art of the bluff, but Terrance shook his head, the lantern weaving and fluttering.

"Oh, I'm perfectly aware of what you *did*, prentice. I was about to ask if you'd read it of late."

Dirk shrugged. "Well, I reckon there's something else . . . *untoward* happened to the scroll, since you want me to read it and all." Swiftly, he broke the seal, and laughed as he read the document.

The scroll requested that King Dragmond of Palerna receive

the physician Valerius from the court of Partha, with the compliments of His Majesty Flavian XII, Imperial Ruler of Partha and Emirate of Mesia, Rightful Claimant to the Green Throne of Umbria, etc. etc.

"It's . . . it's . . ." Dirk stammered, and Terrance laughed quietly.

"Well, not quite, prentice. It's not *quite* what you think it is. Look, if you would, at clause sixteen in the adjoining petition for trade alliance."

"Clause sixteen?" the lad asked suspiciously, running his finger down the page, his lips moving rapidly over the ornate Parthian turns of phrase until he reached the clause in question.

> And let his Imperial Highness Dragmond of Maraven
> attend to the immediate execution of Master
> Valerius' apprentice, who cannot expect his own
> powers of Tarrochio and thimblerig to rescue his
> master and his negligible, sorry self from all
> situations because a simple Aquilan mercenary looked
> for the pea under the wrong nutshell.

"Is *that* so!" Dirk sputtered, glaring at Terrance, who gazed off innocently into the fading night.

"Look," the wizard said quietly. "Off in the distance to the port side."

Flustered, Dirk stared along the wizard's bony finger to a multitude of lights nestled on the deep black horizon.

" 'Tis the Gray Strand, is it not?" he asked, his anger fading.

"Indeed," Terrance replied. "And those are the watchfires of Helmar's army."

But Dirk had returned to the scroll in his hands. Cautiously he turned it over, again and again, reading the scrawl that had changed, while he looked at the distant lights, from an elaborate Parthian script . . .

back to the writing that Dirk had remembered—the ancient print of the writ of apprenticeship.

"Why . . . 'tis the writ again!" Dirk exclaimed, and the wizard plucked the document from his grasp.

"What is it you say at thimblerig, boy?" Terrance asked merrily, the lantern on the brim of his hat tilting and bobbing. "Something about *the hand is quicker than the eye*?"

It was eight miles more to their destination, for Terrance and Dirk turned sharply east when the southern gates of the city came into view, pursuing a roundabout path beneath the shadow of the outer wall. They were safer that way from the companies of Teal Front bravos who, armed with their fathers' dueling sabers, policed the Maravenian walls rather than traveling afield with Helmar's legions. Safe behind the lines, these young aristocrats were notorious for bullying travelers, and Terrance could not risk even the slim chance that one of them might recognize him as the eccentric tutor of the Pretender.

Safer was the East Gate, up by Hardwater Cove where Cove Road passed through the wall and wound eastward toward Stormpoint and far-flung Hadrach. There the walls were crumbling away, the garrisons few, and where the wall tumbled into rubble and sand on the edge of the black beach, Terrance's broken tower lay locked and boarded—a safe and familiar place two wayfarers could pass the night.

So east they rode, the obsidian walls of the city glittering an eerie red with the sunset. Dirk glanced up at the old murder holes, designed by the wall's first architect as a nesting place for archers. The lethal slits in the fortifications had housed only pigeons in Dirk's boyhood, but now cold eyes watched him down the shaft of an arrow as he passed with his wizard master.

"Never fear, lad," Terrance whispered, pulling his hat over his eyes and drooping in the saddle. "My old tower's but an arrow's flight away."

But when they neared the East Gate, they found the wall rebuilt of new flint, glittering and strong from the arch over Cove Road all the way down to the beach, where a guard tower now stood, manned by a squadron of Watch.

" 'Tis an armed camp!" Terrance exclaimed in dismay. A sparrow fluttered from the folds of his robe and wheeled over the wall, traveling north toward the Causeway and Kestrel Tower. "There's no safety at the tower anymore."

Indeed, the old building itself was surrounded by a company of guards. Their red leather armor glowed in the last rays of sunlight as they leaned against the rebuilt and crenellated battlements, looking out lazily over the city and over Cove Road. Lights shone in the tall second-story windows of the tower, and the ancient tree that once climbed the sheer side of the building, snaking in and out through the windows, had been cut down at the roots. Only the tower roof remained as the wizard remembered, covered with empty boxes and broken furniture, its ladders and open stairwells ascending, as they always had, to nowhere.

"This is a quandary," Terrance mused. "I suppose I could bedazzle 'em. Set fire to the waters on Hardwater Cove, or fashion a new constellation in the sky . . ."

"Sign of the Pompous Ass," Dirk muttered.

Terrance pretended not to hear. "But then, that would announce my presence, would it not?"

Suddenly he turned to Dirk, fixing the lad in a fierce and urgent stare.

"As it would've announced my presence as far away as Diamante," he whispered. "Ravenna is waiting for conjuries, scanning the skies for fireworks and omens and strange transformations."

Dirk nodded. "She reckons you're where the magic is. But then, wouldn't that healing we done in the camps give you away?"

"Nothing like that would give us away," the wizard explained, drawing his horse into the shadow of the wall. "Ravenna has forgotten that magic. Forgotten it so thoroughly that she may not even remember it exists. *Hedge wizardry,* she'd call it, if she knew it was about. *Old wives' concoctions.* No, the Great Witch looks for the drama, lad. For blood and thunder in the upper regions, for auguries and necromancy. She wouldn't recognize healing if she stumbled across it in one of her graveyards."

Terrance dismounted, extinguishing the lantern on his hat. Dirk slipped gracefully out of the saddle and took both sets of reins in his small hands.

"There's something else to this, Dirk of Maraven," Terrance said. When addressed this formally, Dirk knew that the wizard was uncertain, that the country beyond him was new and dark. "And part of it is that if Ravenna were casting her nets for us, she could not take us in an act of healing or comfort. Something far deeper than magic sees to that, and sees to it every time."

Terrance's stallion shifted and snorted, and Dirk set his hand to the big creature's muzzle, calming the beast at once.

"And what is more," Terrance added, seating himself at the foot of the wall, "under her nose is the last place Ravenna will look for anything. It's a failing of all enchanters."

In the shadow of the wall, Dirk could not see the expression on the wizard's face.

"Well, I suppose it's time for us to go into Maraven," the lad urged finally. "Though it's a summer wind and balmy enough, I'd fancy a table out of the night air, a mug of ale at the Sign of the Mongoose on Hadrach Road and a bed for the evening—a real rush mattress rather than hard ground, if you understand—and perhaps for breakfast—"

"Indeed, so would I," Terrance interrupted dryly, "but before we plan the menu for the coming week, we must devise a plan to pass by the guards at the East Gate."

"Yes," Dirk agreed solemnly. "The guards."

In the shadows the wizard could make out the faint outline of the lad as he shifted uncomfortably from foot to foot.

Dirk cleared his throat. "I expect that the time has come to show you, then."

"Show me?" the wizard asked. "Show me what?"

Still leading the horses, Dirk tiptoed along the dark wall, westward and away from the gate. After a dozen steps or so, where the new construction gave way to much older flintwork, he stopped, leaned into the stones . . .

and vanished, leaving behind him the horses, grazing serenely on the high summer grass at the base of the wall.

"Dirk!" Terrance called quietly, and as instantly as he had vanished, the lad appeared again, beckoning Terrance to the spot where he stood, to the horses . . .

to the wide mouth of a tunnel that sloped on a gradual incline down into a deeper darkness, as the stone wall shifted back and forth easily beneath the small hands of the boy.

"The Goniph put it here thirty years ago," Dirk announced

proudly. "Showed 'em to me one evening when the Watch nearly caught us by Maraven Wall. 'Twas a good thing that Dragmond was hurried and cheap, else he'd ha' rebuilt the old standing parts of the wall and found it for sure. Telling you is violating the code of silence of the Guild, but I expect I'm not going back to thievery, and the way the King and Lightborn done the Goniph, I'm sure he wouldn't mind, seeing as we're helping the rebels and all."

Terrance was dumbstruck. "Do you mean that this . . . this *tunnel* was here, not fifty yards from my tower, all the time I lived in Maraven, and I . . . I . . ."

"I suppose a body might say you were looking under the wrong nutshells, Master Wizard," Dirk observed, his face hidden in the shadows. "Or elsewhere but under your nose."

So the wizard and his apprentice slipped into the tunnel single file, guiding their reluctant horses into the elaborate underground maze beneath Wall Town. Safely into the city and into the most desperate, ramshackle, and crowded part of Maraven, they emerged in an alley off Hadrach Road, stabled the horses with a reliable old friend of Dirk's, and had plenty of time for the long-awaited mug of ale at the Mongoose. Their journey over and their mugs drained dry, the travelers returned to the stable, where they drank of Terrance's *lethe* so that their dreams would not be invaded. They slept comfortably and deeply in the loft, no rush mattress beneath them, but soft hay that was certainly good enough.

That sleep would have been far more fitful, far more troubled, had they seen what came to pass at the East Gate not long after they vanished underground.

The rider approached quickly on a white horse, the dust scattering behind him like smoke, and only an outcry from the Watch lieutenant kept the archers from firing on him when torchlight shone on his green cloak. Reaching the gate, he spoke quietly to that same lieutenant, who stepped aside deferentially as rider and horse passed through the gate and west on Cove Road, past Hadrach Road and the Street of the Bookbinders, through Grospoint and Ships to the Causeway, then north over the gibbet-lined bridge to Kestrel Tower.

It was only on the Causeway that the rider felt safe. He slowed his horse, leaning back in the saddle, and looked contentedly up at the bodies that swung from the dozen scaffolds, dressed like him, in the mottled greens of the rebellion.

The Great Witch treats her prisoners more efficently than do her enemies, the rider observed. 'Tis a blessing to serve in a practical army.

He laughed quietly and coldly, and burst into song as he neared the gates of the tower.

> Je veux te raconter, ô molle enchanteresse!
> Les diverses beautés qui parent ta jeunesse;
> Je veux te peindre ta beauté
> Où l'enfance s'allie à la maturité . . .

≺≺≺ VII ≻≻≻

As the rider entered Kestrel Tower through its thick oaken gates, Faye, the maidservant of the Great Witch, awoke in her quarters from a fitful sleep.

Her dreams had wakened her again—dreams of alleys and dirty streets, of dried fountains and a path that wound its way through fire-gutted squares and abandoned buildings, and a tunnel. Always the tunnel.

And always the brown-haired lad.

Brenn. She knew his name was Brenn. The name had come to her like an insight, while she labored at the most unlikely tasks—sweeping a floor, strewing rushes, or drawing water for Ravenna. Quickly she learned that her dreams were of the Pretender, and it frightened her, because the Mistress peered into dreams.

And yet it had been a year since the first dream, she told herself, and in that time Ravenna had discovered nothing. Had said nothing.

Time was a curious thing to the tall, brown-haired lass who lay on her cot in the morning's early hours and speculated on years and dreams and time and the Pretender.

Almost all that Faye remembered lay within the walls of Kestrel Tower. She recalled awakening on this very cot one spring morning—two years ago now, as she reckoned it. Without ceremony she was handed a broom and a list of chores, and since that day she had followed the same lonely calendar, rising an hour before dawn and retiring an hour after sunset, her time filled with ceaseless work.

Wearily, Faye raised herself from her cot, setting her bare feet to the cold tower floor. She would be awake for hours now. With a sigh she reached to the foot of the bed and grasped the handle of the rush broom.

"Best get the early chores underway and snatch a nap in the Mistress's closet," she murmured.

Her hair matted, her eyes bleary, Faye slipped from her dark room into the fitfully lighted hallways of Kestrel Tower. A trio of startled grannars scurried away from her down an unlighted hall, chittering and scolding. She peered down the corridor after them, sighed, and swept the threshold, her eyes fixed on the dark ahead of her.

"Like looking back on things," she muttered angrily, and swept the dust into the darkness.

It troubled Faye that she remembered nothing before that spring morning. And yet the dreams of Brenn were too vivid to dismiss as pure fancy, suggesting another life she had forgotten, another time and place far from the Witch and hiding and work and wakefulness.

After all, the very fact she could read spoke to an unremembered past, for someone back there had taught her letters. Sometimes on the Mistress's balcony at nights, Faye would look out over the city, and a distant arrangement of lights would conjure an image of a square, a boulevard, a line of shops. And there were other teachings, so subtle she dismissed them as talents: she could climb a chimney like a sweep and hear sounds that escaped entirely the other servants' notice . . .

and there was this affinity for doors.

Facing what seemed to be a featureless stone wall, the young maidservant played her hands across the smooth surface until her fingers found purchase. "Ah," she exclaimed quietly, and pivoted her right hand . . .

and she was in Ravenna's closet. Through the thin wooden door opposite her, she heard the Great Witch chanting and singing.

"Good," Faye whispered. "She'll keep for a spell."

Smiling at her own surprising gest, the girl pulled a long black robe from a peg and, wrapping it about her shoulders, curled up in the corner of the closet, where she slept lightly, Brenn and a gray-haired man tracing dim paths along the edges of her dream.

She awoke shivering to the sound of another voice.

Cautiously, Faye crept to the closet door, and through the crack in the wood she had widened for purposes such as these, she peered into the candlelit gloom of Ravenna's chamber.

Lightborn was there. Standing by the Great Witch, who knelt on the floor, her pale hands exploring the inlaid marble map over which she conjured and augured.

Faye shuddered, then stared at the Captain more intently. It was like a fascination with snakes, she thought. You know the creature is deadly, so sinister that a coldness falls over a room even at its unseen presence . . .

and yet it is strangely beautiful.

In the week before he left for the command of his legions, Lightborn had visited Faye rather frequently, standing beside her and speaking to her, kindly and at length, as she swept or scrubbed or went about her other chores.

She was certain what he was after. The other maids had told her of men like the Captain, of how the servantry was there for their use, no matter the need or desire. That when your time came, as it did with the Watch captains or the augurers or the King himself, you consented and made the best of it.

Or found yourself on the gibbet, your last true love the voracious kites and ravens.

And she wondered why he was taking so long—why he made courtly talk and studied her habits. Perhaps the Witch prevented his further attentions. He frightened her, this Lightborn, although nothing about his words or deeds spoke yet of such discourtesy. It was something else, remote and shifting and undefinable as a cloud passing over the moon.

She remembered him from somewhere. Of that much she was sure.

"Nothing?" the Pale Man asked coldly, passing before the crack in the door. Faye watched him move gracefully over the marble map.

Ravenna shook her head. "Augury fails me. But it is just for now, just for a moment. The Pretender has his cronies, his inconvenient band of wizards, and it will take but a while to riddle his riddles and pierce his puzzles. The wind is changing, Captain Lightborn."

She smiled weakly as she rose to her feet. But Lightborn, it seemed, was having none of it. He sat in a mahogany high-backed chair usually reserved for diviners and steepled his blood-less fingers.

"The wind may change and the wind may change. But how long, my dear Ravenna, before someone . . . notices the air in the throne room?"

Behind the door, Faye bit at her lip. The words were opaque and elusive. Ravenna moved suddenly from sight, and her voice was faint, as though it came from somewhere near the balcony.

"There were rumors of *your* death, you know," Ravenna teased coldly. "Is it not a good commander who dies fighting in the midst of his soldiers?"

"*Your* good commanders, perhaps," Lightborn answered. "And those . . . even more *dear* to your affections, I have heard. There's a song going about in Wall Town that might interest you. I haven't all the words, but . . ."

The Pale Man rose from the mahogany chair and began to sing, his soft tenor voice clear and melodious.

> "I would do as much for my own true love
> As in my power doth lay;
> I would sit and mourn all on his grave
> For a twelvemonth and a day."

> A twelvemonth and a day being past,
> His ghost did rise and speak:
> "What make you mourn all on my grave?
> For you will not let me sleep."

"Begone!" Ravenna hissed. The room, and Faye's nose with it, glazed over with a thin film of ice, but she still could see the Pale Man through the crack in the door: Lightborn neither flinched nor quivered, though he wrapped his green cloak more closely about him.

"How *dare* you come before me dressed in rebel clothes, one of your legions in bloody tatters!" she cried out. She swept through the room, crossed Faye's line of sight, and vanished again, the air behind her stinging with the bitter odor of smoke and burnt tallow.

"I come to tell you that . . . the forces are evenly drawn, Ravenna," Lightborn answered calmly, pivoting in the candle-light, his silver eyes flickering lazily over the candles, the ornate walls, the closet door . . . .

By instinct Faye moved soundlessly back, burrowing into a drift of robes and furs and blankets.

"The forces are evenly drawn," the Pale Man repeated, his voice muffled now, as though she heard it at the end of a long tunnel. "And even odds are bad for you, nursing a cwalu king to keep yourself in power."

"Lower your voice," Ravenna threatened, but Lightborn continued unperturbed, his voice even more remote than before, as though he spoke through walls and ice and dreams.

"But who better, I suppose, to command the army you will put in the field . . ."

The silence that followed was so long that Faye feared they were onto her, that the movement outside the closet door meant only that they were approaching, preparing to unmask her, draw her into the light . . . .

"Of what army do you speak, Captain?" Ravenna asked finally.

"The army you will raise for me, m'lady," the Pale Man explained, his voice dripping with gelid poison. "For I shall be your champion afield, and carry your cause to your tormentors. But first, you must remember your promise. That when I bring you the Pretender . . ."

"I shall give you enough gold to fill your heart," the Witch conceded. "This I remember, Captain."

"I need an army to do it," Lightborn urged. "And here is how we shall raise it." And as he explained, the candles of the room fluttered and grew dim.

For a moment Faye listened, shouldering the back wall of the closet, but even her sharp ears could hear nothing of what passed between the Great Witch and her captain.

Within three days, it became obvious that Brenn had no intention of pursuing Helmar's legions onto the Gray Strand. The rebel forces stayed where they were, a dozen miles south of Diamante, camped within a mile of the decimated Eighth and Sixth Maravenian Legions, now under the command of young Colonel Flauros. By night, each army could see the watchfires of its enemy, but both stayed put, too battered and exhausted to muster a sustained attack.

For Brenn it was a speculation in great darkness. Twice he sent Bertilak and the reciting owl toward the Maravenian lines, intending that they bring back news of positions and numbers. On both occasions, a squadron of ravens met the two birds over the mile-wide strip of contested ground and drove them back to the rebel lines.

The Black Horse Cavalry patrolled the fringes of the encampments, on one occasion riding through the abandoned center of the once-friendly village of Eildon. All the while, the Second Maravenian Cavalry fended and harried them, so that even with spyglass and recklessness, Ricardo's information was brief and uncertain.

"We outnumber them, sire," he reported to Brenn, not bothering to dismount before he addressed the commander, green tunic and black braid covered with sweat and dust. "But by how much, I do not know."

Nor was the magic helpful. Lapis' lens provided some information, but it was murky and imprecise—not the kind of evidence upon which a commander deploys his green and battered army. And the faeries were but a golden glow at the edge of the camp, distant to Brenn and invisible to all others.

It was then, in the midst of the cloudy aftermath of Diamante, that Helmar seized the initiative. The general surged from his fortified positions on Gray Strand and began a withering forced march across the southern shores of Lake Teal and down the easternmost edge of Corbinwood, four thousand troops in tow.

In the middle of the fourth night after Diamante, a handful of larks flew east over Brenn's encampment, their cries unmistakable and terrified.

Galliard and Sendow glanced at one another in alarm.

"What is it, Galliard?" Brenn asked, rising with Ponder from another fruitless inspection of Lapis' glowing map.

"Send Ricardo and the Black Horse west immediately," Sendow began, then corrected himself at a warning glance from the Forest Lord. "That is to say, begging Your Majesty's permission . . ."

Brenn waved away the courtesies. "Ricardo is far east of here, on patrol by Stormpoint."

"Then I suggest you send his owl, sire," Galliard urged. "There's something afoot at the edge of Corbinwood, some commotion of men and horses if we're seeing the lark by midnight."

Indeed, it was such a commotion, though for hours Brenn and his commanders would not know the extent of the danger. Through a flurry of messengers, Helmar sent orders to Colonel Flauros to withdraw from his tenuous position facing the rebels at Diamante and establish more defensible ground within sight of the city walls. Within an hour of Flauros' receiving the first message, the campfires north of Diamante began to wink out, one by one, and the Palernan front line prepared for a night assault that never came. By dawn, the Eighth had reached the Maravenian gates, where they joined with their erstwhile commander.

And with a legion even more ghastly.

The general's mission, however, was only in part to rescue Flauros. Cutting off Brenn's forces from their stronghold in the forest, Helmar intended to push them east, cutting a wide and destructive swath through the Palernan farmlands, thereby forcing Brenn's army away from the safety of Corbinwood and from their principal sources of supply.

By dawn the general was in position around Alcove, a little village at the borders of the wood whose inhabitants, Palernan sympathizers all, fled when they saw him coming. He established headquarters in the large central hall of the town, and sent out the First and Fourth Cavalries as reconnaissance. Off they rode to the east, the bridles jingling with the silver Aquilan coins minted in the year before the death of Mardonius, when the Duchy of Aquila came under the protection of Maraven.

They did not return for two days. When they did, it was with stories of the Black Horse Cavalry, who harried them from Stormpoint to the edge of the Plains of Sh'Ryll, of the Zephyrian horsemen, their daring Alanyan commander and the ruthless one-eyed Lieutenant Angeda, who melted many of those Aquilan coins to fashion a new blade for his dagger, the first one irretrievably lodged in a Maravenian officer's rib cage.

The rebel army was moving, the Maravenians claimed. Moving west from Diamante, spreading along a two-mile front north to south. Three thousand five hundred soldiers, better equipped now for their battlefield trophies than they had been a week earlier.

" 'Tis a troublesome pass, Danjel," Helmar complained, his eyes fixed on the maps spread over the floor of the village lodge. "Two major battles within a week. Two struggles between battered and exhausted armies. I expect it's going to be like a clash of dragons."

He turned, smiling bleakly at his aide. "I've never seen it, mind you. A clash of dragons, that is. Seen dragons twice, but never two in the same place."

Wearily, the general crouched and picked up one of the maps. Holding it to the lamplight, he turned it over and over, then rolled it into a scroll, slipping it through his belt like a saber.

"They say that dragons fight long past the hour that they can really harm one another. What kills 'em then is their own vanity and stupidity. They fight in weakness and exhaustion, and there comes a point in the fighting where the weakness and exhaustion . . . do one of them in."

He crouched again, weaving slightly, and retrieved another map.

"Let me help you with those, sir," Danjel offered, standing above the general.

"Sometimes the heart ruptures," Helmar continued. "Sometimes the thing goes mad with weariness. Sometimes it kills itself."

He laughed bitterly. "Dragons are curious creatures."

"Curious indeed, sir," Danjel observed, his expression opaque. He took in the scene meticulously and hungrily: the vaunted general on the eve of battle, fumbling over maps and muttering about dragons.

It would be the kind of news that would pass through the camp like a grass fire.

Five days after the Battle of Diamante, the warring armies met again.

It was a day inauspicious for both sides. So the well-paid Maravenian augurers had warned, for not only did the water cloud in the porcelain bowls of the argillamancers, but it thickened and blossomed with the coppery smell of blood.

And east of the Maravenian conclaves the motley assemblage of amateur tacticians in Brenn's army protested the time of battle with a loud and urgent outcry. *Something is imminent,* they said. *Something neither star nor weather nor patterned flight of birds has foreseen.*

Brenn stood alone at the edge of the bickering campfires, his gaze to the west, where the Maravenian army waited like a huge, dormant beast. Tomorrow it would begin, and this was different from Diamante, for he was a blooded commander now, and knew what it meant to order men into battle.

This time, he resolved to leave the tactical darkness, the maps and the messengers. He would be with his soldiers, for he could send them into no country where he would not venture himself.

Helmar's Fourth Cavalry saw the Palernans first, a scattered column of green to the north, weaving rapidly over the sun-browned Palernan plains. Within minutes the general knew of

Brenn's whereabouts, and the Twelfth Legion sprang to action on the left flank of the Maravenian line.

Both armies were advancing when they met.

From a nearby hilltop, Sendow watched as his troops crashed into the charging Maravenians. For a moment the lines—red and green, Palernan and Watch—tangled like coupling snakes. Then the green line bent, dissolved, and scattered, and a cry of triumph rose from the Maravenian legions . . .

a cry cut short when, over a rise to the south, the banners of Galliard's approaching forces flickered like green flame.

The Forest Lord rode at the head of his army, a borrowed bow taut and ready in his skillful hand. Calmly Galliard dismounted, took his place in the ranks of the archers. With a smile and a steady hand on the shoulder of a trembling boy next to him, the rightful Duke of Aquila gave his orders.

"Stand fast. Be resolute. Do not release until red armor passes between you and . . . that stand of poplars in the midst of the field. Better yet, await my command to shoot. Remember to aim high, to reckon the distance."

It was familiar stuff, instructions the archers had received from childhood. And yet the Forest Lord went over it one more time, the old words assuring, reminding, placing the thoughts of the troops in a comfortable, habitual time. Calmly he watched the stand of poplars. His troops began to rock and breathe deeply and draw their bows, all eyes straining for a flutter of red.

Then a column of red-armored troops broke from the ranks and rushed toward the archers, roaring and shrieking, their weapons raised.

Steady, Galliard thought. *Steady, my boys, for there is time to do it all . . . take sight . . . pick your target . . . follow . . . follow . . . there is time . . . there is . . .*

Red armor obscured the base of the poplars.

"Now!" spoke the Forest Lord, and three hundred arrows, launched in unison, plunged into the Maravenian ranks like a fierce, slaughtering rain.

The Palernan archers let out a whoop and reloaded. The field before them was strewn with red armor, Maravenian soldiers twitching and thrashing like so many boiling crabs.

* * *

To the south of Galliard the armies locked as well, the legion Brenn commanded having pushed Helmar's Third Legion back into the fringe of the woods, where pike and sword flashed viciously at close quarters.

Stalking resolutely through the scattered wounded and dying and dead, Brenn drew his sword for the first time on a battlefield. He was not afraid; nor was it simply that he was surrounded by a seasoned squadron of Palernan regulars and flanked by two of his formidable cousins, the poet-archer Thomas and the blond giant Ponder. At the campfire the night before, he had ruled himself, had passed out of the country of fear. He was more king than man now, more man than boy.

"Take half the Palernans and fill that gap in the left flank, Thomas," he ordered crisply. "They've stopped us in sunlight there, and a roundabout road and a sly lieutenant can get us into the forest behind them."

"But these Palernans are *your* guard, sire . . ." Thomas began.

"They'll guard me better in that gap," Brenn insisted, waving his older cousin away with a merry smile.

Thomas turned back once, twice, as he ushered the troops in a wide arc about the southernmost of his own skirmishers. Brenn watched as his cousin vanished into the woods, twenty men following him swiftly and silently.

Ponder glanced down at him apprehensively.

"I think we all would feel much safer if Your Majesty retired to . . . a more strategic position," the big man urged in his most reasonable tone.

"All the strategic positions are ahead of me, Ponder."

The giant shook his blond locks. "Historically, it's imprudent, if you'll give me the liberty to say so. Alexander did it, and the old Philokalian King Cronos, and most of the Zephyrian commanders. So it's not without precedent. But imprudent."

Ponder stopped, pushed his spectacles back on the bridge of his nose, and stared comically at Brenn.

Brenn smiled and kept on walking toward the front. Ponder doubled his steps to catch up.

"I hope you don't imagine, sire, that General Helmar will take to the front lines as well."

"All the more reason I should be there," Brenn replied, and with finality pointed to a swirl of red and green flickering at the edge of Corbinwood.

And they leapt into the ranks like any other soldiers, there where the branches forked over them and the rooted edge of the forest rang with the sounds of battle. Instantly beset, Brenn shoved his Maravenian opponent to the ground. Leaving the fallen Watchmen to the mercy of the Palernans, the young Pretender grasped a low limb of an apple tree and vaulted over a brace of red-armored swordsmen.

The Maravenians turned, but it was too late. Brenn's sword snaked neatly beneath the shield of the smaller man, tearing through his leather breastplate. The man collapsed with a shriek. His companion pivoted away from Brenn and crashed into Ponder, who lifted him off his feet and smashed him into the trunk of the apple tree.

The Palernans around the cousins bellowed with delight, with recognition. Brenn neatly hurdled a fallen log and motioned his troops to follow, then quickly dove into the green light of Corbinwood. Ponder whooped and crashed after him, at his heels twoscore jubilant soldiers, buoyed by the prospect of following the rightful King of Palerna himself in a reckless adventure behind enemy lines.

In his surprise move down the eastern border of Corbinwood, Helmar had guessed at too many things for any sort of comfort.

Surely the other side had taken most of its troops from the forest to effect the campaign near Diamante. Surely the minimal garrison left behind had received specific orders to guard whatever strategic positions there were in the depths of the forest. And surely no aggressive tactics were expected of troops such as these.

Helmar was right on all accounts.

He did not, however, consider that the Palernans in the forest would actually steal the ground from under his feet.

* * *

Left under the command of Brenn's cousin Jimset, the Palernan garrison had honeycombed the ground beneath the forest with an elaborate series of tunnels. Underground corridors riddled the edges of Corbinwood, most of them planned by Jimset himself and carried out by a dozen miners from Aldor, a squadron of Aquilan engineers, and the redoubtable Bracken, Terrance's seventy-year-old dog, who would emerge from the long corridors covered in dirt, sometimes proudly clutching a mole or ground squirrel as his well-deserved quarry.

That same dog emerged from a tunnel in a sunlit clearing, right in front of the Pretender and his small band of raiders. Brenn clutched Ponder by the sleeve, as his soldiers encircled the two of them, waiting expectantly for orders.

"Ponder," Brenn whispered, as his cousin bent to listen. "It's just as I hoped. Jimset's tunnel system runs to the edge of the woods now."

Ponder watched Brenn nervously. Though far from a coward, the big man was a scholar, not a fighter. After his recent encounter, his conscience hurt more than his bloodied fist. Quietly, he sang the song he had heard in the ranks of the army, taken up and passed from one young man to another in the great excitement of approaching battle.

> The forward Youth that would appear
> Must now forsake his Muses dear,
> Nor in the Shadows sing
> His Numbers languishing.
> 'Tis time to leave the Books in dust
> And oyl th'unused Armours rust:
> Removing from the Wall
> The Corselet of the Hall . . .

He turned his sword over and over in his hand. Pummeling the Watchman had been a fit of anger and alarm, and protection for Brenn. He knew that man would recover, even if his head throbbed for days.

He was not sure he could use this weapon. It was absolute.

"There!" Brenn whispered, motioning to Ponder and pointing to Bracken. The old dog turned and waddled from the clearing, stopping where the shadows beneath an old oak tree dappled the ground with unusual darkness. The Pretender followed, and crouched by the dog and the tunnel entrance.

Bracken looked up at Brenn and licked his nose solemnly.

In the distance, toward the east where green shadow gave way to light at the forest's edge, the crash of weaponry and outcry of soldiers deepened and magnified.

"Let's follow it quickly, then," Brenn urged, as Ponder quickly removed the turf, the dirt and boarding, to reveal the steep incline into the dark tunnel. Bracken slid into the darkness headfirst, and Brenn edged toward the mouth of the passage.

The Palernan soldiers, especially those of plains or seaside origins, gasped in amazement.

Brenn tumbled down recklessly. Ponder gasped and plodded in behind him, and before Brenn knew it, certainly before he had second thoughts about the whole endeavor, his company was completely swallowed up.

"Now where, Brenn?" Ponder asked, forgetting the protocol.

Brenn blinked into the darkness. "I'm not sure, Ponder. I'd say the going is slow for the time being. Jimset's a good tunneler, though. I doubt we'll get lost. But we need a lantern."

"Lost?" someone exclaimed behind them, and a chorus of moans arose from the huddled young soldiers.

"Don't be ridiculous, Master Aberra," Ponder scolded, his voice merry and level. "There's such a thing as the King's Guidance, a divinely granted second sight that gives the monarch compass and astrolabe in his reason. *That* will see us through to the end of the tunnel and the backs of our enemies."

The soldiers quieted, taking in this new piece of news.

"Lead us, Your Majesty," urged a rough voice from the darkness, its accents pure Stormpoint, its tone both urgent and confident. "We'll follow ye to Dragmond's gates and wherever ye'd have us go from there."

Brenn reached out into the darkness and felt earthen wall, dried roots, rubble and rock. Quickly, he groped along the corridor, clutching the ruff of Bracken's neck as the big dog lurched and padded through the darkness. It was not long until Brenn felt an opening, and cooler air. The faint smell of juniper filtered through the new breeze.

<<< **VIII** >>>

In Kestrel Tower the Great Witch stood on the balcony and raised her hands.

She was weary already. This was no ordinary spell to raise the cwalu from their rocky graves along the Aquilan coast: those creatures were murderers, criminals all, more than willing to comply with her ghastly summons.

The bodies of innocent youths were altogether a different matter. It took a dreadful and draining conjury to bring unhouseled spirits into those bodies, and her own powers wrestled at the incantations, for everything she said and did in these bleak, nightstruck hours rode against Nature itself, against the laws that bound Creation together.

She did not care. Did not fear the rending of the fabric of things. The throne was worth it. Maraven would be hers at any cost. Weary, weaving slightly in the switching wind, Ravenna began the fourth of the chants:

> Be silent in that solitude
>> Which is not loneliness—for then
> The spirits of the dead who stood
>> In life before thee, are again
> In death around thee—and their will
> Shall overshadow thee: be still.

They would be there by sundown, she thought. And then, as a new and terrible wave of soldiers broke upon the rebels, the tumult of Wood's Edge would become a new battle altogether.

And this time, it would go in her favor.

"Seize to the shirt of the man ahead of you," Brenn ordered. "We'll walk out of here like the Parthian oliphants, clinging to the tails of one another."

A chuckle arose from the darkness around him.

"A most fitting bravado, sire," Ponder whispered, his soft voice surprisingly close to Brenn's ear.

"A most ambitious story, cousin," Brenn hissed back. "All this talk about the King's Guidance!"

"They're ready to follow you, sire," Ponder observed. "That's the *real* King's Guidance."

Brenn smiled despite himself, was glad that the big man could not see his amusement through the dark. "But the other guidance is what they expect," he replied soberly, starting to feel his way up the corridor.

"That's part of being a king," Ponder said.

"A sense of direction underground?"

"No. That they expect it of you."

Jimset's tunnel was woefully intricate.

Brenn guessed that it had been dug in a time when his cousin had explored all of Corbinwood from his peculiar point of view. No doubt Jimset had doubled passage on passage for the sheer joy of digging. Whatever his reasons, the design threatened to lose Brenn, Ponder, and a company of soldiers in a whorling mass grave.

Brenn groped along for fifty yards, no more, and the tunnel branched into three more narrow passages. The juniper smell had vanished in the thick odors of earth and unwashed soldiers, and Brenn stopped to gather his thoughts and brought all of his senses to bear on his choices.

"What is it, sire?" Ponder whispered.

Brenn did not answer. He stood blindly in the intersection of tunnels, staring into untroubled darkness. *Where is the King's Guidance now?* he thought, panic and despair rushing at him through the convoluted black maze.

"Sire?" Ponder murmured.

An uncertain rumbling of voices rose from the darkness behind him. Brenn took a deep breath and steeled himself, as his thoughts wrestled down panic and despair, raced over his rapidly branching options.

He could turn back. Could ask them all to choose which path to follow.

Brenn smiled and shook his head, his right hand absently brushing the hard walls, feeling the packed earth and lodged stone, the bristly tendrils of root. Those options would not do, would show indecisiveness. How would the soldiers follow him into battle if he dithered and hedged?

Better to choose one and tramp on boldly, no matter what. But how?

But which one?

King's Guidance, indeed. When the eyes failed, and the ears, and even the faint odors that had brought him this far faded, what was left to guide *him*? His hand tugged at a loose root and he felt the sword-shaped mark on his palm tingle.

Touch!

He thought of the long winter instructions with Glory, how the Faerie Queen had taught him the King's Touch, the healing by the laying of hands . . .

how she had told him its powers extended . . . beyond what he could imagine.

Quietly, shutting out Ponder's urgings, the soldiers' louder murmurs and grumblings, Brenn descended to a vigilant, silent place in his heart. Descended, as she had taught him, to a place where sound and sight and smell meant nothing, vanished altogether.

He remembered . . .

"Put your hands on your ankle once more," Glory urged.

"But I've done this a score of times already," he had protested.

"Natheless."

He did as she asked, and then closed his eyes.

"Now," she whispered. *"What do you see?"*

"Purple," Brenn replied. *"I see purple."*

"Fabling again, Your Highness," she had scolded merrily. *"What do you see?"*

"Six white points of light, faint in darkness," he answered in jest, opening an eye to look at his teacher.

After all, it had been a time in which he had not known who she was, when he was trying to get her to speak of the faeries.

She smiled.

"Close your eyes."

He closed his eyes, his fingers spreading gently, firmly over the intersection of the tunnels. He waited for color, for blue or purple or healing green.

Black. Black on black, the darkness uninterrupted. He sighed, and opened his eyes. Perhaps . . .

Suddenly, down the central corridor, so rapidly that Brenn feared it was a trick of his eyes, white light flickered in the core of the darkness.

Six points of light, paired and glittering like watchful eyes.

He did not stop to speculate.

"This way!" he ordered, and pushed through the shoulder-wide opening. For a second, Ponder lost grip on him, but Brenn reached back into the blackness, grabbed the big man's wrist, positioned him sideways, and tugged him toward the vanished light, a company of soldiers in tow behind the two of them.

And surely it was the right way, for soon the smell of juniper returned, of juniper and cedar and faint honeysuckle, and a warm wind hurried down the tunnel, and the Palernans rushed to meet the air and sun.

They emerged into marbled sunlight, brilliant and blinding, and for a moment Brenn weaved in the fresh warm air, his thoughts as bedazzled as his sight.

Ponder lifted him effortlessly, carting him to a cluster of taxus and vines. Set down softly in the fragrant foliage, Brenn blinked as his eyes adjusted, made out shape and color and at last the woods' variegated shadows. Swiftly, Ponder pointed out the red backs of Maravenian crossbowmen some hundred yards away, crouching at the wood's edge, showering the Palernan lines with deadly bolts.

They had shielded themselves with an abatis, a deadly entanglement of thorn branches and lumber and cheval-de-frise.

Brenn took in the scene at once. It was a position the Watch could hold for days against frontal assault.

"But not for long in the clamp we'll put on them," Ponder said quietly, reading his thoughts.

"Are we ready?" Brenn asked quietly, and looked about. One hundred eyes were fixed upon his, awaiting his signal, his command. They crouched, poorly armored, brandishing clubs, beaten plowshares, wooden spears, other makeshift weapons—all scarcely a match for Maravenian steel. A stranger might have misjudged them, for he would not have seen them fight at Diamante, would not have known they overmatched Dragmond's troops for bravery . . .

. . . would not have noticed the resolve in their eyes.

"You are an incomparable army," Brenn declared, his voice low and reverent. "Then onward!" he cried, drawing his sword when he broke from cover.

It was what his troops had awaited. Out of the tangled foliage they burst, following their king, whooping and shouting, leaping over root and rock and felled tree in a headlong charge toward the Maravenian lines.

Dragmond's Watch was caught off guard. Startled, the crossbowmen turned to face the surprise attack. Some of them fired their weapons harmlessly into the trees and the ground, a few less fortunate wounded themselves in the confusion. Their commander, a stout little fellow with a Teal Front accent, tried vainly to regroup his men, to organize them into lines, to face the oncoming assault.

But it was too late. Brenn's troops smashed into them with a triumphant roar, scattering bows, bolts, and Watchmen, pinning them against their own abatis. Desperately the Maravenians drew knives, short swords, but this was a company of archers, unaccustomed to close combat, and the Palernans made short work of them.

Of threescore crossbowmen who had manned the abatis, within minutes only twelve were left. Ferreted from the tangles of the abatis by Brenn's soldiers, those dozen men dropped their weapons and fell at the feet of their assailants, begging that their lives be spared.

Brenn stood over the weeping Watchmen, any of whom might have rousted him from an alley only a few seasons ago, might have harassed or beaten or even killed him, given a chance, a whim, and a secluded spot. Any of whom might gladly have brought his head to Dragmond as a trophy.

They seemed different now. The same ruthless patrols he had feared and dreaded during his time as thief and wizard were before him now, humbled and captive. On their knees they blubbered and begged, bringing to his attentions wives and children and invalid mothers some of them had no doubt forgotten until this moment. They praised the mercy and the righteousness of the young man they had sworn to kill.

It was rumored that Helmar himself had said of these men that *they fight well only when the odds are with them*. If so, it was a strange thing for a general to say about his troops.

Nonetheless, their begging was fierce and desperate. It was hard for Brenn to look at these men and spare them. His impulse was to smite them, leave them to the worst instincts of his troops, then discard them lifeless along the fortifications they gave up so readily. These hard thoughts troubled him. Standing on the spikes of a cheval-de-frise, he looked across the thorny fortifications to the Palernan lines, which had moved quickly toward this position when his troops had raised the green banners above the abatis. All around him now swirled the Battle of Wood's Edge, green and red and the flashing gray of weaponry.

He was a long way from that triumphant march across the plains of Palerna. Serenity had been easy then, and forgiveness. Then, astride his horse in the midst of adoring farmers and peasants, he had made pronouncements how the soldiers of both sides, ours and theirs, would all come to the same surprise on the field of battle, for they could discover in the face of the dying or imprisoned enemy a countenance very like their own. It seemed far away now, that pronouncement—the sentiment he wished for but did not share. He tasted dark bile and spat into the ditch.

He grimaced at the realization that war was his wizard now, teaching him the difficult lessons, how the lofty ideals were now so many words and feelings, and kingship was a deed, a hard practice in an imperfect country.

"The outcome looks promising," Ponder said, closing his left eye. Brenn's scholarly aide was standing beside him and at eye level, though Brenn stood on the fortification and Ponder down on the ground.

"Promising?" Brenn stammered.

"Out there," Ponder replied with a quiet smile. "See the swath of green north of us?"

Brenn looked into the distance. What Ponder spoke of was

nearly beyond his view. He nodded, curious at what this speck on the horizon could mean.

"Well, my spectacles are a handy apparatus," the big man announced proudly, tapping his right lens. "Can see with this glass at distances uncanny, and I know for certain those are Sendow's troops, and Helmar's northern lines have been broken."

Brenn looked at his cousin uncertainly.

"We're winning, Brenn," Ponder proclaimed quietly. "It will be costly, but we're winning. Two more hours, perhaps three, and Helmar will either leave the field or face a slaughter."

"A slaughter . . ." Brenn repeated, and the color drained from his face. "What should we do with the prisoners, Ponder?"

"Whatever is right," the big man replied simply, his one-eyed gaze still distant and northerly.

"Then I'll release them," Brenn declared, "all but the officers. Though my feeling is against it."

Ponder turned to him, regarding him skeptically over the bridge of the contraption on his nose. "I believe that a king should be past *feeling*, sir. The heart speaks in other ways besides feelings and thoughts."

"Part of the King's Guidance?" Brenn asked with a rueful laugh.

"A goodly part," his cousin replied. "Look. Here comes Galliard."

The battle of Wood's Edge continued for an hour, and the Palernans fared just as Ponder had foreseen. Sendow's and Thomas' legions hit the strong Maravenian center simultaneously, and at grievous loss of men, turned the red line northward. By noon Helmar had withdrawn to the Triangulo, the notch of land where Corbinwood bordered Lake Teal and the edge of the plains. He had burned the margins of the forest as he withdrew—a tactical necessity, he thought at the time, but one for which the consequences were not yet measured. It was an act of desperation: Of the four thousand men the general had embarked with, only three thousand remained. Frantically the Maravenians assembled their lines, positions, and defenses in open field, at the critical juncture of the Triangulo, awaiting yet another Palernan onslaught.

For the first time since the start of the war, since its origins in the backwoods and hamlets of Palerna, the Palernan army outnumbered its Maravenian foes. Brenn and Galliard rode together now, at the head of a battered but cheerful legion, moving north along the smoldering edge of the woods, framed by two companies of pikemen. At Galliard's advice, Brenn had sent twelve hundred men on a wide, looping arc toward the city, with orders that their commander Sendow descend quickly along the lake shore or establish a position between Helmar and the city, blocking the general's escape. The Black Horse Cavalry would ride to the south of Sendow's marching troops, serving as skirmishers, reconnaissance, as messengers between the two wings of the army.

It was a risky plan. Divided, Brenn's forces were vulnerable. But the end result could be total victory—the entrapment of Dragmond's general and most of his legions.

"The next few hours may be the most crucial of the war," the Forest Lord announced to Brenn, who nodded wearily.

He was becoming accustomed to these announcements. As each event rushed over them, each tactical shift of the armies, each supply line severed by terrain or enemy cavalry, each sudden alteration of weather, even the predictable changes from day to night, a new crisis arose, a new hour became most crucial.

Brenn turned the reins of the horse in his hand slowly, staring absently down at the worn leather. *I expect it will be like this for some time*, he thought. *I expect I have come to a place with no rest, no easeful moments from now on.*

King's Guidance, he thought again, and smiled.

Just inside the cover of trees, Jimset's company of sappers were busy at a new and urgent spadework, collapsing the outermost tunnels and filling them with water, shearing away vast lines of branches, sometimes of trees, so that the fire had no bridge to the heart of the forest.

"Damn Helmar for what he has done to these woods," Galliard said tersely, his eyes on the dwindling smoke.

"The roofs of Maraven are dry this time of year, too!" the brewer from Ransom shouted, and the dirty pikemen around him whooped and cheered.

Galliard smiled and waved at the clamoring troops, but his

royal cousin bowed over the saddle, troubled by the belligerent words.

"It cannot come to this," he muttered in dismay. "Would that Terrance were here!"

It was at this time, with the Palernan army on the march and extended, that the Viscount Halcyon tried to escape for the first of many times.

It was an obligation, he knew, part of the mystery of officers and the unwritten codes of chivalry and battle. He had studied it in military school, had it drilled into his thoughts at the edges of the Plains of Sh'Ryll, where Dragmond had sent the Teal Front boys to make them soldiers.

But putting those lessons into practice had been difficult: there were real captors and sharp eyes. He traveled on foot between two burly pikemen who smelled of fish and laughed when he stumbled. When they camped he was placed under guard as well, in comfortable but visible quarters amid a cluster of tents.

It was difficult to be noble under close surveillance. That was why, when the opportunity arose, he seized it with all recklessness.

Galliard had camped near the edge of Corbinwood, in a sunstruck area loud with birdsong and the whine of gnats and wasps. The heat in the tents was oppressive, stifling, and Halcyon managed to persuade his guards that a walk in the fresh air and sunlight would hurt none of them.

He had no daring plans at the moment. Not really. But while they strolled over the grounds, a cavalry sergeant rode into the camp, bearing intelligence from the Black Horse unit who were busy masking Sendow's movements north of the Triangulo. Dusty and bedraggled, the man slipped from the saddle and lurched toward the Forest Lord, who was crouched in secretive conference with his cousin Thomas.

The sergeant approached the commanders, leaving the horse grazing placidly between two tents. As his guards walked him past the animal, Halcyon leapt into action.

Despite his lack of tactical sense, the Viscount was an excellent swordsman, a more than passing athlete. Wrenching his arm free from the Palernan guard's grip was easy enough, as was the leap onto the back of the black stallion, who, though winded from a long gallop, was saddled and ready to ride.

Halcyon landed astride the animal in a graceful vault and, leaning over the neck of the beast, whistled it into a sudden, fierce gallop through the enemy camp. Soldiers scattered before him; one dauntless boy clutched for the stallion's reins, but Halcyon kicked him away and surged by him, charging toward the camp's edge and the last of the guards and the prospect of freedom . . .

Then the light rose out of the ground.

It was an amber glow, and brilliant, and for a moment the Viscount thought he had turned himself about in the confusion of escape, that he was riding toward the rising sun. Then six dancing lights, paired like white-hot eyes, emerged from the amber heart of the brilliance, and the horse beneath him whinnied and stopped, sending him in a light-blinded somersault over its neck and onto the hard ground.

It took no energy for the Palernan guards to retrieve him. He passed in and out of consciousness for the rest of the afternoon, babbling of claret and cheeses, and Galliard called in a Zephyrian physician who lifted the viscount's eyelids and checked his teeth, lifted his legs to make sure no bones were broken, then turned to address a bemused Galliard, saying that *given a day of rest, the patient would be, unfortunately, roughly the same man that he was before the accident.*

It was neither here nor there to the Forest Lord.

Upon Halcyon's awakening, his guard was doubled, and the chance for escape faded until a later time. He was haunted by that afternoon for days, months afterward. For when the light had risen above him, he could have sworn that he heard voices, as though the light was talking, or the horse beneath him. It spoke of odd things: of axes and hemlock, of herbs and silver and the perpetual changes of the moon, and whenever he thought of that voice, the thought would carry him out of the matters at hand, so that when he remembered who and where he was, even the everyday surroundings seemed freakish, touched by a deep and phenomenal strangeness.

* * *

Through the edge of the woods Anthony walked toward the low cry of the lad.

It was a Palernan boy, his green tunic mottled with blood. He cried hysterically and weakly waved his sword at the broad-winged kites that hopped menacingly toward him, hungering for blood, awaiting the moment when his strength failed him and death arrived.

Anthony stepped between him and the birds. They were wick-ed-looking little creatures, their beaks sharp and their eyes glassy and black. He knelt before them and whispered to them, his voice filled with deference and dignity.

"No. This is not your meat. There are horses dead in the sunlight. Seek your food there."

The birds cocked their heads brightly, regarding his words. They hopped toward the sunlight and vaulted into the hazy air, and Anthony turned to soothe the dying of the man.

In the evening the kites returned, alighting in a nearby haw-thorn. About Anthony and the dying boy the branches of the trees started to wave and darken, and their shadows spread across the edge of the clearing. The branches began to sag with them, black with crows and kites and owls and others Anthony had never seen, and when he closed the lad's eyes for the last time they followed Anthony away, flitting from branch to branch, their calls mournful and soft and low.

Mashoba was the first to see the cwalu.

That afternoon he was riding with Angeda and three squadrons of the Black Horse. Ricardo had ordered them north of Sendow's legion to serve as a lookout if, as the Alanyan said, *anything we do not want comes down from Maraven.*

They rode within sight of the city. Maraven looked squat and gray to the north of them, and twice Mashoba rose in the stirrups, looking through the captain's spyglass at the hated walls, the southern towers in the sunlit, hazy distance.

The adjutant smiled. He looked at the black flint with con-tempt, imagined the red-armored guards on the walls, protecting the decadent life of the city. There was a curse he remembered from his youth—something his father had repeated from the days of old Macaire, who came within a battle of taking that damned citadel to the north, and would have done it, too, had the weather and luck been with him.

Softly, he repeated the old words. The curse was a bard's, overblown and long.

> So blend the turrets and towers there
> That all seem pendulous in air,
> While from a proud tower in the town
> Death looks gigantically down . . .

Mashoba laughed, remembering the words on the tight lips of his cavalryman father, as if a man's voice could not encircle *pendulous*.

The curse went on from there. Something about the dead . . .

> There open fanes and gaping graves
> Yawn level with the luminous waves
> But not the riches there that lie
> In each idol's diamond eye—
> Not the gaily jeweled dead
> Tempt the waters from their bed . . .

Suddenly, Angeda rose in the saddle and shouted, waving his feathered spear. The column behind him wheeled to the north. On the horizon nodded three black banners, then a fourth.

Companies. Four of them. But under whose standard?

Mashoba rode after Angeda's charging column, his pony picking up speed, narrowing his distance to the beaded Zephyrian standards. He would be braver this time, braver than at Diamante, when his hands shook after the charges and he could not hold his bow.

For after all, the Maravenians—even Helmar's vaunted legions—were only Maravenians, only blood and breathing and fear. . . .

He stood in the saddle and whooped—a battle cry his grandfather taught him on the long marches when they moved the city of Agilis, following the seasons, the pasturage, the threat or lure of battle. All of Zephyr would ride into battle with you—the generations who had gone before, back to the Migrations, to the coming of the Horse—if you remembered the songs, the blessings, the curses, and especially the war cry that called them out of forgetful sleep to where their descendants still walked and rode. . . .

The column ahead of him broke and scattered not a hundred yards from the slowly approaching enemy, galloping in all directions. Mashoba rose in the saddle, calming his uneasy horse, and moved closer.

Then he smelled it too. The sweet acrid smell of the charnel house.

The horse beneath him leapt and bucked, wild-eyed. For a moment Mashoba shifted in the saddle, wrestling desperately with his balance.

Then he was falling, the sky above him whirling. He hit the ground, and the life left him.

The Cwalu's March was perhaps the most ignominious passage of the war.

Since her youth, Ravenna had known the secrets, once thought dead with the Empires of Egypt, whereby the criminal dead would flock to the necromancer's banner. And she had mined those secrets at least once before, once on a long night in Maraven when the Pretender, almost in her clutches, had escaped through resourcefulness, through the magic of his wizard protector Terrance . . . and through something else. Something indefinable that haunted Ravenna, that distracted her chanting, her spells and augury, so that now she groped in a larger, surrounding darkness in search of a knowledge that would not come, a magic that sputtered and failed at the edge of her hands.

It was this ancient spell that Lightborn had asked of her. An old spell, and a simple one, once the necromancer had given assent to its horror, its unnaturalness, and its cruelty.

An assent she had given long ago, when she rode in a coach to plague-ridden Rabia, intent to carry the Death to Maraven, to bring back the disease and infest King Albright's legitimate son.

But this time, Lightborn had asked for more. And, had she not been desperate, even Ravenna would not have given in to his terrible demands.

It was the ancient Philokalians, the dwellers in dreams, who had found the houseless dead roaming their early architecture. Soon, the old visionaries had learned the truth of the matter—that weaving among the insubstantial columns of their temples were insubstantial robbers and murderers, those whose bodies were destroyed by fire. And whether those fires were funerary, were the punishment of the stake, or were merely accident, it left them aimless, unhoused.

The Philokalians, supreme masters of the insubstantial, had found the words to banish these flitting creatures to a deep and outer darkness. There they peopled nightmarish fringes of the dream cities, but otherwise did not intrude in the lives of anyone. Indeed, they were as safely confined as things of their nature might be.

It would take a great and heedless sorcery to knit them again to a body. Something past the simple spells Ravenna used to raise the cwalu in her own city. But more than that, to raise an army of such creatures, it would take an abundance of bodies.

That was why the companies moved slowly and clumsily under their black standards. The cwalu were a special sort, and they stumbled as they learned the usage of unfamiliar limbs, of unfamiliar bodies. In ragged columns they marched, red armor by green by no clothing at all, and suddenly the northern fields were dotted with them, as Maravenian and Palernan soldiers alike scratched from their new and shallow graves and joined the dreadful legion.

At their head was a pale rider on a pale horse, his new armor blazoned with the black dragon of Maraven. Lightborn had masked himself with a scented silk handkerchief from the smell of his army and the airborne plague. Still, though hooded and mounted, and sealed in his command by the spells of the Great Witch, the captain was uneasy. His soldiers marched behind him, and he would not look back on them.

By the time they met with Sendow's forces, Lightborn's legion numbered upward of a thousand. Daunted, the Palernans held lines only briefly, then began a hasty retreat onto the plains, the cwalu forces following slowly, unsteadily. By late afternoon, the Palernans had been pushed back to Diamante, and farther southward they retreated, their eyes on the trudging columns behind them, the dark, mottled lines over which wheeled a navy of vultures and ravens and kites.

<<< **IX** >>>

The outcry of ravens brought her the news.

The noon sun tilted lazily into Ravenna's chambers, where the Great Witch sat in the middle of the floor, her dark robes and long black hair fanned wildly over the marble map, her gray eyes bloodshot and exhausted in the smoke of extinguished candles.

One of the larger birds, a dog-sized, gray-winged old coot, perched on the balcony and croaked and boded.

"Ah . . ." Ravenna murmured, tracing her long fingers over the marbled plains of Palerna. "So it did not fail, after all. . . ."

Somewhere to the south, invisible and dangerous, her captain guided his cwalu army toward Brenn and the rebels. It would take all of her regard and intent to manage the coming hours.

She cleared her mind for the next of the incantations—the one that would sustain the cwalu army through a day, perhaps two, of battle. Then she glanced at her hands.

The spots had returned, brown and dry, as though she had spattered herself with some loathsome liquid.

Distracted, Ravenna moaned, fumbled at the three vials she kept on a chain around her neck. No, not the acumen—that was for depth of sight. Nor the red potion, the one for seduction.

She fumbled more frantically.

Here. The yellow elixir. The attar of tithonia. The juice from the blossoms mixed with three herbs, the Alanyan chymist who gave her this formula five decades dead.

She tilted the vial toward the light. There was not much left.

"Hasten! Oh, hasten!" she whispered, and opened the vial.

The smell of the herbs, vigorous and green, filled the chamber, overwhelming the stale odors of tallow and smoke. Ravenna closed her eyes and drank, emptying half the vial with a single swallow.

It was all she could do to seal the bottle once more. The attar swirled in the crystal, taunting her.

"No," she said, quietly but firmly. "For later. In case it does not come."

She turned her attention toward the candles, the map. Deliberately, her thoughts and her body renewed, the Great Witch lit the first of the wicks and, forgetting all other spells and charms and enchantments, stared unblinking into the rising flame.

On the plains of Palerna, the cwalu surged stupidly with a new and sudden animation. Lurching south in battered armor, in cracked boots and bloodstained robes and rags, their weapons broken in their aimless hands, they looked vague and pushed, like a beaten army in retreat.

Except for their eyes. There was no terror in them, neither will nor thought, no sign of weariness. Only a blankness verging on nothing.

On occasion a moan would skitter like the call of a dove through the torn throat of a soldier. Riding above them, tied to his saddle so that he would not be pulled down among them or fall in their midst, Captain Lightborn would tell himself it was only the wind and keep on riding.

Sendow's legion, stationed just north of Diamante, had parted before the army of the dead like water before the prow of a ship. The plains were littered with their castaway weapons. Sendow had tried vainly to rally them, had ordered, cajoled, even beaten the deserting troops, but eventually he was left with a handful of brave but perishable men against a thousand soldiers impervious to weapon or fatigue or fear. Swiftly, reluctantly, Sendow retreated, slipping narrowly through the closing lines of the cwalu as the creatures tried vainly to encircle him.

He would remember it for the rest of his days: the gray hands clutching at his saddle, his boots, the dead men staggering and gaping, some dirt-covered, others still dragging the spears or arrows that were their undoing, toothless, eyeless, clawing at him like they were drowning. Calmly, he had waited on horseback until the last of his soldiers had eluded their circle, the big roan stallion beneath him quivering at the edge of madness, and then, the wall of dead men closing rapidly on all sides, he spurred his horse, hurdling through the sluggish lines, feeling one cold hand clutch . . . then another . . . a third tearing away his sleeve . . .

And then the fresh, bracing air of the plains, and he rode a hundred yards to where his twoscore men had gathered, lighting torches in the broad daylight, waving them grimly at the approaching cwalu. Two hundred of the undead turned toward them, their pursuit mindless and relentless. The others the Pale Man guided southward. Sendow was so hard-pressed that he could not follow them, could not watch their going, could not even send a messenger to warn those whose paths they would cross.

Slowly, in a westward retreat that would take a day and a night of constant movement, constant vigilance, Sendow backed his soldiers toward the village of Diamante, where the rubble and ruins provided fuel for a bonfire that encircled his pursuers, that visited them with the fierce purity of fire. Palernan carried Palernan as the dead followed, and twice when weary lads fell in the path of the cwalu, it was Sendow's courage and the strength of his stallion Camillus that rescued the boys in a blinding, reckless gallop.

Sendow remembered for the rest of his days how the bodies moaned and gibbered, and clutched for the boys, for him, for Camillus, how even when they reached Diamante and set afire the remaining huts and ricks, that the creatures still were relentless, dancing in the fields until the flames consumed them. Of his own forty men, there were ten who spent the rest of their days gazing blankly at the horizon, their thoughts fixed forever on the cwalu, on the burning.

And among them all, there was not a man who slept easily again.

The rest of Lightborn's command reached the Triangulo by nightfall.

In the distance and dusk, they were taken for regular troops. The Maravenians, positioned behind new entanglements of bramble and vine, leapt atop their makeshift defenses and shouted encouragement. The Palernans, on the other hand, shouted taunts and challenges as the reinforcements approached.

From their positions opposite each other in the lines, both Helmar and Brenn smiled wanly at their troops' bravado. For the war was still young, the men still unseasoned. Despite the carnage of Diamante and of Wood's Edge that very morning, there lingered about the coming conflict a jubilant sense of sport, as though red and green had chosen sides for an afternoon's tournament.

"It will be longer than they think, and bloody," Helmar muttered somberly to Danjel.

At the same moment, almost a mile away, Brenn fumbled with his helmet and turned wearily to Ponder. "I almost envy their good time of it," he said bleakly. "I think it would be better to die than to send a thousand to do it for me."

And also at that moment, on the northernmost flank of Brenn's army, the rising moon bathed the new troops in a slanted, silvery light. And the brave foot soldiers of Thomas' legion, battletoughened southerners from the Notches, from Braden Gorge and Painter Falls, dropped weapons and fled the field. Facing them, in the vanguard of Lightborn's army, were their companions-in-arms, lads who had been lost, buried and mourned on the fields of Diamante.

The news of the cwalu reached Brenn indirectly. Far on the northern flanks there arose an outcry, the swirling blare of trumpets that usually signaled a sudden, dramatic change in the battle. Then the first of the messengers approached, alarmed cavalrymen whose tidings were uncertain. Then it was the men themselves, standards and banners discarded, dropping shield and helmet and breastplate as they abandoned the field, unsteady as the cwalu who pursued them.

In consternation, Brenn turned away from the glowing maps into a flurry of aides and lieutenants. Briskly he armed himself. Lapis rushed from the tent and retrieved the lenses, looking long and skeptically at her cousin.

"So you're going to the North, then?" she asked, her question hovering at the edge of a challenge.

"I don't see any choice," Brenn replied, as Ponder boosted him into the saddle. "Something's afoot up there. Thomas' troops are in disarray, and the birds give me no sight of Sendow or his forces."

He leaned over the saddle as the big man handed up his sword. "But what about the center of our lines?"

Brenn was silent, turning the blade of the sword in the air, inspecting its edge. "We'll . . . trust that Galliard can hold the center against whatever Helmar offers."

He looked grimly at Ponder.

If Galliard did not hold, neither Brenn's presence nor his absence would make a difference.

Entrenched in the dark soil of the Triangulo, General Helmar had no intentions toward attack. The courier found him crouched like a bear at the shore of Lake Teal, where the old warrior dipped a handful of water and drank absently, his eyes fixed on the city walls as the darkness rose and swallowed Maraven.

"The first news is good, then," he said, wiping his chin and turning to Lieutenant Danjel, who hovered nearby like a scavenger. Standing laboriously, his knees creaking, the general pushed his aide aside and trudged out of the lake's sunken basin, his muddy boots sliding in the black sand.

"The traitors have scattered north of us," the lieutenant repeated, springing past the general and taking the scroll from the mounted man. Danjel turned, his stare unwavering as he watched Helmar struggle to the higher ground. "The road to Maraven is ours."

Helmar nodded grimly and sat heavily on a felled oak. Puffing and grumbling, he removed his boots and shook the water from them.

Danjel barely masked a malicious smile. "Captain Lightborn sends salutations to the general," he said, offering a scroll to Helmar's extended hand.

The general stretched, unrolled the scroll, and read, his wet hands smearing the fresh ink on the vellum. "His reinforcements have joined with the Third Legion due north of the Triangulo," he announced gruffly, "and the Captain awaits my further orders."

"A most . . . impressive display, sir, if I might be forward," Danjel observed, his bright eyes on the departing courier.

Helmar coughed, set down the scroll, and pulled on his boots. "Says that the Pretender has made a show of force toward his lines. Doesn't know the strength of the troops yet, nor the intentions of their commander, but the Captain expects Brennart to attack at first dawn."

"If I might be forward yet again, sir," Danjel urged with polite impatience, "this may be the opportunity the general has awaited that he might strike with full enforcement the center of Galliard's line."

Helmar glared at his lieutenant.

"Then again, Lieutenant Danjel," the general replied gruffly, "it might be the general's full intention to hie him to that knoll over there and use the spyglass you're in constant danger of breaking to get a glimpse of how the Pretender behaves afield. If *I* might be so forward. And I might."

So the crack Maravenian Twelfth waited away the night and the early morning, encamped near the center of the lines. They were wakened two hours before dawn by their nervous officers, who expected at any moment that word would come down from the general for the legion to break camp and move forward in darkness toward Galliard's green lines. They waited for that word until the sun had cleared the eastern horizon, and the first heat of the day and the first insects hummed about their drowsy heads.

But their general was atop the knoll just north of the Triangulo, alone on horseback save for Lieutenant Danjel, both men recklessly far from Helmar's other officers and bodyguards. He lifted the spyglass, and watched with a craftsman's curiosity as the smoke settled over the green lines to the south, as the Palernans broke camp and prepared for the day's onslaught.

"Why are our men dressed in green as well, Danjel?" the general asked, the spyglass tilting slowly northward. "And why no banners? No standards?"

" 'Tis a militia hastily mustered," Danjel explained with a dry smile. "No time to equip them like the Twelfth or Seventh."

Helmar pivoted slowly southward.

"The Pretender's lines are . . . acceptable," he judged. "Though a bit bookish."

"That would be Ponder's influence," Danjel noted. "Does the general see a blond giant in the company of the Pretender?"

"The *general* has yet to see the *Pretender*," Helmar observed acidly, rising in the saddle, his sharp old eyes scanning the Palernan ranks. "Ponder . . . the scholar of the bunch, isn't he?"

"Historian," Danjel replied. "Of some repute . . . in Aquila."

"Aquilans have history, too, Lieutenant," the general said, lowering the spyglass. "Why are Lightborn's troops so filthily blooded if they have established position without resistance? Looks like they came from the butcheries."

Danjel swallowed. "The fact of the matter is, sir . . ."

Helmar eyed him curiously.

"I am not sure, sir," the lieutenant said sheepishly, and reached for the spyglass.

Ignoring Danjel, Helmar raised the instrument to his eye once again . . .

and turned to the field, where the armies whirled and clashed.

Brenn found himself in the midst of a Palernan column, borne on the back of a green wave, pushed inevitably toward the Maravenian lines. He looked around for Ponder, but his cousin had been swept off in another direction entirely, barely visible over the helmets and shields of the foot soldiers, and the landscape between them was surging with green. Ahead of them the pikemen waited, the bowmen shambled into position, where the swords raised and the spears leveled . . .

and the heavy smell of death rose from the ranks of Lightborn.

The Third Legion was entirely from the city, recruited along aristocratic Teal Front and among the town merchants in Grospoint and Ships. They were used to the best of arrangements, having their clothing dry, their horses and their servants well fed, their tents always upwind in the smoke and stench of the army bivouac.

But now the cwalu had put down among them. Now they stood shoulder to shoulder with brothers in arms they had left dead on the Gray Strand, at Diamante, at Wood's Edge. Former comrades, once a source of companionship, were suddenly and irrecoverably terrible, changed beyond recall by death's hand. Had they not feared the pale Captain even more than the walking corpses who had entered their ranks, many of the Third Legion would have fled like the Palernans, scattering to all parts of the countryside, returning home to the safety of Teal Front and their walled and fortified villas.

So it was with Elazar, as the dead jostled against him, shaking the legion's standard in his hands.

Actually too young for service, Elazar had been forced into the legion by his father, a veteran in the service of Duke Danton of Aquila who had retired to a prospering weapons shop in Grospoint. The front lines were not the place for the lad, the clash of weapons harsh to his ear, but as the Palernans approached and the dead men beside him weaved and clicked, he steeled himself for the onslaught, a perfumed handkerchief wrapped about his face against their foul odor.

Best not look right or left, Elazar told himself. *Best hold high the standard, and let others worry about other things.*

A cry from their sergeant brought the Maravenian troops to attention. At his order they advanced, leaving the cwalu in a listless broken line behind them. To a low rise in the plains the company hastened, pikemen kneeling, extending their weapons, while the crossbowmen stood behind them, gazing murderously down their sights at the approaching wave of green.

The Palernans rushed across the sunlit field, shouting and banging their swords against their shields. Midway in the charge they seemed to slow, and recoiled for an instant when they saw the dead in the Maravenian ranks. But the Pretender was with them, and at their moment of fear he rode before them, a slight young man on a brown horse, a strange gold light descending onto his shoulders. Under his gaze and encouragement, the green-clad soldiers gathered courage and pressed on.

Elazar watched, dumbstruck, envying the Palernans their glorious commander. Behind him Lightborn called out furious orders, and now the Maravenians, living and dead, rose to meet the onslaught. Elazar took three steps back, let the wall of his companions close in front of him as the Palernans closed with his comrades and the battle resumed.

Shield struck shield with a crash, and the Maravenian troops staggered back, digging their boots into the moist, sandy soil. Then, with a fierce outcry, the Palernans pushed through the red lines. Swords flashed in the sunlight, and the air rained blood and screams.

Brenn wheeled in the saddle, shouting encouragement to the Palernans milling around his horse. They overran the Maravenian troops, their charge reassembling as they raced with renewed courage toward the line of the dead. But the cwalu were too strong: the Palernan attack broke against the gray and mottled lines, and suddenly, in that shift of leverage and motion that a general knows, or a wrestler, the dead army pushed back and the Palernans lost ground. Pale hands broke through the circling line of green, blindly groping toward the mounted Pretender. A swift downward slash of Brenn's blade found its home in the shoulder of one of his attackers, but the blow did little good: the dead thing sank to its knees with the impact, but leapt to its feet immediately, clutching at Brenn's saddle and his boots, scoring his leg with its long, yellowed nails. Crying out, half in anger and half in terror, Brenn planted his foot squarely in the face of the dull-eyed creature, who tumbled over backwards and rose again, careening viciously toward him, teeth bared and its fingers arched like talons.

Brenn raised his sword again, this time in desperation, and his horse vaulted and bucked as another of the cwalu tried to climb into the saddle with him—a green-clad boy with an open wound at his throat. With a dry, rasping cry, the creature knocked Brenn from his horse and the two of them tumbled to the hard ground.

For a moment Brenn lay there, the cloudless sky flickering above him. Then the cwalu leaned over him, long knife in its hand, the wind whistling obscenely through the wound in its throat,

> The forward Youth that would appear
> Must now forsake his Muses dear . . .

Brenn cried out, closed his eyes, and prepared to roll and kick in an old thieves' maneuver . . .

and something shoved away the creature above him, a sudden, powerful blow, as though a wild bull had charged, lowered its head, and struck home.

A grim-faced Ponder lifted Brenn to his feet and hoisted him onto the horse he had ridden to the rescue.

"Ride, Brennart!" the big man cried, taking the sword from his cousin and turning to face the oncoming cwalu.

"But, Ponder! What about . . ."

Ponder smiled mysteriously, his blond hair matted to his face by sweat and ash. "King's Guidance," he said. "They'll need it again and elsewhere."

His fist thundered into the face of an enormous Watchman, who toppled like a felled oak into three staggering cwalu.

"I know what to do here," Ponder announced, and slapped the horse's flank.

It was all Brenn could do to stay in the saddle. The big steed, used to carrying much more weight, galloped south back over the battlefield, the young man clinging to the bridle, one foot in a stirrup.

Brenn reined in the horse on the site of the overrun Maravenian position. Looking over his shoulder back into the heart of the battle, he watched in dismay as the cwalu pressed forward and his own men, beaten and overwhelmed and disheartened, turned and ran or slowly backed away, their shields raised and their weapons flailing weakly.

Ponder was nowhere to be seen.

"*I* should be there," Brenn said to himself, urging the uncooperative horse back toward the fray. "What good am I, hovering like a quartermaster at the back of my armies?"

The horse snorted and would not budge. Brenn flicked the reins and shouted, slapped the rump of the big beast with the flat of his hand, but it was as though the animal was mired, there at a safe and kingly distance.

Brenn slapped the horse again. It looked back at him serenely and stupidly, and he muttered a scalding Maravenian curse . . .

It was then that he heard the sobbing.

The red-clad boy was not more than thirteen—perhaps twelve or only eleven. The sword wound was deep in his side, and his assailant had rushed heedlessly on toward the lines of the cwalu, thinking him dead.

Even from the height of horseback, Brenn could tell that the lad was dying. It put him in mind of a winter season years past in Maraven, of the cellars in the Hall of Poisoners, of a swift pale blade that had found its way into the back of an innocent child . . .

Swiftly he dismounted and knelt at the boy's side. For a moment, when the child rolled his eyes and looked up at him, Brenn feared the worst.

There is nothing I can do, he thought. *Nothing but ease the dying.*

Do not think that, a voice returned to him across a distant season. *And above all, do not say it.*

Then his thoughts cleared, and he recalled a sunlit clearing in Corbinwood, his good friend Dirk lying lifeless, stung by the poisonous barb of the wyvern. He had despaired then, had resigned himself to the death.

But Glory had stopped him, her whispering soothing, on her breath a trace of rosemary and mint.

You are *the king, after all,* she had urged. And only the king can lay hands on the ailing without carrying away some of their darkness with him.

This wound is mortal: none other can touch it.

Haltingly, tentatively, Brenn reached out for the boy.

"Lay on the hands," he whispered, remembering Glory's words, "and trust. The healing will come to me . . . when my eyes are closed . . . and my heart is open."

His fingers spread over the lad's torn side, and it was black first that he saw.

Black. Dismal and ceaseless, like the deep tunnels beneath the city. Serenely, his sight probed the depths of the blackness:

fitful images passed before his eyes, whether dreamt or imagined or set before him by a dark malevolence.

A woman weeping, beckoning . . .

A pit, from which pale hands, pale limbs extended, as though a thousand were packed into a shallow grave . . .

A basin filled with clear water, clouding with dark blood . . .

And then, in the vortex of blackness, a glimmer of green.

"Ah . . ." Brenn exclaimed, and his heart went forth to the wound, to the lad, to the infinite green at the core of the dying, a green that blossomed crimson then blue then violet then gold over gold in unbroken and various light . . .

Helmar saw the Pretender kneel beside the fallen standard-bearer. He saw the stillness at the battle's edge, saw the boy stir and rise. Then slowly, resolutely, he cast his gaze on the struggle itself, where the battle's fallen were rising again, impelled by the Great Witch's dark and hideous magic.

He slowly raised high, then dropped the spyglass. Danjel watched in puzzlement as the precious instrument, a year in transport from Amsterdam in the hands of the intrepid lensmaster Ianafitch of Jaleel, shattered on the hard ground of the Palernan plains.

⤙⤙⤙ X ⤚⤚⤚

They had to keep moving, for behind them was the water, and three cavalry companies in pursuit, but the roads were filling ahead of them, none of them corduroy or plank but a plain red dirt that took in the hooves of the horses until the riders felt them slowing down, sinking, drawn into the rising mud.

They had to talk aloud then, because it was so dark they couldn't see the ears of their own horses, and the rain was rinsing away the smell of horse to horse that had linked them in line when human eyesight first failed. So they spoke to the men beside them, and they carried shouts up and down the column, yelling *ho* when someone called behind them, and *deep here* when they felt the horses sink especially.

Finally, not more than an hour or so past Irret, on their way to Stormpoint and higher ground and safety from the pursuing three companies of cavalry, they stopped altogether, horses jostling and bumping each other in the rain and darkness. They stood in the midst of drowned pastureland, once the country of wealthy farmers, now churned and ruined by the passage of ignorant armies. And the snorts and whickers from the horses and the coughs of the men and the incessant downpour were the only things to hear until somewhere up the line came talking, someone from the vanguard walking or trying to walk back to the center of the column, where Captain Ricardo sat on horse, glum and rain-drenched, green cape hoisted about his ears. Peering out through the sagging tent of his broad-brimmed hat, the Alanyan watched as Lesharo and Angeda, his two Zephyrian lieutenants, trudged toward him, framed and visible by the green light of Zephyrian ampules, the watertight globes of fire that were better than lanterns for a mounted company. At their coming, the area defined itself in a nodding light. Steaming horses emerged fitfully from the blackness, and stooped cavalrymen astride them, and out of the impenetrable gloom came outline and movement and breath.

Angeda—if Angeda was indeed the one with the eye patch—pulled at the blanket of a boy riding only two horses ahead of the captain.

"Get down, son. You'll do," he called over the roar of the rain, then turned to a grizzled sergeant who had dismounted and splashed near to investigate what the officers would have.

"And you," Angeda continued, "take the reins of the lad's horse. He'll come with me out to the head of the column, where I'll put him on vedette."

"Not while there are men to ride there, Lieutenant," Ricardo snapped, and lifted his hat. The Zephyrian turned scornfully, prepared to deal with insubordinates, but found the glow of the ampules resting on the dark hair, the long dripping braid on the captain's shoulders. He recognized the commander and nodded briskly.

"As you say, sir. I have chosen him because he is a lad, though. One of the two or three smallest in the company."

Churros sniffed as Ricardo steered him gracefully to the side of the lieutenant. "Perhaps you should explain," the Alanyan suggested coldly. The owl under his cloak stirred and complained and dug its little talons into Ricardo's chest.

"There's a wagon mired to the axles in the middle of the road, Captain," the other lieutenant—Lesharo, was it?—explained, his high voice terse and emotionless.

Ricardo glanced from lieutenant to lieutenant, frowning.

Angeda smiled. For all of his natural gifts, the captain was green to the cavalry.

"The boy is light, sir," the Zephyrian explained patiently. "The idea is that anyplace he begins to sink will be perilous ground for horse and wagon. He's our bellwether through the mire ahead."

"The boy is also a boy," Ricardo insisted. "We are the ones who are supposed to lead this company, and lead we will through our own examples. We'll bellwether like the old ram himself."

Angeda trudged to the side of his commander, setting his hand against Churros' warm flank. "The boy is lighter," he repeated. "The boy is expendable."

Expendable!

Ricardo stared down at the Zephyrian lieutenant. Rain was cascading off his upturned face, his beard, the gray eye patch. The Alanyan fought back the urge to strike him.

"None are expendable in my command, Lieutenant. Where did the wagon mire?"

"Ahead of us."

"I *know* that! North or south or middle of the road?"

"South." The waters were pooling at the man's ankles, in the hoofprints of the horses. It was going to be a long night.

"Then I shall walk south of the road. Lesharo, you will take the north, and Angeda the road itself."

He watched the lieutenants' faces, seeking vainly once again for a nod, a gesture, that would fix name to man.

"We'll serve as our own bellwether," he announced, and, dismounting, handed Churros' reins to the astonished, dripping boy. The reciting owl fluttered from Ricardo's cloak and perched atop Churros' saddle, staring wide-eyed and sorrowfully into the shifting dark. He sang out as Ricardo departed for the front of the company, his thin voice doleful and lonely in the clamorous rain.

> Myrie it is whil somer ylast
> With fowles song;
> But now neigheth wyndes blast
> And weder strong. . . .

The three officers fanned out ahead of the column. As the lieutenants explained it, they were to shout out, as they had done on horseback, to guide those behind them through the darkness. It was the same principle, indeed, but there was more: each man would shout out *deep here* when he reached a spot where he found himself sinking, and the carters would hasten to him, arranging a way to guide the wagons around the mire.

Dismally, Ricardo pulled down his hat even more tightly, because water was running down the brim into his eyes. He could see just as well with his eyes covered, because Angeda had given the ampules to the carters and there was no clear light ahead in the clouds and the driving rain.

He wondered how they would navigate in such blackness, how they would ever find Stormpoint. But soon he understood, as he felt the incline of the road, how the ground began to slope under his feet when he began to stray afield. He would find his right foot higher than his left where there had been no miring, no sinking, and he would move back onto the road and shout *ho* over the sound of the rain.

For hours he shouted. He would hear Angeda's high shout to the left of him, perhaps above him, and then even farther away, Lesharo's booming *ho*, and behind them the shouts would carry down the column, *ho ho ho*, like a laugh in a puppet play. Ricardo could hear it fade behind him into the rumble and slosh of the horses and the creak of wagon wheels, all of it a strange and almost pleasant music, like a chanting chorus from the Temple of the Four Winds.

But it was not a joyous music, this chanting, for the night was sopping and murky and dreadful. Three times Ricardo had to shout *deep here*, had to wait in a spot, one time in mud to his knees, until the carters waded up the road to spell him.

Damned deep here! he shouted on that occasion, and the carters behind him hastened and muffled their laughter.

It was the way the journey went for miles, the water and blackness and shouting until they heard Lesharo say *deep*, and then nothing else. Nothing but quiet in the northern darkness.

Captain, Angeda called out, *I believe that the lieutenant is mired.*

Across the road they went, the both of them, feeling carefully and shouting at every step, because they didn't want to get mired themselves and magnify the troubles. All the while they called out to the lieutenant to answer them.

But no answer came.

Angeda and Ricardo shouted back and forth, each one assuring the other of his safety. Behind them the column had ground to a halt. A faint murmur of men and a shifting of restless horses reached them over the sound of the rain.

Twice it seemed that someone was approaching out of that darkness—the first time a sound grew louder and deeper, and on the second occasion Ricardo thought he saw an ampule bobbing closer through the driving rain. Both times he ordered them back, his voice loud and keen over the noise of the night.

How deep does the earth go? he wondered. *Could the tales of the Parthians be true, that a man could pass through the ground and emerge in another country?*

And where would he be if he did so?

The Alanyan shook his head, stepped lightly and slowly over the rise in the road. It was silly. The world was impenetrable and monstrously large. He stepped again, and he heard Angeda cry out.

Swiftly, forgetting his own danger, ignoring the dark and the unsteady footing, Ricardo paced back down the column to find his lieutenant clinging to a fencepost, waist-deep in the mud and losing grip. For a brief moment, in his ignorance of mind, the captain thought of a teasing comment about expendability, but he let it go, and bracing his foot against the lower paling of the fence, tugged the Zephyrian out by the arms.

They leaned side by side against the sturdy posts, and beside them an ampule neared and widened in the fading dark. Standing over them was a burly carter, his rolled sleeves dripping and his boots thick with mud.

"I reckoned you gents might need a light, regardless of your braveries," he declared, handing the ampule to Ricardo. In turn, the Alanyan tossed the fur hat he had recovered to Angeda, who was struggling to his feet.

"I suspect this hat is yours," the captain said.

But Angeda frowned. "This is not mine," he said.

The carter held the light closer as the two officers inspected the hat.

"Lesharo's," the Zephyrian declared.

Ricardo gasped. "That means . . ."

The officers gaped at one another until the carter shook the ampule, bringing them to their senses.

Instantly, Angeda hooked his legs through the fence rails and grabbed the ankles of the carter, who knelt, stretched over the morass, and felt around in the quicksand-thin mud, grasping for Lesharo or a part of him.

"Well?" Ricardo asked. "Have you found him yet?"

"No, sir," the carter sputtered, wiping the mire from his face. "But I would stand back, because this mud goes forever down and fast." Lying on his stomach, he thrust his arms into the morass, to the wrists, then the elbows, then the shoulders.

"Nothing but wet and cold," he muttered. "Pull me back now, if you'd be so kind, sir. That man is forever part of this road."

Ricardo slammed his fist against the fencepost. To have survived the skirmishes on the Gray Strand, then Diamante and Wood's Edge and this damnable downpour, only to walk down a road and disappear into it . . .

Angeda snorted angrily. He cast a withering glance at Ricardo, who weaved above the railings in a daze of anger. Then Angeda lifted his head and let go a peculiar, shrill piercing wail in the Zephyrian salute to death.

When he fell silent and dipped his head, Ricardo nodded, and he turned in the unswerving darkness, feeling his way horse by horse down the column, calling out until the old man Cosimo, riding the horse in front of him, called back in response. His hands reached the familiar neck of Churros, and he lifted himself into the saddle, weighing the horse down much more with all the mud he had gathered upon him.

And Ricardo was glad for no sunlight or warmth as he rode, for in his dark fancy he could imagine drying up like a brick, so hard and dry and earthed that he would never move again, and be left entombed in clay.

He shuddered to think they were riding somewhere over Lesharo now.

Little by little the clouds cleared and stars came out, and Ricardo watched Cosimo and his horse grow out of the darkness. The last of the rain lifted, and off to the east flickered a few late lamps in Stormpoint.

The Viscount Halcyon, still Brenn's prisoner, seized on the cwalu attack and the rains that followed as his chance to escape. Regarding that escape, there were three stories circulating in Maraven, all of which amused the Thieves' Guild and warmed the rainy nights of the paupers.

The first was that he had broken from his Palernan guards, seized a horse, and ridden east for an hour, his directions disjointed by the battle and the ensuing storm. The downpour had driven him to take refuge in an abandoned cottage in Irret, where he slept for a few hours, then rode through the subsiding rain until he fell in with some cavalry he thought to be the Maravenian Third because of their red capes. He second-guessed himself into a Stormpoint stockade, because it was the Black Horse Cavalry in borrowed garments, and his old Gray Strand nemesis Ricardo of Alanya greeted him the next morning with a smile and a cup of mulled wine.

It was more likely, people supposed, that it happened another way. Halcyon slept at Irret until his snoring alerted the passing Black Horse. The Palernan cavalrymen rousted him from slumber, and he rode out the storm their regained prisoner, finding himself in Stormpoint the next morning, jailed and nursing an oncoming fever.

And yet there was one more version. As in the others, the viscount fell asleep in the cottage, but the water poured down abundantly while he slept, the roof of the cottage sloping until it was swaybacked with rain, the good work of the builder keeping, by one beam and nail, all of that water from crashing down upon Halcyon and drowning him in his sleep. Below him the waters gathered until, around midnight, the cottage came unmoored and began to float, catching a current carrying it north and east. Meanwhile the viscount, as tired as anyone by fighting and movement, slept through it all.

Slept through the birds that roosted on the porch railing—ravens, no doubt, and an owl and a brilliant nocturnal eagle—all waiting for the rain to end and the water to settle, flying off now and then in search of a dry purchase, and settling forever into the Plains of Sh'Ryll, where a false light and warmth had enticed them from the air . . .

Slept as the house floated past village and town, past creeks swollen beyond anyone's memory, in a long arc sailing over the terrible lowlands of Diamante . . .

Slept as he came to ground at last, to the hills south of Stormpoint, with the house wedged among cedars and the viscount unsure where he was in the first place, waking where he had trained his troops in the summer of the year before like the time in between had been canceled. And maybe he thought the year had not happened, the war not started, Stormpoint a Maravenian stronghold, Diamante and the Triangulo places on a map with no history yet. And he stepped from the cottage prepared to give orders . . .

And stepping forth, he found that the lines had changed, the town in the hands of Palernans who saluted politely and took him into custody.

There were other stories, too. Wilder ones than those of Ricardo, than those of the viscount. But only one changed the face of the war.

Brenn slept fitfully the night after the battle at Triangulo. He lay awake on his pallet as the southern skies crackled with lightning and the rain came after midnight, in long powerful waves that swept through the encampment, dousing the fires and toppling the tent posts. The sides of his own tent billowed and bowed, and giving up hope for sleep, he crawled from the bed and drew Lapis' lenses from the pouch at his belt, setting them on the tent floor at the compass points, as she had instructed.

Ricardo was moving east, pursued by three columns of the enemy. Brenn could see that much in the lights at the farthest corner of the map.

It was no cause for alarm. Barring accident or misdirection on the road, Ricardo should reach Stormpoint well ahead of his pursuers: it was a city long opposed to Dragmond, and the Black Horse would find safety there.

The rest of the map was unclear. On its western border light entangled with light, and great gray shadows—Brenn could only guess that they were winds, rain clouds—spattered the map until the arrangement of forces was cryptic as a toss of runes. Again Brenn wished for Terrance, and corrected himself in the wish.

"Meddlesome old wizard," the lad muttered, standing and staring into the candle. "Terrance drew me into this conflict until there was no returning, and left me when the dying started."

He shook his head. That wasn't right, either. A year of absences had softened his anger toward the wizard. Meddlesome Terrance was, and indirect, and there was some unrevealed past with the Great Witch that was bothersome, to say the least.

But Brenn remembered the long instructions in summery Maraven, the ventures into Grospoint. Remembered Terrance bent over the plague-ridden child, drawing away the suffering of the innocent, taking the pain and the fever and the black boils onto himself so that she might breathe again, might have another slim chance in the infested streets of Wall Town.

For a slim chance was a chance natheless, Brenn thought, and smiled sadly. They were losing the war now, with the advent of the walking dead. He saw no way out of the darkness, but a way would come, as surely and as quickly as he believed it. He replaced the candle in its glass globe and, stepping to the flaps of the tent, looked outside into the rush of wind and water.

And where was Faye? The question came to him unbidden, unsettling his thoughts even further. Though the dragon's insinuations in the hot Aralu had been proven lies mostly, Brenn had heard nothing from his old friend—nothing in almost two years.

He had become a king of slim chances.

A nodding green light passed through the rainswept camp. It was an ampule, swaying like a pendulum, its bearer a tall, lean man. Behind him came a dark, hulking form, a shorter man wrapped in furs and helmeted. Brenn squinted, recognized the tall lamp-bearer.

"Galliard!" he called out with a false heartiness, as much for his own good as for any who listened. "Come in out of the rain!"

The two men stood in the downpour, their movements vague and slow. Galliard leaned over his shorter companion and spoke to him briefly, his words muddled by the noise of the rain. Then he walked toward Brenn, wrapping his cape tightly around his shoulders as the wind lifted and yet another tent collapsed across the campground.

"Come in, cousin," Brenn offered, holding the tent flap open as the dripping Forest Lord stepped into the warmth and light. "And as for your foolish friend—"

Galliard raised his hand. "Not so loudly, sire," he cautioned. "My friend is far from foolish."

"Who is it, Galliard?"

Galliard smiled. "You will not believe, sire."

Impatiently, Brenn rushed to the entrance of the tent. "I've had enough guessing games over that damned map of lenses, Galliard! Now if you'd invite the wretch to . . ."

The wretch in question stood at the door, shrouded in dripping bearskins. Gaping, Brenn stepped aside as the man ambled into the tent, his famous limp unmistakable, even beneath the thick blanket of hides.

"Helmar!" he exclaimed, dropping the candle in astonishment.

⤛⤛⤛ XI ⤜⤜⤜

That morning Sendow watched as the smoke from last night's burning settled around the ruins of Irret.

Scarcely a cottage was left standing. Like most of the farmlands in northern Palerna, this land was blackened by war, littered with shards and ash and the remnants of carts, fences, and huts. It was a desolate country, and Sendow tried not to think about it as he peered through the settling fumes, his thoughts on the whereabouts of the enemy.

Through the night they had kept the fires burning—tended the flames buoyed by a vague superstition that the daylight would salvage them from the surrounding armies of the dead, that there was something incompatible about the cwalu and the honest sun. Sendow's company, no more than two hundred men, had all stayed awake, the youngest of them nodding on their feet by the dark hour before sunrise. Everyone was weary past memory, exhausted and sick with smoke and vigilance.

Sendow had watched over all of them, as the night faded along with his strength. He had urged the men to keep watches, so that if there was a battle at sunrise, none would fight without sleep. But he knew better when he urged it, and the vigil had borne him out: it was the rare eye that closed in the long watch of that night, and rarer still the man who lay down and surrendered to dreams.

Sendow coughed in the stale smoke. An old farmer named Tibalt had jostled him to alertness just before sunrise, and he had stood in this spot, between two fire-gutted sheds, awaiting full light and whatever new terrors Dragmond had devised for the Palernans.

But there was nothing. No movement of armies, no black standards or banners.

Unexplainably, the cwalu had left the field.

Breathing a grateful prayer to the Four Winds, Sendow gathered his troops together. Tibalt barked orders at the disheveled company, and bleary-eyed boys staggered into line, the hoes and rakes and scythes they had uncovered in the ruins of Irret in their hands.

They are brave lads, the Aquilan baron thought fondly. *In the fighting and in the larger waiting, where they wrestle with the fears that the night magnifies, they are brave lads.*

They looked at him adoringly, trustingly, as if the longest of their nightmares was over.

He could not have known the silence for what it was.

In the retreat of armies, especially in spring or high summer, the call of larks and the whir of jarflies reclaim the field. Then the landscape is loud and renewed, as though the animals, forced into hiding by the march and maneuver of soldiers, rediscover themselves in song and noise.

But the plains around Irret remained hushed. So Sendow, famous for woodscraft and an ear for the leaves' language, could only listen to the silence and wonder.

Over the first rise, marching in broken lines to the plaintive sound of a single flute, they discovered the enemy scattered on the plains.

Five hundred dead men lay where they had fallen sometime during the long night of watchfires. They sprawled in the midst of ashes and abandoned wagons, and draped over fencerows like rugs, like lapsed banners. Sendow chilled as he noticed that on this field of carnage not a sword had been raised, not a spear hurled nor a bolt launched.

"Something has happened," he whispered to Tibalt, who nodded respectfully, as much in the dark as his commander. "Something has happened, and we will not be safe until we reach the woods."

They hurried west, their steps redoubled.

The first of the men fell around noon, babbling of sleep and dead hands. Sendow ordered his companions to take him up, to carry him on their shoulders.

* * *

The Great Witch, too, was spent and exhausted, worn down by the farthest reach of her magic.

She lay on her back atop the marble map in her chambers, the night air cold on her face. Outside the wind and the rain swept about Kestrel Tower, and a dozen ravens, gloomy and bedraggled, huddled high against the eaves and the crenels.

Cautiously Ravenna spread her fingers, peered intently at her hands, searching for the spots. Satisfied that they had not returned, she gathered her skirts, climbed slowly to her feet, and moved to the closest of the candles.

She would try again.

But she was so weary. Through the long day and into the night she had held up the spell, guiding the cwalu in the battle at Triangulo.

The traitors had been turned by her army of the walking dead. In some quarters, they had even been routed. Had she the strength to continue . . .

Had she been younger . . .

Seething, Ravenna waved away all thoughts of youth and age. Spellcraft such as this day's would tax *any* enchanter, even Merlyn or Roger Bacon or Sycorax herself. In order to animate the cwalu, to breathe life and power into hundreds of them for a day on the battlefield, she had been forced to set aside all other ensorcelment, all augury and divination. And even with those concessions, Ravenna was tired . . . inexpressibly tired.

With a sigh, she seated herself in the throne once reserved for Dragmond, who now lay lifeless in his downstairs chambers, preserved in Egyptian herbs, in wax and mumiyah. Lazily, her fingers played across the onyx arms of the chair, and suddenly she slept, deeply and insensibly, and dreamless for the first time in years.

Below her, drudging in an obscure corridor, Faye stooped above a threshold and suddenly remembered every detail of her life. As the Great Witch slept, the girl crouched, rushes in hand, and marveled at how she ever could have forgotten any of it.

The streets of Wall Town rushed to her recollection, every alley and cul-de-sac as familiar to her as the hallways of Kestrel

Tower. Her childhood returned as well, weaving through those intricate, shabby streets: her time in the Thieves' Guild with the Goniph, who had taught her to read and pick a pocket and speak four languages, and her friendships with Dirk and Randall and Marco.

"I remember him, too," she whispered, and sat inelegantly in the threshold, scattering the rushes aimlessly. For Brenn emerged in her reestablished thoughts like the sun from behind a cloudwrack.

He had told her when they were children that he *was destined for larger things,* and she had laughed and told him that she was Queen of Palerna until she saw the strained, serious look in his face.

How they had broken into Terrance's house, and she had fled when the library erupted in light, stopping only when she was a good distance down Cove Road to look behind and around, as Dirk stewed and Squab chuckled, and the lot of them realized that they would have to return to the Goniph and tell him that Brenn was the prisoner of the mad wizard Terrance.

How for six seasons she spied on him by night at the Goniph's instructions, sometimes standing in rainy Leeside Alley and looking up into the lamplit windows, envying Brenn his comfort and dryness and warmth. How one time she climbed the bole of an ancient black tree and peered in a window, watching him for an hour as he bent wearily over a book. She had almost called to him that night, almost coaxed him from his books back to Wall Town and to the Brotherhood.

But he had been reading—he, who had stumbled maddeningly over posted proclamations and even street signs. And after all, was he not destined for larger things? She had stood there in the black branches and watched and blessed him, returning to the Goniph with the news that *Brenn was still at the wizard's tower, by the way, and I'd reckon there's no return for him now.*

He had returned, though. At the Goniph's instruction, Faye had helped Squab write the note that drew Brenn back to Wall Town, back to the tunnels, back to the Guild.

And in their greeting and embrace, there was something more than the old camaraderie. But she kept herself away from Brenn, no matter how reluctantly, knowing that she had been a willing agent in luring him out of the life of wizards and back into the plague-ravaged streets and the danger of the Watch, back to the thievery that would wear them all down eventually . . .

back to the Goniph's jar, where the crabs crawled over each other toward the edge and freedom, only to continue pulling each other down, back into their glass prison.

All the rest—the night at the Prisoners' Hall, the appearance of the Pale Man, her rescue by the Goniph, and the hard rain on Light Street in which she and Brenn had parted for the last time, with thiefly strategies and jests.

And then . . . something about the wizard Terrance. Something about the dead walking, and a dark coach.

It was no dream or madness that passed through her thoughts as she sat on the threshold of the neglected chamber and cupped her chin in her rough, reddened hands.

"All of it's true," she whispered. "I've been bewitched."

She smiled wryly.

Lithely, Faye scrambled to her feet. It seemed as though her recovered memory had brought with it new vigor and agility and purpose. She cast the rushes carelessly into the darkened room and watched as they scattered and settled in a faint light coming from a door on the far side of the chamber. For a moment she paused on the threshold, her thief's curiosity drawing her toward the light, toward the keyhole, toward the sights beyond the door . . .

And then the top floors of the Tower echoed with Ravenna's shouts. She was summoning servants in the panic that always followed her sleep, when she would waken and look out the window at the sun, at the shifting of stars, at the drained hourglass on the lectern by the door, and realize that more time had passed without her watchfulness—that anything, something, might have happened while she slumbered.

Faye dusted her hands and hastened up the corridor. She was not sure what the return of memory demanded of her, what she was supposed to do or say or even watch for. Yet she knew clearly, as clearly as she knew these corridors or the maze of streets back in Wall Town, that her acquiescence to the Great Witch was permanently, completely broken.

* * *

As Ravenna awakened on the floor of her chamber, there was yet another awakening, miles away on a desolate field.

He was alone in a level, blasted country. The comrades and enemies who had lain beside him had vanished in the afternoon, all of them gone to people Ravenna's army. For an hour or so near sunset, a pair of ravens had roosted on a fire-gutted wagon not a spear's toss from where the big man sprawled, their dark feathers matted with mud and oil and carrion.

Patiently the birds waited for him to die. Around dusk, something in the air shifted and switched, and the birds were distracted, shifting from foot to foot, graveling menacingly. Then they vaulted into the gray sky, wheeling north over Lake Teal, gliding toward the flint-black walls of Maraven.

Ponder's eyelids fluttered as pain returned with consciousness. He tried to rise, but he could barely move: the wound from the cwalu spear, still lodged in his side, had drained his great strength and his energy and almost all his will.

He smiled wearily, resignedly. To his dry lips came the beginning of an old song. He could put no voice to it.

> Even such is tyme which takes in trust
> Our yowth, our Joyes, and all we have,
> And payes us butt with age and dust . . .

But age and dust he would not see. Not now, with this wound, in this dying.

He closed his eyes. At least he had saved the rightful king. There was reward in that, he supposed—a goodness and a glory.

He would go to that reward in peace, thinking of those other heroes. Of Leonidas of Sparta, Horatius of Rome, Cyril and Anthony the Philokalian brothers . . .

There was someone in Umbria he had read about, someone he could not remember . . .

He would join that company of heroes as perhaps its most unlikely member. He laughed softly to think of it—how a gentle, scholarly man whose passion was history and far-flung emperies had settled his life this day and now, on a field close to home, a sword most unsubtle in hand.

Ponder had ushered off his regal cousin, setting Brenn on

horseback, and, with a crisp slap on the horse's flank, sent him galloping toward the Palernan lines. Then he had turned to face the oncoming cwalu.

Slowly, relentlessly, the cwalu marched toward Ponder and the handful of soldiers around him. Already, some of his companions, good men felled in the first assault, now rose sluggishly and joined the ranks of the enemy. They thrust and hacked with their battered weapons, pawing the air aimlessly as the living rushed to meet them.

Ponder shuddered as he remembered. No matter what he did, no matter how brave and resolute the men around him, the cwalu kept coming, stepping over rising bodies, clawing their way up spear shafts toward the wielders of the weapons. He hacked at them, kicked them, pushed them away, but they kept coming. Effortlessly, he lifted one of them, a skeletal Maravenian cavalry captain, and hurled the wretch into two approaching, mud-spattered bodies.

It was then that he felt the pain, lancing white hot from his side through his chest and shoulders. For a moment he stood unbelieving, the blood from the spear wound pouring out between his fingers. Then everything had gone away . . .

to return only now, on this abandoned field, in the fellowship of ravens and night.

The pain subsided. Ponder's legs were heavy and numb. *It is not so bad, this dying,* he told himself, and closed his eyes.

Out of the gray, mottled darkness he imagined a tunnel, a soft, effacing light . . .

then opened his eyes again to the music of pipes and drums as the field vanished in a torrent of amber light, as a dozen brighter globes rose out of the torrent, paired together like sets of brilliant, unblinking eyes.

Ponder laughed weakly.

"Faeries!" he exclaimed soundlessly. " 'Tis almost faerie time . . . ."

The light at Kestrel Tower was harsher by far. It was an hour past sunrise, and the Tower Castelain, a rough-spoken Aquilan by the name of Camarero, was wakeful. A shrewd character with numbers and a ledger, it was his job to keep the place in running order—to make sure that the rooms were cleaned, the larder supplied, and that all things pertaining to the stronghold of King Dragmond of Palerna were maintained, preserved, and impeccable. And run with economy, with thrift. Which was why he paused to consider the offer of the ancient hooded man in front of him, as thin and spectral as the painter's image of the Death, a rake in his left hand, his right hand resting casually on the shoulder of a boy he introduced as "my eyes and legs."

Surely a gardener would do wonders toward the upkeep of the castle, though Camarero was sure that the little plot at the foot of the Tower might escape the notice of the King or the Witch for years, and would be costly in the process. And how did these two get past the Causeway guard?

And yet . . . a garden would be pleasant for *him*, and for those who worked in this black-stoned fortress. In this time of plague and war, pleasantry and herbs and flowers would be most welcome.

Camarero cleared his throat. "Your experience at this, Grandfather, is . . . ."

"Considerable, though none of it in Maraven," the old man answered, his accent thick and rural. He reached in his pocket for a silver flask, tilted it, and sipped. " 'Twas a time in Umbria, a spell to the east in Jaleel, and the longest stay was down to the oracles in the Notches. None of 'em would be without a garden, and it give me fifty years of respectable labor."

Camarero nodded, regarding the old man closely. The flask was a disturbing touch: could make for crooked rows in the garden. And there was something . . . familiar about this Carlo, not to mention the boy who guided him through the grounds of Kestrel Tower.

Familiarity itself gave the castelain cause for misgiving. For this was a suspicious time, and with the traitors besetting the forces of the King on all fronts from Gray Strand to Stormpoint, the orders around the Tower were to turn away all strangers.

Not that anyone could manage a castle that way. Daily, a castelain had to deal with merchants, farmers, laborers, and the carters who brought the lot of them across the Causeway into the protected enclosures of the Tower. Of course. They had come in with some of those.

Camarero shook his head. His desire for the garden warred with his suspicion, but he knew the outcome already. For beyond politics and philosophy, he was a castelain, and as always, his suspicions surrendered to his abiding care for the buildings, their grounds, supplies, and servants.

And after all, was not the Great Witch herself a woman? And did not all women delight in flowers, all witches in herbs?

"Care for a swallow, steward?" the old man offered, smiling and extending the flask. Camarero took it in hand, reluctantly at first, but a polite, delicate sip turned more generous when the fiery contents passed his throat.

"Why . . . 'tis Zephyrian gin!" he sputtered. "And where would an old grannar like you get the likes of this?"

"Even the old grannar has his hiding place," the lad said, his accent thick and Wall Town. "Master Carlo gardened for . . . the Viscount Halcyon down on Teal Front, and even when the Zephyrians cut the trade last spring, His Eminence was never short of nectar, if you understand."

Camarero cursed silently that Master Carlo's former employer was the very viscount who had been taken by the Black Horse Cavalry down at Gray Strand. Halcyon's holdings had been auctioned a month after his capture, and it was said that the King himself had assumed the splendid lakefront villa.

There was no confirming Master Carlo by an absent blue blood. Insight and a generation's experience would have to decide whether or not to employ the old fellow.

Insight, experience, and the option of more Zephyrian gin.

So, an opportunist of the moment and the circumstance, Camarero argued away the last of his misgivings. He imagined the autumn nights grown warmer, the sweet and bracing smell of juniper and the comfortable, addled tilt of the moon.

By the middle of the morning, he had appointed Carlo to the job of castle gardener.

"So it is, Master," the apprentice said, helping the old man into the narrow chamber reserved in an earlier time for the Tower gardener.

"There's a garden in *here*," Master Carlo muttered. "A foot of topsoil, I'd wager."

"There won't be *enough* gin to convince that customer you're a gardener if the herbs don't grow, sir," the prentice cautioned, standing on tiptoe to look out the chamber window onto the dried and unpromising plot, which nonetheless sprouted a gathering of wildflowers.

"The herbs will grow," the Master declared, pushing back his hood to reveal the unmistakable iron-gray brow and beard of the wizard Terrance. "They'll grow, Dirk, because despite your misgivings, I have a country manner. There's herbs enough in the continent, and if not here, then in Europa and Africa and Asia and wherever else a plant takes root in the soil."

He stared long and hard at the little Maravenian thief, and gave him a knowing, mock-serious wink. "The question I have yet to answer," he declared, "is just what herbs we'll plant."

≪≪ XII ≫≫

"And *I* say he is not to be trusted," Ricardo declared flatly. "And all around us is evidence of that."

The Alanyan sat on the blackened stump of an oak, at the edge of Corbinwood, where Helmar's retreating armies had set the landscape afire. Seated on the felled trunk of the same tree, Brenn regarded his old friend with irritation.

Helmar's arrival in the Palernan camp had opened a world of promise to a battered army and its commander. Stepping out of the rain and into the Pretender's tent, the old general had announced, in the presence of Brenn and a dumbstruck Galliard, that he was ready to change allegiance—that night, that moment, if they would have him. And along with his skills and long experience on the fields of battle, he was prepared to bring with him two thousand soldiers—Maravenian legionnaires all, who found their allegiance to King Dragmond at cross-purposes with their consciences.

The offer was simple and blunt. Helmar spelled it out in his gruff, military manner, then offered to retire for the night as his prisoner while Brenn and his commanders considered the proposal.

It had taken the whole night for them to do so. The whole night, the next day, and the night after that. Brenn had tied a message to the talons of Bertilak the tercel eagle, sending the bird to Stormpoint to retrieve Ricardo. Alarmed at the news and what he foresaw in Brenn's plans, the Alanyan gathered a handful of troopers and rode a day and a night to arrive for the deliberations, bearing only his sword and his profound doubts.

Now all of them were gathered, for whatever good it was doing. Brenn, Ricardo, and four of Brenn's Aquilan cousins had debated this news well into the afternoon, and the opinion was still firmly divided.

"You didn't see him when he arrived, Ricardo," Galliard maintained. "When he told me the story about the spyglass, I was touched myself. He's not the kind for emotion, for sentiment."

Thomas agreed. "It must have been the most plain of contrasts. To look out across that field and see Brenn healing the Maravenian standard-bearer with the King's Touch, seeing the boy rise and join our ranks renewed and *inviolate*. Then look across to his own lines, where Ravenna and Dragmond were disturbing the dead."

The poet-cousin closed his eyes. "No poet could find a darker conceit for this war, for the forces assembled and for their handiwork."

"Enough poetry, brother Thomas," Jimset declared. "Enough of your *inviolates* and *handiworks*! 'Tis clear enough to me that Helmar is not to be trusted just because of his touching insight through an optic glass."

Lapis looked slyly at her cousin Brenn. Her soft hair, tied in a single braid, shone in the morning sunlight with a brilliant, glassy luster. "And might I add, Brenn," she coaxed, "that we both know that a lens, such as a spyglass, may refract and distort the light until we cannot see things . . . the way they are."

"You know otherwise, Lapis," Brenn declared flatly, his eyes fixed angrily on his youngest cousin. "You know what Ravenna and Dragmond have done—how they have raised the cwalu and *indeed more*, so that now not even the bodies of the innocent dead are safe. No lens distorts *that*. You have seen it with your own eyes.''

''And who knows?'' Galliard added, his face darkened with the pain of the thought. ''Out on the battlefield, two of your brothers may march with the cwalu army. For we have heard from neither Ponder nor Sendow. Perhaps they, too, are dead. And who is to say that Ravenna will not raise those troops again, and our cousins with them?''

Lapis frowned. ''You don't understand. Neither of you. 'Tis Brenn's personal optics I'm talking about. How he looks on the entire matter—on the battles and the strategy and now on Helmar's defection—with the eyes of one who *wants* to see honesty, *wants* to see an easy way to shift the balance in this war. Guard against wishful thinking, Brenn, against the hope that would only deepen despair.''

''*You* don't understand, little sister,'' Thomas declared, having passed from philosophy into anger. ''For neither you nor that digging brother of mine have spent an hour on the field of battle.''

''But I have,'' Ricardo said coldly, and Thomas fell silent, looking respectfully at the Alanyan.

Brenn noticed how much his old friend had changed through the last year. The lines around Ricardo's eyes had deepened, and the eyes themselves had withdrawn to the depths of his face, so in their glittering darkness you could see expanses of wasteland, thorny desert and endless plains. He had looked upon those landscapes, and he had returned with some inexpressible knowledge—some wisdom that comes on horseback at the turn of the night, when a long ride suddenly arrives at insight and light.

Of them all, it was Ricardo whom he desperately wanted to convince.

''Tell me one thing, my dear friend Brennart,'' Ricardo entreated, leaving his seat on the stump and pacing intently through the littered clearing. ''How will you believe this general when you know of his betrayals? He offers to leave his commander. Will someday he make the same offer to betray you?''

And where were you at the banks of the Eastmark? Brenn thought bitterly. *Leaving me and a girl and a wagon to face the dragon Amalek . . . But no. That was another time.*

Carefully, his eyes never leaving his old friend, Brenn rose and, taking Ricardo by the arm, drew him toward the forest interiors. Together they strolled out of earshot, and while Galliard and the others waited expectantly, the two of them—the would-be king and his cavalry commander—sat in the high notches of an apple tree and, with the air about them fragrant with ripe fruit and humming with wasps, began to settle the matter.

"What it comes down to is this, Ricardo," Brenn proclaimed, after a long, uncertain silence. "If you tell me that you will not accept General Helmar's offer to join my army, I'll refuse that offer."

Ricardo's mouth flew open. It was the last answer he had expected.

"You were right at Diamante," Brenn admitted. "Had we listened to you, a thousand lives might have been spared. I'll not ignore your good judgment again."

"Then . . . then I don't accept him," Ricardo replied, and regretted the words at once, feeling their wrongness in his mouth.

Brenn nodded, and started to climb down from the tree.

"Wait," Ricardo urged. He reached out precariously across the forking branches, seized Brenn by the shoulder. "Perhaps that is too hasty. Too rash."

Brenn smiled. "You're known for that. Helmar is eager to meet *the madman who commands my cavalry.*"

"Oh, he is, now?" Ricardo asked. He threw back his head and laughed, and above him a trio of jays took wing, squawking and quarreling.

"I ask you to do nothing against your judgment, Ricardo," Brenn urged. "Or against your heart."

Ricardo's smile faded at the serious words, but his eyes still glittered merrily as he sized up the young man who had just placed the outcome of the war in his hands. It was a gambler's ploy, an ancient trick from the *tarrochio* game.

But it assured that he would give the matter longer thought.

"Give me this evening, Brenn," the Alanyan said quietly. "By sunrise you'll have an answer that is fair and considered."

"I would expect nothing less of you," Brenn said with a smile, as he dangled from a low branch of the tree and dropped softly to the forest floor.

* * *

From his shadowy perch in the apple tree, Ricardo looked out over the Palernan encampments past the edge of the forest, to the circle of tents and watchfires where Helmar had settled a legion and a half on the dry Palernan plains.

Quietly, as the Alanyan began the longest thoughts of his life, his reciting owl fluttered out of the forest depths and perched on the branch Brenn had vacated. Softly, almost lovingly, the creature began to sing.

> Give me my Scallop shell of quiet
> My staffe of faith to walke upon,
> My Scrip of Joy, Immortall diet,
> My bottle of salvation . . .

Ricardo shook his head. He wished deciding were as easy as it seemed. If all were true and honest, and the general treated with the King in good faith, all Ricardo had to do was give the word, and Brenn's forces would swell by fifteen hundred men. Dragmond, in turn, would lose as many, along with the greatest military commander since Richard of Anglia.

If all were true and honest.

He picked an apple from a branch just above his head, turned it in his hand, examining it for health and ripeness. Satisfied at last, he bit into the fruit and lay back in a net of branches, remembering his alchemical days, his innumerable travels from westernmost Parthia to the markets of Rabia. Those distances seemed smaller, for the decisions he had made during those travels had been, when all was said and done, surprisingly easy.

A wrong choice when you were an alchemist was simply a wrong choice: an alembic might explode, certainly, retort and vial damaged beyond use, but for the most part a failure meant only that nothing happened, that base metals stayed base or the elixir you strived to create remained out of reach.

But these were decisions with soldiers, with people. If he decided wrong, a thousand Palernans could go to their graves.

Or worse. He had seen the cwalu himself, on two fields of battle.

The reciting owl leapt to his shoulder and, regarding him soberly, sang the last notes of its song.

> My Gowne of Glory, hopes true gage,
> And thus Ile take my pilgrimage.

"Perhaps you're right," Ricardo said, regarding the bird seriously and setting his plumed hat askew on his head. " 'Tis dark now, and high time for a pilgrimage to that Maravenian camp over there. If I'm to decide about this Helmar, it wouldn't hurt to watch him on the sly, now would it?"

The owl blinked golden eyes and fluttered his feathers.

Ricardo nodded playfully and started down the tree. He had not reached the next limb down when he froze at a noise below him.

The accents were Maravenian—Teal Front, he'd wager, although he could not be sure. And there were two of them, their soft speech veiled and bloody.

" 'Tis a matter of hours, Cardenio," the first one said, his face still hidden by the shadow of the branches.

The one called Cardenio stepped into the moonlight. The long, livid scar on his right cheek was dark against his face, as though the wound was still fresh. "A matter of hours," he said, echoing his companion. "May our knives be true and our hands steady." They grasped hands in a pact.

Dropping to a thick, forking branch, Ricardo stretched out, trying to see the other soldier. The owl hopped out on a branch and nestled its head beneath its wing in silence.

"Where is his tent?" Cardenio asked.

"At the center of the camp, near the largest of the watchfires," replied the other. "You'll know it by the motley lights from inside: 'tis a map of lenses he favors."

Ricardo caught his breath. They were speaking of Brenn.

Quickly he sized up the odds. They were good swordsmen, those Teal Front lads, but given a little good fortune, he was a match for the best of them. If he had his sword. On the other hand, two were a different matter: though surprise would be his ally, the disadvantage seemed formidable at best. And he would have to use some tricks, having no weapon at hand.

"Guards?" Cardenio asked, and his comrade sniffed disgustedly.

"Of course! The man's no longer a Wall Town pickpocket. But only a pair of them."

Ricardo leaned over the branch, looking for his best drop. Brenn was in danger. It was time to stop reckoning odds and jump the pair of them. If he timed it just right, he could fall on the one before Cardenio drew iron . . . .

But he was too late. They had already started to move, their steps taking them back toward the red-bannered camps of the Maravenians. Not twenty yards away, a third man joined them— a squat, black-bearded character in the red armor of the Watch.

In silent exasperation, Ricardo slammed his fist in the air just shy of the tree. The reciting owl leapt into the air and swooped away.

Helmar. He was sure of it. For had not his instincts warned him? Had not his doubts told him of the man's treachery?

Ricardo lowered himself to the ground and raced after the conspirators. Regardless of the danger, he would protect his friend against the plots of the Maravenians and their general. But at the edge of the trees he stopped. The three men had vanished without trace or sign. He stood staring down on a long level field and, in the distant darkness, the encircled campfires of the enemy. He turned and ran for his sword.

"So you have wanted to meet the madman, Helmar?" Ricardo whispered, sheathing his saber and facing the camp. "Prepare for him, then, and at the height of his madness."

And madness it must have seemed to the Maravenians, as the commander of the Black Horse Cavalry stalked through their midst, brown eyes blazing in the torchlight and the thick black braid wrapped like a scarf about his neck.

They had all heard the stories. How Ricardo of Alanya rode west out of Stormpoint or Hadrach, tying his men to the saddle so that they could sleep at a full gallop, though he never slept himself—not Ricardo of Alanya. And when the Black Horse Cavalry rode a horse down, the Maravenians said, they would not exchange but would stop, and like the wild cavalry of Ungaria, would eat the horse itself, then ride west double in the dust and night, steering by no maps or stars but by Ricardo's sense of smell. And in the villages through which he traveled, he would mark the country folk on their right hands or on their foreheads, so that they would always remember he had passed that way.

They were lies, these stories—lies and legends and the bad dreams of Maravenian officers. But rumor carried Ricardo through the first and second barricade of sentries—rumor and his own bravado, for he was careful of no man on his path to the presence of Helmar. Nobody stopped or even questioned him until he was well into the camp, and all around him the red-armored troops gave way for his angry passage.

Finally he reached the inner circle of guards, those assigned to protect the Maravenian officers against all threats, even those that might arise from mutinies, from their own men. These were Teal Front aristocrats all, schooled in the spear and the sword. Politely but firmly they blocked his way, but Ricardo had even less regard for them, brushing aside the crossed spears of the guardsmen in an impetuous march toward the central pavilion, where the hammer insignia of the general flew on a high flagpost, barely recognizable in the farthest reaches of the firelight. One of the guards—a young one, by his rash action—raised his spear menacingly, fully intending to bury it in the back of the passing Alanyan. But an older man grasped his hand.

"If you toss that, boy," the veteran said, "it's the end of diplomacy and the general's peace. We'll be fighting for that tyrant Dragmond until we all drop before the Pretender's spears."

He found the general's quarters abandoned.

Ricardo leaned against a tent post and glared at the darkened interiors of the pavilion. Despite its sumptuous exteriors, the general's tent was austere on the inside: a simple pallet, one oil lamp, a foot stool that Helmar used as a low desk of sorts, and a floor strewn with papers instead of carpets.

Ricardo fumed. He had come for Helmar rather than gone to warn Brenn of the conspiracy. He had come here ready for confrontation, imagining the general wilting at his hard words and confessing, providing absolute proof to Brenn for Ricardo's doubting assertions in council.

But what if the general had *already* set in motion the conspiracy that had unfolded at the forest's edge? Ricardo staggered at his own idiocy.

What if Helmar was already in the Palernan camp, to . . . The

Alanyan spun about, kicking over the tent post in his haste. Out through the flaps he burst, canvas drooping and fluttering around him like sails descending from a sheared mast.

It might be too late already, and a knife at his old friend's throat. A fine caretaker he had been after all, when Terrance and Delia had entrusted Brenn to his protection. Here he was, half a mile away on a cavalier's jaunt in an enemy camp, braving an absent general while . . .

But that was borrowing trouble, he told himself. *Think the best thoughts and look for a horse.*

As the guards rushed toward Helmar's collapsing tent, Ricardo raced through the firelit corridors of the camp. Around him the shadows of tents towered like shapeless monsters, and the sounds of the rousted army dwindled to a distant clamor, as though a bell of glass had descended over the whole Maravenian bivouac.

To the stables he raced, vaulting the makeshift fence and, as two grooms rushed to obstruct him, dispatching them readily, one with a kick and the other with a crashing forearm to the chin. He untethered a likely-looking horse, freed the hobbles from her legs, and clutched her mane as he guided her back over the fence and into a gallop toward the edge of camp.

She landed gently in her leap, moved fluidly and with a blazing speed. Ricardo had chosen well. He pressed his knees urgently against her flanks.

Then they were free of the light and the noise, and racing across the wide, grassy field toward the opposite camp, toward the Palernan lights. For some reason it never occurred to him to rouse the sentries he met—the tired, green-clad bowmen and the moustachioed Zephyrian riders.

He had decided that only he could undo his foolishness and delay.

Crashing through one campfire, scattering sparks and a sleepy company from Ransom, Ricardo drew sword again as he passed one circle of guards and then another, reaching the dark center of the camp, where the tent of the Pretender lay in humble contrast to the luxurious quarters of the Maravenian command, where he tumbled from the back of the mare and rolled, scrambling to his feet, stumbling, falling, and recovering again before he turned toward the tent and the perils he imagined there.

The lights in the tent were various and low, no doubt the lenses by which Brenn mapped the course of battles. Ricardo crept in the darkness toward the swirl of colors.

Then a shadow intervened, squat and thick and creeping slowly around the side of the tent. Ricardo started to shout, to rush toward the prowler, but a hand seized him from behind, twisted his sword arm in a movement both swift and deft, then pulled him to the ground.

His breath left him in a rush as his assailant sat on him. His opponent was light, but surprisingly quick and strong. Hands wrapped around his mouth, muffling his outcry.

How many *are* there? he thought angrily, struggling to free himself. Disarmed, dismayed, pinned to the ground like a bad wrestler, the Alanyan watched helplessly as the dark shape groped for the entrance to the tent.

The assassin—for surely it was the assassin!—bent, fumbling with the thin silks, and the light from the lenses outlined a long, toothed blade in his hand.

Ricardo lurched beneath his captor, but the man only tightened his grip. Before the Alanyan's horrified eyes, the assassin found the entrance, pulled back the flap . . .

and was struck from behind by a heavy, shambling form. With a curse the prowler tumbled away from the tent and raised his knife, but the newcomer jerked him to his feet and drew him close suddenly, viciously. There was a brief, gargling cry, and the assassin slumped to the ground. Ricardo's eyes widened even further when the light from the entrance danced blue and red and green on the angry countenance of *General Helmar*. Disgustedly, the old man kicked the body that lay at his feet and slipped behind the tent, losing himself in the enveloping darkness.

Immediately, Ricardo's assailant relaxed his grip and stood up. The Alanyan rolled away defensively, groping in the darkness for his sword.

"It's over, Ricardo," the assailant said quietly. "I think our decision is made."

"Brenn!" Ricardo exclaimed. "I . . . that is . . ."

A chuckle arose from the darkness. Brenn leaned over and helped his old friend to his feet.

"What was . . ." Ricardo stammered, "and why did you? How . . ."

"It seems that the general is as true as my hopes," Brenn explained. "Do you think I'm without my *own* spies?"

"You knew of the conspiracy?"

"Since yesterday," Brenn replied, leading Ricardo toward the swirling lights of the lenses. "Well before you learned of it, and before the general learned. I arranged that Helmar would discover it to . . . well, to see what he would do with the matter."

Ricardo rubbed the small of his back, where only a minute before, the Pretender's knee had rested. "How?" he asked again, his face burning in shame.

Now he could see Brenn well, as they stood at the entrance to the tent. The Pretender smiled as he raised the flap, gestured that Ricardo enter before him.

"A fellow named Unferth, trying to steal wine from the Maravenian camps, overheard them and brought me the news."

It was Ricardo's turn to laugh.

He seated himself by the tent post, wincing as he lowered to the ground. Brenn saw his friend's discomfort, and produced a wineskin from his strongbox. The Alanyan tilted the vessel and drank: the skin was full, which did not surprise him, for it was well known that the Pretender rarely drank, if ever.

"That should deaden the soreness," Brenn remarked. "Unferth says it's a good vintage."

Ricardo swallowed hard. "You . . . you certainly have a way with ambush, sire."

"Don't be abashed, Ricardo," Brenn soothed, his eyes once again on the shifting map, where the red swath north of the encampment was turning a sudden, brilliant green. A curious frown passed over his face.

"I wouldn't doubt that in full sunlight," he explained distractedly, "in a fencer's ring or on horseback, you'd make short work of me. But the dark and the back alleys have always been mine."

He stared at Ricardo, his eyes deep and unfathomable.

It is not that he changed the once, the Alanyan thought. *After the plague or the Aralu. It's that he changes again and again, each time becoming something more difficult and strange.*

Each time becoming more thoroughly himself, more thoroughly a king.

≺≺≺ XIII ≻≻≻

The war changed immediately when Helmar and his forces went over to the Palernans.

All through the northern plains of Palerna, from the ruins of Irret and Diamante south to Abertaw and Durain and south farther still, to where the crystalline Plains of Sh'Ryll glittered like summer ice, whole armies shifted allegiance and position.

At the head of the Maravenian forces was a new general. Flauros, the young colonel who had commanded the beleaguered Eighth Legion in the days following the Battle of Diamante and Lightborn's retreat to Maraven, found himself in command of a worse disarray. A general now, the young man withdrew his troops from the Triangulo, moving them to within two miles of the flint walls of the city, where they set encampments, raised abatis and wooden palisades, and awaited the onslaught that everyone knew would come.

For now the Palernans outnumbered the Watch by two to one, and the smell of siege was on the wind.

The autumn came, and colder weather. Soon the Maravenians wakened to crusted ice on the horse troughs and the barrels, and General Flauros gathered his staff for a momentous decision.

Winter in the field would be uncomfortable, perhaps past endurance. Though some of the veterans argued against his policy, Flauros, backed by a strong contingent of aristocrats, decided to retire into the city.

But not before he burned the fields.

October was the end of the rural year in Palerna, when the country folk laid up the barley and, after the first freeze, slaughtered the hogs, leading them from the woods and brakes by dangling bags of mast—a mix of acorn, beechnuts, and beans—before their dripping snouts. It was a simple practice and among the final duties in a slow and simple calendar, when the ordered seasons and expected duties were crowned at last with the long, reflective pause of winter.

That is, if the larder was stocked. From late summer until the first frosts of October or November was a time of putting by, when the farmers stored provender against the cold approaching months.

This year, the Watch disrupted everything: they plundered the countryside, carting grain and swine into Maraven, their wagons packed and brimming, leaving the land behind them barren, the people to face starvation and a vicious winter.

Flauros made the desperate choices simple: all farmers who joined the Maravenian army would have shelter in the city, provisions for their families. Those who refused could watch the fires as the Watch burned their houses, their fields and hayricks, their barns and stables and cotes.

When the Palernans came, the general vowed, they would not forage off these farmlands.

So a pilgrimage began, and for the first time in a year, the gates to the city were opened, and the trade routes flowed with the traffic of refugees. Six thousand people, the historians claimed, flocked from all parts of Palerna toward the great Maravenian gates, drawn to the city like hogs to mast, bearing their possessions on their backs, among them a thousand men between thirteen and sixty . . . a new legion for the Maravenian army in forced enlistment.

The Black Horse Cavalry did their best to obstruct these desperate roundups. There was food to the south, in farmlands beyond the reach of Ravenna's forces, and when they could, the Palernans sent the refugees south, or more often west to Corbinwood, where Brenn's army provided them with shelter and sufficient food to weather the winter, and sustained them with the promise to help restore their lands once the rebellion succeeded.

So the ranks of the Palernans swelled also, but with willing soldiers. And, as this diverting of refugees increased, the Maravenian cavalry was stationed in posts along Hadrach and Cove Roads, to protect the traffic into the city.

It was at this time—late October, two months after the first major battles—that an unexpected reunion took place.

It started simply.

A stretch of Cove Road west of the Palernan strongholds in Stormpoint had been disputed ground for some time. Cavalry passed back and forth over six miles of hard dirt, and skirmishes, raids, and ambushes characterized its daily life.

It was here that the vast influx of southern refugees found the main highway into Maraven. Four lesser trails, no better than drover's paths, joined Cove Road within sight of each other, and the traffic of farmers and burned-out villagers, of carts, of wagons and wheelbarrows and reluctant mules, was as thick here as upon any road in Palerna.

That was why Captain Lubin of the Maravenian Third Cavalry was not surprised to see the young black woman at the reins of a team of horses, guiding a small wagon filled with bundles and bags into a milling line of peasants.

She was Ruthic, no doubt, by her skin's color, and it was rare that people from the Ruthic Islands made their way this far west and south. Rare, but not unique: the scientific community that thrived off the coast of Hadrach occasionally sent its representatives—its astronomers and surgeons, its alchemists and mathematicians—to far-flung lands where their services were demanded. Surely someone—a wealthy merchant, or perhaps the Great Witch herself—had a need for the one in the wagon.

And yet Captain Lubin hesitated, squinted, paused. There was something familiar about this one, and he rifled his memory for a time, a place . . .

The Plains of Sh'Ryll came to mind. The icy air at the plains' edge, and the eidolons that drove their illusory wagons from crystal to crystal, no more than decoys and reflections to hostile eyes.

But this was no eidolon. A flesh-and-blood girl seated in a

wagon, her destination Maraven, her purpose, despite his questioning, uncertain.

Captain Lubin did not press this . . . Delia. If Delia was her name. For you could never tell with a Ruthic scientist or Alanyan augurer, or with a Parthian poet, in whose hire the traveler ventured. Best let her be, and let them reckon with her when she reached the East Gate.

Still, he had a leave coming in November, and she was a likely lass—outlandishly beautiful, and with those golden eyes and the calm demeanor . . .

Well, perhaps the winter in Maraven would be warmer for her presence.

Lubin drew his horse close to her cart, pushing aside a farmer and his family for the proximity. And he had spoken to her again, and she had looked up at him, the light of her eyes brilliant and breathtaking . . .

and there was an outcry in the column behind him, a shout of alarm from one of his sergeants.

Cursing, Lubin wheeled his horse about. It was the Black Horse Cavalry, an entire company of them, riding full tilt from the high brown grass, a plumed and gold-clad commander in their vanguard.

The captain started to draw his sword, to steer his horse from the clogged road to a vantage point, to a place where he was free to wield weapon against the attackers.

Then he saw the black braid of the Palernan commander, and he was afraid.

At the head of the Palernan column, Ricardo gave a hand signal. Angeda wheeled widely right, circling the line of peasants, who had dropped their baggage and were climbing into the wagons for the safety it offered, many of them whooping and cheering. Split in half, the Black Horse encircled the opponent, and the sabers flickered and flashed in the crisp October air.

It was all over in a matter of minutes. Careening in their saddles, their shields raised in panic, the Maravenian cavalry gave way before the Palernans, galloping toward high ground, toward the sloping hills that lined the seaward side of Cove Road. The Palernans pursued relentlessly, Ricardo's wing of the attack dogging the red-armored troopers north, and north still, until Lubin, stationed at a distance from the heart of the battle, saw the design of the Black Horse strategy—to back them into the flanking attack of Angeda's troops.

There was no choice but to fly. Lubin shouted and spurred his mare west, his soldiers falling in quickly behind him. Low in the saddle, flinching at a rain of arrows, the Maravenians rode off toward the shelter of the city, the Black Horse pursuit no more than formal.

Perched atop Churros on one of the coastal hills, Ricardo surveyed the ambush. He had lost only two soldiers to the enemy's dozen, though a third one—a short, grizzled private who had changed allegiance along with General Helmar—lay wounded, attended to by the cavalry barber surgeon. The old fellow was grumbling, trying to rise: he would certainly survive the wound, though the medical attentions might yet kill him.

Of the civilians, none seemed harmed, though some were visibly shaken to have found themselves in the eye of a raging cavalry battle. Two hundred pairs of eyes peeked out of wagon beds, out of the ditch on the south side of the road. Slowly and cautiously, they came out of hiding, brushing the dirt and dried grass from their clothing. Some of them cheered the Palernans; others were quiet and sullen, no doubt resenting the whole business of war and the war's evictions.

Ricardo guided the big stallion down the slope and dismounted, joining in with three of his troopers who were helping an old peasant right his capsized wagon. As the cart shuddered back on its wheels, the Alanyan looked up and saw the Ruthic woman driving her wagon past, her gaze intent on the road ahead of her.

"Delia!" he shouted, and laughed as he raced toward the wagon. "By all the roads and the six lanes of the sea! Is it really you?"

Reluctantly, Delia turned.

"Yes, it is, Ricardo. I would have thought you'd . . . forgotten me."

"*Forgotten* you!" Ricardo exclaimed. "Why, how could you possibly—"

Her stare brought him up short. The golden eyes focused

distantly, coldly, like she was observing spindrift on a far-off wave. The Alanyan slowed, stopped, lowered his arms.

"You had no trouble forgetting when you were at the banks of the Eastmark," Delia accused, and turned to face the road again.

Ricardo was stung and astonished. "But we *both* knew that day was arriving, Delia! We knew that our . . . that our . . ."

He had started to talk of the rightful king, of Brenn and Terrance and the pursuit of honor. But he fell silent, knowing that Delia was not listening for those words.

"I wish you nothing but the best, Ricardo," the young woman answered, flicking the reins and goading her horses into movement. "But we are like essig and aceto: we no longer mix, for we incline toward different things entirely, and our sweetnesses are wasted on each other."

Ricardo's alchemy was clouded, abandoned almost two years before. But it was clear that, regardless of the chemistry, the look on her face amounted to something unhappy and severed, and that regardless of what he felt, his old friend had decided she was a stranger.

But the Alanyan was not the only one who noticed. Wheeling in the air above Cove Road, a brace of ravens dipped their wings, and banked, and turned toward the west, toward Maraven and the Causeway and Kestrel Tower beyond.

The arrival intrigued the Great Witch as much as it vexed her.

She had expected Beladona, the famous apothecary from the Ruthic Islands. Expected her because she had commanded her presence. But the ravens had told the Great Witch that the traveler was a mere girl, that her name was Delia, her elixirs and herbs bundled in packages in the bed of the wagon she drove.

Ravenna stood in the blasted garden, her face uplifted to the October moonlight. Someone had been meddling here: the ground was weeded and covered, as though someone had a mind to grow something in the spring.

She would speak to Camarero about it.

But there were other things to attend to now—things she had let grow over and wild as she guided the cwalu army at Triangulo. That army was gone now, littering fields from Gray Strand to

Irret, nor were her powers strong enough to revive it. But there was time for that, always time when the spring came and the battles resumed.

As for now, she must guard closer to home.

Kneeling, the Great Witch produced a candle from her robes. Shielding the wick against the night wind, she breathed a brief incantation for fire.

> This ae night
> This ae night
> Fire and sleet and candlelight

The candle flickered with a low, uncanny flame, and Ravenna peered into it, looking for the wagon, for the apothecary. . . .

Her gray eyes darkened to a fierce ebony, and she saw Delia leaning over the horses, reins in her hands, her eyelids fluttering as she nodded at the edge of sleep.

"Yes," Ravenna hissed. "And now . . . we shall see, little girl. See the scheme behind this journey of yours."

She stood, and began the chant.

> By each spot the most unholy,
> In each nook most melancholy . . .

Delia startled upright on the seat of the wagon.

Someone was prowling the edge of her dreams.

She knew it instantly as a shadow, an uneasy presence. When you turned to face such things, you always found them gone, though, as though the specter itself was cowardly, would not meet your gaze.

Very well, she thought. If that is what I can expect in Maraven, I shall have to be alert.

Looking back among the packages she had brought, she took quick inventory.

Good. All the components for the lethe were here. And it had shielded Terrance for years, against the prying spells of the Great Witch herself . . .

who, Delia suspected, had come to call while she slept.

So be it, thought the young alchemist, whistling softly to the horses. Ours will be a strange alliance, Ravenna. Strange indeed, and not on your terms at all.

So she kept thinking when the East Gate opened for her in the early morning, when she passed by the guards, who scarcely questioned her despite the hour. She passed Terrance's tower, taking note that the place was dark and desolate, and recalling the black maple whose branches weaved through the second story.

All the time she was waiting, knowing Ravenna would move soon enough.

And indeed it happened on Cove Road, just beyond where the Street of the Bookbinders branched south along the western edge of Wall Town. Two cavalrymen, their faces covered with kerchiefs though the plague had subsided in Maraven since late July, stepped from an alley between the first two buildings of the slaughter yards and approached her wagon calmly, their hands riding lightly on the hilts of their sheathed swords.

"Delia from the Ruthic Islands?" the shorter of them asked.

It was a pure Grospoint accent. The girl marked him as a merchant's son: if she heard enough of his talk, she could tell what his father peddled. But she remained silent.

As she had told Brennart once, there was danger in words.

"Come with us, please," the man instructed.

"It would be wise for you to do so, my dear," his friend urged.

Delia fought back a shudder. She could not place his accent, but something in the tall man's voice . . .

"The Lady Ravenna would be pleased if you would join her for breakfast in the Tower," the short man persisted.

There. The fox was out of hiding. Delia knew the first maneuvers.

She consented at once, her eyes still on the tall man. He did not meet her gaze, but stood behind his comrade, and as they passed the buildings from which the two of them had emerged, he stepped into the alley and returned with two horses, leading the chestnut to his friend and keeping the pale stallion for himself.

Flanked by riders, Delia turned up the Causeway. On both

sides, the gibbets loomed like dark, deformed trees. Ahead of her Kestrel Tower was plunged into blackness, a murky outline against a shadowy sky.

Whatever the hour, the Great Witch was waiting. At the top of the Tower was a cold, solitary light, as yellow and unwavering as a corposant.

Another light, far away and much more gentle, bathed the face of a large blond man.

His eyelids fluttered. He had already been awake: the light was a greeting, a confirmation of the fact.

Ponder stretched, his hands brushing against the branches in which he lay. Books, scrolls, and manuscripts littered the limbs where the Invisible Folk had left them, balanced precariously on thin, resilient boughs and supported by a thick canopy of leaves.

The big man smiled. It no longer hurt to stretch.

The spear wound had taken a good month to mend, but now only a scar remained, a long purple furrow in his side. Sometimes the area twinged and smarted, and at completely unexpected times, as though the wound had a temperament and intentions of its own.

It still astonished him that they had brought him all this way to nurse him back to health. After all, he had been as bad as the rest in exploiting the forest—in hewing the trees and kindling the small, innumerable fires of winter—and worse, he was the skeptic, having studied in their midst and denied them for a dozen years.

And yet they had cared for him. After the battle, he had wakened far from the sandy field where he had fallen. Instantly he had known it was Corbinwood by the stars he could glimpse through the thick latticework of trees. But it was a part of the forest into which he had never ventured. Cobwebs laced the branches of the surrounding evergreens, and weird, glittering streamers fluttered from a ring of mysterious insignia and standards, anchored in a circle at the edge of the leaf-covered clearing.

They had approached him only as amber lights, and for two days they had hovered out of reach, illumining the shadowy branches like a thousand candles. Then, when the pain returned and he cried out in the night, three of them had drawn near, had enveloped him in light, bathing him in a fierce, spectacular glow until he wept and his racing thoughts gave way to quiet and gratitude.

After the second week they had brought him books, and one of them—she called herself Pandora, though Ponder sensed it was not her real name—told him, in a brilliant and silvery voice, that he had been idle too long. So he took up the books and read, and the history and languages, the stories and poetry, the sciences and the mathematics were strange to him, scarcely at the edge of his understanding.

He was delighted by the prospect, enraptured by the challenge. Gradually, the reading became clearer to him, though much of it remained slippery and obscure.

Daily the faeries would visit him, and daily bring him food and reading.

As they no doubt had today.

Ponder yawned and blinked. At once, almost as if his thoughts had summoned them, he saw the three pairs of eyes, staring down at him through the thick, pendulous branches of an evergreen.

"So there you are," he muttered, trying his best to hide the smile. "Late as usual with the food."

"The time is coming that you'll have to gather for yourself, human," warned a high silvery voice from the midst of the branches.

Ponder laughed. "I could do it now, Pandora," he maintained, "but it would leave you with altogether no purpose on earth."

From the secret depths of Corbinwood onto the Palernan plains, from the eastern borders of Stormpoint to the black sands of the Gray Strand in the west, the winter approached in the air. All alike, Maravenian and Palernan, Aquilan and Zephyrian and Alanyan, busied themselves in small preparations—storing food for the season, fashioning mud huts on the plains, building lean-tos to deflect the promised icy winds of December and January.

It would be one of two stratagems, the experts figured: Dragmond would order Flauros and Lightborn to launch a counterattack at the center of the Palernan lines, or they would move on Stormpoint, seeking to divert part of the Palernan army and trying to take that windswept, fortified little town so that Maraven's means to the greater seas remained open through the winter and into spring.

But in early November, the experts shook their heads in wonderment. For at the command of Dragmond, issued from his isolation in Kestrel Tower, three thousand troops swarmed into Maraven, garrisoned in the old Watch barracks and in the emptied slaughterhouses east of Grospoint.

By the middle of the month, they had sealed the gates. Now the only ways out of the city were to the north—over the Causeway or over the ash-gray sea.

"Something is wrong up there," Helmar said, as he and Brenn's commanders pondered the tactics from the high hills north of Triangulo. "Something is dreadfully wrong in that Tower."

"That's good news, then," Galliard declared. "Whatever discomfits Dragmond is to our liking."

"To a degree," Brenn maintained, his brows knit in a deep, uncustomary frown. "To a degree. But it is not safe in that Tower. For those who are my enemies . . .

"And for those who were my friends."

She could not help herself.

The changes had been great since the Battle of Triangulo, when the Great Witch lapsed in a hundred distractions and Faye rediscovered who she was.

It angered her as she continued to play docile Faye the maidservant, masking her newfound knowledge in curtsies and in dutiful compliance. Her hands were red from scrubbing black garments, black curtains, the black arras in Ravenna's bedchambers, and her knees and elbows were chafed from a thousand polishing hours on the floor of that candled observatory at the top of the horrible building.

And yet she smiled, and curtsied, said *yes, madam*, and laughed politely at the grim, humorless jests of the mistress. She awakened at midnight and worked straight through the morning until the afternoon and the autumn sunset, often sustained on only a scrap of bread, a finger of moldy cheese and a ladle of water.

And she continued to smile, and stoop, and drudge, and await her chance. Sometimes at midday, when the Great Witch, propelled by fear and anger and suspicion through forty or fifty sleepless hours, finally tumbled to sleep over the map, in the high-backed mahogany chair, or by the glowing, sputtering fireplace, Faye would stand at the window of the high chamber and look out over Maraven, her view taking in the barracks at the slaughterhouses, Hardwater Cove, the East Wall, and the northern edges of Wall Town. And she would yearn for those places.

Sooner or later, she would be there again.

But there was the matter of Captain Lightborn. It was here, in her dealings with the Pale Man, that Faye could not help herself.

He would stand beside her as she swept, or scoured, or as she washed the Mistress's robes. Always he would find a time when Ravenna was sleeping, so a week could pass without Faye's looking up from her work and seeing that handsome pale countenance, the silver eyes, the disturbing, quizzical smile.

Oh, she remembered him well, now that her stolen thoughts had returned to her. Remembered the Night of the Cwalu, when he and the Watchmen had ambushed her and Brenn and the Goniph in the cellars of the Poisoners' Hall. How he had killed little Marco, killed the Goniph, too, no doubt, in the flurry of knives that followed her escape through the cellar window.

She remembered it all. And still, despite everything she knew and remembered and believed in . . . she was drawn to Captain Lightborn with a disturbing, foreign desire.

At times she thought it was residue from Ravenna's spellcraft, though the idea struck her as foolish, as if magic were some sort of tide that swept over you, leaving behind it flotsam and weed and matters unsettled.

Or perhaps Lightborn himself had captivated her with spells and incantations, for she had heard the other servants say that he, too, was no stranger to sorcery.

Perhaps it was far more simple. Perhaps, after her time of serving the Great Witch, Faye was starved for words and attention, no matter whence their source.

Whatever the circumstances, she found his attentions inviting, her own interest alarming. She would listen as Lightborn spoke, her thoughts carried on the long tide of his voice, and waking she would dream of seasides, of the bright blue of the Mare Nostrum and the impossible greens of Provence, the land of his mother's birth.

His father was Aquilan, the Captain claimed. From his Aquilan blood came swordsmanship, came the skill in stratagem that had made him, a lowly captain, commander over the colonels and the generals of King Dragmond's vaunted army. He could not have done otherwise: it was his inheritance.

And his mother was from Provence, where the poets prospered and song tumbled like rain from the white battlements. He would sing to her, what he said was a Provençal song of courtship.

> Dompna que en bon pretz s'enten
> deu ben pausar s'entendenssa
> en un pro cavallier valen
> pois qu'ill conois sa valenssa
> que l'aus amar a presenssa . . .

It was dashing the way he told what the words said, that a young girl should find an older cavalier as her champion, as her knight, and that she should love him face-to-face. He would look at her longingly as he sang, and she would blush and bend over her work, scrubbing the stone floors as though she could wear them away. But somehow she felt less dirty, less disheveled and hungry.

Always, after the singing and the telling, he would return to the questions. He asked her everything about Brenn, and despite herself, she answered what she knew. By night she would lie on her cot in the servants' chambers, alone with the snoring of the old cook and her own persistent thoughts. Sometimes she would hear the clatter of horses over the cobblestones—sometimes it was Lightborn himself, arriving or departing—and though she always caught her breath and her heart pounded, she would thank her good fortune that she knew so little of Brenn in the first place, and even less since the night the two of them had forced their way into the wizard Terrance's library and been caught at the burglary.

Still, Lightborn would ask. Always when the two of them were alone, in the sunstruck eastern rooms of the tower, in the kitchens and the torchlit corridors.

He asked in the garden, his questions persisting until the old gardener stopped his work.

He followed Faye down those corridors, stopping with her at the threshold of the two rooms she was not allowed to enter. She dusted the threshold to the King's chamber as the Pale Man pried and prodded, and they both stood at the double-locked doorway to that central, secluded room where, day and night, a strange, multicolored light bled from beneath the door.

And at night she would fall swiftly and deeply asleep, worn out from the day's labors and dodges and fendings. She would hear him stalk by, his steps slowing at her door, on his way up the stairs to where the Great Witch plotted and brooded and augured, the strength of her candles gradually returning.

Sometimes he would stop outside her chamber, and linger there, his hand on the latch. She could see his shadow from underneath the bolted door, and there were nights when he would stay there an hour, murmuring and sniffing the air like some ancient, predatory animal.

He never seemed to sleep. At all hours Ravenna would receive him.

At midnight, in her wakeful vigil over the candles, he would knock at her door, disrupting her meditations. The shapes that had almost emerged from the flames would vanish—the shadows of men and horses and moving armies, a closer shadow she suspected was a spy, and one closer still, a gradual turning in the heart of someone in Kestrel Tower. She would labor the night in chant and gesture and the large doses of acumen, until the shapes were like eidolons, hovering at the edge of faces and form.

But at Lightborn's knock, at his first words when he entered without knocking, the shapes would vanish, slipping from her hands like quicksilver, and she would rise from the flames prepared to curse him, prepared to damage and ensorcel him . . .

. . . and be met by those pale blue eyes. Her blood thickened then, and her hands shook, because there was a magic behind the Pale Man, evident in the way that torchlight bent away from him, how the walls whitened with a strange, icy dust as he passed.

Even the ravens were silent at his approach.

M'lady, he would say, *M'lady. What news of the armies has your candle gathered?*

And *None, thanks to you!* she would want to cry out, as she rose to her feet, scattering candles and sconces and light. But instead she would find herself brushing the wrinkles in her dress, straightening her hair as well, silently thanking her own good fortune and the tithonia that her skin was smooth and taut.

For she knew by her own stirrings how the Captain was a lure to women. She had seen it, as well, in the eyes of the officers' wives, in the fumbling manner of the servant girls as he passed, and even in the countenance of her maidservant Faye.

The Captain's talent was undiluted and deadly.

If he kept long enough at Faye, he would find the key to bring Brennart into the city, to the Tower itself . . .

. . . and into her delivering hands.

So Lightborn was useful. When he disrupted her study and augury, when the light sputtered from the candles when he asked *What news of the armies?* she would say, *None. None yet.* And she would smile, would intrigue with and listen to the commander of her armies, as the night rushed on and the traitors encircled Maraven and the siege unfolded.

Lightborn could see the subtleties of the Witch. He knew from the drawn look on her face, from the redness about those marvelous gray eyes, that Ravenna's sleep had unraveled, that this constant vigilance over candle and spellbook was taxing her beyond even her considerable powers. She was eaten with worry.

Three times now he had disrupted her augury. Ravens and candles had scattered, the marble floor dotted with wax and guano and guttering lights, as the Great Witch rose from the flames in a rage, her black robes and blacker hair swirling in the shadows. . . .

And she would see him. And smile. And *No,* she would say, in answer to his questions. *No. Not yet.*

She expected him to deliver the Pretender. He knew it by instinct, as a raptor, high in the air above the plains, knows where his prey hides trembling on a spot of earth.

Expected him to succeed where she had failed, for it was not magic that could draw Brennart back to Maraven. That much they both knew. Terrance still watched over the lad, and the Queen of the Faeries labored tirelessly in Brenn's behalf. Indeed, Lightborn suspected that it was from their agency that Ravenna's candles had gone mute and opaque.

What the Great Witch needed was a confidante wise in the dark ways of the heart, who could plan her visitors and their arrivals.

He was working on that. The girl Faye was the bait in the trap.

Let Ravenna wait, he thought, riding his pale horse up the Causeway for yet another night of argument and augury. *Let her expect it, then.* Through the December moonlight and the shadow of the gibbets he approached the gates of the Tower, his cloak wrapped tightly about him against the wind off the Bay of Ashes.

Let her wait, because she will not have long to enjoy her triumph. My reasons to procure the death of the boy go far deeper than her own . . . back to a vanished time and a vanished country. . . .

He had been cold since childhood.

His widowed mother Rosamond had taken the newborn boy into her arms and instantly felt the chill about his heart. She was a sheltered darling, little more than a girl herself, and when she touched his clammy blueish skin, at once she thought him stillborn.

Hysterically she cried out to the nurses, who had rushed into her ship's cabin, pushed aside the midwife, and flocked around the poor girl like a convent of geese, passing the baby from one pair of manicured hands to another, until the midwife, a sorciere from Languedoc, had calmly set the glass before the baby's lips and wordlessly, scornfully, showed them the mist of his breathing.

Lightborn swore he remembered his first hour: the rocking lanterns, the smell of the bilge in the belly of the boat, the looming faces of the women, how he came to rest in the sly stare of the witch and how the glass fogged with his first breathing. When the Lady Rosamond told him the tale years later, it was as though it was already a family story, repeated at a fireside until children knew it word for word.

Nothing his mother told him, then or ever, surprised him.

Not even when she told him about his father.

For the Lady Rosamond was widowed while still carrying her child. Lightborn's father, she told him, was Count Julian of Arbor and Orgo, scion of the great Aquilan ruling house and the reigning Duke of Aquila, undone by assassins in the hire of his brother Mardonius.

She had left the palace in Orgo before her pregnancy showed, smuggled to a dark pier where a ship awaited, her entire staff of servants on board, along with a handful of guards. They intended to sail back to her homeland, docking in Marseille and traveling north overland, but the plague that would ravage Palerna years later had already struck in Provence and in the Aquitaine, and the port cities had been hit especially hard.

They were forced to keep to the sea, to sail along the southern coast of the Mare Nostrum where port after port refused their entry. Finally, at the edge of despair, their food supplies dwindling, they turned back toward Aquila, prepared to face the intrigues of the court at Orgo rather than become ghostly voyagers, manning a tattered ship.

Lightborn swore he remembered this, too: how each cowardly harbor had turned his mother away, how, before they docked in the teeming port of Rabia, where the Pale Man would pass his childhood, twenty people on board had died of starvation, even after half the servants had been jettisoned so that what remained of provisions would last all the longer.

He grudged that infancy of deaths against the cold ports of Europa, against Marseille and Nice, against Barcelona and Cartagena. But most of all, his hatred stayed close to home: he despised the black-walled city of Maraven, whose worthy kings, his distant cousins, had blamed his uncle Mardonius for the murder so that they might hand the Aquilan throne to a more compliant branch of the family.

He despised Maraven, and he coveted it. For he was as much cousin to Brennart as Galliard or Sendow or any of those Aquilan impostors. And as Brenn's cousin, he stood in line for the throne—indeed, could lay better claim to it than any of those made duke or baron by a vanished king's appointment.

That was why he rode to the Tower by night. Why he watched every movement of the Great Witch, why the death of Dragmond had delighted him secretly, though he feigned shock and anger.

That was why Lightborn had promised to bring the Pretender into the clutches of the Witch. For when Ravenna disposed of the boy, the captain's claim on the throne would be better than any man's.

When that moment came, he would know what to do. After all, he was the scion of two lines, heir to a joined Aquila and Maraven. The King's Guidance ran flawlessly in his blood. He was the rightful wielder of Danton's sword Libra, the blade that ancient tradition said *singled out the crown of the line*.

For he was the balance of power.

The old man watched the Captain cross over the Causeway and enter the massive gates of Kestrel Tower. He had been standing at the entrance to the gardener's shed, his wide-brimmed hat covered with dirt and dried leaves and the first vestiges of a midnight snow.

Behind him, crouched in the little lean-to, his apprentice tended the low fire that was their one solace against the freezing December weather.

"Better get back in here, sir," the lad called. "Afore you freeze whatever parts are useful to a gardener."

"Hisst!" the old fellow scolded, waving a gnarled hand at the boy, at the fire.

"Gin and promises ain't going to stand against the likes of the Northwind," the apprentice warned again, producing a blanket to cover the mouth of the hut.

The gardener said nothing, but shielded his eyes against the rising wind, the nettling snow.

With a sniff of disgust, the lad covered the entrance to the hut and settled warmly inside, his thoughts on the city streets across Needle's Eye and the winding labyrinth of tunnels beneath them, warm and musty and out of the coursing wind.

"Terrance'll kill himself before this is over," the boy muttered, his Wall Town accent emerging more thickly in his anger. "Freeze himself blue in the garden, so that he's useless unless they prop him at the gate to scare away the crows."

He laughed bitterly at his own imaginings, extended his hands toward the fire.

"I expect the rest of 'em are warm," he muttered. "Enemy and friend, they've got them fires and blankets and steadier walls than these. And what ha' we got? A fist full of roots and a pension."

Outside, Terrance could hear Dirk muttering, but paid it little attention. He warmed himself with a swallow of Zephyrian gin, with a short spell or two that raised a little temperate wind about his ankles, lifting the hem of his robe and melting the snow in a wide circle.

He sang softly to himself, his words misting and condensing upon his gray beard until it glittered with ice. The wizard's voice was thin, but gained strength in the singing, and had Dirk the courage to brave discomfort and peek outside, he would have seen Terrance rising to full height against the cold wind, seen his back straighten like a young tree with a springlike infusion of song and youth. *Now winter nights enlarge,* the wizard sang, closing his eyes and recalling an earlier time, an earlier incantation. His voice tumbled through the garden, bathing the dormant soil with warmth and light.

> Now winter nights enlarge
>   The number of their houres,
> And clouds their stormes discharge
>   Upon the ayrie towres;

> Let now the chimneys blaze
> And cups o'erflow with wine,
> Let well-tun'd words amaze
> With harmony divine.

He opened his eyes. The garden around him was ablaze with violets and primroses, sweetpeas and cowslips, and the evergreens that bordered the little plot of land filled the tower grounds with their sharp, watery fragrance.

Terrance chuckled to himself. It would be gone by morning: the snow would cover it all, and he knew a spell or two to divert the disaster of early growth and blooming. Through his song, there in the winter night, had come a brief prophecy of spring, where he could look upon the place and know what it would look like, what it was bound to be in the turn of the season.

"If only the human season were so . . . divinable," he murmured, squinting south through the driving snow where an approaching wagon was outlined against the distant lamplight of Ships. The driver was bent over the horses, bundled and diminished by the night and the hard weather.

Terrance prepared to enter the lean-to, but something—call it intuition or magic or fortune or simply idle curiosity—kept him outside, leaning against the ramshackle building, staring off across the moonlit Causeway. The wagon passed, and he saw the driver more clearly: the glitter of silver bracelets against dark skin, the familiar profile . . .

"Delia!" he whispered in disbelief.

 **XV**

As midwinter passed, and with it the worst of the weather, both armies prepared for the inevitable siege. Into Maraven supplies came by ship—livestock and grain, stones from the Aquilan quarries, and oils to hurl on assailing troops. By February the city was well-stocked, able to stand a year-long siege according to the estimates of its commanders, Flauros and Lightborn.

The supplies came into the Palernan camps as well. From the countryside, the farmers brought what provisions they had hidden in an angry winter—bread and cheese, corn and salt pork and eggs. The supply wagons were heavy laden, though never over-flowing. Still, it was enough: Brenn was ready to last the year as well.

There were, however, chances to cover, possibilities to con-tain. For thoughts of the cwalu lurked in Brenn's mind, in the mind of his men. Even if the cwalu never returned, if Ravenna's powers had faded or turned to other things, the walking dead remained a powerful weapon, a deadly alliance for Dragmond. For they infested the fears and imaginations of the Palernans, and a soldier of double mind is scarcely a soldier at all.

And so the Pretender traveled into the depths of the forest, like a king in an old folk tale, his escort of Zephyrian cavalry nervous but brave as Brenn led them into the heart of fabled Corbinwood, among the lairs of manticores and wyverns and chimeras.

Or so they had heard. And yet despite the forest's dark reputa-tion, the lad who guided them seemed at ease, even carefree, as though he had long awaited this journey.

"Keep an eye to the branches," Brenn said, ducking beneath a bare oak limb that jutted across the horse path. The seasoned Zephyrians smirked secretly at the lad's order. For where was the cavalryman worth a horse beneath him who had been felled by an overhanging branch?

It was the stuff of comic tales and Parthian satire, a warning that would pass for an insult, were the Pretender not so young, not so . . . inexperienced in the ways of . . .

And yet the branches seemed to move. Slowly, perhaps, but they moved nonetheless, and if you looked away for only a moment, sometimes you turned back to a great, brain-addling limb, which seemed to have stretched itself from nowhere straight across the trail ahead of you, as though the forest were descending on Brenn and his band of troopers, trying to bar their path into its depths.

"Here," the Pretender declared, raising his hand.

The Zephyrians halted. To a group of plains riders, it was a wooded spot like any other wooded spot.

"Here is where I leave you," Brenn said. "You will wait for me here."

Angeda, who was leading the cavalry escort, started to protest. But a brief, commanding glance from the Pretender checked his words. "Very well . . . sire," he replied reluctantly, and looking uneasily about, dismounted slowly, as though he were stepping into bottomless mud. Following their lieutenant's example, the other soldiers dismounted as well, each no doubt asking himself why, of all possible patrols a man could draw at the beginning of siege, it had fallen to him to escort a lad in a search for the Queen of the Faeries.

This was the spot.

Brenn remembered it fairly well, as he brushed aside oak branches and tendrils of fir and juniper until the ground almost gave way beneath him, and he found himself looking down into the deep ditch of one of Jimset's collapsed tunnels.

This was the spot where he had fallen, had damaged his ankle and knocked himself unconscious in the process. This was the spot at which he had first met them a year ago, the place from which they had guided him out of grave danger back to Galliard's camp.

If there were faeries to be found in Corbinwood, he would find them here.

He seated himself at the edge of the trench, the ground hard and cold. For a while he thought on the business of sieges, on the westward and secret journey of Ricardo and Galliard now underway, of Maraven and of Faye and of the prospects of returning to both of them.

Then he thought of the day he had first met the Invisible Folk. It brought a smile to him at once—what was the song he was singing, that night in the haunted forest?

> The leopardes savage,
> The lyons in theyr rage,
> Myghte catche the in theyr pawes,
> And gnawe the in theyr jawes!

> The serpentes of Lybany
> Myght stynge the venymously!
> The dragones with their tonges
> Myght poyson thy lyver and longes!
> The mantycors of the montaynes
> Myght fede them on thy braynes!

And at that particular gruesome juncture in the song, he was startled by the sound of applause.

Spinning, reaching for his sword, Brenn lost his balance. With a muffled cry, he rolled into the ditch, striking the hard ground with a blow that set his teeth clattering and his breath to flight.

Glory stood above him, her eyes bright with merriment.

"Th'art in good voice, Majesty," she observed, and Brenn sat up, the air whining about his head and a thousand lights fluttering between him and the Faerie Queen.

"You . . . you could scare a man to early age with your surprises, Glory," he protested, still too dazed and winded for anger.

"Surprises?" she asked, sitting on the edge of the collapsed tunnel. "I would have sworn by my own lamps of reason that your journey here was to find me."

Brenn closed his eyes. He had forgotten the double-talk of enchanters.

"I have news for you," Glory announced. "Good news regarding your cousin Ponder."

Brenn's eyes fluttered open, widened. "Ponder? We searched the battlefield. We had given him up . . ."

"Rest easy, Majesty," the Faerie Queen said. "For he is among us now, in the depths of Corbinwood where neither man's eye hath seen, nor ear heard."

"That is heartening news, indeed," Brenn said, standing and brushing the dirt and dried grass from his tunic. "We had feared that he walked among the dead."

Glory considered. "A common fear in this day and time, when the dead, it seems, have lost their dignity in the hands of necromancers."

Brenn climbed up the bank of the ditch. "That is why I have come to you, Lady."

"To see what I can do about these necromancers?" Glory asked through a smile. "Long ago, Brennart, when I saw this war begin to unfold in the high houses of Maraven and Aquila and deep in my own woods, I made a vow to the forest itself that, once army clashed against army, I should not venture therein. I would take no sides, I vowed, no matter how clearly the lines were drawn between forces of dark and light."

"But you have already done so!" Brenn argued. "You remember as well as I do that afternoon on the Eastmark River, when you put the dragon to flight . . ."

"A time before the war's coming," Glory reminded him. "Before the mustering of armies and the call to battle. Now that the war is with us, I must keep my vow."

"I don't understand," Brenn protested. "The fate of Maraven, of Palerna, of this continent—"

"Will twist and stumble its way from century to century, regardless of war and the rumor of war," Glory interrupted, her eyes distant, abstracted. "And a thousand years from now, when historians gather to tell the story of this age, who can say if they will even remember Palerna? Or you, for that matter? And who can say if they will care who won a war in a nameless country? Meanwhile, a thousand young men, perhaps two thousand, will follow you blithely to early death."

She paused and looked up. Overhead, in the branches of a knotted old maple Brenn recognized as the tree from which he had fallen on the night he first met the faeries, a cardinal perched, red against the black bark and slate-gray sky. Its crisp, chipping song was the only cheerful note in the forest.

"They will know somehow," Brenn murmured, surprised that the argument came forth from his muddled thoughts. He stared at Glory, his voice gathering strength and confidence. "History will know we've passed this way, no matter if our names and countries and wars are forgotten. Surely something is different because of the boys we have lost, because of the loss of that singing lad from Murrey, or Ricardo's aide, or the rest of them. You may be right: the big outcome may be the same, and the future may not rise or fall on the lives of even a thousand of us, because I've read enough history in Terrance's tower to know how large that history is.

"But the feel of it, of what had come to pass, I like to think would be a shade different because those men are no longer here, like the air might be a shade colder in a winter house when one more shingle falls off of the roof—not enough so you could tell, but a shade colder so that somewhere on your hands or between your shoulders before you put on your shirt in the morning your skin could notice."

Glory smiled and nodded, and Brenn continued.

"And that these changes add up and will add up until something changes so much that things are very different on account of them, though we may never stop to figure how things might have been otherwise because those changes had come so very slow."

He stopped, shook his head.

"Rightful king I may be, but this uncrowned head is no philosopher's. Not yet."

"Oh, I think you have done quite well by those thoughts, Master Brennart," Glory observed amiably. "And I also think that I shall not break my vow."

Brenn started to speak, to argue, but the Faerie Queen raised her hand for silence.

"However," she said, "there is this matter of the cwalu. Which is a thing against all nature, a mockery of life and of the dead. Therefore, we shall find an end to that, at least."

Brenn breathed a sigh of relief as Glory turned to the north, toward Maraven, and lifted both her hands. She sang into a chorus of birdsong, and for a moment Brenn thought that spring had made an early return to the forest.

> Call for the robin-redbreast and the wren,
> Since o'er shady groves they hover
> And with leaves and flowers do cover
> The friendless bodies of unburied men.
> Call unto his funeral dole
> The ant, the field-mouse, and the mole,
> To rear him hillocks that shall keep him warm
> And, when gay tombs are robbed, sustain no harm;
> But keep the wolf far thence, that's foe to men,
> For with his nails he'll dig them up again.

"Ravenna is the wolf," Glory added, as the air around her gilded with a warm, yellow light. "The foe of men. And though I have sworn no allegiance to a warring faction, it does not grieve me to see the Great Witch discomforted."

Brenn shielded his eyes. "Thank you, Lady," he whispered. "For your kindness and your justice. And for the freedom of your thoughts and enchantments."

"You had only to ask," she replied.

The effect of Glory's spellcraft was instant.

Throughout the Palernan countryside, the bodies of the dead, buried or unburied, stirred briefly, almost indetectably, one last time. Then they all were still, peaceful, and the more visionary of the country folk, walking by graveyard and open field, saw a curious light rising from the ground and into a cloudless sky, where it hovered for an instant like a burning mist, then dissolved.

Back at Archimago's cottage, the Irish bureaucrat, packing his saddlebags for his trip to Hadrach and home on the earliest ship, swore he could hear bells in the air. His traveling companions, Geoffrey the Englishman and Saavedra the Spaniard, laughed at his impressionable ear, but they both agreed that something strange had come to pass that evening, and that the road ahead of them seemed somehow shorter and less steep.

Throughout Maraven and the outlying country, the war's survivors felt a greater sense of restfulness and peace. Widows and orphans, Palernan and Watch, awakened that next day lighter of heart, as though a long night of mourning had ended and winter itself was fading into March. And even though a siege awaited them all, and the prospect of more and greater bloodshed, most of them believed that something had turned in the spirit of the war, and that there was a brightness visible in the dark days ahead.

Most, that is, felt that brightness and peace. But it was more rare in Kestrel Tower. There, the Great Witch woke from unsettling sleep, from a dream that the edge of her dreaming was raveled and that the city was burning around her, and that the spots on her hands were large, festering, and swollen like the black boils of the plague. She awoke, shivering, the blankets tossed to all corners of her bedchamber. Instinctively, she called for Dragmond, then remembered . . .

As she remembered every morning . . .

She rose, bleary-eyed, and the weakness she felt at her rising told her that something had drawn her power while she slept. Alarmed, she raced to the looking-glass, imagining the wrinkles, the spots . . .

Indeed, there were lines around her eyes, a faint purpling at the throat. Desperately, she tugged at the cap of the vial, fumbled it open, poured the last of the attar of tithonia hungrily down her throat. Relieved, her eyes heavy-lidded, Ravenna watched as the spots and wrinkles faded from her reflection in the bronze mirror.

'Twas a good thing that the Ruthic alchemist had answered her summons. Perhaps there was also something in those eastern herbs and tinctures and mixtures that could do something about the smell of the King.

For though the cwalu may be compliant to the will of the necromancer, they are never pleasant company. Peasant and king, wise man and bumpkin, they all . . . *turn* after a brief time, and no amount of perfume or incense can forestall the fact of their turning.

Ravenna turned from the mirror and opened the door to the chamber, stepping into the well-swept corridor and shivering at the cold draft of wind that greeted her. She headed for the King's chambers, where she kept the animated body at a distance from courtiers and counselors, showing Dragmond on rare occasions from the Tower balcony, where great distance and height masked the fact that the whole city of Maraven, from General Flauros and the leaders of the guilds down to the lowliest plague-threatened peasant, looked to a dead man for guidance.

For something was wrong, and though she could not put words around it, Ravenna knew it concerned the King. And whatever concerned the King concerned her cause. Her steps quickened down the stairwell, and within sight of the door she broke into a run, her dark robes billowing, her weariness replaced by fear.

Fumbling with the first lock, then the second, she gave up the keys altogether, hurling them up the corridor in rage. They rang against stone and vanished into the shadows, and the Great Witch turned, setting her hand on the door.

She felt more energy, more virtue drain from her as she spoke the incantation:

> And farewell cruell posts, rough thresholds block,
> And dores conioynd with an hard iron lock.

Into the chamber she wobbled as the door burst open before her. Dragmond lay sprawled on the stone floor, empty of even the false and fitful life her spells had given him, and no amount of incantation or conjury or pleading could make that body move from its dark and forgetful rest.

Ricardo and Galliard felt the change as they settled for the night in the Zephyrian camp. It was a strange feeling of strength and rescue, and it gave them heart for the negotiations that followed the next day.

For out of the east would come Antal, the Prince of Partha, at the head of a company of Parthian officers, philosophers, and strategists the likes of which had not been assembled in two centuries. They were come to the plains of Zephyr, and coming to meet them in turn would be Castra Agilis, the moving city of Zephyr, its atheling and commander Baron Namid of Aldor.

And at this great meeting of nations, Ricardo and Galliard would try to strike the first bargains of a lasting peace.

A year ago, none would have hoped for such a peace: the enmity between Parthian and Zephyrian had been passed down from their grandfathers. The border disputes were as fierce and bloody as they had been a century past, sometimes erupting in out-and-out war, but the conflict was even deeper than that—a clash of manners and of bearing and, quite simply, of the way that the people of each nation looked at the world around them.

For the Parthians fancied that the Zephyrians were spear-carrying drudges, doomed to nomadic cities and constant war because they lacked the imagination to understand productive peace. And as for the Zephyrians, they considered the Parthians soft and weak and accustomed to leisure, warring for no principles beyond extending their riches and comfort.

It was not the most promising basis for treaties and alliances.

Yet the Pretender of Maraven had sent two of his most trusted commanders east into Zephyr with a handful of men, riding cloaked and armed up the southern, wooded shores of Lake Teal and onto the black sand of Gray Strand, where the notorious Alanyan had guided the little squadron between three companies of Maravenian cavalry. They had arrived the night before at the appointed spot on the Zephyrian plains, carrying with them little but their own wits, a week's provision of winter rations—dried grain, pemmican, and nuts—and a string of gleeful stories about being chased up and down the strand by a cavalry too slow and stupid to catch them.

It was the kind of riding the Zephyrians liked, though they frowned at the boastful talk. And the Parthians, arriving late the next morning, delighted in the stories but found a certain foolhardiness in the risks that Ricardo had taken.

That afternoon, Ricardo and Galliard sat alone in a gabled Parthian tent, a single lamp their only source of light—and of warmth—in the wintry, desolate plains.

"This had better work, Ricardo," Galliard said with a shiver. "I had always thought that living in Corbinwood was braving the elements, but the trees were a shelter against winds such as this, and next to the Zephyrian plains, a winter in the forest seems rather balmy now."

"But neither of us is here to talk of the season, Your Grace," Ricardo observed quietly, "though peace between these nations may be as changeable and beyond control as the weather itself."

"What have you in mind, Ricardo?" Galliard asked. He had decided some time ago, when the two of them embarked for Zephyr, that he would be guided by the gambling judgments of the Alanyan. Diplomacy was hard for the Forest Lord, who saw his truths clearly and spoke them without reserve.

Ricardo leaned forward with a conspirator's smile. His white teeth glittered, and from somewhere—Galliard was uncertain—he had produced a gold earring, now agleam in his left earlobe. He looked like a corsair, like a road agent, and once again the

Duke of Aquila was uncomfortable, remembering he had cast his lot with a good-hearted band only one step removed from thievery.

But I was a thief, myself, he recalled. *In a time not all that long ago.*

"We won't be able to draw a treaty," Ricardo whispered. "For Parthians are Parthians and Zephyrians are not."

Galliard nodded. He felt naive, if not stupid.

"So . . ." the Alanyan continued, "we'll trick them into peace."

"*Trick* them?" Galliard gasped. "But—"

"Trust me," Ricardo proposed with a wicked smile.

When Antal and Namid convened in the neutral tent, they looked first to the Aquilan. He was the royal representative, after all—the Pretender's cousin and the rightful Duke of Aquila by most reckoning.

But when Duke Galliard was strangely silent and the Alanyan cavalry officer did the talking, Antal and Namid settled back, scowling at each other across the lanterns, both dreading the long night of haggling that lay ahead. All the usual proposals were set forth and rejected—that the Parthians cease their *defensive maneuvers* in Zephyrian country, that the *preemptive raids* by Zephyrian cavalry upon the Parthian farmlands come to a complete and permanent halt.

Both dignitaries sighed, their thoughts beginning to wander. Then Captain Ricardo spoke one last time, and both Antal and Namid paused, sensing something new, something possible, the end to a long conflict that both men loathed and neither was willing to give up.

"It is the same ground between the two of you that was between old Antal and Macaire," Ricardo announced. "Between their fathers before them, and between each prince and atheling back beyond memory."

"You knew it would be so, Alanyan," Antal replied sharply. "Why did you ride so far?"

Namid raised a blunt finger, pointed at the Parthian, started a harsh reply, but Ricardo stepped in.

How devious he is! How dangerous!

"I rode at the command . . . of m'lord Galliard," he said, regarding the Forest Lord with a cool, appraising glance. According to their arrangements, Galliard said nothing.

Instantly the nobles turned to the Aquilan Duke. For he was like them—of royal blood, a commander of armies, a man of principles . . .

who smiled, and offered them a game.

≺≺≺ **XVI** ≻≻≻

"Since nothing has changed for generations," Galliard proposed, "and Partha offers one version of the truth, while Zephyr offers yet another, and neither years nor force of arms has proven one more true than the next . . ."

"To the point, Aquilan!" Namid urged between clenched teeth.

Galliard sat back and took a long moment before resuming his speech.

"The point is, either truth will do."

"Oh, surely the duke has not brought me this far into the unenlightened east for . . . a philosophy lesson," Antal remarked dryly. The Zephyrian glared at him across the wavering light, and muttered something contemptuous about philosophers. The room again would have erupted in accusation and hard words, had not the duke stepped in once more.

" 'Tis not philosophy, but a contest to which I have called you," Galliard announced. Casting a quick glance at Ricardo, who winked slyly, the Forest Lord continued, according to their plan.

"Since argument has not settled this conflict, perhaps . . . competition is the better way. I shall propose to you a riddle, and you will have a brief span of time to guess the answer. If Prince Antal guesses correctly, the Zephyrians will meet his demands and cease forever their raids within the borders of

Partha. If, on the other hand, the Baron Namid solves the riddle, then all Parthian maneuvers, parades, exercises, and shows of strength shall cease within five miles of his borders.''

"*Ten* miles," Namid insisted, never lifting his eyes from the Parthian prince. "Not that I choose to riddle away a kingdom."

"Not that you would care to match wits with a Parthian," Antal observed.

"I do have a sword here, Prince Antal, if you're of a mind to match something with a Zephyrian atheling . . ." Namid offered angrily, and this time, both Galliard and Ricardo stepped between the bristling leaders.

"If you both answer the riddle, each grants the other his demands. Your borders will be peaceful for generations because of your wit and inventiveness. And if both fail to answer—which is the possibility that delights me the most, since it means that *I* am the winner—you shall ally with one another under the banner of Brennart, rightful King of Palerna . . . ."

Namid reached over Ricardo's shoulder, clutching vainly for the throat of the Parthian prince, and Antal growled menacingly.

"Very well," the prince conceded. "Pose the riddle. I trust implicitly in the wits of Baron Namid."

Galliard watched carefully as Namid mulled over Galliard's challenge. If he knew Zephyrians—and he believed he did, having commanded them for a full year in the field—the baron would be honor bound to take up the challenge.

Secretly, the Aquilan breathed a prayer to the gods who look after charlatans and gamblers. And whether or not those gods were listening, his prayer was answered.

"Let it never be said I backed down from a Parthian challenge," Namid declared. "Pose the riddle, Duke Galliard."

And so he did, as Ricardo had prompted him, with the warring parties listening intently.

"Your riddle is a task," Galliard said. "You must show me a thing that no one has seen before and none will ever see again."

"That is all?" Antal asked, and the duke nodded.

The disputants retired to opposite corners of the tent. There they mulled over possibilities, each offering, after the allotted time, his answer.

Namid suggested the breasts of a priestess, since many were

the orders in which the woman kept herself from men, reserving sight of her flesh to her order and the gods alone. Galliard pointed out swiftly that the riddle had said "no one," not "no man."

And who, after all, could guarantee the honor of the priestess?

"But the honor of a snowflake, Your Grace, is indisputable," Prince Antal suggested slyly and with a wide smile. "As is its purity, its uniqueness, and sadly its transience."

Namid frowned, and Galliard's glance flickered uncertainly toward Ricardo. He was silent—silent a long time—as Ricardo and Namid watched and the prince's smile grew hard and wolfish.

I cannot rescue him now, the Alanyan thought. *The next time I bargain with Parthians, may I be graced with an oil peddler and a tarrochio player as my companions!*

Then Galliard met the stare of the prince, and replied in a low, almost melodic voice.

"Show me that snowflake, Prince Antal."

"I beg your pardon?"

"Show me the snowflake. You were asked to show me a thing that no one has seen before and none will see again. You can tell me of it, and I can trust you because you are the Prince of Partha, but the task before you is to show me that thing, and unless you do so, you have not solved the riddle."

Desperately, the prince cast his eye toward the open flap of the tent. Outside, the sky was sunny and clear, as though the weather itself conspired with the Duke of Aquila.

"Very well, then," Antal conceded. "According to your rules, you *may* have won the contest, Galliard of Aquila. However, it is my verdict that you have won on . . . a technicality, on asking me to show forth the item in question instead of merely naming it, as any honest riddle might demand. I shall command my legal scholars to review the wager, and abide by their decision as to who has solved the riddle."

Galliard winced. When Parthian legal scholars were brought into any issue, it expanded and extended and tied itself into knots that it would take an old Philokalian philosopher years to unravel. They were back at the beginning, back at the impasse between Zephyrian and Parthian . . . .

But then Namid spoke.

"To let a Parthian lawyer determine my defeat or victory? I think not, Prince Antal! I would imagine that if you are willing to break one promise, that I may break another. I have three hundred cavalry within earshot of this tent—"

Alarmed, forgetting where he was, Prince Antal leapt to his feet. The high crest of his helmet collided with the canvas of the tent, and the headgear slipped down over his face.

"Cavalry!" he sputtered angrily, his voice muffled by plated metal. "You . . . you *never intended* . . ."

"But I fully intend now," Namid declared triumphantly, "if you refuse to abide by the terms of honor."

"And what might be an honorable solution, Baron Namid?" Ricardo asked. Galliard turned in surprise toward his companion. For a moment he had forgotten that Ricardo was there.

Namid cupped his chin in his hand, mulling the Alanyan's question as the prince wrestled the helmet off his head. Finally, as though he had seen the idea at a great distance, the Zephyrian brightened.

"Let Duke Galliard show us!" he shouted. Then, remembering his listeners were at close quarters, he spoke more quietly.

"If Galliard can show us a thing that no one has seen before and no one will see again, then I say that he should be declared victor and we the losers, and that Prince Antal and I seal our alliance here and now!"

"Is that to your satisfaction, Majesty?" Ricardo asked, nodding toward the prince.

"I suppose," Antal blustered. "I suppose with fifteenscore cavalry prepared to pounce on me, that my choices are limited. But yes . . . cavalry or no, it is a just ruling."

Galliard smiled. Opening the pouch at his belt, he drew forth a walnut. Cracking its perfect shell, he plucked forth the light-brown meat from the heart of the nut and held it aloft for all present to see it. Then, with great ceremony, he placed it in his mouth.

"Welcome to my brotherhood, Parthian," Namid said quietly. "And to our new alliance."

"How could you know, Ricardo? The Parthian was clever: He almost slipped our noose."

The two of them were on horseback, riding east along the edge of Corbinwood, their Zephyrian escort riding some fifty yards behind them, too far away to eavesdrop. To the north, at a great distance a column of Maravenian cavalry circled and watched, too far away to give sporting pursuit.

"I had no honest idea, Your Grace," Ricardo said with a laugh. "That is why it is called a gamble."

Then the Alanyan regarded the Forest Lord with new seriousness. " 'Tis less of a gamble when you trust in those who venture with you."

Flustered, flattered, Galliard stammered his brief, barely coherent gratitude.

But Ricardo laughed again. "You were part of the mixture, sire. But only a part."

"I don't understand, Ricardo."

As the Forest Lord spoke those words, an outcry rose from the ranks behind him. Ricardo and Galliard turned in the saddle, just in time to see yet another company of Zephyrians, at their head a young man with an eye patch, emerge from the wood's edge and join ranks with their party.

"Namid!" Galliard exclaimed.

The Zephyrian atheling approached Ricardo, his expression, as usual, unreadable.

"Greetings to my brothers in arms," he declared quietly, his eyes flickering toward the northern edges of sight, where the Maravenian cavalry paused, wheeled, and vanished.

"Greetings as well to the High Atheling of the West and the Baron of Aldor," Galliard replied, gracefully negotiating the dance of honors and titles. "It is our hope that friendship or joyous news leads you to meet us on the roads."

Secretly, he dreaded that the truce had already been broken.

But Namid smiled, and nodded, and extended his hand.

"Joyous news, indeed, Duke of Aquila," the atheling announced. "In gratitude for your games of peace, Prince Antal of Partha places under your command five hundred archers, that the Pretender may be given winged power at the siege of Maraven. I shall send five hundred cavalry as well, so that the ranks of the Black Horse will remain as famed and honorable as they are today."

Galliard blinked. It was more than expected. Not only had a truce been struck, but now both nations had sided with Brenn.

"I believe," he said softly, "that the crown of Palerna has passed to its rightful king."

Ricardo drew the sword Libra and extended it, blade first, between the two nobles.

"Let us set hands to this ancient blade," the Alanyan announced.

"The blade of my old fathers," Galliard said.

"The blade of my old enemies," joined in Namid.

"And let us vow a lasting friendship between the kingdom of Brennart of Palerna and that of the Atheling Namid of Zephyr."

"Sworn!" Galliard exclaimed, his hand on the engraved letters.

"Sworn as well," the Zephyrian agreed.

Galliard's heart swelled at the moment. It was too good, too noble, the stuff of poetry and old romance, of coblyn bards and Umbrian saints.

"I expect Prince Antal will be . . . less likely to swear," Ricardo said. Strangely, he and Namid burst into laughter, the stocky Zephyrian shaking so hard that for a moment Galliard feared that his mirth would throw him from the saddle.

"Gentlemen? Gentlemen?" Galliard asked, beginning to chuckle himself, though for the life of him he could not find the joke in a solemn oath. Ricardo leaned over Churros' neck and recovered his dignity, but another snicker from Namid set off the laughter again, great whooping guffaws.

"What? What?" the Forest Lord asked, and as his patience began to unravel, the Alanyan righted himself in the saddle and took a deep breath.

"Prince Antal hadn't a chance, sire," Ricardo said. "With three such minds in conspiracy against him."

"*Three?*" Galliard asked. "How . . ."

Then Namid laughed again.

There on horseback, miles from the rebel camp, for the first time Ricardo revealed the whole plan to the Forest Lord. Stunned, gaping, Galliard learned that he had been fooled as deeply as had the Prince of Parthia.

It seemed that Ricardo and Namid had arranged the whole

stratagem hours before the meeting with the Parthian. Ricardo would stand in the wings, preparing scheme and counterscheme if Prince Antal proved a difficult dupe. Galliard, as spokesman for the Pretender, would lend authority and respectability to the enterprise, and Namid . . .

Namid's mere presence was strategy enough. For the two things that could hoodwink a plotter like Prince Antal were his pride in his own invention and his contempt for his opponent.

That the enemy was Zephyrian made it all the easier.

"When all was said and done," Ricardo explained, "you'd have to confess that Antal won the riddling. *Snowflake* was a good answer. No arbiter, whether Palernan, Aquilan, or Zephyrian, would have found him a loser. Certainly his own scholars would have sided with their prince."

"What could we have done about that?" Galliard asked, still a little breathless with the revelations. "You . . . you couldn't *plan* for his answer."

"Of course not," Ricardo agreed, pushing his plumed hat back on his head, squinting in the winter sunlight. "But you could plan for other things. When Namid played along, pretending to be the blustering fool, the prince did just what we thought: He gave up his victory by gambling it on a foolish challenge to you, simply because he would not back down to an enemy."

Ricardo smiled triumphantly and winked.

"Why didn't you tell me?" Galliard sniffed, at once regretting the whine in his voice.

"Why, you're much too honest, my friend," Ricardo explained. "One deception was plenty for the likes of you."

The two companions skirted Lake Teal, riding toward the rebel camp with uplifted hearts. On occasion Galliard had broken into song, and Ricardo joined with him gladly, baffling the cavalry escort that followed them—stern, closemouthed Zephyrians who stood in the saddle and watched for the enemy.

To the Aquilan and the Alanyan, though, it felt like the night two summers back, when they had crossed the Gray Strand alone and raided Dragmond's castle, bringing back with them the sword Libra.

They had stopped, warmed themselves at Barco's Ferry, then crossed over black oily water to the Maravenian walls. Deftly, guided by Ricardo, the two of them scaled the flint walls and found themselves in the gardens of Kestrel Tower.

Galliard replayed the whole swashbuckling adventure in his mind, down to the flamboyant planting of wildflowers in the castle gardens. It was there his remembrance dwelt on a strange image—King Dragmond on the balcony.

The memory was a haunted one, the usurper leaning perilously against the stones, his eyes fixed on a great distance, an unhealthy turn in the air of the garden as the Forest Lord slipped into shadows and watched and wondered.

It had been a brief, disturbing pause in a hectic undertaking, and until this moment, his horse weaving through the sparse northern borders of his beloved Corbinwood, Galliard had forgotten about it, or had placed the thought in his mind's recesses.

All in all, though, these escapades were bracing, exciting. And this journey, the ride west to settle a treaty between Parthian and Zephyrian, had all the same feel of a past and adventurous time—the deception and the daring and the long ride afterward.

Soon they would settle into a new adventure, Galliard thought, the wind of the February afternoon knifing cold across his face, carrying with it a distant and encouraging birdsong. Soon Brennart would win, would be crowned in Maraven, the old king and his witch cast aside, and then the lot of them—Brenn, his cousins, Galliard himself—would turn to the daily business of rule and governance.

There at the margins of the forest, with the horses weaving among the trees and the first, forward smells of spring in the air, Galliard was not sure he was glad about it.

Ahead of them the horizon bristled with green banners. Ricardo rose in the saddle, lifted the spyglass as they approached the Triangulo.

A squadron of cavalry rode to meet them, at their head Lieutenant Angeda. It was as it should be—the Pretender confident and alert, his army growing.

Surely the news they brought would only add to the joy.

* * *

They met due north of the Triangulo, on the very spot where Brenn had launched his first attack against Lightborn and the cwalu. Ricardo extended his hand in a time-honored Zephyrian greeting, and the lieutenant grasped it slowly, almost reluctantly.

The Alanyan set his teeth. Something was wrong.

"His Majesty requests that Captain Ricardo of the Black Horse Cavalry be brought to him at once. He would have news of their westward venture."

It was Galliard's turn to frown. "And what would King Brennart have *me* do, Angeda?" he asked.

"He would have you meet with him afterward, sir," the Zephyrian said, his gaze unable to meet the Forest Lord's. "But before that hour, he would ask that we inspect your belongings."

"I beg your pardon?"

"And I yours, sir," Angeda replied, as three of his cavalrymen dismounted and approached the Duke of Aquila. "Trust that my duty is done reluctantly. But I am ordered by the commander of our armies, and for good reason."

"Good reason?" Galliard asked coldly, his hand moving to the hilt of his sword. Intently, he searched the lieutenant's face for sign of drug, enchantment, or betrayal. "I have rarely known Brenn to act against good reason, but I am hard-pressed . . ."

"The . . . curse has returned, sir," Angeda explained, his announcement almost an apology. "My countrymen have found saddles missing, the Palernans everything from shoes to weaponry. General Helmar's spyglass was taken, and with it two medals from the wars against good Baron Macaire.

"All of these things they have found in the tents of your cousins."

"Surely there is some mistake . . ." Ricardo began, dismounting himself as the cavalrymen approached Galliard. He set a gloved hand firmly on the shoulder of the foremost Zephyrian, a lad, as he recalled, from West Aldor.

"I am your commander, boy," Ricardo urged softly, turning the young man around to face him.

"And his orders are from *your* commander, Captain Ricardo," Angeda replied.

Reluctantly, Ricardo stepped back. Nor did Galliard offer resistance. The Forest Lord lifted his hand from the sword hilt as the Zephyrians moved to his saddlebags, untying the cords that bound them closed.

Nobody was really surprised when the jewelry—the seal ring and the gold medallion of Antal, Prince of Partha—tumbled from the bag onto the hard plains of Palerna.

The Zephyrians stepped back as though they had uncovered a suspected viper. Expressionless, Angeda stared at his captain, who finally spoke, as though from the depths of the forest.

"Good friend," Ricardo said, his voice unwieldy with sadness. "Know that no other choice is mine. I must take you into custody in the name of Brennart, rightful King of Palerna."

⤚⤚⤙ XVII ⤙⤙⤚

"But why would it return?" Ricardo asked angrily.

The three commanders sat on horseback, within distant view of the Maravenian walls. The morning's haze over the city had been burnt away by the sun, and Maraven squatted on the northern horizon, its flint walls ugly and glittering like the wings of a monstrous insect.

The Alanyan turned to Brenn and General Helmar. A study in opposites, they seemed—the lean young man with a trace of a first beard and the burly old general, his uniform and goatee crusted with the dirt of a morning's ride.

And yet, they shared a common puzzlement.

"I know nothing of curses," Helmar offered. "And perhaps even less of magic." He grunted, moving back in the saddle.

"I was at the Aralu," Brenn said, his gaze on distant Maraven. "It was from there I brought the Bag of Ladra from the lair of Amalek. Terrance told me it would lift the curse, that final thievery. I suppose he was wrong again."

It had been a trying night for the young Pretender. He had rounded up his cousins (even little Lapis, in whose possession they had found Helmar's spyglass) and placed them together under a house arrest of sorts, guarded by a stalwart squadron of infantry from Braden Gorge. The five of them now rested uneasily in the center of camp, the subject of a rising suspicion among the troops—especially the Zephyrians.

Ricardo stared sympathetically at the young man. To be this close to total victory, his army growing, and then, suddenly and unexplainably, to lose half his officers to an ancient curse—it was a hard thing to endure. Now those same forces stood at the edge of disruption: The cavalry circled the camps daily, herding in would-be deserters, and even the ranks of the Black Horse themselves seemed to dwindle as the days pushed sullenly into March.

Only Brenn's constant presence, Ricardo's jokes and good humor, and an underlying fear of General Helmar kept most of the troops from wandering away. They were fed up with winter and dreading the prospect of the siege without Galliard, Sendow, and Thomas. And, as the time passed, those prospects appeared even more meager.

"There was nothing you could have done, Brenn," Ricardo soothed. "You did what we knew. That is all—"

His voice trailed into silence, as Brenn continued to stare off toward Maraven.

Finally, the Pretender smiled slowly and stroked the neck of his horse.

"Of course it isn't," Brenn murmured. "My fault, that is. I haven't the time for faults and blaming and pitying myself. Let us set our heads together, gentlemen. Spring approaches, and as swiftly as we can, we must take a city."

Ricardo whooped, and Helmar snorted in gruff approval. The boy had a general's spunk, an infantryman's endurance. They knew he would wander the camps that afternoon tirelessly, spending his time among the common infantry in storytelling, encouragement, laughter, and in losing the occasional game of dice. Most commanders would have lost heart over the last fortnight, but if anything, the boy seemed more assured, more straight in the saddle and cheerful among the men.

"Siege and swiftness don't usually go together," Helmar observed. "But there are ways to find the most unlikely matches."

"Then we shall find them," Brenn declared, looking back at

the city walls for signs of movement, changes in wind and rising smoke—for the evidence of things he knew he had yet to see.

By the end of March, though, even the unseen things were ominous.

Twice the Maravenians had issued forth from the walls. General Flauros himself had led a swift, effective sortie into the heart of Sendow's old legion. Those rebel troops, still demoralized from their struggle against the cwalu, retreated in dismay, and only the lightning-swift support of Angeda's cavalry kept a Palernan defeat from turning into a rout.

Two days later, it had been Captain Lightborn, emerging from the East Gate with six hundred men, striking with willful savagery against the flank of what once had been Galliard's legion. Without their accustomed leader, their chain of command disrupted, the Palernans made their stand nonetheless. They wrestled back the Maravenians, killing fifty of them in the process, but at a loss of more than three hundred men.

Helmar stomped furiously through the camp, kicking over the bivouac fires and scattering armorers and quartermasters. It was said that his words would drop the new leaves from trees, could curdle the milk in the udders of the mares. He could not be everyplace at once, he maintained, and where he was not, events tumbled rapidly toward chaos.

Brenn was insulted by the general's bluster, by his high-flown assumption that the army would unravel without him. Yet "It will be better soon" was all he said, watching in frustration as the March rains swept through the camps and another six hundred men vanished outright.

"Surely when the weather warms," he told himself, "the spirits around here will lift."

Ricardo listened sullenly, the canvas from an old tent draped over his head. As the weeks dragged on and the army dwindled, it was harder and harder to trust the King's Guidance.

Then, on the first of April, as though it had kept a cruel appointment, the plague arrived in the Palernan camps.

The first to fall were the lads from the country and the mountain provinces, inhabitants of more remote areas where the plague had never touched. Within days the wagons carted the dead from the campsite, burying them in a burned wheat field south of Irret.

Brenn moved through the camp, accompanied by Anthony the Shepherd, the strange man from the East whom the predatory birds followed, docile as doves. The two paced around the smudge fires the physicians had lit to check the spread of the plague. Brenn's hands dispensed the healing touch until he tired, and he slept fitfully, guarded by masked infantrymen, his dreams of the strange cavernous room beneath the fires of Dame Sorrow's kingdom.

Those he touched recovered, but it often seemed futile: the plague had settled in the camp and would not leave, and the sick were likely as not to contract it while Brenn slept, or while he was elsewhere, tending to others. Daily, he fought the plague's profusion, standing over red fires, the smells of jasmin and garlic lacing the open air as the physicians tried desperately to aid him. But by night many of those he had healed in the morning had fallen ill again. A mile's trip north toward Galliard's troops or west toward the archers that Thomas once commanded would exhaust him by evening, and as he returned to his quarters in the center of camp, he would meet a cart trundling off toward the Widow's Field, filled with men he had thought on the mend that morning.

Soon the physicians themselves could not stand before him for the boils and the fever.

All the while, Brenn moved from man to ailing man, his hands extended, his thoughts of ice and of the green ocean depths, his courage untroubled by the profusion of disease and dying.

He remembered the forest, Dirk's terrible wound, and the words of the Faerie Queen to a reluctant lad who, for the first time, had set his kingly hands upon a soul mortally ill and sinking.

"But my hands haven't the power," he had said then, holding them vaguely, fingers spread, above his dying comrade. "At least not yet. And this is Dirk, Glory! This is my friend for ten years—more than half my life! What if my hands should fail my friend?"

"There will come a time," Glory said, resting her ruddy hand on his shoulder, "when you will ask that question with every wound you touch, unless you answer it now. The time is coming when every plague-ravaged face is lifted to you in hope and yearning. You will love them all then, as much as you love this lad before you."

It had not seemed possible, this love for all of them. And yet tirelessly he rose before sunrise, and, guided by one of the Parthian physicians, a young woman named Jolanta, would trudge toward the latest outbreak of the Death, his prayers already on his lips, and the blue, sword-shaped scar on his left hand already aglow.

Sometimes the light from it would keep him awake at night.

And always he concerned himself for the fires, the drums, the odors of incense. It would not be long before they knew atop the walls, if they did not know already.

Of the seven thousand men assembled in Brenn's camp south of Maraven, three thousand were dead by the end of April. It was a time of sudden hope in the city of Maraven.

At strong suggestion from the Great Witch and her captain, General Flauros confined the entire Maravenian army to its barracks, in Teal Front, in the residential areas, in the old slaughterhouse at the eastern borders of Grospoint. Perpetual fires smoldered on the streets around those buildings, and the army lived under quarantine, fenced in except for the times that they were masked and, under a covering cloud, led to the gates and out onto the open field of battle.

For with spring the plague had come to Maraven again, as violent as anything seen around the distant fires of Brenn's camp. Six thousand townsfolk were dead by the end of April, though thanks to the devices of Ravenna and her commanders, the army was kept virtually disease-free.

Nonetheless, the troops could not help but be demoralized, for they saw the Death ride in with April wind, and they saw the dead ride out on the Corrante.

Scores of bodies were set adrift in the Bay of Ashes, keeping the boatwrights in Ships busy day and night producing the cheap wooden coracles fast becoming known as *Dragmond's coffins*.

At night the dark waters were dotted with a hundred small boats, rowed slowly by the becchini toward the ashen southern coast of Aquila.

Trading ships now unloaded farther north, sometimes even in Orgo, impelled by fear of the plague. Carters would carry the goods south over the Causeway to the merchants who waited eagerly in Ships and Grospoint. And now, the weather much warmer, food would perish and spoil on the overland route, and in Maraven the first rationing of a siege time began to take its effect on the populace.

Wall Town was hit the hardest. The poor in Maraven's slums had always been ill-fed, closely housed. Now the plague tore through them like a fire raging over their cramped buildings of dry and brittle wood, killing half of the people who had no choice but to stay in that wronged and wronging district of the city.

Among those was one Amilcar Squab of Grospoint, a sturdy lad of merchant stock, his given name outrageously grand for his humble origins. He was no older than Brenn himself, and though his influence was great he was much less admired and loved, even in a city supposedly hostile to Pretenders and rebels.

Amilcar Squab was worthy of mention only because of his sudden and curious rise to power.

After the Night of the Cwalu, when Faye was captured and the Goniph killed and Brenn and Dirk fled the anger of Ravenna, the searching hand of Captain Lightborn and the Watch, the guild to which they had belonged—the Noble Brotherhood of Light Fingers, the Fellowship of Ladra, the Company of Thieves— had altogether vanished. Its leaders either fled, were taken prisoner, or were executed by the roundup of dangerous folk the Great Witch encouraged in the week that followed.

In that time, Squab was the eyes and ears of the King; the Guild became Dragmond's instrument, his intelligence in the depths of the city, in the slums of Wall Town and the ramshackle alleys of Ships, and in the maze of tunnels that underlay all of Maraven, from the southernmost walls to the honeycombed coast of Hardwater Cove.

Three hundred alleged thieves were brought to the King's justice in the next year. Some of them were indeed of the Brotherhood—cutpurses and burglars, con men and looters. But most were innocent folk, merchants or tradesmen whose business the King coveted, seditionists or firebrands or rousers whose names, at the King's command, would enter the Guild lists in the cramped, scarcely literate hand of the new First Master, Amilcar Squab.

He would watch from the bronze dome of the Burghers' Hall as they brought out the thieves. He crouched in the arch of the bronze pendentives, a tattered coat wrapped around his shoulders, though surely he could afford a better, could afford fine wool or even furs if he chose. And from his vantage high above the northernmost streets of Ships, he could see all the way to Kestrel Tower, to the West Wall and east to the slaughterhouses where the troops were barracked, far from hunger and cold and the plague in the streets.

From the dome he watched the hangings on the Causeway, scratching a tally with his knife on the weathered bronze. It was high theater to him, a distant story in which his was a small but important part.

Indeed he must have felt it there in the Burghers' Tower—the craftsman's surge of pride at the results of his handiwork. For of those brought to the scaffold in the year after Brenn's escape, half were recommended by the First Master himself.

It was the way he kept order in the Guild. For by the end of the first winter, all the Brotherhood knew that any contrariness, any defiance of Amilcar Squab, could bring with it the night visits, the manacles, the stay at the old Maraven Keep, and from there the short walk in full sunlight to the gibbets on the Causeway, your escort a squadron of Maravenian guards, masked against the plague and armed against your rescue.

By the end of the first winter, they had learned a grudging silence.

They kept that silence in the long spring of the plague following the war's outbreak. For the hangings continued, though the First Master complained that the King had long ceased granting an audience, that now even the Witch and the Pale Man would not see him.

That duty had been given to a Sergeant Danjel, who it was said had the ear of Captain Lightborn. Squab was not sure what that meant—a close confidant? a friend? a second-in-command? But he fancied that this Danjel was a party to the most secret dealings in Kestrel Tower, if only because the news that the sergeant brought along with the informant's reward of a dozen silver marks was the First Master's real payment for selling his guild and his friends into the hands of the King.

Whatever the station and power of young Danjel, he was not reluctant to give away secrets. They understood one another, sergeant and First Master, or so Squab told himself. Twice a week, in the dead hours of the Maravenian morning when not even the Watch patrolled the streets, the two would proceed to an honored meeting place—the cellar in the Poisoners' Hall— where Squab would leave a list of names for the sergeant in return for money and *regular intelligence*.

It was an unlikely place for meetings of state, this wide cellar of the Poisoners' Hall. Shelves filled with old clay bottles and dusty vials and flasks lined the far, windowless wall. The racks in the center of the room had been splintered and crushed in a long-ago struggle, and the cellar smelled of astringents, of deadly herbs, of medicinal alcohol and vigilia root.

On the nights they met, the whole place was bright with candles. The sergeant stood behind a screen and a wall of incense, remote as a Parthian idol. From there he spoke of the castle intrigues, of Ravenna's plans and the captain's strategies.

Squab attended hungrily. Often he asked himself, *Can I believe this?* and *Why do they want me to know?* but the stories themselves banished his wisdom and misgiving, and Squab knelt on the cold cellar floor and listened, the sweet smell of incense bathing him, smothering him.

What of Faye? he asked. *She and I . . .*

Were friends, Danjel said. *Yes. So you have told me. She is a fortunate girl, working for Ravenna.*

Squab nodded, though he did not believe.

More fortunate still, the sergeant continued, *in her choice . . . of new friends.* And so the story, carefully crafted by the great Witch and the Pale Man, passed into Maraven, its unlikely carrier the First Master of the Brotherhood of Thieves.

According to the tale, the girl shared the bed of Captain Lightborn.

Had he thought for even a moment, Squab would have doubted that parcel of news as well. But it was alluring, seductive, and he was not one to resist any temptation.

Why? he asked, his imagination racing. *And . . . and how?*

I expect the "how" is in the usual and time-honored way, Master Squab, the sergeant observed dryly. *But as for the "why," I have my own conjecture.*

Squab leaned forward, squinting against the sweet smoke. He loved conjecture.

So Danjel spoke, and there in the Poisoners' cellar, he filled the ears of the First Master with the lingering venom of his words.

Oh, for a while she held out, Sergeant Danjel began, his voice melodious, enticing. *For a while the girl Faye insisted on proprieties, on some strange behavior one would not expect from a street urchin. But she returned to form, and it was short work when the Ruthic alchemist arrived.*

Squab drew back. *Ruthic alchemist? I know of . . .*

The voice rose from the smoke, low and insinuating. *Delia. An old friend of the Pretender. A traveling companion. Or so it is claimed.*

The First Master rocked back on his ample haunches. He would not have thought such things of Brenn.

It was delightful, the scandal of it all.

The Great Witch knows things, Danjel continued. *Knows the sleep and the waking, the visions of day and desires of night. She saw them west of the Eastmark River, their encampment after the Alanyan left . . .*

Amilcar Squab smiled wickedly. There were those in the Brotherhood who held out an allegiance to Brenn—a romantic notion, born of the starving Maravenian streets and the plague and the luxury of armies. He had seen it in the tunnel graffiti: *Brennartus Dux* and *De Latrone ad Regem* the signs read, defiant slogans that led the First Master to believe there was rebellion brewing in the Guild.

When they heard how their paragon had betrayed poor Faye in the arms of some exotic alchemist . . .

Tell me more, Squab urged. *Tell me more, Sergeant Danjel.*

So the sergeant apprised him of other things: that the wizard

Terrance was in Rabia, where he had set up a school for the black arts, that all of Brenn's cousins had deserted him, flying back to the fastness of Corbinwood and their lives of robbery . . .

Of that you will see evidence, the voice intoned. *And soon.*

Squab rubbed his hands in delight.

As for now, though, Danjel concluded. *Your list.*

The marks, Squab insisted.

In the bag. Behind you. Now the list.

Fumbling in his worn, tattered coat, the First Master produced the vellum roll. He stood, his intent to walk past the curtain of smoke, past the screen, to hand the document to the sergeant . . . .

Wait. Do not approach me. Set down the scroll. Take up your money and leave.

I don't understand, Squab insisted.

What is there to understand? Do as I ask.

The First Master gaped stupidly. He awaited some sign, some explanation, alone with the rubble and the silence and the billowing incense. Then, hastily, he dropped the scroll, picked up the bag behind him, and wedged his way through the narrow cellar window back onto the moonstruck cobblestones of Light Street.

Eagerly he opened the bag. He could not have done so in front of the sergeant, where it would have seemed mistrustful, faithless. But here, in the open, the *gahlo* sound of the echoing sea wind in the streets bringing to him voices, laughter, the creak of a distant cart and the murmur of raposa dogs, the First Master opened the bag . . .

and withdrew the gold florins, wrapped in a wrinkled sheet of vellum. At first delighted, then with a growing confusion and dismay, Amilcar Squab read the note scrawled on the wrapping.

For Amilcar Squab, First Master of the Brotherhood, from his constant admirer Captain Lightborn of the King's Watch.

And everich of thise riotoures ran
Til he cam to that tree, and there they found
Of florins fine of gold, ycoined round

Wel neigh an eighte busshels as hem thoughte—
Ne lenger thanne after Deeth they soughte.
But eech of hem so glad was of the sighte,
For that the florins been so faire and brighte,
That down they sette hem by this precious hoord.

"And after Death . . ." he murmured. "I don't understand this."

The sound of hoofbeats interrupted his reading, his reverie. He scrambled into the Starboard Alley and looked down Light Street, where the riders approached, two of them carrying torches against the shadows of the overhanging buildings. The riders neared him, passed, and were lost in the winding thoroughfares of Grospoint.

But Squab had seen their faces, the face of one in particular.

"By the four winds, 'tis true!" he muttered excitedly. "The cousins *are* leaving him!"

He told them all of the defections—of Brenn's infidelity, of Faye's new liaison, of the Aquilan in the company of the red-armored Watch, on his way north toward Maraven Tower.

Enraptured they listened, for it is the first nature of all, not only of thieves, to believe the worst betrayals, the most dire treacheries.

And it is the first nature of all to enjoy their telling.

At first Squab thought he had spoken far too long, that his delight in gossip had carried him past his knowledge and invention and voice, for when the other thieves left, no doubt carrying the news through the vast network of lairs and passages beneath Ships and Grospoint, his throat felt suddenly dry and sore. Perhaps the climb through the narrow passage from the cellar and the swift journey to the Anacreon and the stairs had tired him, had winded him. The rich food and wine . . .

then suddenly the coughing, the sweat. Amilcar Squab sat in the tunnel, his head against the cool subterranean stones. For a long time he sat there, his eyes closed, his fever rising, hoping that whatever it was would pass over him suddenly.

But it lingered, the sweat beading uncomfortably on his neck, on his brow.

The florins. He thought of the florins and smiled. They would buy him . . .

What? A physician's attentions? For the fever rushed over him again, and the street whirled. Dizzily, Amilcar Squab extended his hand toward the torchlight at the mouth of the tunnel. It shone down upon his exposed fingers, his surprisingly graceful wrist, and there, mottling his forearm, was the first unmistakable sign of the dark boils.

He coughed, his eyes rolling in terror. From somewhere— farther along the tunnel, perhaps, or perhaps from within his own horrified thoughts—a voice rose, whispering, taunting.

Ne lenger thanne after Deeth they soughte.

The florins poured from the bag in the First Master's hands, chiming absurdly in the echoing dark.

Lieutenant Meresin guided the horses onto the rocky ground of the Alanyan coast. In the dark bed of the wagon, his three companions steadied their ungainly bundle, and when the wagon creaked and rattled to a halt, hoisted it among them, carrying it awkwardly toward the Potters' Field.

"I never knew he was this large a man," Agares said.

"The heaviness of policy, Agares," Lightborn quipped darkly, and Danjel laughed nervously as he set the body on the ground.

Meresin and Agares carried shovels. Furtively they began to dig, in a shadowy spot not even the moonlight touched.

"He's already turning," Agares muttered to the men behind him. "I can smell it from here."

"Your duty is to dig the grave and to notice nothing," Lightborn reminded him coldly. The lieutenant shivered and returned to the task at hand.

No words were spoken when they laid King Dragmond to rest, when they covered his remains with scarcely six inches of dirt. For the Potters' Field seemed haunted at night, and the shadows of the wild raposa flitted hungrily at the edge of the torchlight.

Finished with their rushed, perfunctory task, Agares and Meresin leaned on their shovels and recovered their breath. Behind them, his back to the moon, the Pale Man moved closer to the fresh gravesite.

"You have done your duty, lads," he observed, smoothing the dirt with his foot. "In part."

"In part, sir?" Meresin asked, turning toward the captain. "We have dug the grave, and you can rest assured we shall notice nothing."

The knife slipped into his ribs before he could block the thrust. Agares cried out, tried to run, but Danjel leapt on him, dagger flashing in the wavering moonlight.

In a moment it was all over. The two survivors climbed into the wagon, turned the horses toward Kestrel Tower.

Danjel laughed nervously again. "For a moment, sir, I thought I was destined for the Potters' Field along with Agares and Meresin. The look on your face—"

Lightborn smiled grimly. "I have other duties for you, Lieutenant. You and I will be together . . . for a long time."

<<< **XVIII** >>>

Of course, the stories that Squab had died believing were not altogether true.

Though Brenn and Delia had been companions on a lengthy and dangerous journey from Corbinwood to Hadrach, theirs was a friendship born of the road and a common cause. Delia would have been as surprised as Brenn to hear rumors of a great romance that had blossomed on the plains of Palerna.

But it was the story Faye heard as well, in the depths of Kestrel Tower.

"And she is lovely, Faye," the Great Witch would say, as the girl swept her chambers, washed the tinted glass mosaic over the mantel. "They say . . . ah, but who knows what to make of rumor? and yet they say that she and the Pretender . . ."

The words were always around her, in the air like candle smoke, like the forgotten odors deep in the heart of the castle. She resisted them at first, told herself they were yet another spell of the Great Witch, yet another wicked enchantment. But the stories continued, subtle and sinister and falsely sweet, and Captain Lightborn repeated them, hovering above Faye in his attractive and unsettling manner as she spread the rushes, aired the rooms, kindled the evening fire.

Though she was drawn to him, drawn past her own believing and good sense, the Captain never touched her, despite the rumors. And strangely she was glad of it, would sigh in relief when he left on the Tower business and when he was in the field—when she could be assured of a stretch of days without his morbid attentions and her bewitched response to them.

In one of those stretches of days, when her chores were lighter and the cares of Ravenna and Lightborn were apparently fixed on some remote council on the plains of Zephyr, Faye saw this Delia for the first time—in the Tower bailey, at the edge of the surprising garden that was now in full green below the King's balcony. And indeed, the alchemist was beautiful—the type of dark looks that would turn a lad's head. Faye leaned against her broom, feeling old and abraded and common, as the woman, glittering in the gold cloth that was the badge of her trade, walked to a shady spot in the garden and, looking about, knelt and peered amid the herbs and flowers, intent on something minuscule and obscure—an alchemist's attentions, usually reserved for measurement and mixture.

Crouched above the dark earth, Delia tilted her head, as though she listened to a distant music. The diamond in her ear caught the edge of the sunlight, and for a moment thoughts more generous flickered in Faye's suspicion.

He spoke highly of her. Of her . . . breeding and honor, if I'm not mixing her with someone else.

It has been long indeed.

But breeding and honor . . . do not sort with Ravenna's words.

In a roundabout way, after innocent talk of the weather and vegetables and herbs, she asked old Carlo what had brought Delia to his garden at the foot of the tower.

He was a bright-eyed old sort, and secretive, and though

something in his face was faintly familiar, her Wall Town days had taught her not to ask after resemblances. At any rate, when she told him of Delia's presence in the shadows among the herbs, his gaze, usually direct and honest, was suddenly veiled and dodging.

She knew at once that her news of Delia had surprised him.

And that it would be wise of her not to press it further.

So they talked of other things: of the growth of the flowers and the circle of varied evergreens the old man had tended back into health. His apprentice, who kept at a great distance from Faye, stirred from the cottage as they spoke and turned to the farthest edge of the garden, to the shadows beneath the Tower walls, where he crouched above the same patch of herbs, stirring Faye's recollections once more. But she and Carlo continued their idle talk, speaking of the weather again, and of the plague's progress, and finally of the news that one of the Aquilan barons had been captured near the Triangulo.

All the while Faye rummaged through her thoughts and remembrance, seeking a face to match with Carlo's. Her memory was returning quite well, in the time since the Witch's spell had lifted, and she remembered many things, many people: the old becchini she met five years ago, in the plague's worst season until this spring, the officer in the Watch who had goaded her with harsh words off of Hadrach Road when his company passed and she was in the way, the Alanyan visionary who had come before the King to read the entrails of hawks.

None of them. She could not place old Carlo yet.

So they talked of the weather yet again, and of the captured baron, and Faye let her suspicions of Delia, her memory of that single moment in the garden, settle into a dark place in her thoughts, where other concerns shrouded and covered it.

As the girl left him, Terrance breathed a spell of blessing, his eyes misting with an old regret.

> Also these freshe somer floures,
> White and rede, blew and grene,
> Ben sodeinly with winter shoures

> Made feint and fade, without wene:
> That trust is noon, as ye may sene
> In nothing, nor no stedfastnesse,
> Except in women, thus I mene.
> Yet aye bewar of doublenesse.

Dirk stood behind him, a shovel in his hands, shifting from foot to foot, awaiting politely the end of the spell.

"And what was that you were castin' about?" he asked Terrance, as the last of the wizard's words tumbled and died in the fresh garden air.

"Doubleness," Terrance replied quietly. "Doubleness is all around the girl. May she be enough of a thief . . ."

"Oh, I can tell you *that* much, sir," Dirk assured him, setting down the shovel and hobbling to his side. It was that same time of spring in which the wyvern had stung him, and every year the wound returned, in a way—a stiffness in his young limbs, a flurry of night fevers. "She's as much of a thief as you'll need in the time you'll need it."

None of those who spoke together in the garden had heard of Squab's untimely passing, nor of what had transpired with the renegade baron. None knew that these events, conducted at night and in the greatest secrecy, would come to daylight in the weeks that followed, changing the face of the war forever.

For the baron was Sendow, next to Galliard the most valuable of Brenn's cousins on the field of battle. Commander of the legion that had first met and bravely fought against the cwalu, he was one of the favorites among the Palernan troops—more stern than the other leaders, but more forest-smart and a master of rock-ribbed defenses. Helmar admired the young man as well, remembering always a mired coach in an earlier winter, how Sendow had captured him and treated him with the greatest courtesy before releasing him in what the grizzled old general called "the first chivalrous act of a nasty war."

But on that field after the Battle of Triangulo, when his troops had been forced to the high ground south of Irret, ringing themselves with fires, keeping a sleepless watch as the cwalu circled them relentlessly . . . something had turned in Baron Sendow of

Aquila. He had not slept well in the months that followed, and when the Curse of the Lifting returned, he was the first to steal.

And when Brenn had ordered the cousins confined to their quarters, placed under guard at the center of the camp, it was Sendow who was first to rise up.

He did so quietly. Late in the evening on the day that Amilcar Squab made his crooked way through the streets of Ships toward a veiled meeting with Sergeant Danjel, Sendow dressed quietly in the candlelight of his tent. A plain black robe he put on, the better to merge with the deepening night, and he left his armor for Jimset, who stirred in the cot opposite him, dreaming no doubt of roots and spades and the dark directions of tunnels.

Sendow looked lovingly down at his sleeping brother. He would not leave Jimset—would not leave Lapis, or any of them, for that matter—were it not for this imprisonment. A dozen years in Corbinwood had been enough confinement; he had thought himself free of it, of the curse and all the restraints that had come with it, but when it returned every bit as strong as it had been in the days before Amalek's defeat, Sendow was the only one of the cousins to despair.

Their cheeriness seemed like a burden to him—Jimset's foolish babbling about how he would be Brenn's chief engineer *when the curse was again lifted,* and Thomas' and Lapis' happy return to quiet times, to poetry and lenses, as they waited for their larger duties to be restored to them. Even Galliard, who Sendow had been sure would be grievously scanted in this dull cage of house arrest, was reasonably content. Daily, Brennart would send him messengers and maps, and the Forest Lord kept abreast of the tactics and positioning of troops, always planning for a time in which he could resume his place at the head of his legion.

It was all too much. Each of them clutched at the smoke of an outlandish hope, and after a week's confinement, Sendow had removed himself to a small, isolated tent at the edge of their circle. There he spent his time in solitude, except for the occasional visits of Jimset, who was hard at work on a network of tunnels to connect all of the cousins' tents, and on the third night of Sendow's exile, had burst through the sod into the middle of his tent, dripping earth and the tendrils of roots. He would stay there some evenings, and on the fifth day of the confinement had dragged his cot into the premises, setting it up in the presence of a despairing Sendow, who knew now that he would find neither solace nor privacy in the midst of his family.

He was headed for Zephyr on the night he escaped. The Atheling Namid, he had heard, was searching for a passage through the edge of Corbinwood, by which he could transport cavalry and supplies rapidly to the Palernan armies. It seemed like a good pursuit to Sendow—a way to escape, and yet to assure Brenn that he meant the cause no harm, that indeed he intended to continue in the service of the rightful King of Palerna.

Perhaps on the plains, in the midst of the Zephyrians, who traveled light and tied their belongings about their waist, his curse would go unnoticed, unpracticed because of the lack of occasion. He would have to learn to ride better, of course, and to live off dried fruit and pemmican like a raven in a wasteland. But he could not live here, his talents going to waste, in the futile hope that Brenn would find some solution, that the curse would be removed and that all of them could go back to the way things were before.

Why did it return? he asked himself, as he slipped the guards easily and made his way through the sleeping soldiers to the corral in which the black horses were kept. Seizing on a likely mare, he saddled her and mounted, his woodsman's senses alert to every shift of sound, every movement of the shadows. Twice litter-bearers trudged by, carrying bodies to the plague cemetery that had grown up a mile away from the camp's edge. Sendow did not stop as they passed, paid them little attention: they combed the camp daily for the dead, and often crossed his path, for the plague had touched the surrounding tents and even taken one of the men assigned to guard him.

They would be hours in returning, and by the time they reached the corrals they would forget entirely the dark shape moving amid the horses. By then he would be well on his way—past Diamante, perhaps, and even within sight of the Triangulo, where Galliard and Ricardo had left their Zephyrian escort a few days back. With any luck, there would be stragglers, outriders.

It was a dim hope, but better than this infernal waiting.

He rode past midnight, approaching the Triangulo from the north. To his right he saw the huddle of trees, black on the moonlit field, and he shuddered as he recalled that spot—the place where they had first retreated from the marching dead.

Never. He would never go back there. Nor to any place on the Palernan plains. It was a haunted landscape to him, and he longed for the forest's safety, for the undiscovered lands to the west . . . .

As he had suspected, the cavalry approached him. Six men, perhaps seven, riding out of the squat woods he had passed and shunned. Sendow reined in his mare, stood waiting for them.

I am at the edge of new adventures, he thought. *And so I always shall be.*

I will wait for nobody and nothing.

It was in the next breath that he realized the cavalry was wearing red and carrying Dragmond's standard.

Sendow's ride to the city was brisk, relentless.

His captors were Teal Front boys, skilled riders from endless lessons and races. Of all the men in Maraven, these were the best suited for the cavalry, and Sendow had trouble riding with them, keeping pace over the rising terrain as they galloped toward the distant flint walls.

The captain of this squadron was subdued, respectful, when he found he had captured Sendow of Aquila. Time and again he tried to strike up a conversation as they rode, but his prisoner would have none of it, closemouthed and sullen as the city leapt into view on the moonlit horizon.

As bad as Halcyon, Sendow thought, his dark meditations accusing him, scolding him. *Even worse.*

And look at me in the saddle. If I cannot hold with these dandies, what alienado stoked my brains to make me believe I could ride with Zephyrians?

He hung on in silence, his thoughts coiling and tangling, until suddenly there was a warm gust of night wind and he broke into a sweat.

These black robes, he thought. *Uncommonly heavy for spring.*

He looked to the young captain who rode unruffled beside him. Full Maravenian armor beneath a gray cape. It would seem that, if any man were heated . . .

The stars in the northern sky flashed and blinked and wavered.

Is it . . . what . . .

Sendow weaved in the saddle, his hands unsteady on the reins. Desperately he gripped the sides of the mare with his legs, prayed for balance . . .

and recovered, his breathing forced and shallow. To the southernmost gate of Maraven the cavalry rode, as the fever rose in the veins of their captive.

They stopped for inspection at the gate, and the sentries examined the Palernan commander with wonder. Sendow glared at them, shrank into his robes, stifled a cough. Up through the residential district they clattered, the lamplight flickering in the narrow streets, and for the first time he could see the faces of his escorts, could discern features, hair color, scars . . .

and finally, as he had feared he would discern, the discoloration of his left hand.

He had learned enough of the Death to know it worked quickly, that the sole hope of his recovery was the King's Touch.

But the one man who could save him was in the Palernan camp, miles and hours away.

For a moment Sendow thought of escape. His captors were good riders, but hardly tough and wary. One quick turn of the horse, one push to unseat the nearest rider, and he could be free in the Maravenian streets. Providing he could find his way to a gate and out of the city, he could elude pursuers for hours.

But he no longer had hours. The fever was mounting, and the buildings of Light Street seemed to swim around him as his party passed the Hall of the Poisoners, their destination no doubt the prison at the old Maraven Keep . . .

where they would find him dead tomorrow morning.

Sendow grimaced. Dead and useless. The meantime was everything.

Slowly, a desolate plot took form in his fevered thoughts.

If he could get to the Causeway, the Tower . . .

But what of the Tower? Once he was there, he would undergo intense inspection: because of the plague and the wars, nobody would approach Dragmond's presence without being poked and probed and mulled over head to foot.

They would discover he was ill, would kill him on the spot or take him away before his new plan could bear fruit.

There was a better way. But he had to act fast, before his escort brought him to the Maraven Keep.

I am at the edge of new adventures, he told himself again. *And so I always shall be.*

I will wait for nobody and nothing.

Taking a deep breath, he spoke to the commander of the squadron.

"Take me to the slaughterhouse."

Startled, the man turned rapidly in the saddle. Sendow had been silent for over an hour.

"I beg . . . your pardon, sir?"

"The slaughterhouse. 'Tis where the barracks are, is it not?"

The man nodded stupidly, then caught himself, sniffed, and turned away. The horses trotted up Light Street, the Maraven Keep now in sight, beyond it the scaffolds of the Causeway . . . .

"Come now, Captain," Sendow urged. "You've betrayed no state secrets. I want to go to the barracks. To be met by my opposites, my rival commanders in the field."

"We—we were taking you to Maraven Keep," the captain stammered.

"To rot dishonorably in prison?" Sendow asked, his voice mimicking outrage, hurt pride. Intrigue was a kind of forest, entangled and complex, and as he played his part and misdirected the Maravenian captain, he found that he knew the country well. "But surely, Captain, you know the strictures established by the Umbrian Accords?"

"Why . . . of *course!*" the captain replied, "but perhaps the Baron Sendow would care to . . . refresh the memory of my troops."

In the dark of his hood, Sendow smiled. This captain was poisoned with pride, so thoroughly that he pretended to remember fictional accords—accords Sendow invented one breath ago. The vision of dead men is remarkably clear and precise, he mused.

Well, if the captain *remembered* the Umbrian Accords, he would *remember* their principal point.

"The Umbrian Accords," Sendow explained, secretly exulting in his own dark joke, "declare that an officer taken prisoner is allowed immediate audience with the supreme field commander of the capturing troops."

"That would be General Flauros, sir," the captain prompted. "And right y'are that he's bunked in the old slaughterhouse, but I'm not sure that . . ."

"What you're sure of has no bearing here, Captain," Sendow insisted, his voice cold and commanding. "The Umbrian Accords take precedence over all treatment of prisoners, over siege rules and the conducts of chivalry, over the Philokalian Treaty and . . ."

He paused. He had reached the dangerous edge of a lie, where if he said any more, there was a chance that the captain would begin to question him, would find the gaps and holes in the fiction.

"So take me to the slaughterhouse," he concluded breathlessly, his head whirling with fever.

And fitting it is that I shall die in a slaughterhouse, he thought, as the captain nodded, and, reining the horse about, led the party east on Cove Road through Grospoint, the smell of smoke and creosote fading into the old smell of blood and much dying, as the squat buildings ahead of them took on a crimson outline in the rising sun.

But of some use in this death, I shall be, Sendow thought, settling into a curious peace as they passed the barrack guards and entered the quarantined grounds. *Of some use.*

I carry more than amenities and messages.

≺≺≺ XIX ≻≻≻

The news reached Kestrel Tower by midday.

The woodwise cousin, it seemed, had died on his feet. Standing between two astonished guards in the slaughterhouse barracks, he clutched their arms fiercely, deadlocking himself upright after the breath had left him.

When the soldiers drew back his hood, they saw the lifeless eyes, the black sores. Then they knew why he had insisted on passing through the officers' quarters, why he had brushed against the cavalry commanders and clutched at Captain Amiens.

Alone in her lofty chambers, having dismissed servants and advisers, having dismissed even the hovering ravens who now circled the tower aimlessly, the Great Witch stirred above the map, above the dormant candles.

Fifty feet below, on the front steps of the Tower, Faye basked in the afternoon sun, a book on her lap. Only a light shawl covered her shoulders, for the wind was warm off the Needle's Eye, and yet it was still a sea wind, carrying in its depths the faint hint of cold, the last memory of winter waters.

Captain Lightborn sat two steps above her, shielding his eyes.

"The first reports," he said, "are alarming. Fifty men already show signs of the plague. Fifty men, my dear, and 'tis less than eight hours since Sendow passed among them."

Faye nodded, thumbing the pages of her book. She tried not to listen to the Pale Man.

" 'Tis the kind of unfair strategy the Pretender prefers," Lightborn coaxed. "Infecting innocent men with a deadly disease, against all the rules and reverence of warfare. I do not doubt it was all his plan, the 'capture,' everything!"

And summoning forth the dead? What honors do you find in that, Captain? Faye thought, but did not say.

For to say would be to challenge the man, to set herself against him in a way she could not do. She hadn't the courage or she hadn't the heart—she was not sure which it was.

"What are you reading?" he asked, his voice soft and reconciling.

"Oh . . . plants, mostly. Plants and herbs." Instinctively, she held the spine of the book away from his eyes—away, so he could not read the title.

"He's dangerous," Lightborn said. Faye blinked, lost for a moment in his shifting conversation.

"Oh. You mean Brenn," she said, sneaking a glance at him. *How handsome he is! How dangerous!*

She took pains to banish that thought, resting her mind on the old man, on the garden.

Carlo's garden had been her refuge over the last few weeks. Faye had found herself retreating to it when the Witch was distracted, helping the old man plant alyssium and marigolds, listening to his chatter about his plans for the turnips. It was soothing talk, free of politics and magic and gloom, and Faye looked forward to those moments with eagerness, almost with hunger.

The boy—the gardener's apprentice—was never there. Always on errands, or sent for something back south of the Causeway, his absence left Carlo shorthanded. Faye joined in the work merrily, so often that sometimes she fancied herself the gardener's apprentice.

Yesterday, Carlo had asked her about the herbs.

"I'm not from these parts, girl," he confessed, "and no matter how long you work a garden, there's some things come into your knowing late, or come not at all. Long as we have them, and long as they interest the Mistress upstairs, I expect I should know more of them. You're a Maraven girl? How does petrial grow here? and scintilla and marelle?"

She had shrugged and stammered. Faye was a city girl, after all, and the gardens she had seen were on the other side of high fences. Nonetheless, she had promised the old man whatever the Tower library offered on the subject, and he had seemed eager, even excited at the prospect.

She liked Carlo. He did not browbeat and frighten her, like the Mistress, nor unsettle her, like Captain Lightborn. She wanted to help him, to make him happy.

That was why she had smuggled the books from the Tower. Two of them—smaller volumes about specific herbs—she had concealed in her robes. This other one, enormous and arcane and almost indecipherable, was too large to hide, so she had brought it out in clear view, pretending to read it and hoping whoever saw her would find her interests innocent and boring.

For the life of her, she could not say why she knew she must hide the title.

Lightborn rested his gaze on the battlements. "You

must . . ." he began, then paused, shaking his head. "Never mind. Not now."

Never mind? Not now? What? Faye looked directly at him, and their eyes met.

"Faye," he said, and she felt a warm flush on her face. "Faye, the time is coming when you will grant me a great boon . . ."

What does he mean? she asked herself, closing the book and sliding it beneath her skirts. Treating with Lightborn was like a journey at the intricate edge of a forest, where shade and root and entangling vines reached out to grab you, draw you in, engulf you in darkness.

She stood.

"I had best be going out to the garden, sir," she said, then realized he had seen the book, would know she was taking it, would know . . .

But what difference did it make? She had known thieves before, dozens of thieves, who were charming and honorable and . . . stole things. Was the man on the steps any different?

She would tell him. Who would care?

"I'm . . . I'm taking this herb book to the gardener. At his request, of course, and with the Mistress's permission."

She felt fragile, vulnerable, as though she had revealed some horrible secret. But Lightborn leaned his elbows against the stair and slowly, almost wearily looked away.

"Did Ravenna speak to Sendow?" he asked.

"I don't know. I had best be going, sir."

"Did she send him a message?"

"As I said, I do not know. Please, sir."

Silently, the Pale Man waved her away. As Faye descended the steps, carrying the heavy book, he looked up from his reverie, his eyes following her lazily, playing over the slim line of her thighs.

"Good afternoon, little gardener," he murmured. On his lips, the farewell was leering, almost obscene.

She would grant him a great boon. Sooner than she thought.

And who would not follow a girl like that, even into the jaws of a nightmare?

* * *

"These are all that the library holds," Faye said, setting the three books on the gardener's table. He stared at her from the corner of the shed, and for a moment she thought she had recognized him finally, placing the face in her memory.

Something about storms . . . a borrowed cloak . . . the Night of the Cwalu . . .

But it vanished, she could not retrieve it, and she turned instead to the books she had brought him, laboriously displaying the titles for his view.

"*Lenimenti naturalis,*" the gardener read with a frown, turning one of the small volumes in his hand. "*Usus cicentae.* The usual stuff. Poisons and palliatives."

With a grunt, he lifted the large book, held its spine to the light.

"*Folia Morrigana,*" he breathed. For a moment Faye saw a brightness pass over the old man's face, as though a new moon had sailed into the sky, shedding light in the darkest corners of the castle yard. "The *Leaves of Morrigan.*"

"A mystery, for the life of me," Faye added hastily. "Written in some outlandish tongue that hasn't the decency to go by an alphabet . . ."

She would have gone on, but the gardener was no longer listening. He set the book gently, almost reverently back on the table, and opened it to the very first page. Faye called his name once, twice, and on the third time he responded with a vague mutter, as though he had suddenly remembered his name.

"What? Oh, yes!" he sputtered, his eyes darting back to the page. "These will do nicely, Faye. I'm very grateful."

The girl could see that he wanted to be alone with the book. A little miffed, she nonetheless smiled and nodded, and backed from the gardener's shed into strange weather.

A rack of black clouds had passed over the sun, and for a moment Faye thought she had spent far too long with the old man, that without her notice the afternoon had passed into evening. It was with great relief that she looked up to see the sun begin to peek out of the gray billows, and the garden recover its fragile, airy light.

Quickly she lifted her skirts and ran up the steps to the Tower, her brown hair trailing in the warm April breeze. The Captain was gone—long gone, she guessed—and if she reckoned rightly by the sun's position, Ravenna's hours of augury would begin shortly, and the high chambers would need airing, the candles replacing. She took the stairs two at a time, her thoughts racing as well, away from the old gardener, the shadowy shed, and the books she had left behind.

From the battlements a dark figure watched the girl scamper into the Tower. Larger than a raven, he was, and precariously perched on a high station, weaving in the strong breeze and waving a spyglass like an awkward baton.

When the doors closed behind her, the figure vanished as well, lost in the glitter of flint and the rising night.

They stood above the pages in wonder. In the lamplight Carlo's features seemed to shift and change, and the quick-witted lad noticed at once.

"You've the look more of a wizard than a gardener, sir," he whispered.

"Very well," the old man said. "We shall undo the spell, then. For what is a mask when you know the true face behind it?"

Quietly, with a half-smile, he spoke the initial words of the counterspell:

> Ye old mule, that thinck your self so fayre,
> Leve of with craft your beautie to repaire,
>> For it is time withoute any fable
>> No man setteth now my riding in your saddel;
> To much travaill so do your train apaire,
>> Ye old mule!

Dirk laughed softly. He loved the words of the spell. Quickly, he recited his part, as the gardener's face began to blur and soften:

> With fals favoure though you deceve th'ayer
> Who so tast you shal wel perceve your layer
>> Savoureth som what of a Kappurs stable,
>> Ye old mule!

It was always a little of a surprise, even when he participated in the spell. For at the reciting's end the old man's features took on new lines, new clarity, and Terrance the Mage stood before his marveling apprentice.

"Now," Terrance said, wiping his hands on his robes. "Let's take a closer look at this volume."

"Why, Terrance?" Dirk asked. "What is it you expect to find? A book on herbs is, after all, a book on herbs . . ."

"Carlo," the wizard prompted. "While we are in these walls, my name is Carlo. This will take close reading, take hours of study, for my Umbrian isn't as good as his was . . ."

" 'His'?" Dirk interrupted. "The man who wrote this?"

Terrance nodded. "It's in Albright's hand."

"Albright?" Dirk asked. "You mean Brenn's *father*?"

"*Grandfather*, damn it!" Terrance hissed. "What *is* it with you lads and lineage?" Impatiently, he pointed at the scrawl of runes on the old vellum page. "It's Albright's script, for sure: I recognize the *unciales*. And it's in the code, all right."

Dirk shook his head in frustration. "Beggin' your pardon, Master T—Carlo. But what's this of kings and codes and uncles . . ."

"*Unciales*," Terrance corrected, lifting his gaze from the book. For a moment the lad before him seemed hopelessly ignorant and foolish. It was now that he needed bright wits as well as young eyes beside him—Delia's, perhaps, or Faye's.

But no. He needed Brenn.

As skilled as Terrance was in the laws of magic, in the intricacies of rune and language, he would have trouble reading Albright's ancient encoded note. The code was a royal code, ingrained in the blood line of the Maravenian kings: reading it came to them as second nature, almost as instinct, and it was a true test of royal blood and kingly anointing. In the old days, when there had been dispute over who should ascend the throne, all pretenders were given encoded passages to read, and it was a sure sign that the one who could decipher the cryptic messages should be crowned.

Terrance had no doubt of Brenn's anointing. He had seen the boy's hands set upon the wounded, the dying, the dead. His was the King's Touch, no doubt, not the ministrations of some hedge healer.

And with that anointing, with that touch, came a knowledge of the code. What would take the wizard years to decipher, while innocent folk died of starvation and plague and battle, could be solved by the rightful king in a matter of hours.

There was no question. Brenn must come to Maraven. But there was the matter of the lad's command, not to mention that his parting with Terrance over a year ago had been on less than friendly terms.

"It must be laid aside," Terrance mused aloud, his fingers passing over the fading ink on the page. "The lad must forgive me, must leave his armies leaderless awhile, must find his way through a city where his old friends have turned against him . . ."

"Beggin' your pardon again, Sir," Dirk interrupted. "But I haven't the foggiest notion . . ."

Terrance stood upright, his hat brushing against the ceiling of the shed. He smiled wanly, and a murmuring sound—that of a bird, perhaps, or a small mammal—arose from his robes.

"Call the girl back, Dirk," the wizard said, forgetting his own warnings and calling his apprentice by name. "Call her back, and pray to those who look after burrowers and thieves that *she* is not one of those who has turned against our Brenn."

She was in her quarters by the time Dirk found her.

Faye was napping, her sleep light and her dreams shifting and fitful, when a soft calling from below the window awakened her. Immediately alert, she rose from her cot and padded to the window, leaning over the sill toward the sound of the voice some thirty feet below.

"Who is it? Who's there?" she hissed.

Dirk stepped out of the shade of the wall.

She recognized him at once. Stifling a cry of delight, she waved excitedly, and Dirk lifted his finger to his lips.

"Where have you *been*?" she whispered, as the little thief clambered up the sheer wall until his hands gripped the bars in her window and he pulled himself comfortably onto the sill.

Dirk could come no farther into the room: in the last week, Ravenna had seen to it that Faye's quarters were private, her windows fitted with iron bars—*to prevent intrusion*, she had said. For Faye, it had made the place seem even more the prison, especially since the door was locked now, during the hours that the Great Witch slept. Instead of the freedom she had once enjoyed in the corridors and stairways of Kestrel Tower, Faye was ushered into the narrow cell of her quarters at times unpredictable—whenever a drowsiness fell over the spent and exhausted witch.

For the first time in months, this little room seemed less confining—seemed almost cheery—as Dirk dangled his legs between the bars and spoke quietly, amiably, as behind him the eastern sky darkened toward a clear spring night.

"I've been in the woods, Faye," Dirk explained. "And in training to be a sorcerer. Hold your laughing tongue, I swear!"

Faye looked at her old friend long and hard. Dirk had always been prone to exaggeration, multiplying the numbers against him in a fight, subtracting severely the number of florins in his purse when she asked to borrow money. But she decided that separating lie from truth was impossible after a year's absence, and that she had better believe him if only to spare herself the guesswork.

"Sounds as though you've done well for yourself, Dirk," she whispered ironically. "As for me . . . well I always told you I was the Queen of Palerna. Welcome to my palace."

Dirk glanced around the room and shook his head. "Not like our quarters under Wall Town, is it now? The Goniph would be spinning to know that Dragmond treated you this way."

"Dragmond's neither here nor there," Faye replied, glancing nervously toward the door. "Haven't seen him for months now, 'cept on the balcony of an evening, and not even *that* of late. Don't be mistaking, it's Herself that runs the premises now."

She paused, listening to herself with surprise. The Wall Town accents had returned to her voice.

Dirk smiled and leaned back in the windowsill, hooking his knees around the bars. "Then it's the Witch you'll be dodging for what I have in mind," he said with a wink. "There's someone I want you to meet again."

"Meet *again*? And even if I wanted to, how . . ."

"The Goniph would spin over that as well," Dirk taunted. "The fat man's favorite, fretting over a simple lock and a plain barred window."

Faye smiled, remembering the old First Master. Something in Dirk's words goaded her, and something about his mysterious *someone* whetted her curiosity. For a moment she hovered in caution, thinking of Ravenna's temper, of the Captain's cold and piercing eyes.

But Faye was never coward, and adventure seemed all the more delightful given her old friend's challenge.

"The Goniph would be pleased on one account," she declared, reaching under her cot, producing a ball of wax, and tossing it to Dirk. "From Ravenna's own candles."

Deftly, the lad plucked the ball from the air. "Proud indeed, he'd be, to see his prentice of prentices roguing tallow." He turned the wax in his hand, saw the imprint of the key. "And I suppose you'll be asking me to find someone who'll fill this with metal?"

Faye winked dramatically and seated herself on the cot.

"I'm asking if you're asking me to meet a *someone*."

Dirk held the ball of wax up to the fading light. "This time tomorrow even, then," he said, and lowered himself from the windowsill. Behind him the sky was nearly dark, and the first stars were winking in the ominous sign of the Adder. Alanyan astrologers could tell you by a glance at the moon and planets that it would be a poor week for travel, for Coluber the Adder was the sign of betrayals, of misfortune in dark places.

There were dark places indeed, in the shadow of the walls, as Dirk placed the wax in the pouch at his belt and scrambled like a lizard down the wall. He touched the ground lightly, already on the run, and slipped through a high topiary bush. Within minutes he was in the garden, gliding silently from shadow to shadow toward the crack of light from the gardener's shed.

Back at the Tower, something stirred in the darkest shade of the wall. Against the black flint of Kestrel Tower, the full moon flickered on a white sleeve, and a man stepped into the light beneath Faye's window.

He had seen it all, and heard most of it. Heard at last the time of appointment.

It was an assignation he would keep to himself.

He stepped out from the window, clear of the Tower's shadow, mounted his horse at the edge of the Causeway, and sang to himself in a soft and melodious tenor:

> Je veux te raconter, o môlle enchanteresse!
> Les diverses beautés qui parent ta jeunesse;
> Je veux te peindre t beauteé
> Où l'enfance s'allie à la maturité . . .

The song reached the ears of yet another, hard at work in a windowed room high in that same Tower.

Delia carefully moved to her window. A balcony of granite and wrought iron commanded a lovely view of the spring sky, the tilting constellations, and a low, orange moon above the smoky Sea of Shadows.

The alchemist rubbed her eyes. Time was when she would have looked on herbal studies as a lark, on a stay in a Maravenian palace as a luxurious holiday. But the Witch was a tiresome employer, asking persistent questions, sending out spies, and urging that the work move more swiftly and toward more definite answers.

Delia sighed and looked over her shoulder to the cluttered table. Books were stacked upon scrolls, scrolls upon sheets of vellum and papyrus. A small but well-designed alembic rested in the center of the table, beneath it a low and steady fire. The air was filled with the fresh smell of leaves brewing, and the faintest hint of a bracing Alanyan spice.

The alchemist smiled. Were Ravenna to peer through the keyhole, she would see pay being earned, work being done, things boiling and bubbling and an entire alchemical machinery unpacked in the corner, ready for use within the next several days.

But there was no philosopher's stone in the making on the table, no elixir vitae. There *was* a good strong bracing tea, for Delia was thirsty after four hours at equation and Arabian algebras, and the tea needed strength to keep her from sleep, for the Witch relentlessly pried the edges of her dreams.

Delia walked to the table, poured a cup of the strong brew,

then turned back toward the balcony, her steps weary with study and the hour of the night.

XX

Dirk was on time with the key the next evening.

He whistled softly and tossed it through the window. It bounced once on the stone floor with a muffled ring and Faye, ready and waiting, caught it before it rang again.

She was out the door in an instant, down the steps to an unguarded side entrance, locked from the inside. Carefully, quietly, she opened the door, set it ajar with a hand-sized piece of flint that lay in the rubble at the base of the wall, then circled the Tower until she came around to her window and Dirk.

He took her hand, and together the two of them raced through the gathering dark to the gardener's shed. Faye started to protest, to say she had been here before, that they would wake old Carlo, but Dirk shook his head and signaled for quiet.

It was Carlo and yet not Carlo, the man whom she saw when she entered the shed. He was taller, younger, straighter of back and brighter of eye, yet somehow he was the same man, and this time she recognized him at once.

She remembered the lightning-crazed sky, the trooping dead on Cove Road, the door opening . . . .

"Terrance!" she exclaimed. The wizard glared at her, and she lowered her voice. "I—I thought you were in Rabia."

Terrance smiled. "I am not in Rabia, Faye. I am here."

Faye curtsied awkwardly. She was at a loss how to greet the wizard.

For over a year Ravenna had spouted nothing but venom about this man. A traitor to his master, she'd said, to his fellow prentices, and to his own prentice Brenn, whom he had abandoned plague-ridden at the edge of Corbinwood.

That was the way the Witch had told it. Now, looking at the

pleasant old fellow in front of her, Faye once again doubted Ravenna's version of things.

"I am here," Terrance repeated. "I am also glad you are here."

Faye stepped back. Prefaces like these usually led to impossible demands, to great danger.

"You see, Faye," the wizard continued, "I need your help."

Exactly, she thought, and awaited the story. No doubt he would ask her to spy on Ravenna, to poison the Captain or bring him the keys to the Tower. Well, she was not ready to be a sorcerer's go-between. She was not . . .

"I need you to bring me Brenn," Terrance said, and the girl gaped at the boldness of his request.

In the hour that followed, the wizard outlined his plan. Faye was the logical choice, he said, to pass through the lines and reach the Pretender's camp. It was she who could set aside any hard feelings, any hostility that remained between Terrance and his former apprentice.

Nor did it take Faye long to think over the request. She accepted at once, glad to do something that might set at ease the great unrest in her heart.

For weeks it had plagued her—her long struggle against spell and fatigue to remember her friendship with Brennart, their history together in the tunnels under Maraven and how that friendship had only begun to blossom into something deeper when he had returned from his apprenticeship with Terrance. But she was forgetting again, her memories replaced by images of Captain Lightborn.

Lightborn is a criminal, she told herself. *It is folly to feel these things about a criminal.*

But then she would look at herself—the skilled apprentice thief, the Goniph's darling—and a dark voice within her would make her wonder how such a creature could speak so righteously of folly and criminals.

You're no better, it would say. *The Pretender has his alchemist, and no doubt dozens as beautiful and skilled as she. He has not thought on you in a year. Expect no more for a Wall Town girl, and thank whatever stars brought a handsome captain to a wretch like you. Just look at yourself.*

As Terrance spoke to her that night in the gardener's shed, the dark voice spoke as well, and Faye, struggling against its words of diminishment and doubt, of handsome captains and lucky stars, consented at once to the wizard's plan. Perhaps, she told herself, she could do something of worth, so that when the words returned to condemn her, she could remember and assure herself with something she had *done*.

Together, the three of them plotted Faye's escape from Maraven. With the death of Amilcar Squab, the tunnels were once again a refuge for Palernan sympathizers. Dirk knew the passages and people to get Faye out of Maraven within an hour. From there she would have to find Brenn's lines on her own, although Terrance would shroud her in spells so that her journey would be safe from the eyes of the Maravenian Watch.

It seemed like a good plan, daring but not impossible. Heartened, at last with something to do beyond scrubbing and brooding and enduring the scorn of the Witch, Faye rushed back to her quarters to gather the few belongings she intended to take. In the side door she slipped, removing the stone she had set there, taking the steps and the dark corridor back to her little room.

Silently, her fingers moving nimbly, she found the lock and opened it. Breathing a great sigh, she stepped through the door . . .

and was seized by hard, cold hands.

"Where have you been, my little dear?" the Captain asked her, his breath sweet and winesodden at her ear. She struggled to free herself from his grip, which was tightening, painful. But he would not let her go.

Swiftly, casually, he flung her onto the cot, as though she were an old coat. For a moment a strange darkness passed over his eyes, as if thoughts so black he could barely imagine them arose to greet and embrace him. Then he leaned back, braced himself against the door of the chamber, and smiled.

"The Guild, is it not?" he asked. "The Guild and the tunnels. They want you to go to the Pretender, show him the way he could bring troops into the city."

Faye's eyes widened. The Pale Man had it all wrong. "That was not it at all," she said, cursing herself at once for saying anything.

"No matter. It would not work," Lightborn said. "One of the last deeds of that despicable little First Master was to show us the places along Hardwater Cove where the sea laps at the mouths of the tunnels."

He took a step toward her, his blue eyes glinting unnaturally.

"It is only a small task. Our engineers are more than capable."

His long white fingers reached out, stroked Faye's hair.

"It would not take them long to fill the entire system with water."

Faye gasped, scrambled off the cot. She imagined the tides rising in the underground labyrinth, the thieves—always some of them were children—struggling for exits they would not find, coughing and sputtering as the waters covered them.

"Unless?" she asked, her eyes downcast.

"I beg your pardon?"

"What is the 'unless' in this, sir? If you were planning to do it, come hell or . . ." She stopped, shuddering at her own figure of speech. "You would not have told me. You would have done it without warning. Things like that work better without warning, don't they?"

"Ah. Such bitterness!" the Captain exclaimed ironically.

"What do you want of me?" Faye asked, her jaw set.

"The Pretender Brennart," Lightborn said. " 'Tis as simple as that. Go for him, as your friends in the Guild requested. But bring him instead to me."

"I can't," Faye protested. "Brenn is my friend. He's . . . he's . . ."

" 'The rightful king'? Is that what you think, Faye?" Lightborn sat beside her on the cot. He smelled of jasmine and leather and something fierce and menacing that underlay all of those pleasant smells.

Faye shuddered as he caressed her shoulder. Whether from fear or pleasure, she could not tell altogether. She suspected it was both.

"He's no more king than I am . . . Duke of Aquila," the Captain said with a curious laugh. "But what if he were? What if, indeed, your friend and fellow street urchin *is* the King of Palerna? Does that make him worth the lives of . . . oh, a thousand Wall Town paupers? Because we know, you and I, that the waters would cover at least that many in the tunnels. Unless.''

Faye thought rapidly, taking into account all she knew of the tunnels, the cove, the tides. She wasn't sure: what Lightborn was saying just might work. It was not worth the risk of all those lives.

"Very well," she murmured, looking sadly toward the window, where through the bars the tail of Columbar shone mockingly bright against the dark sky.

An ill sign for travelers indeed.

"I knew you would understand, Faye," Lightborn said. He leaned forward and kissed her lightly on the lips. "You have a great compassion that not even a king can ruin. It is what I admire the most in you."

Sitting beside her, clutching her hand with a mocking tenderness, the Pale Man offered a simple plan of deceptions and deep betrayals. And distracted by fear and sorrow, her eyes averted as though avoiding his gaze would be avoiding the whole sorry mess of lies and misdirection set before her, Faye listened, and learned her part.

From the window they watched her leave. Faye was a dark spot on the Maravenian plain, her movement unnaturally swift, propelled and covered by a simple magic to elude the scouts of Dragmond's vaunted army.

But the Witch, her eyesight braced by acumen, followed the cloud as it passed south toward Diamante. In its midst she could see the outline of the girl, though nothing was clear, nothing identifiable.

"And you know this girl, Lightborn?" she asked.

A pale arm snaked about her waist. "A girl of little consequence, Lady. Never mind who she is. A messenger only."

"A powerful message it must be, Captain, in order to draw him here." She inclined her head, her dark hair brushing against the Pale Man's shoulder.

But he was not forthcoming. "Trust me, it is powerful enough," he said, his large hand spreading to cover the span of her waist. "And trust as well that I shall hand you the Pretender soon, and you, in turn, shall give me . . ."

"Enough gold to fill your heart. I remember my promises."

" 'Tis well that you do, Lady," Lightborn said. "For indeed, my heart is bottomless."

The Palernan lines were easy to find, stretching as they did in a wide semicircle about the city walls. Faye stepped among the tents of a company of Helmar's pikemen, hard men who had defected with him after Triangulo. The cloud evaporated, and the astonished soldiers found themselves staring at a brown-haired girl dressed in the leggings and tunic of a woodsman—clothes she had borrowed from Dirk.

"Who're you? And what're you about in our camp?" the sergeant asked.

Faye was relieved to hear the Wall Town in his voice.

"It's here to see King Brennart, I am," she replied. "I have something to tell 'im."

"We all have something to tell 'im," the sergeant said dryly. "But the Death is havin' our say, mostly."

"But I'm sure he'd listen to you afore us!" a foot soldier quipped from the shadows. "I know I would!" Several of his companions leered and laughed appreciatively.

"Then you'd best be concerned what I tell him," Faye snapped, and keeping her back to the fire, turned to address the sergeant.

"I'll be taking your guidance now, sir," she insisted politely. "As to where I can find King Brennart, I mean."

The big man scowled and rose to his full height, towering over her.

"You should know better than to sauce a soldier," he growled. "Don't be so high and mighty, girl! My ears can tell me where you're from."

It could have grown worse from there, no doubt. Angry words can spark danger for a solitary girl in the midst of a rough band of men. But as Faye and the sergeant glared at each other across the campfire, a horse approached, and the face-off dissolved when the rider spoke.

"What seems to be the matter, Sergeant?"

The burly man turned to the rider and blushed. "No matter,

Captain Ricardo, sir. The lady here was askin' directions of us to King Brennart's headquarters, and we was questioning her.''

Questioning, indeed! Faye thought angrily, glaring at the sergeant, then at the Alanyan officer on horseback at the edge of the fire. From what she could tell in the wavering light, he was a handsome fellow, his long dark hair tied in a single braid. He didn't look altogether trustworthy, and were she in Wall Town or Grospoint this time of night, she would do her best to put a street or two between herself and him.

But these were other circumstances, other times. The sergeant had shown himself for a Wall Town hooligan with too much power for his own good, and next to him and his band of knaves, this Captain Ricardo looked like a model of chivalry.

''Well, if your questioning's done,'' Faye said quickly. ''Perhaps the Captain would be so kind as to escort me to King Brennart.''

Ricardo raised an eyebrow.

''At your command, of course,'' he replied, smiling. He guided the horse next to Faye, and lowered a hand to help her into the saddle. He trotted toward a cluster of tents at the center of the camp, Faye clinging desperately to his waist and wishing, as she always did when forced to ride, that she were anywhere except on the back of a horse.

''So she's in the camp, you say?'' Brenn asked the slovenly character standing at the back of the tent. ''Tell me about her.''

Unferth swirled his wine in the cup, gave the Pretender a cautious, sidelong glance.

''Come in overnight from Maraven,'' he claimed. ''That's what they're telling me.''

''What do you think, Unferth?'' Brenn asked. ''You've been at Kestrel Tower a fortnight. You've seen her there. How is she?''

Unferth smiled. The first question was easy.

''Well, she ain't the Witch's thrall, sir. Got a mind of her own. I seen her with the old gardener, with others as well, but never with the Witch. And if she's Ravenna's personal servant, she's got abundant time on her hands.''

"And Lightborn?" Brenn asked. "What about him?"

Unferth paused, his thoughts racing. He had seen the two of them on the steps of Kestrel Tower, had noted the glances that passed between them. He had a dozen guesses, but none of them spoke of distance and unfamiliarity.

He also knew the Pretender suspected nothing.

The spy cleared his throat. When the truth could imperil you and a lie was even worse if discovered later on, there was always one way out.

Pretend to be ignorant yourself.

"Lightborn? Oh, yes, sir. I think he's back in charge of a legion or two, and my wager is that he's still in Ravenna's favor."

"That's not what I meant," Brenn began, but Unferth placed a grubby finger to his grubby lips, slipping quietly to the back of the tent.

"Hist, Majesty! She's comin' as we speak!"

Brenn never received the last part of Unferth's report. When Ricardo's voice hailed from just beyond the tent flap, the spy held his tongue and awaited Brenn's permission to continue. But Brenn saw Faye, and that was the last he wanted of secondhand information.

She came into the tent and Brenn swore later that the light of every lantern surged and shone forth twice as brightly.

He had no words, and so for a moment, she thought he had found her out.

"Brenn", she began, "I'm sorry—"

"I know, Faye. I know she had you enchanted. You would never have willingly served her or any other that sought my ruin. You are my most loyal confidante."

She nearly collapsed, and he rushed to catch her.

"It's put aright now, Faye. Whatever has happened, whatever has been said or done, it will not stand. I've learned so much about people, so much about myself. Just let me hold you and it will all be fine."

It was Faye's turn to lose her words. She clutched at him tightly, as if it were the last time she should ever be this close to him. Brenn mistook her desperation for relief and thought about how pleasant it was to touch her, to wrap his rough and hardened arms about her body.

"Dirk," she whispered.

Brenn held her out from him and looked wondrously into her eyes.

"Dirk? Dirk has spoken with you? What? Is Terrance in Maraven, then? Of course! That's why you could get through the lines! You can go now, Unferth."

Faye gasped and first shook, then nodded her head. Ricardo craned from the tent door where he stood a perfunctory guard duty as Unferth melted through that same door and into the night.

For a moment Brenn almost told her about Terrance's stupidity or oversight or betrayal—whatever it was. Then he stopped himself. It would be needless. Besides, he had forgiven the old man—had told himself time and again that Terrance's mistakes, if mistakes they were, should be a part of the past only. Like all of their mistakes.

Though his heart had not worked out that forgiveness, his mind and his will and his words had set aside long ago the hard thoughts he had for the wizard. So he held himself to a silent promise, and kept that silence as Faye went on and on about her escape.

Finally, she gave him Terrance's message—that he had found something that needed Brenn's attention.

"Something, he said, that *needed your eyes. The key*, he said, *to this whole muddled business*."

Brenn frowned. The words were familiar, faintly. He mined his memory for a talk of eyes . . .

He remembered a firelit winter room. The shadows. The glowing scar on his hand . . .

"The Leaves of Morrigan!" he whispered. "Terrance has found the Leaves!"

Faye frowned. "I suppose so," she said, "seeing as I gave the book to him and all. But what does . . ."

"A book!" Brenn exclaimed. "How simple! I should have known it was a book all along!"

At the doorway Ricardo shrugged, baffled by all this talk of leaves and books. He started to step out into the darkness, but Brenn called him back.

"Stay, Ricardo. We need you in this."

Ignoring the Alanyan, Faye pried her old friend with questions.

"Just what's so important about the Leaves of Morrigan, Brenn? And why does Terrance need *you*? I mean, if it has to do with reading and all, no offense, but surely . . ."

"I don't know, Faye. And again I don't know, and I don't know. All I *do* know is that the Leaves are a thing of great moment . . . that he has been waiting a long time to find them. And so it's simple: I'll be there."

Faye nodded dumbly, her thoughts dwelling on her narrow chambers in the Tower, on the pale eyes that probed and menaced her, and on promises and loyalties of her own. On the tunnels and a rising tide.

She could not think of it very long.

"Then we've no choice," she said, a slight tremble in her voice. "It's on to Maraven. Best go while we've still enough darkness to cover our journey."

Brenn smiled. "It will be like the old adventures, Faye. And now, Ricardo," he said, turning to the Alanyan. "Now for your part in this enterprise."

He smiled again, the old thiefly words coming fluidly to his speech. *Enterpriser*. It was what he had called himself that faraway night when he and Faye had broken into the tower library of an old, distracted wizard.

It had been the start of a great adventure.

‹‹‹ XXI ›››

Twice, maybe three times, Faye almost revealed the betrayal.

The first time was in the tent, when the two men sat at the table and set forth a brash plan to smuggle Brenn into Maraven while concealing his absence from the knowledge of his troops.

It was an old thieves' ruse of disguises and doubles.

"You can wear this hood and stay at a distance, Ricardo," the Pretender explained, removing his own cloak and handing it to the skeptical Alanyan. "Since the setbacks of this spring— the cousins, the plague, and . . . what happened to Sendow— people are wary of approaching me."

Ricardo muttered as he took the garment in his hands.

"What is it, Ricardo?" Brenn asked. "What's wrong?"

Ricardo stared at the hood, his thoughts on Brenn's dangerous venture. Something nagged at the Alanyan, troubling his better judgment. But beyond the recklessness of the whole enterprise, there was nothing he could name.

And who was he to caution against recklessness?

"Nothing. Nothing is wrong, sire," he replied, breathing deeply, dismissing his great unease. After all, he was following the orders of the King, and the King alone should worry if those orders were farfetched or foolhardy.

It was an unaccustomed faith. He would keep telling himself that Brenn was right.

Having settled the matter in his thoughts, Ricardo looked across the table at Brenn, folded his hands, and flashed his broad and disreputable smile. "I was only thinking how you dress me more drably at each stage of this play."

Faye almost disclosed it all then—Lightborn's plan, the threat of the flooded tunnels, her own guilty complicity in the bargain. But Brenn laughed and rose from his seat, already moving away from the moment.

She held back her words. If she told him, what could Brenn do? Raise an army? He had already done that. And no matter his action, by the time it was underway, Lightborn would have called out his engineers and the waters would be flooding the tunnels . . .

and a thousand would die.

So she remained silent, as the Pretender and the captain of his cavalry exchanged outer garments. It surprised everyone in the tent, for each man's cloak fit the other well: Brenn, it seemed, was no longer the slight wisp of a lad that everyone remembered and kept imagining. And Ricardo, never one to settle for the somber greens and browns of the Palernan clothing, had conducted a quiet rebellion of his own: the lining of his cape shone a bright crimson in the lamplight.

"I have found that red lining useful on night journeys," the Alanyan explained with a wink.

"I shall fly Bertilak with me," Brenn said, nodding toward the tercel eagle, shifting eagerly from foot to foot on his low perch. "I'll send you back word by him, no later than this time tomorrow, as to my safety. Along with instructions as to how you should next proceed."

Ricardo nodded, drew himself to attention. It was a general who addressed him.

"If you do *not* hear from me," Brenn continued, "guide your plans and those of the army according to your own judgment."

"But don't sell the army to the Parthians?" Ricardo jested thinly.

"Oh, anything but that," Brenn replied with a smile. "And if you do not hear from me, disclose this plan to Galliard. He may be a thief again, but he's greatly honest and trustworthy."

"Should we be going, Brenn?" Faye asked a little hastily, her face suddenly flushed. "It's not long until sunrise, you know."

They were both light, and the black horse carried them easily.

With Brenn's skillful guidance, they circled an incoming night patrol of Maravenian cavalry and, following from a distance, closed the gap with the last horseman and entered the heavily guarded South Gate not a dozen yards behind the enemy column. At the last moment, in the shadow of the great South Tower, Brenn turned his cape inside out, looking to the casual eye just like a Maravenian cavalryman, returning from the field with a young woman behind him on the saddle.

Leaning over his shoulder, her face nestled against his neck, again Faye almost told Brenn of the treachery. *Go back!* she wanted to say. *There is still time!* But her words faded at the thought of the brimming tunnels.

The guards, lulled and sleepy with the time of morning, were suddenly alert at the sight of the strange young woman. One of them, a corporal by the markings on his armor, stepped forward, intending to stop them, until Faye leaned over Brenn's shoulder, kissing him and trailing her finger along the curve of his ear.

The corporal laughed knowingly and waved them through. It was not unusual practice for the cavalry, especially on night patrol, to bring back more than information. More unusual was the bird that wheeled overhead at such an early hour, gliding north into the city on the last wind of the night.

"Hunting by dark?" the corporal asked himself. "The next thing will be owls on the wing at noon." He shook his head, taking it for an omen. Surely it had something to do with the siege, with the spreading plague, though he was neither scholar nor naturalist enough to figure it.

But the world was changing. The old things had capsized, and in their stead was something he did not understand.

"Chaos come again," he whispered. "I'll ask my diviner next time I'm in Grospoint."

"You surprised me. My face was nearly as red as this cape," Brenn muttered as the horse clattered up the cobblestoned incline of South Light Street, headed toward Ships and, he supposed, across the Causeway from there.

But there was no teasing in response. Instead, Faye was strangely businesslike, strangely cold.

"Stop at the Poisoners' Hall," she whispered. "Red cloak or not, there's no getting you over the Causeway without more of a disguise."

"I don't like the Poisoners' Hall, Faye. The memories, you know. The Goniph and the double cross."

They rode on in silence for a long time. Deeply Brenn inhaled the air of the city, the distant salt-and-fish smell of the coastal water, the peat smoke from the chimneys along Teal Front. He had missed home more than he imagined, his memory restoring his childhood map of the streets—which alleys were dangerous, which blind, the quickest way from this lamplit thoroughfare to the heart of the tunnels.

He did not even notice the silence of the rider behind him.

Light Street narrowed as Brenn urged the horse north. The buildings were taller, closer together, more run-down as he passed from the residential district into the craftsman's quarters of Ships.

"Here," Faye said finally, as the horse passed beneath the masts of a galley, propped on its side in the middle of Light Street before being hauled to the harbor. "There's Starboard Alley up ahead. The Poisoners' Hall—"

"Is on the left," Brenn interrupted. "Surely you don't think I've forgotten."

Again Faye was silent.

Brenn reined in the horse by the tall building, abandoned for years but still marked by the sign of the inverted skull—the ancient symbol of the Poisoners' Guild.

Brenn shuddered at the faded sign. "Well . . . where do we go from here?" he asked.

"You'll stay," Faye said, her voice peculiarly flat and lifeless. "Terrance is on his way. I have to be going. The Great Witch will boil me if she finds me here."

Brenn slipped from the saddle. Faye took the reins and shifted into his place, her gaze never stirring from Light Street and the Causeway beyond it.

"Is it something I did, Faye?" Brenn asked, looking up at her one last time as he made for the alley, for the cellar window she said he would find open.

"I know not what you speak of," she said formally, awkwardly, and spurred the horse into the shadows.

Left alone, Brenn shrugged and made for the sheltering darkness. Too much hinged on this night in the city to bother his senses with speculations as to the moods of young women. Whatever he had done, obscure as it might be, there would be time to undo it later.

The window was smaller than he remembered. Someone had tried unsuccessfully to board it up, but the boards had been kicked away—perhaps by a burglar, or maybe a wretch seeking a shelter. Brenn squeezed between the splintered boards and dropped into the cellar. Instantly the cold memories of that spring night two years ago rushed over him, and his hand moved to the knife at his belt.

The cellar was swallowed in a dense darkness, its only light creeping in from the window. Brenn moved through the blackness, his hands extended. If he remembered correctly, the stairwell was in front of him, the tall shelves somewhere off to his left, but it had been years since he had ventured into this cellar, and he could not be sure.

Finding the center of the floor, Brenn lowered himself to the soft, cool earth and waited. Moving around seemed unduly dangerous. Better to wait for Terrance and the light he would no doubt bring. The cellar was silent except for the dripping of water somewhere, the occasional scuttling of a rat among the shelves.

It was darkness such as this that drove prisoners mad. The place held a great sadness as well, for he remembered the night two years ago, when he and Faye and Marco and the Goniph had entered this cellar, three of them intent on a simple burglary, while the Goniph . . .

Well, as always, the First Master had known more.

And of the four of them, only two had emerged into the moonlight.

The room felt suddenly cold. Brenn realized that his thoughts had taken him far away from the here and the now—a dangerous lapse in a dangerous place.

"Perhaps a little light would not be *so* bad," he confessed. "At least I wouldn't doze off or daydream."

Brenn cupped his hands, breathed into them, and chanted a little spell, more for his own solace than the light it provided:

> *Sol de stella.*
> The sunne that ever shineth bright,
> The sterre that ever yeveth his light,
> *Semper clara.*

A blue light shone in the palm of his left hand. The sword-shaped scar, his heirloom from his father and grandfather, had begun to glow. By the light of his own hand, Brenn surveyed the dark cellar around him, the jumble of shelves and cobwebbed rubble.

"*Sol de stella,*" he breathed again quietly.

"*Semper clara,*" a voice behind him echoed ironically.

Brenn spun about, startled, drawing his knife, but the red-armored thugs were too large and too many. Four of them wrestled him to the hard floor of the cellar, their knees resting painfully on his back and arms. He looked up in astonishment as the Pale Man descended the steps.

"By now," Lightborn said with a smirk, "you should find this a familiar place." Slowly, he drew a long stiletto knife from his belt, and the Watchmen leaned menacingly over Brenn as the light in his hands faded.

"The sword. Where is the sword?" the Captain asked.

His prisoner was silent.

"Very well, then. Silence runs only to the edge of pain. I shall have the sword, regardless of what the Witch intends for you."

Perched at the top of a gibbet, shivering a little against the cool dawn air off the Sea of Shadows, the eagle Bertilak peeked out from beneath his wing as Brenn rode north on the Causeway, surrounded by a dozen Maravenian cavalry.

The Pretender's hands were tied behind him, the gag in his mouth tight to assure that neither spell nor incantation might avail him. A knot above his right eye, purpling and swelling, revealed that he had not been confined without a struggle.

Bertilak launched himself from the scaffolding and, aloft on a gust of salty sea wind, banked and circled above the riders. The smell of rosemary and apple and juniper was borne on the air from the Tower grounds, and the keen senses of the bird placed the familiar odors at once.

The old man. The wizard. Bertilak would find him.

Following the smell, the eagle glided around the eastern side of the tower, carefully skirting a flock of ravens perched on the uppermost balcony. Below him a patch of green, surprisingly lush and arboreal, stood out like an island against the black and rocky coast. Instinctively, the bird descended toward the green, toward sheltering leaves and the sweet smell of lavender and marigolds.

With a loud, insistent hammering of wings, Bertilak shrieked as he alighted atop the gardener's shed. In the darkness beneath him, someone awakened with a curse and a clatter of tools, and in a breath, in no more than three beats of a frantic wing, the wizard emerged hatless in the last glimmer of moonlight, rubbing his eyes and inventing new names for eagles.

Faye, too, watched Brenn's progress up the Causeway from her barred room on the second floor of the Tower. She saw her old friend slump and weave in the saddle, saw rough hands set him aright, slap him to wakefulness.

They passed under the arch of the gate and were lost from sight.

With a scalding Maravenian thieves' curse, Faye leapt from her window and rushed into the hall, pushing aside two linkboys and another maid as she raced for the stairwell. Up three flights she ran, stumbling in the dark and cursing again, until she reached the topmost floor, the little hall that encircled the Great Witch's closet, and, shifting the smooth stone in her hand, slipped almost silently among the black robes and dresses, panting with exertion, her gasping muffled by the thick, dark cloth. There she waited for arrivals, for words, for familiar voices, for news of Brenn.

Squinting, Faye shifted her weight for a better look through the crack in the door.

And saw someone moving toward her, hand extended for the latch.

With a brief, heartfelt prayer to whoever looked out for thieves when their luck ran out and the light shone on them, Faye pulled the coat from its peg and burrowed beneath it, making herself as dark and small as possible on the floor of the closet. Soon, after her own panic had stilled and the coat had settled in a warm scratchy heap over her, she heard the man breathing not a yard away from her.

Whoever he was, he was busy at something. Peering out between the folds of the cloak, Faye saw by the narrow light the long, slim fingers of an aristocrat, something gold glittering in the palm of his hand. . . .

A thief? A Brother of the Guild?

She dared not risk notice, whoever it was.

Instead, she waited. Heard a muffled knock at the chamber door. Heard someone enter the room.

"I have brought him, m'lady," a voice declared—a voice refined and cold and familiar. Moving aside a black winter coat, stepping carefully around the Witch's arranged rows of slippers and boots, Faye peered through a crack in the closet door.

It was Lightborn, certainly. She saw the pale hair, the white cape, the gloves. He moved quickly through her line of sight, then back again, his voice level and soothing as he explained to Ravenna the circumstances surrounding Brenn's capture.

"And the girl?" the Witch asked, a note of malicious eagerness in her voice.

"Just a thief. A pickpocket from Grospoint the lad knew in his larcenous days," Lightborn assured her. "You need not concern yourself, Ravenna. She's back in the tunnels now, somewhere in the dark under Wall Town."

Faye breathed a silent thanks to the Captain. For all his ruthlessness and greed, his lie had protected her from Ravenna's wrath.

But to what purpose? What expense?

Slowly, the conversation in Ravenna's chambers filtered back into Faye's ears. The subject had not changed—not altogether.

"I shall have the name of the girl, Lightborn."

"What does it matter? She is in the tunnels by now."

"And you are sure it is no one . . . closer at hand?"

Lightborn laughed. "You would *love* it to be your maidservant, wouldn't you? Do your sense of poetic justice a good turn, would it not? The maid betrays the Pretender as the prentice betrayed the promising girl . . . how long ago was it, Ravenna?"

Faye shuddered. The Captain was dancing close to the edge, and he knew it. Hours on end at Kestrel Tower were filled with Ravenna's raging against Terrance, over some murky past that the two of them shared in a long-ago apprenticeship on the edge of Corbinwood. The Great Witch thought she was obscure, was secretive, but no woman mustered such anger over . . . *professional* slights.

And there was the matter of Ravenna's amazing youth. . . .

"You will tell me, Lightborn," Ravenna commanded. "Tell me, or I shall visit great punishment upon you."

The room beyond the door fell silent. Faye peered out from

the coat; there was movement in the shadows beside her, and shallow breathing.

"Rosamond," the captain said. "Her name was Rosamond."

"Was?" Ravenna questioned, her voice mocking and contemptuous. "And *Rosamond*? Quite an elegant name for a cutpurse, wouldn't you say?"

"She is gone, though," Lightborn murmured, and Faye strained to catch his words through the door, the thick wool, the fumbling and snuffling of her companion.

Almost mournfully, the Captain told the story.

"Lost in the flooded tunnels, she was. At your prompting, m'lady, I ordered the engineers to work last night, and through the day the tunnels have filled with water, the last dykes and barricades we set under Cove Road holding only until . . . oh, an hour ago."

The flooded tunnels! Faye thought, panic and anger and disbelief all warring in her mind. *But he lied to Ravenna about my name . . . surely . . .*

"Good," Ravenna said. Faye could hear her move, the rustle of her gown as she crossed the room. "Good work. Never mind the girl, then. You've rid me of that nest of thieves."

"And brought you the Pretender," Lightborn reminded her. "I trust you remember what you promised me in turn."

"How could I forget?" the Witch asked, her voice muffled and distant. The mysterious eavesdropper beside Faye moved suddenly, silently, placing his hand against the closet door.

Something is happening! Faye thought. *This is more than spies and eavesdroppings . . . something . . .*

" 'As much gold as would fill your heart'? That was what you wanted, dear?" Ravenna's questioning was seductive, insinuating.

"My very words, madam," Lightborn replied confidently. "But my heart, as I told you, is depthless."

"So you told me," Ravenna said, and suddenly the doors opened and the closet flooded with light.

For a moment Faye thought she had been discovered. In a panic, she rolled toward the darkest corner of the closet, carrying the wool coat with her. The man in the closet—for it was a man, she could see clearly now—sprang into the light and lifted a readied crossbow, its bolt glittering unnaturally. Without hesitation, the man fired the weapon, then stepped confidently into the room.

Ravenna's chamber tumbled to a deep, sepulchral silence. Faye was afraid to look, but she looked nonetheless, peering around the half-opened door to a spot by the balcony, where Ravenna and the bowman stood over a white, huddled form on the floor.

"That should be sufficient gold for your heart, Captain," Ravenna said quietly, exultantly. "I had a jeweler in Grospoint fashion it yesterday."

Numbly, absently, the Pale Man tried to rise.

"I could share everything else with you, Lightborn," Ravenna said, her voice soft over him, almost loving. "Command of my armies, my kingdom . . . for a while my affections. But the Pretender has come, and though you have brought him to me . . . I share him with no man. He is mine and all mine."

The bowman turned. Faye thought she recognized him—a man she had seen once in the ranks of the first legion mustered, a hardened man with a livid scar on his chin. Ravenna stood over Lightborn as his eyes glazed, as his head sank to the cold stone floor, the golden arrow strangely bloodless in his chest.

The man behind her grew impatient.

"M'lady?" he asked finally as, lost in reverie, Ravenna knelt to stroke the cold cheek of her victim.

Absently the Witch turned, her heavy-lidded eyes focusing at last on the hired killer.

"Beggin' your pardon, ma'am, but the matter of my payment . . ."

"Payment," Ravenna said. "Yes. Your payment. We settled on what figure?"

The man stepped toward her, his gaze downcast, his demeanor polite. "Twenty florins, I believe. Twenty florins and the bolt."

Ravenna smiled. "Oh, you will be paid more richly than that."

And she began to scream.

Faye burst through the secret panel and into the dark of the hallway. Nobody saw her in the commotion of rushing guards, of the bowman's futile attempt to escape, of the drawn swords flickering in the torchlight as the man fell to his knees, onto his face, as Ravenna kept screaming, screaming . . .

"Assassin! Help! Assassin!"

XXII

Ario the ragman stood in the streets of Teal Front shortly after sunrise, marveling at the fury above him in the crimson sky.

As usual, he was up before dawn, winding through the broad and airy streets to recover whatever was cast away from the villas and summer houses bordering Lake Teal. To the south, over the broad blue-green expanse of water, Corbinwood rose into light, faint and colorless at this distance, like a low cloud.

Today Ario's pickings had been slim. A wooden bathtub, its bottom splintered. A rusted iron kettle. The prize of the morning, a chair entirely restorable, thrown away solely because of the laziness of its former owner.

Praising the wastefulness of the rich, Ario hoisted the chair into the bed of his wagon. Then the sky exploded with shrieks and feathers.

An eagle, it seemed, had fallen foul of a dozen ravens—big ugly gray-winged birds from the Tower grounds. Ario watched dumbfounded as the raptor wheeled between the Tower birds, its instinct to rise above them thwarted by a fierce dark canopy of wing and razored bill.

Lower and lower the eagle circled, and with each pass of the lake more birds plunged in pursuit, until ravens whirled over the water like flies, and the eagle rose again, outstripping most of them in a desperate lunge back over the city, where the flight and pursuit vanished into the rising smoke of the Grospoint shops.

Ario shrugged, decided that whatever the fate of the big noble bird, it was beyond his ever knowing, lost in the heights above the city, where it would take astronomers to reckon the battle's outcome.

Coughing, pulling at his tattered gloves, the ragman climbed into the wagon. Grunting and muttering, he rolled the iron kettle to the middle of the bed, balancing his load for the trip back to Grospoint. He heard the shrieking again, but faintly, weaving low through the streets like the echoing, deceptive *galho* sounds of the city. Shaking his head, he wiped his gloves on his tunic, turned to gather the reins . . .

and out of the smoke and the shadows burst the eagle, skimming the ground, scarcely a foot from the cobblestones, six ravens in close pursuit.

Ario was not a complicated man, but he had a sense of the potential of things. As the eagle approached, weaving through the buildings and, on one occasion, in and out of two corner windows, his heart soared with the bird, with the achievement and mastery of the thing. He found himself applauding the eagle, cheering for it in the deserted streets as windows opened and bleary-eyed aristocrats who cursed and sputtered and ordered him to be silent.

Quickly, as the birds circled the spire of Teal Academy, the officers' school four streets from the lake, the ragman took stock of the situation. Always, the broken things could blossom into renewed usefulness in his eyes. The plight of the eagle was no different. Suddenly, wildly, as if none of his daily business would ever matter again, Ario began to call out, to whistle, to motion wildly to the darting bird.

And Bertilak heeded him.

Since he had left Terrance, the message to the Palernan command embedded deep in his thoughts by the wizard's most intricate magic, he had been pursued by ravens. They had started to follow him over the Causeway, their pursuit more intent and more intentional the farther south he had flown.

Three of them had swooped onto him as he passed over Grospoint. Bertilak had pivoted in midair, his talons and curved beak extended, and one of his pursuers had seemed to explode, vanishing in a dark spatter of feathers and cries.

It had given him room to escape, as the ravens had followed

him more distantly for a while. But then, their numbers increased to a dozen, they had pursued him back into the city's heart and north over the water, where he had lost half of them in a fog bank over Palern Reef. The other six tailed him back through the residential districts, closing the gap when Lake Teal came back into view.

He had passed through alleys, shuttled through the window of a widow's bedroom, emerged with a tearing cry through the thin parchment that covered her other window, then soared over the roofs of the humbler inland villas, the hot smell of the ravens behind him, their cruel gibbering in his ears.

Y' ain't half the gallant y' fancies y' self, they were saying, their voices a menacing chorus. *Y' ain't even a right eagle, we can tell . . .*

And then, of all absurd prospects in this absurd and relentless chase, here was this ragpicker standing in a wagon, whistling and calling and motioning to him, hauling a ridiculous wooden tub from the bed of the wagon.

The taunting behind him rose in volume, in pitch, and suddenly, to his left, the rest of the ravens fluttered from an alley like monstrous, gray-winged bats. They would intercept him before he reached Lake Teal, would cut off his escape . . .

and his odds had suddenly moved from bad to grievous.

Just as suddenly, his threadbare supporter, who hopped and beckoned from the wagon bed, seemed like a godsend, like a kindly gatekeeper at the borders of freedom. Bertilak understood now and dove toward the wagon, drawing in his wings so that he sailed through the smoky air like a golden bolt. . . .

shooting beneath the wagon and out into clear skies, a clamor of caws and cries behind him. He wheeled for a split second, looked back, saw the ragman standing on the cobblestones, wrestling with something beneath his ramshackle bathtub. Dismayed at their comrades' capture—for the man had three, maybe four of the big birds trapped in his makeshift snare—the other ravens swirled about him, clawing and slashing the air, but afraid to draw near him, for Ario had produced a fireplace poker from the jumble of rags in the wagon bed and wielded it like a sword or mace, standing on a wooden tub, keeping Ravenna's flock distracted and at bay.

* * *

The raid began south of Diamante, when the eagle, intact and unbloodied, but wearied by a long swift flight, perched on the Pretender's tent post and shrieked. A caped man, hood lowered to cover his face, stepped from the tent into the sunlight and, seeing the bird, extended his arm like a falconer. Bertilak hopped on the man's wrist, and the two of them disappeared into the tent.

"Now the message," Ricardo said eagerly, brushing back his hood. Seated on Brenn's cot, Galliard rose to his feet, awaiting eagerly the news from Maraven.

"There's . . . there's nothing tied to him," Ricardo said despairingly, examining the eagle's legs, wings, and beak for the sign of a note or letter, trying to turn Bertilak upside down in a frantic search for a small scroll.

"If it's Terrance who sent the message," Galliard offered, "I expect it's more . . . *obscure* than a note. Look, the poor thing is winded, and there's blood on its talons."

"Ravens?" Ricardo asked, squinting at Bertilak as though the eagle might speak, might tell him what transpired.

"I would guess ravens," Galliard agreed. "Which means that there's magic in or on the bird we have here. There's not a raven alive who would take on an eagle, lest something provoke or prompt it."

Ricardo nodded. Ravenna's scavengers were notorious for pursuing transformed, enchanted, or otherwise magicked creatures. Wherever the magic lay in the city of Maraven, whether the incantation of sorcerers or the healing charms of a hedge wizard, if it persisted long enough, the Great Witch would find it. And if it was strong enough, or unusual enough, she would send her birds to find it out, to bring back word of what they had seen.

"So old Terrance has tricked the message into you, eh?" Ricardo murmured affectionately to the eagle. The Alanyan remembered that this was a man transformed, who had chosen to return to his birdlike state after terrible, bone-bruising tribulations in the forest, where he fell from trees and found no satisfaction in venison or pork. Since his change, Bertilak had shown no real signs of humanity: on occasion he seemed to have more wits about him than the average bird, but his movements and thoughts were alien and opaque.

As was whatever he tried to say, hopping along Ricardo's arm and squawking harshly as the two commanders listened and frowned at one another, and listened yet more.

"I'm damned if I can understand a syllable of it," Ricardo muttered. "If Terrance intended to keep the news from prying eyes and ears, he's done a good job of it."

"Don't give up so readily, Ricardo," Galliard said, producing a huge magnifying glass, through which he regarded the bird curiously. At a puzzled stare from Ricardo, the Forest Lord blushed and hid the lens.

"Lapis," he murmured. "She . . . she *loaned* it to me."

Ricardo shrugged, turning once again to the eagle. "Whatever the message, it's doomed to the language of birds, I'm afraid."

Galliard smiled slowly. "Which is why he knew only we could decipher it."

The eagle whistled and shifted from foot to foot.

"How?" asked Ricardo. "I don't follow."

Galliard burst from the tent, on his way to a shady perch at the edge of the campsite. "Who do you think could interpret that language?" he called back triumphantly, as he leaned forward and gently awakened the reciting owl.

For once, it was a hard task to coax the owl into reciting.

The birds sat side by side on the perch, regarding each other skeptically. Again, Bertilak whistled and screamed, and the owl danced away from him, pivoting its head and flapping its wings.

"Now, now," Ricardo soothed, tickling the distraught bird's feathers. "What did he say? Come now."

The owl stared dimly at the branches above it. Bertilak shrieked again, and the poor creature leapt from its perch, pulled back harmlessly by the long leather jesses Ricardo had tied to its feet the night before.

"Come now," Ricardo coaxed, offering the owl a scrap of bread.

Galliard stood in the sun, a few steps from the birds and the negotiations. He drew an apple from his pocket and reached for the knife at his belt, only to discover it missing.

"Thomas!" he muttered angrily and tossed the apple toward the perch, sure that the knife rested comfortably in his cousin's possession. The owl's enormous yellow eyes widened even further as the fruit rolled past, and Ricardo knelt, picked up the apple, and dangled it before the bird.

"At last," the Alanyan said. "Some goods to bargain with."

Sure enough, with the apple in clear view, offered and withheld, the owl remembered a song neither Galliard nor Ricardo had heard it sing before. Hopping on the perch, tilting its head to listen to the eagle's whistle and cry, it began to recite:

> "Nay, be my trouth," seyd Robyn Hode,
> "So shalle hit neuer be;
> I make thee maister," seid Robyn Hode,
> Off alle my men and me."

> "Nay, be my trouth," seyd Litull John,
> So shalle hit neuer be;
> But lat me be a felow," seid Littul John,
> No noder kepe I be."

> Thus John gate Robyn Hod out of prison,
> Sertan withoutyn layn;
> Whan his men saw hym hol and sounde,
> Ffor sothe they were ful fayne.

The commanders stood in grim silence. The song was clear enough: Brenn had been taken prisoner, like this Robyn Hode, and his right hand man, this Litull John, was fully expected to rescue him.

" 'Tis a reckless undertaking, Ricardo," Galliard cautioned, though the time for cautioning was past. "You know full well that they'll hardly keep a rare bird like Brennart in a prison as frail as the Old Maraven Keep: it's Kestrel Tower for him, and a thousand guards between us."

"That doesn't concern me nearly as much as . . . the other thing, Duke Galliard," Ricardo replied, his hood concealing the glint of a smile. "For you see, I shall leave this camp in the command of a thief."

* * *

The cavalry embarked at noon. Ricardo took only a hundred troopers—crack Zephyrians who hungered for the chance to ride through Maravenian streets.

One hundred was a formidable number, the Alanyan decided: enough to fight their way through most patrols, as long as surprise was their ally. Still few enough to be mobile and elusive.

His good-byes to the camp were few: As far as the men could tell, the Pretender Brennart was riding out with a band of cavalry to survey the Maravenian walls. They hardly noticed him, except for the cousins, who knew who was the hooded man at the head of the column.

Ricardo took along the sword, the double-edged Libra. It seemed only right that the weapon, once a prisoner itself in Dragmond's chambers, would return to free yet another held captive to an evil warden.

"*Libra potestatis sum,*" he whispered, turning the blade in his hand. For a moment, the glittering sword seemed to reflect a dark, hovering shape in the tent behind him, but when the Alanyan turned, nothing was there.

An apparition, he thought. An eidolon.

Or his own restlessness and misgiving.

For Galliard was right. It was a risky undertaking. The walls of Maraven bristled with red-armored soldiers, and even if the cavalry made it into the city, it would be a pitched battle, street by street, before they reached the Causeway and Kestrel Tower beyond.

But he had always been one for risks. Had not General Helmar thought him a reckless madman?

Galliard, Thomas, Jimset, and Lapis stepped from their tents to bid him farewell. It was sad to imagine the absences, to think of stern Sendow, dead of the plague in Maraven, and of Ponder before him, missing on the battlefield at Triangulo. The four survivors, too, were in straitened circumstances—confined to their campground, forbidden to mingle amid the other Palernan soldiers.

Ricardo vaulted into the saddle. The Zephyrian troops wheeled and milled on their ponies at the northern edge of the camp, awaiting his presence, his instruction.

There have been great losses for you, Brennart of Maraven, the Alanyan thought grimly, as Galliard hoisted the sword to him, Thomas his shield, and Lapis the spyglass she had given him when the war began. *Great losses, my friend, and these your cousins can tell you most closely.*

Great losses, and yet I would do my part all again. If only for the freedom and the feel of the horse and the speed of the ride.

Ricardo rode from the camp, his hood raised over his face. The soldiers by the campfires saluted him as Brennart. The black stallion Churros surged beneath him, and above him the eagle Bertilak banked and soared.

The cousins watched him leave, and Lapis lingered awhile outside the tent as the distant rider joined his company, as the column circled and wheeled to the north, to Diamante and Maraven beyond.

Thus John gate Robyn Hod out of prison, the Alanyan sang to himself. *Sertan withoutyn layn . . .*

He had led the column on a wide and dangerous arc eastward, looping through Irret, until they reached undamaged land and the smell of the sea came to him from a distance. From there, it was only a mile to Cove Road, where they stopped and rested the horses and prepared for the perilous ride into the city's heart.

Ricardo had decided to ride through the East Gate, as he always had before. It was the least fortified gate, being the farthest from the Palernan troops, and the sun would be low behind the walls by then, so the archers would be clear in outline on the black battlements.

Once inside the gate, they could turn south into Wall Town or brave the more dangerous and direct route along Cove Road, where the barracks lay, and the secondary defenses of Grospoint, and the strongest civilian support for Dragmond and Ravenna.

But for now, he would breathe a space, would walk in the fragrant Palernan countryside he had learned to love as a traveling alchemist, when he had followed this road on a score of journeys, his destination the shops at the mouth of the Causeway, his motive the florin and mark alone. He thought to rest under this old black maple tree as Churros grazed tranquilly and the sun dipped beyond the distant black walls.

With a sigh, Ricardo drew forth the sword Libra, examining it again in the afternoon sunlight. He would see to it that the blade was returned to Brenn, to the true Balance of Power who was its rightful owner.

And he *would* rescue Brenn. He would pass through a rain of arrows and a hive of daggers, would pass through death itself if necessary, but at the end of that passage the lad would go free. It was that simple.

Ricardo laughed softly. In his alchemical days, he knew little of loyalty. So Delia had told him, then and in their last meeting months ago on this very road, when the vacancy in her eyes said he had vanished from the inside of her thoughts. And yet he had changed, like a base mineral in an alchemist's conversions, refined by heat and time and magic toward gold, toward silver, toward the noble metal that was always the goal of cleansing science.

A shadow passed over him, and for a moment the blade of the sword darkened again. This time it was only Angeda, coming to rouse him from his rest and reflection.

"The sun, Captain. It's best we were going if we're to reach East Gate by nightfall."

The Zephyrian's eyes were haunted, eager. Hated Maraven was an hour's ride from his sword. All around him, the cavalry plucked branches and leaves from the maples and chestnuts, tying them to their hair, their beards, to the manes and bridles of their horses, in an old Zephyrian rite as ancient as those trees themselves, born when the forests were impassable and the plains went on to the edge of the world.

The *kerim*. The celestial war against evil. Where the Zephyrians believed that their people would fall like leaves autumnal, where all of nature would join in the battle and the people would stand a last time against unraveling evil, would fulfill the land's renewal with their deaths.

"Yes," Ricardo replied quietly. "Yes, Lieutenant. And perhaps in rescuing the King, we can give him the city as well as his freedom."

⋘ **XXIII** ⋙

The guardsmen scattered as the Black Horse Cavalry, bristling with leaves, approached the East Gate. Ahead of them rode a hooded man on an enormous black stallion.

The Maravenians were Wall Town and Grospoint boys, pressed into service by the King's decree and the strong arm of the Watch. Unwilling conscripts at best, theirs was the least likely outpost to receive the brunt of an attack. Instead, the young men lazed against the battlements, drank wine and ate sausages and cheese, and exchanged lies and legends, especially during the long and quiet night watches.

Every single lad at the Eastern Gate remembered the old stories about the King's arrival—that *he would come to the city up Cove Road, carrying the forest with him*. At the sight of the hooded man and his arboreal company on the eastern horizon, they quietly slipped from the walls and returned to their homes, or cast their hats in the air and their lots with the approaching cavalry.

It took that cavalry by surprise, and its commander especially. Ricardo had expected a struggle for the gates, had appointed a score of his best men to scale the walls, fight off the guards, and open the huge oaken doors to admit the rest of his troops. Instead, it was smooth passage, the doors flung wide and thirty or so red-cloaked infantry joining him, cheering him on.

Ricardo guided his horse onto the black sands of the beach, and a dozen veteran riders followed.

"Take the rest, Angeda!" he called out. "Spread confusion to the south and draw the Watch away!"

The Zephyrian raised his cutlass in response, and with the shrill, quivering whistle that was the ancient call of the kerim, galloped down the Street of the Bookbinders, south toward Wall Town.

"Now," Ricardo said, turning toward a gap-toothed, freckled young man who had been part of the East Wall garrison. "Young man, I would like you to set this tower afire." He gestured toward Terrance's old tower, the topless monstrosity near the wall's end, its uncompleted ladders and stairwells rising into thin air, into nothingness.

The young man regarded the structure stupidly. " 'Sbeen here a long time," he said. "Use to be a crazy man lived here."

"Natheless," Ricardo urged. "You have torches, and the stairway itself is kindling enough. I need confusion to the side of me and behind me, and you're just the man to provide it, by the looks of you."

The boy turned his slow-witted gaze to the man on horseback.

"Whatever you say, King Brennart," he declared, and jostled a large man beside him.

"Get me 'at torch, Shagga," he said, a sudden authority in his voice, a wide grin spreading across his face. "We're about the King's business, you an' me."

Up Hardwater Cove Ricardo and his dozen comrades raced, fires to the east and the south of them. Over the black sands galloped the black horses, shrouded by the rising night, the Zephyrians crouched low in the saddle, their bows and swords at the ready.

The stockyards were glowing with lamps, loud with alarms. As he passed to the seaward side of the huge renovated barracks, Ricardo watched the confused Maravenians muster and assemble, crying out to each other, their weapons jostling and rattling. Then the town before them was a still, unnatural dark—scarcely a lamp in a window against the dusk.

Where the beach ended in the hard cobblestone streets of Grospoint, Ricardo slowed his horse to a trot, and slowly, almost leisurely, the thirteen men stalked through the harbor streets until between a shoemaker's shop and the guild hall of the augurers, the last red sun on the horizon caught the outline of the Causeway gibbets.

They emerged from the alley, startling the half-dozen Watchmen who guarded the southern end of the Causeway. Three of the men turned and ran, while the other three surrendered, dropping their weapons dully on the packed earth.

Ricardo did not stop for questions. Ignoring the trembling foot soldiers, he led his squadron on a gallop over the Causeway, leaving the cobblestones, the district of Ships, the city itself behind them, as the dark walls of Kestrel Tower loomed ahead like the architecture of a mad Philokalian, inhabiting the dark edges of a nightmare.

In her own nightmare, the Great Witch stood on the battlements and watched the rim of the city burn.

Far to the east, flames licked at Terrance's old tower. Long the target of her surveillance, her augury, her failed spellcraft, it was conquered at last by a casual torch. And far to the south, where the streets issued onto Lake Teal, the dark blue waters glittered red and orange with still more fires, as the traitor cavalry ransacked the wealthy villas.

And yet, Ravenna was exultant.

The Pretender was hers, locked in Dragmond's old bedchamber below, his only possible escape a drop of seventy feet or more from a stone balcony overlooking the garden.

Nonetheless, her smiths had constructed an iron cage over that balcony. There were rumors, no matter how farfetched, that in his struggle with the dragon Amalek in the depths of the Aralu, her prisoner had assumed the form of an eagle. If these stories were true, and not Alanyan double-talk or the last mad words of the dragon, the cage would prevent a transfigured Pretender from taking wing again.

Ravenna smiled almost winsomely. She had foreseen all possibilities, all perils. Her army held the city fast against the rebel attack, despite the burnings in the farthest districts. She had removed the vexing Lightborn, who lay in state in the throne room, attended by his mourning officers, and she was again in sole control of Maraven and the Watch.

All she needed was the crowned head to fill with insinuation and sorcery. Standing at her balcony, looking out over the Causeway, she began the long process, that would, over the course of weeks, bend Brennart's mind to her will.

The first incantations had been used before, in other service, but since the cwalu had failed, Ravenna had turned the spell to newfangled use, as Archimago had told her she could in the waning days of her apprenticeship. For not only did the words give life to the dead, but they were a road by which a spirit might enter a susceptible body, might crowd the original life-force out and set up its own sinister occupation.

She was not sure how long it would take. Some of the ancient texts said a year, some only a season. But she had the time.

Let the soldiers die and the citizens starve. Let them all burn and fester.

If she could not govern the king, she would *be* the king.

Quickly, almost muttering, she began the incantation.

> At the round earth's imagin'd corners, blow
> Your trumpets, and arise, arise
> From death, your numberlesse infinities
> Of soules, and to your scattred bodies goe . . .

Her voice grew louder as her confidence waxed. Brenn shivered on his balcony as the words cascaded from the Witch's chamber. He had been weeping, thinking of Sendow, of that needless and terrible death, and when the incantation reached him he felt a dizziness, an alien breath in his ear, and the thoughts of his cousin's great wrong gave way to still more evil, and he braced himself against the railing until it had passed, had tumbled by him . . .

down to the vaulted throneroom of Palerna, where the body of the Pale Captain lay in state, guarded by a company of the Watch, by Lieutenants Amiens and Danjel. Amiens heard the Witch chanting faintly, like the humming of hornets in a distant dark grove. The noise unsettled him, but he pushed it aside, more relieved than mournful at the death of Lightborn.

Danjel, on the other hand, had lost his guidance. His eyes swollen, brimming with tears again, he stood above the still body. The incantation reached him but faintly, though somewhere below thought, in the depths of his grieving heart, he heard and understood the words.

On the bottom floor of the Tower, in her barred and sequestered room, Faye stood at a window as well, tearful as Danjel.

She had heard that the tunnels below Maraven were filling with water, that already sewers had overflowed in Grospoint and cellars were filling in Wall Town, that few of the thieves had escaped the deluge alive.

She should never have trusted Lightborn. He had bargained with lives for Brenn, and he had not kept his word. Now Brenn was imprisoned above her, Lightborn was dead, and Ravenna virtually ruled the city, as she had before the war and the disruptions at court.

No matter that you did not see Dragmond. Not anymore. Not for weeks. The rumors said simply that he was *in seclusion*, commanding from hiding, from somewhere deep in the castle recesses.

Perhaps in that central room, the one always lighted and locked . . .

But what did it matter? Wherever he sat or hid or governed, the war was hers now, the kingdom restored to her thrall.

Faye speculated long and bitterly, condemning herself for frailty and trust. She scarcely heard Ravenna's voice, and when she did it was remote, stripped of words, creaking like a door in a distant corner of the bailey, swung randomly by a directionless wind.

In the midst of her dark meditation, the girl heard hoofbeats on the hard earth of the Causeway. Leaning through the bars of the window, looking south, she saw the cavalry approach at a gallop, the hooded man at the head of the column surge past the last two sentries, drawing his sword . . .

Jankin, the lad from Wall Town assigned to burn the wizard's tower, had run into great difficulty in the process.

He had started on the bottom floor, where the empty library shelves and the desolate solar ignited like kindling with a single sweep of the torch. Rapt by the fire, fascinated by the curious alcoves and facets of the building, Jankin bounded up the stairwell as the flames converged on the lowest steps.

Whooping, brushing the glowing ash from his tunic, the boy peered into the abandoned bedrooms. Everything was ransacked, capsized, and emptied onto the floor—trunks and boxes and broken crockery, where once a wizard had no doubt kept a thousand concoctions and herbs.

Snickering in merriment, watching the flames surge up the stairs after him, Jankin leapt onto a ladder and climbed to the attic, where a low ceiling and an ill-placed litter of boxes caused him to bump his head, to cry out.

And then, as though the blow had finally knocked some sense into him, the lad realized that he could not return the way he had come. The flames were high on the second floor now, the boards beneath his feet were hot, beginning to smoke and catch fire themselves.

With a desperate whimper, he ascended another ladder, finding himself on the roof, beneath a clear spring sky and a canopy of stars. The smoke billowed after him through the trapdoor entrance, and soon the roof of the tower was clouded, lost in acrid fumes.

From below his comrades, Shagga and the others, called to him. Jankin coughed and reeled, then coughed again. At last it dawned on him that the fire in the wizard's tower might consume him as well. Peering over the edge of the roof he looked down a sheer drop to streets of hard cobblestone, of glassy flint.

The fall itself would kill him. There was no way down.

Apprehensively, his fear rising toward panic, he looked about him for another escape. The incomplete stairwell offered itself to him—a column of stairs that spiraled up from the roof and seemed to stop nowhere, as though the builder had started the project and tired of it in process.

But now the stairs looked anything but failed and forbidden. They led to a height, and that was enough: a place above the rising smoke and heat. Jankin took the steps in long, athletic strides. Halfway up the flight he stopped, weaved, and looked up.

Instead of a stairway that rose ten feet and stopped altogether, Jankin saw that the path before him had extended itself, spiraling around behind him toward a narrow landing on which a large door rested. Smoking and steaming, a little heat-blackened and charred at the edges, it sat on a film of glittering air, as though it were afloat on a layer of ice.

The door seemed to lead to nowhere. Behind it lay an expanse of cloudless sky, as though while the boy had nodded the same ghostly builders who had erected the stairwell had come back and finished it, with no concern for its use or destination.

And now, it was the only portal left to him.

Ricardo would have taken gladly any portal, any door. The cavalry had crossed the Causeway, entered the Tower bailey before the astonished guardsmen could close the gates, and dismounted at the edge of the Tower gardens. The laughter and whistling and whooping had faded at once when they cast about for a gate, a passageway indoors, and failed to find it.

The garden beyond them rippled with shadows, with the outcries and fitful torchlight glinting on red armor. The Tower Guard, the best of the Watch by far, had been alerted, were combing the castle grounds for the trespassers.

"What now, sir?" asked Hega. He was one of the younger cavalrymen, a tough fellow from West Aldor who revered the Baron Namid and handled a sword with the skill of a fencer twice his years. "Shall we climb to a window?"

Ricardo looked up. A single balcony jutted over the garden, its high railing a crenellated battlement of flint. If they could reach that wall, that overhang . . .

But it was thirty feet up the sheer side of the Tower. No grave task for the men with him, but a slow one. He stood at the fringe of sapling fruit trees next to the Tower wall—frail apple and pear, planted that very spring, no doubt, encircling a little fountain, in the midst of which an obsidian elf danced and poured water over its shoulder back into the bowl of the device. Cooled by the spray from the ingenious font, Ricardo examined the flint for foothold, for purchase.

"No," he breathed in disappointment. "Like black glass, this Tower wall."

Then the first arrow flashed over his head, striking the flint with a crack and clatter. Across the garden the Watchmen were approaching—threescore of them, he guessed, all armed with sword and bow. The Maravenians knelt, drew their bows, and riddled the air with arrows.

One of the horsemen fell, clutching his leg, and the others, trapped against the flint walls, raised their little cavalry shields awkwardly against the deluge of whistling iron.

Then, suddenly, as though the ground itself had allied with the raiders, a great mist rose from the garden. Ricardo, standing at the edge of the white tendrils, heard a voice from the midst of it, maintaining an intricate chant.

> Hie therefore, overcast the night;
> The starry welkin cover we anon
> With drooping fog as black as Acheron
> And lead these testy rivals so astray
> As one come not within another's way.

Shouting and cursing arose from the garden, as the Watchmen lost their footing, bumped into one another, launched their arrows harmlessly into the air, the ground.

Ricardo laughed at the sound of clattering armor, the bumps and curses behind him. "Terrance!" he said to himself. "I'd recognize that voice in my sleep!"

The incantation repeated and swelled in the depths of the garden, as the covering fog thickened further.

Then Brenn leaned over the balcony. "Ricardo!" he whispered.

The Alanyan looked up. "Brenn! I had fears that . . ."

He could not find the words.

"No fear, Ricardo," Brenn soothed, his smile tranquil and assuring. "There is no room for fear. Gather the men at the wall."

"What?"

"At the wall," Brenn repeated, his voice level and low. He extended his hands through the bars, and Ricardo could see the blue scar glowing on the Pretender's left palm.

The Alanyan let out a low whistle. It was proving to be a night of spectacle.

"Clutch to the saplings at the foot of the wall," Brenn urged.

The Zephyrians looked foolishly at one another.

"You heard him, damn it!" Ricardo hissed. "Do as he says."

As the Zephyrians laid tentative hands on the saplings, Brenn began a chant of his own, echoing out over the garden where the words entwined with those of Terrance's, until it seemed like something choral, a duet between the two enchanters.

"Here at the Fountains sliding foot," began the Pretender,

> Or at some Fruit-trees mossy root,
> Casting the Bodies Vest aside,
> My Soul into the boughs does glide:
> There like a Bird it sits, and sings,
> Then whets, and combs its silver Wings;
> And, till prepar'd for longer flight,
> Waves in its Plumes the various Light.

Suddenly, the little fruit trees began to burgeon and grow, surging from the ground as the work of years took place in a matter of seconds. Astonished, Ricardo clutched the bole of a young pear tree as it spread and stretched, bearing him aloft in its branches.

It was a short climb and step to the balcony. Ricardo leaned into the railing, pushed and pulled against the metal bars.

They would not give. Cursing, the Alanyan pulled again.

"Use the sword," Brenn insisted.

Ricardo frowned and drew the weapon. "But Brenn. The cage is iron. This blade could work at it for years . . ."

"You brought it here for some reason," Brenn insisted.

"But I don't know why."

"Use it, then." Brenn's command was assured, insistent.

Solemnly the Alanyan hooked his feet around the thick trunk of the apple tree and, leaning back dizzily over a seventy-foot drop, whirled the blade once, twice, a third time over his head, then brought it crashing against the iron bars with a clanging that the Maravenian soldiers heard at the slaughterhouses, that they thought was an alarum bell ringing in Kestrel Tower. With a shrieking, rending sound, the iron bars ruptured at the impact.

Brenn scrambled through the huge, ragged hole and vaulted into the branches above Ricardo. Silent and wonderstruck, the men climbed down to the garden, where a dozen more Zephyrians stood gaping, enthralled by the lofty feats of their commanders.

Ricardo gained his footing, and turned to Brenn. They were

a brief ride from freedom, from the sands west of the Causeway and from Barco's Ferry, where the wizened old boatman had no doubt been waiting an hour, if the courier from the Palernan camp had reached him according to plan.

From there it was the Gray Strand, and the shelter of Corbin-wood.

He almost laughed to think of it . . . the sheer exultant daring of it all.

Helmar would think they all were thoroughly mad.

At that moment, as the Alanyan boosted Brenn into the saddle, the quiet garden erupted with the roar of a hundred charging troops. Out of the fog rushed a company of Maravenian soldiers, Captain Amiens in the vanguard. One look told Ricardo that these were no shivering boys at a defenseless gate.

These were the Watch—the high guard of Kestrel Tower.

Quickly the red-armored warriors circled the dozen intruders, and then the circle narrowed.

Brenn steadied himself atop Churros and held forth the sword Libra. The Zephyrians, already mounted, drew their sabers as one. No Maravenian onslaught would buy cheap victory from the rebel cavalrymen.

Brenn's orders were calm, almost conversational. "Follow me, gentlemen. Neither relent nor figure the odds." Then he spurred the horse toward the thinnest point in the Maravenian circle, toward a squadron of pikemen who knelt and prepared to receive him.

It was headlong, sudden, even more mad than the rescue. Churros hurdled the first row of pikemen before they had lifted their weapons, Brenn dispatching a swordsman gracefully with a single stroke, then wheeled in the saddle to face two charging officers. Hega pulled Ricardo up into the saddle behind him, and the two of them plunged after Brenn, ducking a spear and kicking a burly sergeant away as they weaved through the scattering pikemen.

It may well be over, Ricardo thought, as he bobbed behind the saddle, *and if that is so, I'll be damned if I'll be outdone this last time by a man twenty years my junior, whether he be King or not!*

With a clattering of hooves, the cavalry galloped through the tower bailey, making for the Causeway under Brenn's leadership. Now from the castle walls, Maravenian archers rained arrows on the hapless squadron, and Hega clutched at his throat when a dark bolt struck him, driving him from the saddle with its impact. The horse slipped, recovered, and galloped into the fog, leaving Ricardo behind, clutching his ankle.

Seeing his friend in danger, Brenn wheeled Churros and galloped back to retrieve the Alanyan. With the big black stallion at full stride, leaning low over its flanks and extending his hand, he grasped Ricardo's wrist and pulled his companion up. Turning the horse about in a volley of arrows, he sped to catch the others, who were already passing through the Tower Gates onto the Causeway.

"Some riding, that was," Ricardo shouted in his ear above the outcry of the soldiers, the clatter of arrows. "Surely there's a traveling circus that—"

His words were cut short with a sudden gasp. Brenn turned, then clutched at the Alanyan's cape as Ricardo fell from the saddle. Ricardo's weight pulled Brenn after him, and the two of them struck the hard earth of the bailey as Churros galloped out through the gate, following the other horses.

Brenn scrambled to his knees. For some reason the downpour of arrows had stopped, and the red-armored men above on the battlements gaped at the scene below—a hooded man lying mortally wounded, an arrow deep in his side, his smaller, slighter comrade crouched above him.

"By the Four Winds!" one of them cried out. "I've killed the Pretender!"

<<< **XXIV** >>>

"It's not that bad, Ricardo," Brenn urged, trying to help the Alanyan to his feet. "Get up. I'll help you into the fog."

He looked around. From all sides the Watchmen were descending from the battlements, swords drawn. Slowly the Tower Gate was closing ahead, and there were lights now in every window of Kestrel Tower.

"Leave me, Brenn," Ricardo said weakly. "I know it sounds foolish and heroic, the kind of thing that the hero's friend says in the story . . . But look at the odds, boy! You've a kingdom to carry away from here! Let me pay my taxes."

"I'll not!" Brenn exclaimed, recalling Ponder and the distant battlefield of Triangulo. "*You* won't send *me* . . ."

"Nonsense," Ricardo said, his eyes fluttering, his breathing shallow. "Make a run for the garden. I heard Terrance there, and he'll spirit you away. Come back for me. Turnabout, you know. Honor among thieves."

"But Ricardo—" Brenn started to attempt the King's Touch.

The Alanyan pushed him away, drawing Libra menacingly from its sheath. "Get away, Brenn!" he urged, handing the sword to the desolate lad above him. "And waste no sorrow for me. I'll be back. With your help, I'll be back."

"I believe you will," Brenn declared, and his hand trembled as he placed it on Ricardo's forehead.

Then he took the sword, as Ricardo had asked him. The Maravenians had reached the bailey grounds, were closing on him rapidly, Lieutenant Danjel in the vanguard, brandishing a long knife.

There was no time, no helping Ricardo. Brenn turned and raced toward the garden, toward the sheltering fog, and he did not look back.

In Corbinwood, asleep in a hammock, his shovel leaned carefully against a black maple tree at his feet, Jimset was jostled awake by a long, sorrowful howl.

It was Bracken, Terrance's old dog, left in his custody while the wizard and his cousins wandered the edges of the world. Generally, the portly creature, some seventy years old and showing no sign of decrepitude or age, spent his days merrily chasing squirrels and rooting for mushrooms in the dark soil of the clearing.

But now the dog sat on an ancient oak stump, his fat haunches curled beneath him, looked to the north, and bayed solemnly, as a great cloud passed over the clearing, obscuring the moon and stars.

Jimset scratched his head and rolled out of the hammock. He ambled toward the dog and rubbed its ears.

But Bracken was inconsolable. Wrestling away from the perplexed young man, he continued to howl and bay, always facing north, toward the rising mist and the black walls of Maraven.

"What's happened?" Jimset whispered, burying his face in the dog's warm fur. "We've lost one of 'em."

And the dog continued its baying, a sound so plaintive, carrying so clearly through the moonlit night that miles away, in the deserted streets of Maraven, the wild raposa dogs stopped their foraging and listened.

Listening, too, was the big man in the branches of the oak tree, miles to the south where the woods were thickest and most wild.

He knew the sound for what it was—a cry of hapless mourning—and he knew that it was Bracken instantly. Resolutely, despite his pain, he climbed from the branches, and crouching by a dead maple, broke off a leg-sized branch to carry with him as a walking stick, a shillelagh.

In a swim of lights, Ponder of Aquila trudged north through the tangled paths of Corbinwood, with the faeries calling to him as he left the bright clearing behind.

> Who doth ambition shun,
> And loves to live i'the sun,
> Seeking the food he eats,
> And pleased with what he gets,
> Come hither, come hither, come hither;
> Here shall he see
> No enemy
> But winter and rough weather.

"The time has past for that!" Ponder muttered, waving them away with his enormous branch. "The enemy has struck a blow against mine own, and I must go north!"

He crashed through the branches into the dark of the woods,

and the faeries that followed him circled a while, glittering and unheeded, before they returned to the clearing.

Brenn was not fifty feet into the garden, wading among vines and tubers and the thickening fog, when a strong hand clutched at his elbow.

The Pretender turned, Libra raised, but breaking through the mist was a familiar face, a familiar voice.

"Keep silent, prentice, and come with me."

"Terrance!" Brenn said, "Ricardo . . ."

"I know. I know, lad. Keep silent."

The shed lay oddly in the center of the garden. Brenn had seen it by daylight from his window, and it seemed a foolish place to hide, here beneath the nose of the enemy. But Terrance led him inside nonetheless, and closed the door behind him.

Brenn fell onto the narrow cot. He knew his friend Ricardo was dead: he had seen that look on two battlefields and on the plague carts, in the eyes of soldiers he had not been able to save.

For a moment the hot tears rimmed his eyes. He could not believe the price of kingship. Let Terrance or Galliard or Helmar run this miserable war, and let them sit the throne afterward, for all he cared. He would just go away—back to Corbinwood, perhaps, or to far-flung Hadrach. Venice and Genoa and glittering Constantinople were not impossible destinations . . .

But he could not set it aside, any more than Terrance could take command of the army or Helmar the crown of Palerna. He was the king when the war struck far from him, and he was king when it struck far too near. It was as indelible as the glowing scar on his left hand.

With an enormous breath, his eyes red and hurting, Brenn sat up and looked around him.

"It's . . . *larger* than it seemed from the outside, Terrance," Brenn whispered, his voice husky, as the wizard lit the lamp.

And indeed it was. The shed was every bit as large as the Goniph's chambers, as the room where they had held him in Kestrel Tower. Four tables and a lectern, all littered with books and parchment and scrolls, sat side by side in the spacious room, a lamp on each of them, glowing with a muted green light.

"It's like the old library," Brenn murmured.

"The old library is burning now," the wizard said, lighting the last of the lamps. "And good riddance to it all, I say. Especially since not a book was touched by the flame."

"I don't understand," Brenn persisted. "How can we expect to remain hidden . . ."

"In the midst of the enemy? I have set a table for you here, King Brennart of Palerna. It is not your concern how we escape detection. Instead, you are to concern yourself with this."

With a grunt, the wizard laid the heavy volume on the table before Brenn.

"Folia Morrigana," Brenn read.

He looked up at the wizard, who stared back at him expectantly.

Brenn muttered, searching his memory for the Latin. "The *Leaves of Morrigan*?"

"Of course, you ninny!" the wizard thundered. "Didn't you get my message? Why do you think we risked everything to bring you here?"

"But . . . *Latin*, Terrance!"

"I know. You were always terrible in Latin, *discipulus terribilus*, or whatever the damned adjectival ending is in the masculine nominative. . . . No matter. It's not *in* Latin, or I'd have read it myself."

The wizard opened the book, and the musty smell of the pages raced out over Brenn. He sneezed several times uncontrollably. Undaunted, Terrance took him by the ears and turned his head back to the page.

" 'Tis a language only the rightful king can read," the wizard claimed, a strange authority in his voice. "So *read*!"

When Dirk called from beneath her window, Faye slipped the key in the door and padded down the hallway.

Brenn was waiting for her, the little thief had said. Wanted to see her. It was not the most cheering of prospects.

Everything she had done had ended in disaster. And though she deeply regretted her betrayals, and would have done far otherwise given another chance and a time redeemed, she was sure that Brenn summoned her for reproach at best, but probably for outright rejections.

For the first time she ever remembered, she went toward punishment willingly, because beyond Brenn's anger lay the hope of mending things with her old friend.

' Faye slipped through torchlight and shadow, ducking into a side corridor once as a trio of Watchmen passed, their talk of the raid and the skirmish in the bailey. The Pretender was dead, so the rumors went, but Faye knew what Dirk had told her, knew that the body by the gates was that of the Alanyan Ricardo, Brenn's companion in his Palernan adventures.

She crouched in the shadows and waited for the Watch to pass. Throughout the Tower, Dragmond's soldiery was on full alert, swarming like an anthill with the red-armored Watch, archers manning each window and patrols on the stairwells and in the halls. The simple path from her room to the garden became an intricate passage through a labyrinth of swords and spears, as she avoided a dozen outposts and stations.

In a side corridor on the second floor, she detoured twice and then a third time by the presence of troops ahead. Faye stopped for a moment and gathered her breath.

A steady light shone in the depths of the hall behind her. Faye heard noises, the approach of a guardsman, and crept back toward the light, ducking into an alcove next to the door. As the Watchman passed, his footsteps fading up the corridor, Faye looked around.

It was the door she had passed a hundred times as she swept and scrubbed the floors of Kestrel Tower. This chamber and that of the King were the only two into which she was never allowed. Dragmond's privacy she understood, or thought she understood, crediting the locks and the bans to the secrecy of kings. But what lay beyond this door remained a puzzlement.

Crouching beside the keyhole, her curiosity overwhelming despite the urgency of her errand and the danger about her, Faye peeked into the room. . . .

Where all she saw was a fierce, prismatic swirl of light, a shifting spectrum of reds and indigos and deep violets.

Finally out of the Tower, into the sheltering darkness of the bailey, Faye could not find the gardener's shed. Though she walked to the very spot where it had been that morning, that afternoon, there was no building—not even the *sign* of a building—and the ground on which the shed had stood was furrowed and planted like the rest of the garden.

Faye sat on the moist earth in distress. Dirk had told her to come here, after all, and from the looks of it, *here* had become no place in particular. She thought of calling out, but remembered that the bailey was as busy with the King's troops as the Tower itself.

Maybe that's what he wants, a dark voice inside her said. *For me to be "caught trying to escape," handled the way that the Watch handled Ricardo. . . .*

It was then that the air in front of her buckled and swirled in a thick, metallic light, from the center of which came the voice of the gardener Carlo, calling her, calling her into the whirling, glittering vortex. . . .

"Come closer, Faye," Brenn said, motioning to her. "Terrance tells me you've had your nose in it for a year, on and off, and I expect you'd like to know what it's all about."

He stood with Terrance beside a lamplit table, a huge book spread open in front of them. Dirk perched on a stool in the corner of the shed, paring his fingernails with a long knife.

Faye's first step was cautious, almost fearful.

What does he know? He acts as if nothing . . .

"Hurry up, Faye," Brenn urged. "We haven't all night."

Her head bowed and her footsteps shuffling and slow, the girl moved to his side.

His eyes were red and swollen, and there was a heaviness about his movements that Faye had not seen in a long time—not since the Goniph fell in the cellar of the Poisoners' Hall.

But he was a king now, and he ruled over his grief as well.

"First of all, it's obvious that we have a map of the garden," Brenn said, tracing with his finger the green outline on the second page of the book. "Evergreens at the northern border, juniper forming a colonnade into a little circle at the northernmost part of the bailey grounds. The shade trees line the garden's southern borders, flowering wood to the east and the fruit trees westerly, against the wall of the Tower."

"Where the sunlight makes 'em grow prodigious, I hear tell, even at night," Dirk observed. Despite himself, Brenn smiled.

"But it's all in disarray," Terrance said. "I've been at work on it since we arrived, but it's the restoring plan of years I'm after, rather than a quick mending."

"I'm not here to garden, Terrance," Brenn insisted, and Faye noticed the old thinness in his voice that he had always shown as a lad, when the dallying and ineptitude of the younger thieves had taxed his patience.

"Then what of the map? Symbolic associations?" asked the wizard. "Druidic speculations? The language of trees?"

"Or perhaps it's just a map," Dirk said with a yawn.

"What do you think, Faye?" Brenn asked.

Faye took a deep breath, stepped toward the open book. She heard no condemnation in Brenn's voice, no slyness. Perhaps he did not know that she had brought him to the Poisoners' Hall at Lightborn's request.

Timidly, she stepped between Terrance and Brenn and peered down at the map. Carefully she examined its edges.

At the top of the map, at the east, a bold hand had inscribed the word *fiore*. It was *sempreverde* to her left, with the colonnade that Brenn had described trailing to a circle at the edge of the page. To her right, half obscured in the gutter of the book, the inscription *foglia*, and at the bottom of the page, where the outline of Kestrel Tower formed a huge half moon on the face of the parchment, the same hand had written *alberi de frutta*.

"It's . . . it's like you were sayin' it was, Brennart," she agreed. "But if you squint a mite, it's like a map of the city, it is. See, the evergreens form a coastline, and that colonnade, why . . ."

"Of course!" Brenn exclaimed, his eyes bright at the discovery. "The garden plot is a city map!"

"That's all well and good, Majesty," Terrance observed dryly, "but it's a penchant for a garden to *resemble* things. I've seen them in the shape of lozenges, of hourglass and the quincunx, of latticework and spiderwebs and one of Europa in its entirety, where all of Provence was an orange grove and the Sicilies spice and flowers."

"But it's Maraven, Terrance!" Brenn protested. "Don't you think that *means* something?"

"Oh, surely it does," the wizard conceded, pointing to the next page. "But probably nothing useful. The handwriting in these margins is another matter."

"You mean all of this debate about herbs?" Brenn asked.

Faye and Terrance looked at him in puzzlement.

Blissfully unconcerned with the matters at hand, Dirk was drawing circles of silver light with the point of his dagger, chanting easily the little song Brenn had stumbled over time and again in his apprenticeship:

> Ignis vivi tu scintilla
> discurrens cordis ad vexilla
> igni incumbens non pauxillo
> conclusi mentis te sigillo . . .

Blocking his ears to the song, Brenn pointed to the thin scrawl at the top of the page. "See? The concern with the shifting sunlight of late summer, with planting the feverfew in the open, the eyebright by the Alanyan perspicacia root so it can draw nourishment and provide *enough acumen to see to the Notches*, as the writer says."

Brenn looked up at a gaping girl, a smiling wizard.

"Then it's true," Terrance proclaimed. "If ever I had a doubt . . ."

"About what?" Brenn interrupted. "You *know* all these apothecary matters, Terrance."

"Oh, yes. But I can't read the writing," the wizard replied, a curious catch in his voice. " 'Tis the palace code. 'Tis the handwriting of your grandfather, Brenn. You know it by inheritance, by your blood."

Faye's eyes widened. It was true after all. All the commotion and concern about her old friend and his claim to the Palernan throne came down to these gardeners' instructions in the margin of a musty old book. She could read five languages herself, and yet these letters were incomprehensible, as alien as the pattern of tides or the cry of birds.

Something in her had held back from believing, something that told her *he is your friend and grew up with you in the tunnels, on the streets. He is a thief.*

What kingdom is there for the likes of you?

And yet it was true, as impossibly true as the Palernan victories and her own breaking from the Great Witch's enchantments. She looked at the young man beside her, trying to find the boy thief, scarcely a memory now amid power and resolve and calm.

She blinked, shook her head. He was speaking to her.

". . . in the Witch's chamber?"

"Wh . . . I beg your pardon?"

"The herbs," said Brenn. "Eyebright and yarrow. Have you seen them in her presence, mixed or pure?"

"In the blue vial," Faye replied. "The *acumen,* of course. My chymistry is better than you remember."

Brenn glanced apprehensively at Terrance. "Acumen. She has acumen. Are we safe?"

The wizard shrugged. "She can't see us. There are more magics than my own concealing this shed from her eyes."

"There's another vial," Faye offered. "Attar of tithonia. She thinks I can't read, but I've seen it in a bottle at her vanity."

Brenn glanced anxiously at Terrance, who smiled.

"Cosmetic. At least that's what most use it for. In the wrong hands, though, it's far more than that—a storehouse of blight and charm, things that appeal to the likes of Ravenna. I don't know much more than that. If you hadn't noticed, I myself have little use for cosmetics."

Brenn smiled at the wizard's rough features, the crow's-feet when the old man smiled back.

"Attar of tithonia's a good one, I've heard," Terrance continued. "Takes thirty years off your appearance. Volatile stuff, though. Knew a woman who exploded from it." He laughed softly. "But do not burden yourself with thoughts of Ravenna. Read the *Leaves,* and tell me what you see there."

They were bowed above the book for hours, as the girl watched them and Dirk slept in the corner.

After a while, the search lost its interest for Faye. After all, she read no royal encodements, and without Albright's notes, the book was ultimately dull to a city girl—nothing more than a thorough herbal.

And yet Brenn and Terrance pored over it, silhouetted in the lamplight, their shadows tall and menacing. It was an arcane language they spoke, the cant of alchemists and apothecaries, mixed with a strange history and gossip that continued to intrigue her after the book had lost its allure.

"From Myrra, you say?" Brenn asked.

"How *else* could he have gathered it?" Terrance replied, leaning so close to the text that Brenn had to brush his beard away from where it covered one of the margins. "She was ever jealous of her sister, you know."

"But Myrra was Albright's mistress," Brenn insisted.

"And Ravenna was the powerful one," Terrance said. "Old Gauderic's daughters, Ravenna and Myrra. You should have heard the Witch talk of her little sister. Venom, it was, and bile. *Brood sow,* she called her. *The King's whore.*"

"From what I read here," Brenn said, "the little sister had no kinder words for Ravenna."

Tracing his finger along the page, he read his grandfather's scribbled notes.

And Myrra saith that her sister is a nest of calculation, a bad mixture of bad mixture, sustained by acumen and invention and the attar of tithonia. That Ravenna holds powers especiall over men and over boys, allurements and enticements beyond her magick and beyond their knowing and resistance.

"How very true," Terrance murmured with a sad little laugh.

"Hist, Terrance!" Brenn ordered, waving his hand before the wizard's face. "There is more.

But do not fear, the sweete girl saith, for the Witch hath alway a mortal wound in the midst of her strength, death in the middle of youth."

"What does that mean?" Faye asked, her curiosity piqued by anything that promised death for the Witch.

Brenn turned the page, his lips moving silently as he read another inscription.

> Her death in the middle of youth, and all our youth in
> the middle of her death. 'Tis the attar that undoes the
> witch, the poison asleep in the arms of tithonia . . .

"What *does* it mean, Terrance?" Brenn asked. "I can read the code, but it still seems encoded to me—all double-talk and paradox."

Terrance chuckled and scratched his head. "And so, no doubt, you come to me for the translation. I don't know whether to be flattered or affronted, Majesty. Read on."

Brenn rubbed his eyes, continued.

> Four winds sow the garden. Four branches stir the attar.
> North and south, east and west, the attar the heart at
> the center.

"Well, *that* clears everything up," Faye muttered, then blushed deeply as the eyes of the two men rested upon her. "It sounds like a recipe. All that sowing and stirring."

With a sniff, Terrance turned back to the book, his face lost in the shadows around the edges of the lamplight. But Brenn continued to stare at her, his frown transforming suddenly into the bright smile of the lad she remembered.

He is still here! Faye thought exultantly. *There is still a Wall Town under those tactics and royalty!*

"Of course, Faye!" Brenn exclaimed, laughing delightedly as he bounded across the room, lifted her from her stool, and hugged her fiercely, almost painfully. "That's it exactly!"

"I beg your pardon?" the wizard grumbled, turning from perusing the book, his hat awry on his head and his beard frayed and tangled, where he had used it vainly to mark pages.

Dirk snorted and tumbled from his stool in a heap.

"Aconite!" Brenn exclaimed, setting Faye down gently and

wheeling to address Terrance. Delightedly, he slammed his fist on the table. "Aconite!"

Terrance and Faye exchanged worried glances. Dirk rose blearily from the floor, fumbling at his belt for the knife that he had lodged harmlessly in the shed walls.

"Don't you see?" Brenn asked. "It's . . . it's like Glory taught me back in Corbinwood. I'm surprised I remember any of it, I was such an inconstant student. But I remember aconite. Monk's hood. In small doses—infinitely small—good for pleurisies, neuralgias, whatever. And poison deadly as an adder's bite if you use too much."

"I see . . ." Terrance mused. "The attar of tithonia."

Brenn nodded. "All in the way it is mixed. Mixed right, it keeps her young. You said something about *volatile*, about explosions."

"So mixed another way," Faye chimed in excitedly, "it destroys her."

The three of them gaped at one another. It was as if a new star had risen in the eastern constellations, and with it the prospects of new time and new future.

"Well . . ." Terrance began, pulling back his sleeves. A squirrel leapt from his robes and scrambled up the beams to the ceiling of the garden shed, where it perched and chattered loudly at Brenn and Faye. "Well. Let's find out what is in this elixir of youth."

Three ingredients were easy. All they had to do was to examine the contents of the garden—what plants and herbs were generally alien to the hard coastal soil—and work from there, by the process of elimination. Brenn's instruction at the hands of Glory served him well, as did Faye's keen eyes and memory, for the girl recalled to the box, bag, and vial the herbs Ravenna kept in her chambers. Terrance, of course, knew how things fit together: what herb mixed well with what potion, what extract with what oil.

"Alanyan fire," Brenn concluded wearily. "The red evergreen from east of Rabia. That has to be the first. What else is there on the garden's northern edge that you wouldn't see in a Teal Front arbor?"

"It makes sense," Terrance agreed. "Alanyan fire's a cordial. Stirs the blood. And no doubt the others are pirum and primula."

"But what's the fourth?" Brenn asked. "After all, the book says *four winds sow the garden.*"

"Read on," Terrance urged.

"There's a whole library in this book." Brenn sighed. "Do we have days?"

"Read."

Resolutely, the young man turned back to the *Leaves of Morrigan.* He skimmed a dozen pages idly, started to close the book. Then his eyes fastened on another passage.

"It's here. I don't know what it is . . . not yet . . . but I know it's here.

> Four directions there are in the blood, four seasons, four elements, all turning and awakening to a stirring of leaves. The primula from the earth, the watery pirum, and the annealing blaze of Alanyan fire, and finally the air we breath, which rises from the earth and bears the water, and into which the fire vanishes, the island polychrest . . ."

He looked up from the book. "Polychrest?"

"A two-barbed herb," Terrance explained. "Shaped like that sword of yours, thorny and sweet. Used medicinally and for poison by apothecary and chymist . . ."

"Like aconite!" Brenn exclaimed.

"But greater," Terrance said, an odd look in his eye. "And native to but one place in the entire continent. The Ruthic Islands."

<< < **XXV** > >>

The Ruthic Islands meant only one thing. Delia had brought the polychrest to Kestrel Tower.

That knowledge brought them out of the swirling shed, out of the collapsed time into which Terrance's magic had placed them. The old wizard produced an hourglass from his robe—a broken instrument, evidently, for the sands had stopped flowing from one chamber to another. The useless thing discarded, Terrance stood on a table, rocked and weaved and gained his balance, then, with his hands extended, began to chant the spell.

> Those hours that with gentle work did frame
> The lovely gaze where every eye doth dwell
> Will play the tyrants to the very same
> And that unfair which fairly doth excel . . .

Brenn gasped as the hourglass lying on the floor beneath the table began to empty its sands, magically restored to use.

"The time has returned," Terrance whispered, a surpassing weariness arising in his eyes. "And whether it takes an hour, or a day, or a year, the end of our journey is in sight."

It was early morning, a little before sunrise, as the red-caped soldiers reckoned, and the search for the Palernan had subsided in the castle grounds. A trio of Watchmen passed by the shed at a distance. Recognizing the gardener Carlo as he stepped into the moonlight, they gathered that nothing was out of the ordinary, really, and after exchanging a few words at a distance with the old man, returned to their posts where they would wait out the last hours of darkness.

Had they looked around, they would have seen the gardener change, the years slide off him and his back straighten. They would have seen his little apprentice follow him from the shed, as they might have expected, but then, surprisingly, the girl would follow, and the elusive young man they had searched for most of the evening.

No doubt, since they were far away from the shed to begin with, they would not have seen the tercel eagle perched on the top of the ramshackle building—a strange sight, the daytime raptor taking to the darkened sky! Nor certainly would the Watchmen have heard the young man speak to the bird, seen the bird take wing, vault and vanish into the mist over Grospoint, bearing a message for Galliard and Helmar.

Brenn had ordered an attack on Maraven. At sunrise, and with the full unbridled power of the Palernan army. As the bird vanished behind the row of deciduous trees that marked the southern boundary of the garden, the Pretender breathed a prayer for its safe flight, for the wisdom of his commanders and the courage and resourcefulness of his armies.

If all went well, Helmar would assault the East Gate, drawing Dragmond's attention, as well as that of the Great Witch, to eastern Grospoint and to the warrens of Wall Town.

Then, with the eyes of the powerful averted, Brenn would follow the plan he and Terrance had hatched hastily, there in the ramshackle shed.

Silently, efficiently, as though they were a host of thieves, the four in the garden shrank into the shadows of the newly grown fruit trees by the wall. There they would wait until the eastern horizon was red, until the edge of the sun peeked over the black rim of the Sea of Shadows.

Then Delia came, as they figured she would, crouching in the shade by the herbs, kneeling over the dark earth.

Brenn watched her coolly. Her steps were slower this morning, as if she had risen from a deep, oppressive sleep.

"There, I expect, you'll find the polychrest," Terrance whispered contemptuously. "Where she's brought it for Ravenna."

"Now that we know where it is," Faye hissed, "I expect we can put that turncoat out of the way."

Brenn looked at his old friend in puzzlement. *Out of the way?* Faye's gray eyes glittered malignly in the shadows. You would almost think they were black, instead of the gray he knew they were.

Now Dirk joined in the rising chorus around him. "After all, Brenn, she has gone over to the Witch and all. Why else has Ravenna been givin' her food and board over the last month? I can take her."

Slowly, with the silence of a trained assassin, he drew his knife. The air hummed with violence, Zephyrian bees, the Goniph had always called it—that tension that preceded the hardest words, the drawn knife, the razor under the cloak. A good thief could sense the bees even in a strange crowd.

Brenn had not lost that sense. "No!" he whispered, seizing Dirk's wrist, disarming his friend with a quick turn of the hand. "There will be questions only—no knives."

In the shadowy distance the Ruthic woman rose, wiped her hands, and started toward the castle.

"Then I would gather her in and begin asking those questions," Terrance urged. "Before she returns to her quarters."

"Or before you break a man's fingers," Dirk muttered angrily, rubbing his hand.

Brenn caught Delia before she left the garden. With quiet authority, he took her by the arm, his other hand on her mouth, and led her quickly toward the evergreens. She started to wrestle away, but he held to her firmly, and when she turned toward him, ready to cry out, to struggle, to draw knife if need be, she saw at last who he was and fell silent.

And at that moment, Brenn saw who *she* was.

It was a disarming sight. Delia's eyes were red, her hair disheveled. She staggered, and Brenn held her up.

At once the mistrust and the anger fled from Brenn. He knew that Delia had been weeping, and he guessed that she had been weeping for Ricardo. There had been harsh words about her— accusations of betrayals, rumors that she had allied with Ravenna for some malign purpose—but Brenn no longer believed any of it.

Gently, almost lovingly, he wrapped his arm around Delia and ushered her toward the others.

"I understand," he whispered.

Faye watched them approach from the shadows. She flinched when she saw Brenn embrace the Ruthic alchemist, gather the girl in his arms and whisper something to her—something inaudible, scattered by the rising morning wind.

Ravenna was right all along, the dark voice told her. *Something happened between them on the plains, something . . .*

She chose not to think about it, but the dark, accusing voice would not leave: There was nothing with which to replace it. Brenn brought Delia into their midst, introduced her to Dirk and Faye. Then the five of them made their way to an arched entrance on the northern side of the Tower, where the grounds came to an end in the sheer abutment of black rock that bordered the whole Aquilan coast.

It began to rain, the soft, cooling mist that was native to April in those parts, and huddled in the arch amid the darkness and the smells of moss and moist earth, the infiltrators planned their assault on Kestrel Tower and the Witch who lived there.

"Not to aid her," Delia insisted to the persistent questions of the wizard. "You should know that."

Faye walked to the mouth of the arch and stood there, her back to the alchemist, the wizard, the King. Shivering, her face beading with the rain, she leaned out and watched Dirk scramble up the black rockface, settle himself like a bird in an eyrie, and, producing Brenn's spyglass from beneath his cloak, peer out over the bay for signs of erupting battle at the East Gate.

She did not want to hear the alchemist's lies, especially since she suspected they were no lies at all—that Delia was telling the truth.

It would have been better to believe she was a liar, that she had nothing but ill will toward Brenn. That way her deceit could be unmasked, she could be exposed for what she was, and disposed of immediately, no longer a factor in Brenn's mind and heart.

The other prospect was strangely more frightening. If Delia was helping Brenn here, if she guided him to victory with her learning and ingenuity, then, when it was all over . . . when they were all triumphant and safe . . .

Cease with your mournful auguries, Faye! she told herself, as the rain picked up, washing the bailey and the Tower in thick, driving sheets. *Cease with your borrowing trouble!*

It was jealousy, good and proper. Faye dreaded the prospect of romance between Delia and Brenn because . . .

Because you want him yourself! Admit it!

She stepped into the rain, heard Dirk cough and sputter and curse above her. She did not notice Brenn's eyes follow her, even in the midst of the grave matters that unfolded as Delia explained the workings of the polychrest.

"An infusion, it has to be. Mixed in your healing hands, Brenn, and boiled over a low flame. The steam will rise from it like a fog on the coastline."

"A steam?" Brenn asked. He was unfamiliar with matters alchemical.

"It will cleanse the city," the alchemist insisted, "ridding it of all disease, malignity, and curse."

Faye laughed aloud.

"What is it, Faye?" Brenn called to her.

She turned and faced him, her brown hair dripping with rain. Her eyes rested on Delia for a moment, on the alchemist's dark hair and amber eyes. She felt slovenly and rough.

"Oh, nothing, Brenn. It's just an impossible order, cleansing things entirely." She was surprised at her own venom, tried and failed to fight it back.

"Faye's right," Delia conceded amiably. "In the long run, that is. Such a cleansing cannot hold forever, but it can work for a while. And a while is long enough for your purposes, Brenn."

"How's that?" Terrance asked curtly. Brenn glared at him, seeing the wizard's skepticism, his mistrust of the gentle, serious girl in front of him.

"Simply put," Delia explained, "a moment of perfect peace will be enough to destroy Ravenna."

Dirk stepped through the arch, dripping and sputtering. "It's begun," he said. "I seen smoke down around Wall Town."

Begun it had. Helmar had received Brenn's message scarcely three hours before, when Bertilak perched, wet and shrieking, on the footstool as the general nodded in his chair, tired with waiting and planning his considerable memoirs.

He understood what the bird had said by instinct, even before he sent for the owl to translate, and as the verse spewed forth from the excited creature, the general disregarded the rhyme, the meter, and went straight for the message.

Insurrection in the city. Launch an attack to the East Gate that will summon attention and buy me time.

Immediately the camp sprung into life under Helmar's iron hand. Raising alarums, he stomped through the infantry bivouacs himself, scattering troops to their weapons—men who would rather face a wave of Maravenian pikemen than the anger of the grizzled general who moved among them.

He woke Angeda by kicking over the Zephyrian's tent. Angeda emerged, livid, his sword drawn, but he blanched in the presence of the general. Helmar sent him at once on a diversionary raid along the southern walls of the city, drawing General Flauros' attention so that the infantry assault, against the East Gate as Brenn had ordered, would create even more confusion.

Confusion was epidemic in the tents where the cousins were kept under guard, for Helmar's next task was to release them from house arrest. Thievery or no thievery, he placed Galliard and Thomas at the head of their former legions and sent them at once to the front.

It was only later that the guards discovered their rings were missing.

Within an hour, Thomas and Galliard had resumed their commands, joining with their forces along the seacoast. At a signal from Helmar—a circling eagle in the sky over the East Wall, Galliard's infantry marched forward, their confidence renewed under their old commander. Thomas' archers took their place on the flanks, and behind the wide column advancing toward the Maravenian gates, Jimset's engineers and sappers trudged along deliberately, their orders to burrow into the Maravenian tunnel system and thereby breach the walls and defenses of the city.

They sang as they marched into battle, and beat their swords against their shields, and the larks startled from the fields in front of them, and the gulls along the rocky coast banked in the rain, and fluttered and cried.

* * *

Dirk saw this movement as a distant wave of color at the edge of sight, dark green against the gray abiding fog. At first he thought it was a trick of tide, but the spyglass confirmed the hopes of those who waited and planned in the arch below him. Nimbly, he scrambled down the rain-slick rocks to Brenn, to Terrance, and announced that the assault had begun.

"So now we prepare the infusion?" Brenn asked Delia, who nodded gravely.

"Just a moment, Brennart," Terrance protested, pulling the edge of his robe away from the sopping Dirk, who was toweling himself down with it. "With all respect to Delia . . . how can we be sure all of this is truth?"

Faye leaned forward intently, grateful that the wizard possessed the courage to ask what she had wondered all along.

"I'm not *sure* that you can, Terrance of Keedwater," Brenn replied, rising to his full height beside the wizard. Accustomed as he had been to their relationship as sorcerer and apprentice, teacher and student, man and boy, he was a little surprised that he looked Terrance in the eye.

"I'm not sure that you can," he repeated, "but I *command* the three of you—you and Faye and Dirk as well—to behave *as though* you believed her."

There was a long silence beneath the arch, as the clamor of the rain swelled around Brenn and Terrance, and from somewhere near the barracks of Kestrel a trumpet sounded, and the clatter of armor echoed through the nearby garden.

"Very well, then," Terrance conceded with a strange half-smile. "I suppose that's all believing is, when you come down to it. If I've done aught in the past to school a king, 'tis the least I can do now to obey him."

He rolled up his sleeves and stepped into the rain.

"You'll need time for the business at hand," he maintained. "This rain is going to make fire-starting downright vexatious, though you can do it magically, desert or deluge. Dirk will help you if you need the helping."

Brenn nodded. The time of deadly magicks was close at hand. As soon as Ravenna realized what they were doing, every spell, incantation, chant, and illusion would be hurled in their direction as she plumbed the desperate depths of her dark gifts. What they would need was time before that, distraction on distraction.

It dawned on him that Terrance was giving him the time.

"Wait, Terrance!" he cried. "If Ravenna sees you, she'll . . ."

"Pursue me with every ounce of energy and rage she has." Terrance chuckled. "Which is the idea."

"You'll be safe, though?"

Terrance smiled as the rain cascaded from the wide brim of his hat. "Of course not. You have a foolish confidence in my magic, King. Spell to spell, charm to enchantment, Ravenna's more than my match. But that doesn't take *you* into account. And Dirk and Faye. And Mistress Delia."

Terrance bowed to the Ruthic alchemist. "My king has asked me to act as though I believe you. I cannot believe you more than to stake my life on your honesty."

He turned and tramped into the heavy rain, breathing the first of a dozen incantations. Reaching deep into the folds of his robe to where it lay, tied to the string around his neck, he drew forth the glowing claridad fruit he had carried with him, on and off, for fifty years. Many times he had tried to put it aside, to lose it under scrolls and books in his library or bedchamber in the old tower by the East Wall, but it seemed to return to his possession like a loyal apprentice—or perhaps like a pain he could neither subdue nor outlast. In Corbinwood, sitting by the Forest Lord on a moonstruck night in the clearing, when he felt the fruit being drawn from the pouch at his belt, something in him had rejoiced: the old life seemed behind him now, and with it the times with Ravenna that the claridad had reminded him of for over half a century.

But Galliard had wrestled with his conscience, had returned the damned thing by Bertilak when the curse had lifted. The eagle had dropped the claridad from a great height and with amazing accuracy, and when Terrance had awakened later that afternoon, head throbbing and facedown on the river bank, the first thing that caught his eye was the green glow of the claridad.

Might as well tie the blasted thing around my neck, he had muttered angrily to Dirk, who retrieved the thing from the dark road to Maraven and thought the whole business to be great sport. And then Terrance had done so, in an almost rueful joke.

Now he was glad it was there. For if anything would push Ravenna's anger beyond its furthest boundaries, it would be the sight of that glowing fruit and the memories that sight would bring to *her*—how Archimago had betrayed her a half-century before, giving a journeyman's job to the less experienced Terrance . . .

And how Terrance himself had left her.

In Ravenna's chambers, the candles burst suddenly into flames.

She leapt from her chair and raced to the balcony. The rain swept over her as she threw open the doors and rushed to the railing, leaning into the downpour and the wind off the Sea of Shadows.

Someone was standing in the garden, his arms extended toward her. She recognized the voice at once.

"Terrance!" she shouted, reeling dangerously at the railing. For a moment she teetered over the sheer and lofty drop, her hands clutching at air . . . at nothing. . . .

Then, grasping the rail in a fierce grip, she called forth the first of her most potent spells against the figure in the garden.

> His sense thus weak, lost with his fears thus
>   strong,
> Make senseless things appear to do him wrong,
> For briers and thorns at his apparel snatch,
> Some sleeves, some hats, from yielders all things
>   catch . . .

At once the evergreens along the northern edge of the garden surged toward Terrance, extending their spiny branches like long, entangling fingers. Quickly the wizard turned, stepped aside, but the branches of the deciduous trees rushed to meet him from the other side, closing over him like an enormous wicker cage.

Ravenna leaned against the balcony. She had him. Beyond her wildest expectations, she had captured the wizard easily, without a struggle. Laughing triumphantly, she spun from the balcony into her chamber, rushed to the closet for a cloak against the rain.

She had always known that her magic was superior to his. Suspected in those early days with Archimago, even unto the time when the gangling lad from Keedwater had usurped her rightful place as court enchanter for Duke Danton of Aquila . . .

She had believed these things assuredly when Terrance's ward, that simpleminded Aurum, had matched wits with her beautiful Dragmond. And though Dragmond was dead now, dead past recovery and necromancy, smuggled by night to a shallow grave in the Potters' Field along the Aquilan coast, Aurum was . . .

was beyond recovery and recall himself.

Ravenna laughed again, a high-pitched, hysterical giggle as she opened the door of her closet. She would descend into the garden, would take the wizard into her custody. Without him, the boy would be nothing, his escape fruitless, his cavalry commander dead and his adviser captured. And there was always a dark hope for Terrance. Perhaps, after months of charm and enchantment, he would join his powers with her. . . .

Then she would need no figurehead king, no monarch through whom she would speak and govern. They would govern together, she and . . .

Ravenna stopped at the opened doors. A thin line of light shone at the back of the closet. Frantically, she shoved aside the rows upon rows of black garments, her long-nailed fingers fastening on the secret door, pushing it open into the corridor behind the chamber . . .

and she knew then she had been watched. For how long and by whom, she could not tell.

That slut of a scullery maid, for certain.

And no doubt the wizard outside.

Angrily, Ravenna paced back to the window, stared down through the rain into the entanglement of branches. A green light danced in the midst of the natural cage, weaving back and forth like a firefly under glass.

It took only a moment to recognize the claridad, to know that Terrance was taunting her.

"You bastard!" she screamed, and the lightning flashed as her voice shrilled and crackled. "You insolent . . ."

She could not find the words. They tumbled away from her like a thousand scattering locusts, like sprites glittering on Hardwater Cove. Then they came to her, the right words, as fierce and raging as the fire she summoned, as she muttered, spread wide her fingers . . .

and the cage of trees below her billowed with smoke, with a torrid magical blaze.

<<< **XXVI** >>>

The nightingale perched atop a blue juniper, careful not to stray too close to the Alanyan fire tree. There was no telling what curse or blight or thunderbolt Ravenna had in her command, and above all, the patch of polychrest below had to be kept safe from the accidents of her wrath.

Beside him the trees writhed in magical fire, and the claridad apple turned brown, then black in the whirling flame. The bird turned his head away from the withering light and continued his song.

He had to keep singing so the Witch would notice.

For, of course, it was no ordinary bird there in the midst of the evergreens. When she noticed, Ravenna would know him on sight as Terrance transformed. When she recognized him, realized he had escaped her burning, she would not rest until she had destroyed him.

It would be a merry chase, and it would buy time for Delia and Brenn.

Fluttering his wings to shake away the coursing rain, Terrance trilled a merry little love song from Keedwater, reverent and bright—just the kind of thing to infuriate the Witch. Though the melody sounded sweet and wordless in his bird's throat, Ravenna would recall the tune and the words that went with it.

And if the claridad had not been enough . . .

As soon as he began the song the Great Witch turned on the balcony, fixed him with her darkening gaze, and saw through the magic to the wizard hidden in the bird's body . . .

as her shriek became a hoarse, inhuman cry. In a gust of black smoke, her robe dropped to the floor of the balcony and an enormous raven wrestled out of the dark folds and perched on the railing, clutching with its sharp claws, its razored beak dripping with rain.

Sullenly, it eyed him from its flinty perch, and then with a cry launched itself into the downpour, swooping toward the north end of the garden, toward the evergreens, toward Terrance himself. . . .

Immediately he vaulted into the rainy air and vanished into the smoke and mist, his song dwindling into the rush of the rain and crackling fire. Veering and steadying, gaining control of her newly acquired wings, Ravenna closed the gap between them rapidly, and Terrance, skimming over the rocky coast of Aquila, heard her cry close behind him.

Out to sea he flew, the wind off the water smelling of salt and kelp and ash, the black waves below him boiling in rain, and then she emerged from a bank of clouds, tumbling from the sky like a diving falcon, croaking malignly, her talons extended.

Terrance swerved, and Ravenna plunged by him, righting herself not a dozen feet from the water. She climbed back toward him, resolutely, her wingbeats strong and decisive now, and Terrance knew he was lost if he kept up this flight, this struggle in the air. . . .

So he murmured the second incantation and, folding his wings to his sides, plummeted into the icy waters of the Sea of Shadows.

Into the churning waters Terrance descended, deep into the alien darkness. Words and song fell away from him, and everything was unspeakably silent. He imagined a colder current beneath him—the Corrante that encircled the Aquilan peninsula, its waters a million years in the making—as below him the white skeleton of Palern Reef ghosted forth from the murky waters.

For a moment he almost forgot Ravenna, almost forgot the flight from the garden, as the lost light danced on his dwindling back, as wing and feather became fin and scale, and from the water came his strange liquid breath. Terrance surged through the eddies, rising toward the surface and the light.

He was a flying fish, and the nightingale wings, though transformed into fin and spine, had not quite left him. That was humbling: when he had cast the spell to change himself, he had imagined he would become a formidable, noble creature—a marlin, perhaps, or a sailfish . . . like the dark gray mass that glided beneath him in the water.

Ah, Ravenna! he thought.

She stayed at the edge of his sight, barely distinguishable from the ocean shadows and the ash borne along by the cold Corrante. She was moving with a blind hungry will. Slowly she rose from the opaque depths to the translucent upper waters, where regardless of cloud and shadow, the fractured sunlight hinted at her enormous outline.

Terrance rose, fluttering closer to the surface. Ravenna was a jackal shark. Mariners said they infested the reef from the harbors of Orgo all the way down to Stormpoint. Nearsighted and witless, more scavengers than predators, they were wary, almost skittish, except for odd occasions when the currents switched and the plentiful reef-dwelling fish ventured out into deeper waters, leaving the jackals sole inhabitants of the hard white coral. They were aggressive then, and ill-tempered.

She circled Terrance menacingly, twice moving dangerously near him, once so close that he weaved and bobbed in the wake of her passing.

It was in that second pass that Terrance saw the glitter in the shark's eye. When she turned for him again, he launched himself toward the surface, toward air and flight, his bony wings vibrating in expectation.

He broke the water and skipped across the surface. Ravenna's dark form advanced through the depths, gained substance and bulk and momentum as it closed the gap, its dark mouth opening. . . .

And he propelled himself up again. Hearing the jaws crash behind him, feeling the surge of displaced water, he skipped about until he could fly no more, dropped awkwardly onto the predator's back, then tumbled into the water as the shark buckled and thrashed in pursuit.

Terrance dove beneath the foam and, reciting a spell in his most dim memory, leapt once more into the air, as Ravenna leapt after him, as she opened her cavernous jaws, as her prey coiled and curled . . .

and buzzed away merrily, a seaside squinchfly no bigger than a housefly, around whom the shark's jaws clacked harmlessly.

It was a long flight to land, as Terrance weaved and shuttled through the rain. In the distance he could make out the black shoreline of Palerna, the porous pumice that dotted the black beaches along Hardwater Cove. The water churned and thrashed behind him, as Ravenna raged at her slowness, her failure. Gradually the commotion ceased, and the squinchfly flitted over the beach, over the rocks . . .

and skidded to a landing in the mouth of a seaside cave.

Terrance gathered his breath and looked around him. The water brimmed in the recesses of the little cavern, but where he sat was dry, comfortable.

It seemed he had eluded the Witch. He only hoped he had held her attentions for long enough.

For a moment he was tempted to sleep, but he struggled toward wakefulness, fully aware from his own zoological studies of the great dangers awaiting small insects in the seaside food chain. He fluttered toward the mouth of the cavern, intending to rest under an awning or eave on the Street of the Bookbinders. . . .

But as he reached the light, something caught his wing and tangled him in midair. He struggled, tried to free himself, but he was only bound more securely, more tightly.

It was a rope that held him, a tacky, viscous fluid. . . .

Then he saw the spider, scaling the web from the sandy floor to where he lay caught in her clinging spirals. She approached, each of her eyes black and glittering and intelligent and triumphant. . . .

She's won after all, Terrance thought, closing his eyes, drawing his wings about him as he awaited the fangs, the swift searing poison. *But I pray she has lost the greater struggle.*

If only I could have seen it.

The spider arched above him, her forelegs extended, her fangs as black as her eyes. Then, inexplicably, she stopped, wavered on the web, her claws racing along the strands as she felt the distant vibration Terrance could also feel, and she cried faintly and tumbled from the web to the floor of the cavern, became a raven, and in a billow of black smoke, arose and departed, wafting toward Kestrel Tower, gaining speed over the dark waters.

Immobilized by the clinging strands, Terrance chuckled nonetheless. Something was happening at Kestrel Tower. . . .

And Ravenna did not like it at all.

"This is for Marco and the Goniph," Brenn said quietly, sprinkling the dried pirum leaves into the steaming pot.

"Not too much, now, Brenn," Delia warned, "or what you will have is perfume."

The beaker the Ruthic alchemist had set in the arch was half filled with salt water. Brenn started the fire, drawing on all the skills he had mastered in Corbinwood, and when those had failed, turning to minor spellcraft.

> This ae night
> This ae night
> Fire and sleet and candlelight

The fire beneath the beaker sputtered and lit.

"The best kindling known to man," Dirk muttered appreciatively, and drew his sword. If the Great Witch returned, he would be ready.

"And this—how much, Delia?"

"Primula? A blossom and a pinch."

"How much is the pinch?" Brenn asked. "Show me."

Delia shook her head. "I cannot handle any of the ingredients. Else it doesn't work. The King's Touch, remember?"

Brenn nodded, held up a bit of the primula for her inspection.

"Good enough," Delia said.

"That's for Ponder," Brenn said. "And Ricardo."

"Thank you," Delia breathed. "When he fell before the Kestrel Gates it was all I could do to keep Ravenna from dumping him on the midden. He's lying in state beside that fiend Lightborn. . . ."

"Better company in the midden," Dirk muttered, stepping out into the rain.

"It is good to know he had your friendship," Delia said wistfully. "The last time I saw him . . . on the road to Maraven, I could say nothing pleasant to him. He had to think I loathed him, or my plan would not have worked. He'd never have let me go to the Witch."

Brenn smiled at the alchemist. "You had no choice," he said. "It was a time when voices carried."

He glanced at Faye. "It's sadder still when little fears add up to silence."

Delia cleared her throat. "Now the Alanyan fire branches. Four of them—one for each point of the compass."

As Brenn dropped in the first branch, the garden before them filled with a ghastly yellow light. The bent trunks of the trees emerged in stark outline like a skeletal rib cage, and in their midst, clad in branches and weeds, the pale figure of the Great Witch rose to her full height, staggering, lurching toward the arch, toward the huddled company and the boiling infusion.

Swiftly, Brenn dropped in the other branches, then looked to Delia for instruction.

"Now the polychrest," she said calmly.

Ravenna stumbled, raised her hands, and began to chant,

> Young soul put off your flesh, and come
> With me into the quiet tomb,
>> Our bed is lovely, dark, and sweet;
> The earth will swing us, as she goes
> Beneath our coverlid of snows,
>> And the warm leaden sheet . . .

"No!" Faye cried, and, startled, the Witch spun about to see her maidservant, rain-drenched and muddy, step toward her angrily, a large menacing stick in her hand.

"You'll not have Brenn!" Faye shouted. "Not have *any* of 'em!"

"Not even the one who *steals* him?" Ravenna asked cruelly. "The Ruthic girl who shares his bed?"

Brenn looked up, astonished at the lie.

"Remove the leaves of the polychrest, Brenn," Delia urged, her voice quick and fervent. Brenn snapped back to the task and stripped the leaves from the strange, purple plant.

"Whatever the alchemist Delia *shares*," Faye said, "whether it's beds or brooms . . . she won't have to share Brenn with the likes of *you*! Not as long as I've a breath and two legs to stand between ye." And she rushed at the Witch, sliding in the thick mud.

"Begone!" Ravenna shouted, and waved her hand. Instantly a wall of rain tumbled over Faye, pummeling her, toppling her, passing over her and over her again. The girl cried out desperately, trying to stand, but the water beat her down, filled her mouth and nostrils, and suddenly she was drowning—drowning horribly in the midst of a castle garden.

Brenn looked up from the boiling beaker, the stem of the polychrest in his hand. Ravenna was turned toward Faye, but still regarded him from the corner of her eye.

"Cast the polychrest aside," the Witch warned. "Else the girl will drown."

"Do as I say," Delia urged, "and no harm will come to Faye."

"Oh . . . harm will come to the girl, Brennart," Ravenna said. "Trust me. I have sufficient magic to dispose of her."

Faye tried again to rise, slipped to her knees as the water swirled around her like a whirlpool.

"You're King, Brennart of Maraven," Delia said. "It's yours to decide."

"Then I decide to win on all counts," Brenn declared, and breathing a silent prayer, dropped the polychrest stem into the bubbling beaker.

The steam rose and spread like a hot *alienado* wind, racing to all corners of the garden and grounds, over the Causeway in an instant, coursing through Ships and Grospoint on a swift tidal surge toward Teal Front and Wall Town, to the farthest battlements of Maraven and to the troops who fought there.

Guiding the second wave of his infantry toward the East Gate, Galliard rose in the saddle as the bracing mist passed over him.

Instantly he felt cleansed, repaired, and he shouted in triumph, standing in the stirrups. From somewhere off to his right, along the black beach where the archers were stationed, Thomas returned his exultant cry, and from behind him, in the ranks of the engineers, Jimset echoed the call.

"The curse is lifted," the Forest Lord shouted to his men, as the infantry cheered and doubled their steps, racing now toward the battle, their hearts confident and committed and light.

"Now nothing stands in our way," he whispered, and spurred his horse toward the flinty walls.

Before the Palernan troops, the red Watch gave way like a scattered company of recruits. As they retreated west along Cove Road, as the Palernans scaled the wall and the East Gate buckled against the battering ram, even the Maravenians felt the freshness in the air, smelling the salt, the infusion, and strangely, below all of these, they knew at once that the plague had left the city. Some of them dropped their weapons instantly and ran to their homes in Teal Front, in Wall Town, in the central residential districts. Others turned and raced toward the East Wall, shedding the Maravenian armor and preparing to fight at the side of Galliard and the Palernans.

In the alley by Terrance's burned tower, at the side door, its lock picked long ago when Brenn and Faye had entered the wizard's library, a shimmer of light buckled and bent and resolved itself to a human form. The boy Jankin sat dumbfounded on the alley stones, gaping, looking around him.

"The things I seen!" he exclaimed in wonder. "And I done some of them, too!" He paused, scratched his head. "But I don't know why I seen 'em or done 'em."

With a shrug, Jankin picked up a fire-blackened ceiling joist, shattered it heroically against the tower stones, and, with a club-sized weapon in hands, trudged toward the East Gate, his mind and heart in full allegiance with the Palernans.

Closer to home, another lost servant returned. Ricardo's eyes napped open, dislodging the coins that had been placed on his eyelids. He rose up from the makeshift catafalque, blearily trying to remember his whereabouts, to remember what had brought him to this room and why. He stepped from the platform with a joyous shout, and, clutching his side, staggered toward the other body.

Lightborn lay as still as he had when life had left him.

"You always were an ugly bastard," Ricardo observed, gazing at the pale body. And yet his words were not without pity, not without a certain strange understanding.

Ricardo remembered where he had been, and the memory unsettled him . . .

"The things I've seen!" he exclaimed. "And done! Ah, Brenn! I told you I'd be back!"

His last promise made good, he hobbled, then walked, then ran down the Tower steps toward the garden . . .

Where the mist touched the Great Witch, and she began to wither. Huge brown lesions mottled her white skin, and she wrinkled like an ancient dried fruit. "No!" she cried out, and again "No!" as the infusion aged her, far past her own seventy years, for corruption and plotting and sleeplessness now rebounded upon her in one terrible moment.

At last, after all these years of scheming and wickedness, her appearance came to match her soul.

From the battlements a flock of ravens swooped, their natures restored by the purifying infusion. As though they had waited a century for vengeance, the birds descended on the Great Witch, rending her parchment-thin skin with their beaks, tearing her hair, grasping at her eyes with their furious talons. She whirled and screamed, flailed at her tormentors with her tattered arms . . .

Then, as suddenly as she had aged, Ravenna was gone, a heap of dried leaves skipping and scattering over the garden as the rain subsided, rising in a spiral, borne on an eddy of wind through the window of her old balcony, where they skittered across the marbled map of Palerna and into the ring of candles. There the flames consumed them, and they dwindled to ash, to a foul odor briefly borne on the air—the legacy of the Great Witch in a country cleansed and delivered.

* * *

Brenn gathered his fellows close under the arch, and for a moment they stood clutching one another in wonderment, shaken by what they had brought to pass.

He put his arms around Faye, embracing her in quiet joy, in relief, and in a deeper emotion he understood now, around which he had finally put thought and word. For when he had seen her at the mercy of the Witch, in danger of drowning in the rainsoaked garden, he recognized that every victory would be less triumphant without her, every defeat less bearable. She would be Queen of Palerna.

They heard a great commotion on the Causeway as the Watchmen passed. North over the land bridge they came, skirting the castle walls in their retreat north into Aquila, where they would hold out for days until Helmar's army had surrounded them, had ensured their surrender.

Already to the east, Brenn could hear the triumphant Palernan army singing as they approached Kestrel Tower up Cove Road, as they passed into the outskirts of Grospoint, and the people of Maraven rushed from their houses, waving green banners and white flowers, and singing as well with the advancing legions.

> The forward Youth that would appear
> Must now forsake his Muses dear,
>> Nor in the Shadows sing
>> His Numbers languishing.
> 'Tis time to leave the Books in dust,
> And oyl th'unused Armours rust:
>> Removing from the Wall
>> The Corselet of the Hall . . .

On it went, as it had when they marched for the first time into battle, the song taken up by duke and commoner, by Zephyrian cavalryman and Parthian archer, Teal Front merchant and Wall Town peasant, by John the Shepherd, who was strangely at peace, the healing of his thoughts and hands extended to the comrades who marched beside him, and by Unferth the Apprentice, who joined in the song because everyone else was singing,

> But thou the Wars and Fortunes Son
> March indefatigably on;
>> And for the last effect
>> Still keep thy sword erect:
> Besides the force it has to fright
> The Spirits of the shady Night,
>>> The same Arts that did gain
>>> A Pow'r must it maintain.

"We've won!" Dirk whispered proudly.

"Not yet," Brenn cautioned, drawing his sword. "There's still a king to reckon with. Lead me to Dragmond."

His three companions regarded one another curiously.

"I haven't seen the King for months," Faye said finally, as the others nodded in assent. "But I suspect a place we can find him."

≺≺≺ XXVII ≻≻≻

Faye was wrong, of course. Dragmond was long buried in his shallow grave, miles from the castle. Even so, the suspicion that he was alive and had fled Maraven would linger for months after the final battle.

But the place to which Faye led them was the door she had passed so often in her tedious labors—the door in the darkened hallway, under which the variegated light shone forth day and night. She had always suspected that even if the King had not vanished into the mysterious room beyond the portal, there would be something worth attending to in there.

Outside the door they waited, Brenn and Faye standing bravely in the forefront, Delia a few cautious steps behind them, and Dirk at the end of the hallway under the guise of guarding them all against attack from the rear.

"Be careful, Brenn," Faye whispered, as he crouched by the

door. "If Dragmond's behind there, it's my good money he'll be armed and spoiling to fight."

She had run out of warnings.

Brenn shifted to his knees, holding his left hand so that the blue light from it fell on the latch, the pick in his right hand. He growled and shrugged.

"Faye, get down here."

Faye looked at him curiously.

The King of Palerna flushed and gritted his teeth. He offered the pick to the girl at his side.

Laughing softly, Faye crouched beside him, and in an instant the door flew open, the girl scrambling to her feet as Brenn burst into the room, sword drawn, expecting his dark uncle, the cwalu, or whatever sorcery and evil could muster in a last, desperate stand. . . .

But instead he found ice. Or the inside of a diamond.

The candlelit interior chamber glittered with crystal, with elaborate glasswork reflecting the light to a central table, another catafalque where yet another body lay, still and silent, covered by a faceted globe of glass.

Brenn moved cautiously toward the body, sword drawn and at the ready, Faye following him closely, her hand on his shoulder. Delia stood at the door, and a joyous cry from Dirk in the hallway behind her signaled that friends were approaching.

Brenn was breathing more easily now. He knew he would need no support. Cautiously, he peered into the glass case, where a slight, middle-aged man lay with his hands at his side, lifeless on a huge green map of Maraven.

Something about the man's features was familiar. Brenn peered at the line of the face, the nose. . . .

"Look!" Faye whispered. "His left hand."

Brenn followed her gaze to the man's palm, pressed against his left thigh. Through the thin skin that webbed between the fingers a blue light was glowing—a constant source of radiance as the candlelight flickered and shifted and faded.

"It's like yours!" Faye exclaimed. "Like the light you . . ."

She did not need to complete the sentence. In wonder, Brenn extended his hand toward the glass.

"This is Aurum, Faye. The missing king. This is my father."

* * *

The connections were easy to make, the puzzle easy to decipher. The map on which Aurum lay was the first and most necessary clue, leading Brenn's eyes and thoughts back to the *Leaves of Morrigan*.

"Bring me the book, Delia," Brenn muttered. The alchemist, who had carried the volume from their huddled conclave beneath the arch, handed it to him eagerly. And he had opened it and read.

It was on the last page, where he had expected it—Albright's final discussion of the King's Touch.

> It is like sunlight, the touch of a King, or like the course of water from a great river, for within it is solace and nourishment and life itself. I have seen health course through my fingers, and I have seen the death drawn by my hand. Such is the great office of the King, for the power that is solace and life can twist and turn upsodoone when it touches and is touched by an evil hearte, and indeed can sustaine that heart a while in the dreams of darkness, in wounding and death.
>
> But the anointment is the author and finisher of the power, and such power, though refracted, though bent, must bend and refract finally to the good of the Crown, of the Commonweal, to the good of the Good itself.

"He was Ravenna's power source," Brenn proclaimed, unsure how he knew, but sure that he spoke the truth. "She kept him here, and fed her magic from his anointment. And Grandfather was right finally: Ravenna's evil undid itself."

"That's philosophy enough," a voice boomed behind him. "What're you going to do about rousting him?"

"Ricardo!" Brenn shouted. The Alanyan, dried blood still crusted on the side of his green tunic, stalked into the shimmering room and, his left arm around Delia, reached for Brenn with his right. The three of them stood before the crystalline bier of Brenn's father, embracing, weeping, heads bowed in the posture of mourners, though in fact it was jubilation and gladness that flickered and danced off the crystalline walls of the room.

"What . . . what *shall* I do, then?" Brenn asked huskily, drawing away from Ricardo and staring down at the faceted casket.

It was a seamless catafalque, or so it appeared—as impenetrable as the diamond it resembled, except for the strange, tilted slot in the crystal by his father's head, crowned by an inscription engraven in gold.

"*Corona generis* . . ." Brenn read, his irritation rising that it was Latin again. Of all the things he had never quite mastered, Latin and locks topped the list, and they both returned to rankle him at his moment of triumph.

"*The crown of the line,*" Ricardo prompted. "At least, that's what my chymist's Latin tells me."

Brenn pondered the slot for but a moment, for the answer was no farther away than his hand could reach. In triumph, he drew forth Libra, and touched the blade to the crystal canopy.

"This sword is the balance of power," he said, "and not as a weapon. Pure and simple, it is a key."

He slipped the blade into the slot, and with a turn of his wrist, the keyhole righted itself, the tumblers balanced, and the crystal coffin opened.

"This is all well and good," Dirk observed dryly. "But now what? Aurum's as still as the stone itself."

"The King's Touch," Faye whispered, stepping to Brenn's side. "What was it your book said? *It is like sunlight . . .*"

"*The author and finisher of the power,*" Brenn repeated reverently, extending his hand toward his father. "And after all, doesn't sunlight dispel the deepest winter?"

The scar on his hand glowed blue and violet and deep deep red as he touched Aurum's hand. Suddenly, all of them—Aurum and Brenn, Faye and Delia and Ricardo and the catafalque itself—glowed with an intense and magical light. At the doorway Dirk whistled, started for them, and thought better of it.

Then the light faded to a soft glimmer, the encasement disappeared, and Aurum stirred on the bier.

He was a weakened man, a pale shadow of the healthy, jovial king some in the court remembered. Brenn and Ricardo helped Aurum into the King's old quarters, musty and dirty from Dragmond's negligence and the month of sequestering following his death. Dirk and Faye rushed ahead of them, sweeping and airing the room, spreading fresh rushes.

He would lie there for a fortnight, passing in and out of wakefulness. Brenn sat by his side most of the hours, as physicians attended him, as Aurum traveled the slow, long road back to health.

When he is king, so be it, Brenn thought contentedly. *There's something to be said for being a prince, after all.*

Gives a young man time to grow into wisdom.

In the meantime, more good news reached Kestrel Tower. The Maravenian forces under General Flauros, routed to Aquila by the Palernan armies, surrendered just south of Orgo. Flauros, a changed and humbled man, handed his sword to Helmar with the promise of service and fealty to the new king.

Helmar accepted the promise and cordially imprisoned his hapless adversary.

It was only a matter of hours, however, until Galliard arrived, whose good sense and ducal authority prevailed with the grizzled general. Flauros was set free, and well over half his troops joined the Palernan forces on the spot. The rest, diehards and malcontents, disappeared into the mountainous blasted heath in the north of Aquila.

Helmar and Ponder, newly arrived from Corbinwood, were all for going after them, for *finishing the job,* as he gruffly maintained. But the King's Mercy, decreed by Brennart of Maraven after his triumph, was extended to all—even to those who did not altogether wish it.

Harmless for now, Galliard told himself, looking back as he guided his legion south toward Maraven. *But Aquila is my country, and this muttering is eventual trouble. The King's Mercy will last a good while, though—longer than most mercies, and longer than most peace.*

Peace it was, and the last of the resistance was cleared from the city. The body of Lightborn was given a funeral all quite honorable, considering the man's treachery and betrayal. Brenn even allowed the Pale Man's companion Danjel to accompany the body to the crypt on the Aquilan coast. The young lieutenant remained there for a week—in mourning vigil, went the rumor at Kestrel Tower.

Old Barco the ferryman told his sons otherwise. He was passing westward, he claimed, along the Aquilan coast, when he heard the chanting from the rocky tombs where the captain was laid to rest. It was a young man's voice, he said, and the words were mysterious and unsettling.

> At the round earth's imagin'd corners, blow
> Your trumpets, and arise, arise
> From death, your numberlesse infinities
> Of soules, and to your scattered bodies goe . . .

It might have been only the wind, Barco told his sons and himself, as they circled the campfire on the Gray Strand. Only the wind, and so the ancient ferryman sent no tidings to the castle.

But a sudden change had come over Lieutenant Danjel. When he returned to Maraven he was quiet, strangely chastened, as if something had passed away within him.

It was a time of other arrivals.

Terrance, it seemed, had resigned himself to a slow death by starvation in the abandoned web of the spider. Try as he might, he could not break the web by force of body or force of magic, for the strands were too thick for the strength of a squinch-bug, and Ravenna had endowed them with a magic that resisted his incantation and spell.

So it would have ended—the wizard undone, reduced to a lifeless husk in the thin webbing—had it not been for the elf.

Terrance swore it was the one he had healed that long-ago time in the attic of the tower, when Brenn had capsized a boiling beaker upon the dirty, curious thing. At least it looked like the same creature, and the wizard thought he remembered that the floppy left ear of the elf in question had been chewed a bit.

But whatever the case, there was something bordering on gratitude in the creature's gesture. Crawling from the recesses of the cavern, covered in soot and mud and seaweed until it looked like a huge mound of refuse cast up on the Maravenian beach, the elf slipped toward the web and peered at Terrance, its rancid breath overwhelming his insect's senses.

Do they eat squinchflies as well as raw eggs? the wizard thought, as the creature extended a grimy finger toward him. Terrance wriggled, struggled, tried to escape, but the creature only burst the webbing around him, and waited politely as Terrance transformed himself back to a very human wizard.

The two of them, sorcerer and elf, arrived in Kestrel Tower the next night. Their welcome waned a bit when Ricardo found the elf in the plentiful wine cellars of the tower, facedown in a barrel of sack; it took Brenn's healing touch to rescue the wretched thing from drowning, and ultimately, as Dirk observed bitterly, the wine was ruined as well.

But Terrance had returned, and he took his place in the King's company as loyal subject and trusted adviser. The elf stayed with him and made an uneasy peace with old Bracken—a peace disrupted temporarily every year or so, when the dog decided that his small, dirty companion might very well be edible.

Aurum did not want the throne.

He made it clear from his sickbed, when his son announced his own impending marriage with the Lady Faye.

"My blessings go with you, Brennart," he said, waving away an overattentive surgeon. "And to the glorious girl at your side."

"You have no misgiving, then?" Faye asked. "That your son marry a commoner?"

Aurum laughed weakly, reclining onto his pillows.

"Surely my personal history should teach you," he maintained, "that I've a warm spot in my heart for Wall Town women."

He chuckled, his laughter like the creaking of a door. Terrance fell into the humor, then Galliard after him, and around the bedside was mirth and joy and merriment as the old king held his final court.

Brenn watched his father with concern: even though those who should know—the physicians and Terrance and Delia—had assured him that Aurum was well on the way to recovery, the man still looked pale, almost transparent. The draining thefts

Ravenna had made over the years had ruined his health, and though he could be expected to live a long life, he would never be the hale and active man he was before Dragmond and Ravenna seized him.

Aurum would advise, he said, but no more: and he maintained that, given his own checkered past as the ruler of Palerna, the best advice he could give his son was a simple two sentences:

Look at what I have done. Now don't do it.

In the days before the wedding, a thousand guests convened from all over the continent and beyond—folks Brenn had never expected to see again, and folks he had never seen before but delighted in meeting beneath the doting eye of his newfound father and the prideful glance of his wizard adviser.

All the cousins were in attendance, each bringing unusual gifts from obscure sources. Brenn knew the curse was lifted, believed it was lifted for good. . . .

But he also knew not to inquire all that closely as to where his cousins had acquired the curious objects they presented the bride and groom.

Among the most surprising guests was an Alanyan crystalmaster, a compact and angular man by the name of Ianafitch. Through the wedding feast, the crystalmaster seemed preoccupied, and indeed his thoughts *were* elsewhere, dwelling on the occasion years ago that Dragmond brought him here to fashion the catafalque for the kidnapped King Aurum. The usurper had paid him in gold florins, all of which Ianafitch handed over to Brenn: when he had discovered the use of the crystal he fashioned, he had refused to spend his wages.

He had brought the couple a mirror—a wedding gift from the Great Witch Sycorax, whose lodgings in Hadrach had expanded to accommodate her ever-increasing size—and when Ianafitch confessed his complicity to Brenn, the young king forgave him readily, appointing him to the task of fashioning stained glass windows for Kestrel Tower.

By far the most touching gift came from the couple's old friend, Dirk of Maraven. The wizard's apprentice produced a coat from thin air and smoke—a threadbare garment that Brenn recognized instantly.

"Why, it's the one I let you *borrow*! The night we broke into Terrance's tower!"

Dirk smiled and nodded. "Let it never be said that your friend Dirk backed out of his debts!"

They looked at one another across a gulf of years and absences, and as surprised as they were at the changes that had befallen them, they were all the more amazed how their friendship had grown to contain those changes.

It all seemed too good for Faye to believe. As the dogs danced and as Dirk, clad in the midnight blue of an apprentice wizard, made a fruit tree in the garden vanish and reappear, and finally as Thomas sang and the guests joined in and the King lifted his own sweet, damaged voice to the chorus around him, she could scarcely contain her joy.

One time—one unsettling time—she looked into the depths of the surrounding crowd and saw Lieutenant Danjel by the old gardener's shed. His was not a welcome face, but he was a guest nonetheless on this night of the King's Mercy. Faye smiled at him as well, and nodded, and for a moment she saw a new and eerie look in his eye, one that was disconcertingly familiar.

She turned away at once. Nobody had seen the exchanged glance. Except for Unferth, faceup under the wine barrel, who regarded the festivities—and everything that went on—with a bleary but thorough attention.

When Brenn called Faye's notice to the silver chain he had stolen from Galliard's neck while the Forest Lord flirted with Delia, she lost sight of Danjel altogether, and when she looked back he had gone, in his place the old mage Archimago, who had traveled north at the prospect of gambling, fresh beer, and young girls. And yet she could not forget the odd look on the lieutenant's countenance, one that had held her gaze on him despite her mistrust and dislike of the scheming little man.

"We can rest for a while, Faye," Brenn assured her, touching her hand softly. His smile made her forget Danjel and her discomfort.

Indeed, made her forget everything else.

Tonight, she vowed, she would tell him about Lightborn. Their marriage would not begin with concealment, and Brenn would know about her complicity in his capture and imprisonment, and how she had repented for that mistake in every moment since. Surely he would understand.

For after all, did not the King's Mercy extend to the Queen herself?

Faye finally smiled. For a moment she thought she heard another melody over Thomas' lute, a snatch of a little song drifting away into the Maravenian moonlight, but she dismissed it as the last dark feeling in an evening of lights.

But Bertilak heard it, and Bracken noticed, and the elf as well, who had toppled Terrance's winecup in a greedy search for the last amber drop. The owl upon Ricardo's shoulder rolled its great head, stared at the captain with huge, unblinking eyes, and translated the song out of the summer air, out of the revelry and the Maravenian moonlight, so that Ricardo shivered unknowingly before he returned to song and conversation.

But he would remember the words at the edge of his dream that night, and rise toward wakefulness in the dark hours of the morning with the first verse still on his lips, though he did not know what it meant:

> Je veux te raconter, o môlle enchanteresse!
> Les diverses beautés qui parent ta jeunesse;
> Je veux te peindre ta beauté
> Où l'enfance s'allie à la maturité . . .

‹‹‹ **Epilogue** ›››

Anthony of the Ravens went home from the war on the longest road because he had not finished his duty. He moved now among the living, as he had among the dying, with Bertilak and the kites, and Ravenna's disenchanted flock for company. In every town of Palerna, someone waited for news of the soldiers who had not returned. Anthony remembered them all, remembered the last things they said, remembered the names of whom to tell it to, and so he searched out the survivors, town by town, farm by farm, and delivered his messages.

The night was well fallen when he reached Murrey. The chandler's shop gave every appearance of having been shut up for the evening, but Anthony strode toward it nonetheless. It was his last stop.

Albert the candlemaker stood in the dark of his shop and stared hard at the latch he had left raised since Gabriel had gone to join the Palernan army and become a hero and make something of his life.

The moment the door swung open, when Anthony of the Ravens came through it, Albert knew that he could lock the shop hereafter.